FIVE CENT RETURN

In memory of Tukey Cleveland

For Samia, Jim, and Cleo

Published in 2009 in conjunction with createspace.com. The author may be reach at 1078 Nix Lane, Santa Fe, NM 87507

Prologue

When Joe Evans turned fourteen, his grandfather decided the boy was old enough to learn about his mother. He had been born overseas and not one member of the Brings Plenty clan knew the child existed until a man found his way down the sandy track that led to the grandfather's house and gave him an envelope. The Agency man stood there while the old man opened the clasp and touched the papers. He raised his head but his eyes were blank and the Agency man thought he understood.

"This is my grandson?" The man nodded; "Yes, Mr. Brings Plenty, while your daughter Anna did not register his birth correctly, she left notice of the day and date at the Agency. However, we received no further proof the boy was alive until now." Isaac handed the papers back unread. The two men stared at each other and their thoughts were similar. Anna was a known drunk and highly irresponsible, but this one time she had done it almost right. The silence lengthened, until the Agency man startled Isaac by saying, "The boy was born in Wales." Isaac shook his head. "Wales."

The man continued; "The Agency cannot find your daughter, and you are the boy's only living relative of record." There was a pause and Isaac knew he would not like what was to be said. "The father's family has refused to acknowledge the child. We thought it best to have him live with blood." Then that time again, when men's thoughts went to the unthinkable. "She is either dead or has remarried, Mr. Brings Plenty. We have no way of knowing unless she wants us to know."

That woman they spoke of had been his child, his beautiful daughter filled with laughter, riding her pony in the sand hills, helping with the brood mares, teaching the young colts to wear a halter and to lead and stand. That had been his daughter; this woman who would abandon her son was not of his family. Yet the child, a boy, was hers by written word. "How old is he?"

The Agency man had to shuffle through papers, holding several up close, then sliding them behind more papers. Isaac Brings Plenty was content to wait; he had learned patience in his sixty-eight years.

"The boy will turn eleven in two weeks. He is in foster care in Lincoln. If you sign here we will bring him tomorrow." Again Isaac Brings Plenty was silent. The Agency man fumbled his explanation; "The boy speaks only in a strange language although we know he understands English. And he grew up with horses, which is why the Agency believes you will offer the most suitable place for him to live."

Isaac studied the painted Agency vehicle, one of those high-wheeled monsters needed to cross this land when the snow came or the winds blew and the shallow track to his house disappeared. A grandson. Isaac turned slowly; careful on the leg where the sorrel horse had kicked him and split the bone and the doctors chided him for taking too long to get to their services. He did not explain to them, there was no point; these doctors always lectured as if their superior ways could change reality. It had been winter and with a broken leg and alone, he could not drive the high-wheeler so he waited until the snow cleared, as it always did, and he could climb into the small reasonable car where he did not have to use both legs to drive. It had been a long wait for the snow to clear and the break had begun to heal.

Standing now, aware of the outward turn of that leg, Isaac Brings Plenty thought that a grandson would be a fine thing to have. A boy to bring life back to the ranch, once owned by a white man, before the family left and Isaac Brings Plenty was able to purchase the old Norris place.

The boy arrived as promised the following day. He was let out of the Agency car, given a large canvas bag and told to go to his grandfather who waited for him. The papers had been signed; there was no need for further Agency interference. Only when the Agency car had gone, leaving behind that faint taste of fuel and dust that reminded Isaac why he did not like cars and trucks but preferred the smell and sound of the horses he raised, only then did he realize he needed to reach this child. He had a chance to right what had once gone wrong. "Boy." The child had not yet moved except to drop the canvas bag. Isaac tried again; "I am Isaac Brings Plenty." He waited, leaving open that space where the other person offered their name. The boy said nothing.

Isaac moved very slowly. His shoulders raised and then fell, and he turned his head enough that the boy could hear the words but they were not being spoken directly to him. "The mare who gave birth this morning, I need to check on her colt, to put iodine on the cord stump." His walk was uneven, and he made a show of swinging the injured leg. Not asking the boy to follow but letting him know that his grandfather was an old man. What happened now would tell a great deal about the child's heart.

There was a sliding noise, a misstep on a stone and then the boy appeared beside him without the awkward bag. Not speaking or asking questions but walking head down, studying the ground. When they reached the pens, Isaac was glad to lean on the sturdy fence, and even as he did not stare at the boy, he watched carefully. His eyes ached with looking sideways for he recognized that the boy would spook at anything more.

He did and did not look like his mother. No one could doubt his Indian blood, with skin the color of mahogany against the black hair. Isaac knew that the Welsh themselves were often dark-haired. But not with skin that color; they were Anglos, white people. There had been no chance to see into the boy's eyes. He had been clever, not quite looking in his grandfather's direction, not allowing entrance into his soul. The boy slid through the rails of the fence before Isaac could stop him.

The mare was angry and scared. Joe recognized her fear, he could hear his father tell him to be quiet and gentle and not frighten the young Thoroughbred filly who'd given birth and would not allow the foal to suckle. This bay mare was older, and it wasn't her first foal, but she did not like strangers, she did not like humans at all. Joe walked a few steps and the mare's ears went back and behind him he could hear the old man fuss.

His father's hands and voice guided Joe as he walked around the mare to find a sturdy post, where he slid down to sit on his heels, resting his back against the fence. The old man had built well; there was no give to the posts, no bend to the rails. He huddled there, head low, never looking straight at the mare and her foal; if this was what his grandfather bred, then Joseph Evans thought he might stay for a while.

It was a song his father taught him in the old language, for gentling foals and small animals and frightened children. It was hummed with sounds to fit the notes and yet as he sang, the old man behind him found a few of those sounds and brought in a deeper note, with differing repetitions but the mare seemed to hear them both. The foal touched Joe's hand, which hung between his hunched knees. A childish hand, nothing unusual about it except for scars and nicks belonging to an adult. The fuzzy colt rubbed his lips on the dark flesh, then raised his small muzzle and opened his lips to expose pink gums.

The boy laughed, and his grandfather laughed also. The mare moved forward with her ears pinned back in maternal fury and suddenly Isaac worried. The boy did not move and the colt walked away, his mama hesitated, briefly touched her muzzle to the boy's black hair and followed her colt.

It was the week after his birthday that the boy began to talk. He had nodded, shook his head, stared blankly at his grandfather but would say nothing, until Isaac asked the boy if he would work with the colt to get him used to the halter and a soft lead line, help him learn to pick up his feet. The boy studied him for a moment, and gave Isaac his first real opportunity to see into the boy's eyes. They were black like his mother's, with thick eyelashes that were not hers and the face despite its dark coloring was from a separate tribe. His father would have been handsome in the white man's way, with a good chin, those eyes rounded, open, a high forehead. Their child would become a handsome young man, and neither world would accept him for he would not fit their rules.

"I like that colt. Thank you, Grandfather, I will teach him as my father taught me." Isaac did not change his face, did not smile or make a comment other than: "Good." It went from there in short words about details and nothing of his loss. Only hard work, and eventually, as the fall returned, Isaac told the boy he would go to the local school. It was the first time Joe defied his grandfather. "I do not go to school. My father teaches me at home." Isaac did not like the boy's refusal;

"Child, your father isn't here to teach you so you must go to school."
Joe Evans stood almost as tall as his aging grandfather now, angular
and in need of muscle but growing, and it took very little for the boy to
raise his head and look into his grandfather's eyes.

"You can teach me."

When the boy was fourteen, Isaac had a letter from Anna Upthegrove,
addressed to her father in care of the Agency. It was a brief letter,
stating that she was remarried and sober two years now and wanted to
see her son. It was then that Isaac told the boy about his mother.

Isaac put the boy on a bus going east, for Anna lived in New
York. Her new husband was Native, she said, from a Maine tribe, and
he'd settled them near an upstate reservation. Isaac was not
comfortable letting the boy go, and for the first and only time Joe
Evans, standing an awkward six feet tall, leaned down and gently
hugged his grandfather, as he hugged any one of the new-born foals he
comforted and trained in the past three years. "It will be all right,
Grandfather. I will come back."

It would be eighteen years before Isaac Brings Plenty saw his
grandson in the small home again.

One

When he asked what happened next, they laughed and said 'go home'. They gave him two hundred dollars, as if the amount would be enough to get him across all those states to the one place in this country where for a while he'd been safe. Joe guessed that qualified it as home.

One of the guards who had not been cruel in the passing years; indifferent yes, especially when at eighteen Joe had been moved into the adult population at Wende, that same guard who read the rules to the newcomers back then, took the time now to explain that if Joe was careful and rode the bus, ate simple meals, he would get to the Midwest in decent shape.

Beyond that, the guard said, it would be odd jobs and begging that would take him home. Folks around here or anywhere for that matter weren't keen on hiring those who'd been in prison half their life. And incarceration always showed. The man stood there, belly first, uniform not quite fitting, a caricature whose compassion was at odds with every preconception of a prison guard.

Joe'd learned not to talk back, learned that a long time ago; he had rarely passed time with the other inmates. He had fought for silence, and knew his look and manner gave rise to the belief that violence came to him naturally. When he'd first been jailed, he'd been a child of fifteen. He had been fearful but well-mannered, taught by his father and then his grandfather. He could hear the old man's voice those terrible first days of cell doors and inmates, rules and fighting.

That he was so young brought him trouble. That he was half Indian, black hair and eyes, dark-hued skin, seemed to either fascinate or frighten off the worst transgressors. He'd been sixteen when he was tried as an adult and sentenced. Since then, Joe read everything he could access in the prison libraries and then he petitioned for more books, specific titles, so he could continue to learn in the empty time.

Now he'd served fifteen years for Murder Two and hadn't lived outside prison walls since he was a child. He had two hundred dollars and nothing that belonged to him. The clothing was church-donated, and they had attempted to give him suitable clothes. Two pair of faded jeans, a jacket, worn boots someone had waxed and polished but could not hide their age, and three garish shirts, a faded purple, a multi-striped monstrosity and a red and white stripe.

Someone with a sense of humor or a good memory had donated a black cowboy hat. Pushed down, it stayed on his head, but Joe doubted that it would last through a good rain or a high wind. The money was different; the first time he had a fistful of twenties and he did not want them. A gift from the State that confined him, then turned him loose with a pathetic amount of money, his reward for fifteen years of good behavior.

Joe's father had been born near the town of Hay-On-Wye, and Joe never knew how his father and mother met, did not want to know why they had conceived him or why she abandoned him. His mother had been mean-tongued and wild during the few months he'd known her; the memory of his father was of a quiet and kind man, who raised his son for ten years at a yard in England, where he trained horses to race over jumps. Even at ten Joe had been tall enough to be the size and weight of a jump jockey. With hands of gold his father told him, hoping for a grand career first as a jump jockey and then a trainer. When Joe was almost eleven, his father was killed by an overturned lorry.

Standing outside the lethal rolls of wire surrounding Wende Prison, he was no longer that child. Muscle broadened his shoulders, thickened his hands. He was dark, darker than the pureblood Mohawks imprisoned with him, and they refused his story of white blood until he spoke in the lingo of his father, and added Lakota insults learned from his grandfather and the Mohawks simply ignored him.

The Spanish gang members and the city blacks with their rules and gestures, they eyed his oddity and felt his strangeness. Word got out of his crime, the killing of his stepfather and why Joe had killed him. He would not allow such depredations again. His eventual size, his insistence on continuing to study, earned him the nickname 'doc' and he became the one to ask if an inmate had trouble spelling or trying to set down his plea to a new lawyer. Knowledge, Joe learned, was useful in many ways.

He was an oxymoron, which was one of the words Joe liked; at thirty-one he had a strength of character as well as face and body that received too much notice, but he was innocent of women, the curves and places within their bodies. He knew the talk, saw the pictures circulating through the cell tiers. And he felt his own body respond; he was not that innocent. But he'd had no chance to learn about physical love.

He stood outside the walls; a donated suitcase rested at his feet, money burned his hand. 'Go west, go home' echoed inside his mind. He could hope the way was there, the ability to keep his fear to himself and his temper in control.

A prison psychiatrist, one who specialized in violent-crime prisoners, set up appointments with Joe, asking if he felt now, with the years behind him, that he could control his temper, had he come to the point where he knew what he'd done was wrong. Joe studied the doctor, another one of those colorless men, thinning hair, tweed coat, as if he too were playing a part. Joe knew the truth would overwhelm the doctor but he could say no less.

His voice was monotone; "He beat his two sons and raped them, he tried to fuck me. He was about to kill their mother." The doc interrupted; "She was your mother too, Joe. That's why you were there." Joe shook his head; "She birthed and left me. That does not make her my mother. But he wanted to kill her and I was the only one who could defend any of them so I hit him and he died." He took in that breath; "No I don't regret what happened. Only that I was the one to do it. He would have been killed, or killed himself with drink, but if I hadn't stopped him right then, he would have murdered her and the two boys."

Joe was tired of saying this, tired of no one listening. He had said the facts too many times; a fourteen-year-old boy, a newcomer to a family that was never whole, was the only person to keep three other people alive. His mother hated him for her husband's death and killed herself with drink. The boys had gone to live with their blessed grandfather and they had a new life. Joe paid for their lives, like an older brother putting the younger ones through college.

The doctor wrote frantic notes, barely lifting his head to listen while Joe described what happened. When Joe had been silent for several minutes, the doc looked up. "So, you're saying you have no regrets for taking a life?" Joe answered harshly; "That wasn't what you asked me." It stood between Joe and an early freedom but he could not lie. He shrugged; "You write what you think you heard, doc. They always do."

Over the years his attitude did not change. He never altered his answers to their endless and mindless questions, their badgering him to admit what he did not believe.

Joe heard the dulled engine, began to feel others behind him pressing to get on the bus; the few released from their prison. The system provided transportation to take them some place, to family, a job, a halfway house where they could try to learn how to live among the law-abiding population.

The fortunate had cars waiting for them; cousins, a buddy, a wife with haunted eyes, children bouncing in the back seat, hands grasping at the window for their papa. Joe stood to the side and watched the line move slowly, men stepping on pocked silver steps, hunched over as they entered the long tunnel of seats. Then it was his turn and he raised a foot, brought back it down in place, looked up at the driver's worried face. "Thank you. No." He backed up and swung to his right, in front of the battered vehicle, smelling the stink of diesel and hearing the mistimed valves. Engine heat added to the day's hot air blasted him, and a voice called; "Evans, you get on that bus."

He had a choice. Joe stopped and looked back at the pot-bellied guard. "No thanks, I'll walk." The guard glared at him; even from a distance Joe felt the impulse to look down as was proper for a con. Then he found a grin, shook his head as he said the words again; "No thanks, I'll walk." The guard yelled with that tone demanding obedience; "Evans, it's thirty miles before you find a town. You stop at a house and they'll call the cops, they'll know you're a con. It's all over you." The guard's words meant nothing.

Taking or not taking the bus was Joe's first real choice in over fifteen years. He chose to walk, to not shut himself inside any thing or place at this one perfect moment. He knotted the jacket through the suitcase handle, pocketed the two hundred dollars and started down the road, same direction as the bus would pass, and he would endure the shouts and curses of the men shut inside but he would walk, feeling the movement of his body, feet going ahead, legs working, using strength and energy controlled by others for too long.

He didn't look over or hurry as the bus glided by. The driver slowed, honked once, then hurried on as Joe did not respond.

It was the glory of walking; a bumpy dirt shoulder, in places dropping off to thick grasses folded from the weight of their richness, over a buckled culvert where marshes gave up the stink of rotting fruit, skunk cabbage earning its name. It was the air on his face, against his eyes, pushing over his half-open mouth to coat his tongue with fine dust. Dust rose from his steps, not from others in line marching on orders, going to another place and other chores, hard work, dull work but at least work done outside.

It was an illusion he knew, that there were no walls except what he raised on his own. Between himself and anyone who came in too close. He could not afford mistakes. He could not let caring enter him for it caused destruction. His brothers, half-brothers he reminded himself, had been too young to know what he'd done. Yet as they grew, they wrote to him in a slowly maturing hand. At first their efforts were from their grandfather's insistence, their letters holding the old man inside each word. Then one of the boys, Quent, wrote and said their grandfather had given them his name, Brings Plenty, allowing them to shed their father's inheritance.

The rage he'd felt then no longer mattered; Joe Evans was breathing air, knowing that to hurry would lessen the pleasure. He did not need food or a roof over his head. He walked along the road, staring out to the ruined fields, bought and left barren as the prison grew. No one wanted to live near the steel and concrete reminder of failure. Broad-leafed sumacs had begun their theft; seeds blown from a forest's edge growing into spindly trees, producing more trees to move in until the once fertile land was rendered useless. Joe'd taken out books on the local species and studied them, tried to name what he saw as he and others worked for local contractors.

His grandfather's presence walked with him on the narrow road; the old man who would never chastise his grandson and kept his thoughts private about what Joe had done. In his letters, Isaac Brings Plenty spoke only of every-day matters. Joe had no intention of explaining to anyone again why he had committed the crime. For he was in truth a murderer, and now that he was free, with nothing to fight against, he was not sure how long he could bear his life. Grandfather wrote in a spiky hand, never asking but offering advice among sentences telling Joe about the new foals, the rains that did or didn't come to wash the land. Then he stopped writing; the boys wrote a few more letters, and for the past four years there had been no word.

Joe shivered at the thought of approaching the sand hills ranch and looking down into faded dark eyes that knew him too well. Even worse, he did not want to reach his journey's end and find a grave.

Eventually the sun scorched him until Joe smelled himself grow riper with each step. He had showered yesterday, and the prison barber had clipped his thick hair. Now he smelled honestly of sweat, and he kept walking, hungry too, but not willing to stop. He wanted miles and exhaustion to draw him into the small world of muscle and air and no one and nothing to hold him. Then he approached a gift offered to him from whatever being watched over newly-released inmates; a pond glistening with quiet water, surrounded by bent rushes where a duck nested. His approach to the water brought her out of hiding, squawking and beating the water with her wings before taking flight.

The pond was low, leaving a dry slope for Joe to cross until he reached the water's edge, which moved gently toward him and then away, stirred by the duck's departure. Joe struggled to remain upright while he removed his clothes; the boots stood to accept the burden of the jeans, socks, underwear and then he carefully laid the shirt over everything from a peculiar modesty. Barefoot, toes curled against the sand and pebbles, eyes closed to feel the damp air, taste the algae-rich water. He brought his head up, tilted back in silent and universal thanks. Slowly he realized the open air, the silence, even the smallest sound of the water patting land, scared him. This sudden ability to do as he wished, to stand naked with no one watching, was unnerving.

He moved quickly into the water, gasping at the chill, disliking the soft footing thick with green scum and a few large rocks. When the shallow waves reached above his knees, he leaned forward and slid into the murky liquid, drowning what threatened to become tears.

Eyes open, the water was thick, filled with spirals of vegetation, but it was clean and cold and Joe rolled over to float on his back, laughed at his belly, then looked up to see the vivid sky, the sun that burned him so he rolled again and swam across the small pond, scraped his knees on the unexpected shallow water, pushed backwards and landed belly-up again, floating, then swimming in awkward strokes, rolling, pulling his body together to dive, conscious of presenting his butt to the insects and birds that rightfully resented his intrusion. He jack-knifed, went deeper into the middle, lost his breath and struggled for the surface. The duck had returned, skating across the water to settle in, wings folded. Joe tried to be unassuming, taking up only a small part of the pond until the duck swiveled her head, watched him briefly before she disappeared back into the rushes.

Slowly, pulling water to him and dragging his body, he headed toward his clothes and the barren shore. The duck rustled in her hiding place but was no longer disturbed by his voyage. He stood, letting water drip from him, breath slowed, heart pumping without fear. He listened, heard only insects, birds overhead, somewhere a cow bellowed for its calf. No metal, no anger, no orders or fighting.

As he stood naked and letting the sun bake him dry, he had the briefest sense of what it might have been to grow up from boy into a man in a life suited to him, with his grandfather's horses and the sand hills of Nebraska as playground and school house. Joe shook like a dog, then bent to put on the red striped shirt and the faded jeans. Now he was hungry and it was May, with few crops producing anything to eat. Perhaps if he kept walking, he would find an untended vegetable garden, a patch of half-ripened berries. Anything to ease the pangs in his belly.

He walked easily, studying what he saw, looking for familiar leaves and some kind of food. There was a growth of blackberries tamed by the rock confines of a family cemetery, but the immature berries were inedible and he knew it, knew his quest wouldn't produce much but it kept him walking.

Walking gave him tired feet, and an ache in his gut. He found an algae-covered water trough and drank directly from the dripping intake pipe. The water was bitterly flavored by rusted metal but he was thirsty. More miles, maybe four hours of step after step; he had no watch but the sun was headed west now and he was still hungry, still walking.

He found a ragged garden from last year; it offered early radishes, some grainy red lettuce. He pulled carefully, not wanting his theft to be noticeable, for he would be easy to describe and easier for the cops to hunt down. Two radishes and a few lettuce leaves didn't seem like much of a theft but men had been imprisoned for less.

In the dark he wadded the shirts under his head and lay back to see the sky he had missed. And then he drew in a deep breath and found beyond the grass and trees a scent that held even deeper memories, and brought water to his eyes. He wiped it away, embarrassed although no one could see him. It was the smell of horses; a tang of salt and digested grass and their hide, the rot found in their hooves, the ammonia of stalls not cleaned often enough. He'd find them tomorrow, he'd ask for a job. To clean stalls, repair fences, drive a tractor. Anything he could offer to be around horses.

Hunger left him light-headed as he started walking in the morning. His muscles weren't ready for the miles ahead, but he stretched his legs, made himself walk until the rhythm returned and he could appreciate his first morning waking up free.

There was water in a small brook; he knelt and drank, watching indescribable elements flow downstream, and as he drank he sifted out bits of wood and gravel but it was clean water for him, no chlorine, no muddy coffee or burned food. There were dandelions rolled up, ferns tightly wound. He picked a few; tonight if he had not found work, he would find a tin can, start a fire and boil the greens, chew on their fragrance and use them to partially fill his gut.

He stood, inhaled air, smiled to himself; not far, he thought, up the slight hill in front of him. It was a large barn and separate paddocks; things from his far past barely recognizable; the scent was manure with shavings, urine, brushed hides and burnt hoof parings. He walked along the carefully tended driveway lined with sculpted trees. This was his first test and he was terrified; only hunger pushed him forward.

A woman stood near the barn, in the middle of the driveway. She was the first sexual woman he'd seen. There'd been a nurse at the hospital wing, one psychologist who had more chin whiskers than he'd ever grown, and the lady who ran the mobile prison library. She had been kind to Joe and he could have no thoughts about her other than gratitude. This woman was generically familiar from the illegal girlie magazines. The parts of a woman did not surprise him, he'd helped his father and then his grandfather birth out foals and those parts were all similar through the necessity of purpose. It was the flash and glitter, the hard blond hair and eyes colored to make them prominent, the tight jersey that showed off what didn't seem real. He was uncharitable, a trait his grandfather had tried to remove. It was easy to use it in prison; sarcasm gave him distance as long as he didn't push it into a fight. For all his noble thoughts, Joe knew he was afraid of women. It was that simple. He had made his place in the prison, he had become comfortable, mostly safe, always miserable but fortified with the knowledge that he had killed a man and deserved the punishment.

This female thing, this joining of two beings terrified him more than the biggest con holding a filed knife and waving it at Joe's belly. He could grab that knife and twist; he'd broken an arm on a con one time and the fight had been over a book of all things.

He choked and swallowed, looked directly at the woman.

Two

The man, her husband Joe guessed from their matching rings, tilted his head. Joe inhaled; "You got any chores I could do for a meal?" He hated his voice but he was hungry. "I know...been around, horses." The words didn't come smoothly. "I can strip and clean stalls, or repair fence. For a meal." He was begging, his hands clenched and the man stepped forward as if to put himself between his wife and Joe. Joe looked down, wet his mouth; "It's all right, mister. I'm leaving." The man smiled, then shook his head. "You clean the stalls like you say and we'll feed you. It's a deal. I'll come down to the barn in a few hours."

Joe was given a wheelbarrow and a manure fork and the man pointed to the manure spreader hunkered between cement walls. "It goes there." Joe kept his head down and only nodded. By the time the eight stalls were cleaned, limed, and bedded with fresh shavings, Joe was light-head and dizzy. He waited for the man's appearance, hoping it would not be the woman but he needed the meal they promised. When no one showed, he leaned on a stall door to find his balance, and went exploring. A door stood part-way open and he went in. Another door to the back of the long room showed the guts of a bathroom. And on a counter there was a tray.

A bottle of milk, slices of cheese and ham, an unopened loaf of bread. He picked up the loaf and held it to his nose; rich, sturdy bread, not white pap. There it lay, once hidden by the bread, a check made out to cash in the amount of fifty dollars. The writing was female, flourishes and illegible but on the stable account.

Rather than remain inside, Joe cradled the bounty in one arm and took a door that stepped directly onto the driveway out of sight of the house. Ten minutes later he sat in an overgrown pasture and carefully drank some of the milk, ate three slices of bread and lay back. His belly gurgled, his head ached and he waited patiently until he thought the food would stay down.

One piece of ham, a corner of cheese, and he slept briefly before eating a similar amount of each delicacy.

He spent the night watching the stars while thinking of the woman and in the morning he wanted a pond of cold water to clean his thoughts as well as his skin but the land was hilly and dry. As he walked from place to place, there were times when he wished he could accept a ride. The few signs still said New York State, until he hit a sign giving distances to Olean and then the Pennsylvania border. Joe knew he'd walked a far piece, and now it was time to reach for that promise he'd made. He'd seen the place on a map: Gettysburg in Pennsylvania. That's where he was going.

It started with a rainstorm with sudden thunder and lightening and he was walking the road, beginning to search for the night's resting place. Hard pellets of ice scarred his face before softening into rain as more thunder startled him. He knew better than to huddle under a tree. He could see the opening to a level field and maybe there was a ditch where he'd lie flat while he was rained on but stayed alive. Storms like this one went over fast, leaving behind water and random destruction.

Fresh tire tracks led into what he realized was a hay field. A woman with long hair tied in a scarf was throwing bales onto the back of a truck, an old Chevy that had a gear so low the vehicle would crawl while the woman struggled to throw what looked to be sixty-pound bales. If the hay got soaked through, she'd lose the crop.

Joe dropped the suitcase and jacket and ran, stopping just short of scaring her. "Ma'am." He had to yell over a clap of thunder. She saw him but didn't slow in her efforts, just nodded. He picked up a bale, slung it high onto the truck bed and she threw in the next bale.

The silence was a blessing, the work an old friend. Joe threw his head back and laughed and surprisingly the woman laughed with him as they threw bales in turn, until the truck was about to climb the rock fence and Joe slipped into the cab and caught the gear, turned the truck and pulled it back into granny, using a rubber cord to bind the wheel to the gear shift.

The short end of the field held a few more bales and they were done. Joe grabbed the suitcase, knowing everything inside was soaked. He headed toward the edge of the field until the woman and the old truck nearly ran him over and she yelled for him to get in. He swung up on the running board as the rain turned to hail and he felt it against his back, his skull, and yelled as the weather cleansed him. It would take a lot more of these storms to renew life but this short, brutal one had scratched and clawed at the first layer of prison filth.

The woman got them to a barn, wood ramp and all; a grand barn like they didn't have in England or South Dakota or Nebraska. The truck lurched, gears winding down; she popped the clutch and he fell off the running board, landing butt first on the planed flooring. He let his fingers run over the raised knots, the softer wood worn away from use. The woman stuck her head through the rolled down window; "You all right, mister? Didn't mean to throw you." He looked up at her, finally able to see her face; "Ma'am, I've been thrown from horses and a top bunk but never from a truck." That didn't seem to satisfy her; "I'm fine, ma'am. Only wet is all."

She wasn't pretty, not in the brittle way of those magazine photos; her long hair was tied with a scarf and she wore a sleeveless jersey showing far too much of her body. Her wet face held no hint of makeup, she wiped her forehead and mouth on the back of her arm, and when she got out of the truck cab, she stuck out her hand. He took her hand as if she might break. It was the intensity of her grip that eased him, for this was no protected female.

"Ma'am." That was usually enough. He'd realized over the past month he never said 'sir', only nodded to the men who hired him and didn't want to learn their names. But women deserved better treatment. She laughed, pushed a damp curl out of her eye, cocked her head. "Well you're a knight in wet armor. Thanks for the help, I hate to lose even ten bales, and that was the last of a good first cutting."

Then there was a change in her face, the unadorned eyes tightened, her smile disappeared. "What're you doing walking these back roads? There's no work around here, most of the farms are sold for those damned developments. I can't afford help and barely get the work done alone."

Joe bungled his first real conversation with a woman; "Ma'am, a woman like you should have a husband. Then you could work this place, it's good land, that's nice hay..." He stopped, tongue thick, embarrassed by his unwitting stupidity." My husband died six months ago. This farm belonged to his family. His great-grandpa built the barn."

She immediately forgave him his well-intended blunder about a husband; what an absolutely beautiful man to arrive just when she needed him. And here she was soaking wet, no bra so everything showed and he stood there shirt open, jeans hanging on him. My god he was any woman's daydream. She and Davy had talked about this at the end of his suffering. He knew his wife, loved her, and respected her appetite. He told her, until she wanted to be angry with him but realized he didn't remember what he'd already said.

He'd turned ornery and told her again, to take a man, find a partner, keep his love in her heart even as she felt another man's touch. She shied away from such talk, held his hand, and was there when he died, his body bucking against the fatal invasion, thrashing, eyes wild then without life but the body would not stop until she lay herself over him. Rested on his new corpse and held his flesh until it stopped the fight and she heard the escaping air and cried.

No one, no man she'd met, not even the one woman who'd been a close friend and offered more, none of these people roused her interest. Until a black-haired wild man helped her buck hay bales into the old Chevy flat bed and brought them into the barn's hold. She saw the damage her quick comment had done; his face tightened and he looked away as if he'd crossed an invisible line. "Ma'am, I'm..." What, she thought; embarrassed, sorry, grieving for her because of a loss he didn't know. Couldn't have known and yet it hurt him. That knowledge reminded her that she was half naked with a stranger.

"Let me get us each a towel, I hate water dripping into my eyes. Then we'll get to the bales. They go up into the loft and it's no easy job even with two of us." She didn't think the work ahead would bother this one at all. She couldn't stop herself; "What are you anyway? I've never seen the likes of you." She slapped her hand over her mouth, inhaling wet pieces of hay. Those eyes studied her; he sure enough wasn't much of a talker. "Ma'am?" And he wasn't as rude as she'd become. Living alone eroded her manners. She gave him points for his try; "Me. I'm someone going home." She laughed; "That's not much of a story, you can do better than that."

He didn't seem to understand the concept of polite conversation, for he stood mute, head turned away, eyes down. If she didn't know better, she would think he was afraid. Then she gave up waiting; "What's your name? I'm Jackie Weeks." She pulled off the soaked scarf and shook her head. His voice was rough; "Ma'am. My name." He seemed very careful now, even taking a step back. "My name is Joseph Evans. Joe." As if there were a secret within his identity she couldn't comprehend.

She smiled and her face was beautiful; she blew at a dangling strand of hair and he almost laughed but it didn't seem right. "Yes, ma'am, a towel'd be nice." She slid between the truck and the vertical boards that formed a pen for small animals under the loft, almost touching him. He could smell her, something unknown combined with sweat and the richness of new hay. He wondered, as her tied-back hair touched his shoulder, if that light touch against his skin was meant to cause such a ruckus.

She brought him a light blue work shirt and a thick white towel. He took them while being very careful not to touch her hand. He wadded up the soaked red-striped shirt to hide it in the suitcase and she took the mess from him.

"Mr. Joe Evans, after we're done here, I promise you supper and a hot shower as thanks for all the hard work. You put that shirt in there wet and all your clothes will stink of mildew." He quickly used the towel to wipe his face, scrub at his hair that had begun to grow and eventually got to wiping the damp hay stuck to his chest and back.

The shirt was a joke; he couldn't get more than half an arm into its place and the material hung up on his shoulders. "Ma'am?" It was all he knew to say. He dug out another one of those shirts, this one a multi-stripe that for unknown reasons made him laugh. But he could slip it on, and even button it across his chest and belly.

His look stunned her. The bright shirt on any of the men she knew would look effeminate; on this man, against his color and the steadiness of his eyes, the angles of his face, the colors were clean, making her want to touch him. He stepped back in the confined area, held out one hand as if to keep her away. "What do you raise here, ma'am? That's decent hay but there's no smell to these stalls."

Trying to redirect her, she decided. He was so used to women acting this way that he was indifferent to another opportunity. Oh well, Jackie thought, at least she had some response left, for the first time since Davy was diagnosed. She climbed up on the truck bed and then to the loft, and gestured for him to stand on the flat bed. Getting the bales to the loft and stacking them was much simpler with two people, and even easier with a man who knew what he was doing. He hefted each bale up to her. It was the last of the first cutting, the only bales to get wet, and it would feed the goats all winter, so she stacked it separate from the sale hay. It was when the work found a rhythm that she thought to answer his question as if the asking and the answer had meaning.

The words came in short bursts as she picked up a bale and swung it into place. He moved gracefully, shoulders twisting, arms picking up the sixty pounds with little effort and then raising the bale overhead to slide it into her grasp. "Davy, my husband, he wanted to make the farm pay even though he inherited it. We raise goats for their milk, and have vegetables available all summer and into the fall. People can buy shares in the crop, and come to pick their own or we, that is, I will pick for them and deliver for an extra fee. It works, or it did until...Davy died."

She stopped and he did not change the rhythm of lifting the bales, which forced her back into the work. It was what she needed, to get that last bale on the top of the pile and dust herself off, look down at the man who turned away from her stare. He shrugged and stepped from the end of the flatbed where his boots cracked on the wood floor and she winced.

Supper was fish chowder from yesterday, made with their...Jackie shuddered; made with one of the stocked trout pulled from the farm pond. Cornbread of course, hot from the oven, and glasses of chilled goat's milk, which her guest seemed to study before trying. He said nothing about the chowder, but was curious after the first taste, something new for him, she figured. She already knew better than to ask.

It was growing dark; Jackie turned on a lamp for Davy had not wanted to use the florescent overhead light fixture his grandfather had installed. The lamp stood on a tin-lined milk sink with a flat top, where she often kneaded bread. They had a sterile milk room in the addition to the barn, where the goats lived and where she milked and boiled and bottled. It was the most difficult thing to do; every place in the milk house had Davy's signature, his carpentry, his laughter and stories about his grandfather and the great aunt who had run the place with the old man. Now the milk shed was quiet, only the bleating of reluctant goats and a few kicks against the stainless steel pails kept up any music; the remaining flow of sound was inside her head.

She looked across the table suddenly, expecting to see her husband's face and was startled, then frightened; a stranger was in Davy's seat. A man whose past was blank. And she had in her insanity invited him into the house. The farm was at least five miles from the nearest neighbor. Jackie put her hands on the table, sharp and hard, one on each side of her half-empty soup bowl. He raised his head from concentrating on the food and saw into her. He did what she would not expect; he stood, moved to the back door that led to the barn. "Ma'am, I won't hurt you, what I did was buck hay or the bales would spoil."

He stood with his hands away from his body, their softly colored palms toward her. His face was frozen, those beautiful eyes showing nothing, willing her to accept him as he was. Voices mixed in her head; her mother warning a teenage daughter about men, and especially strangers. Davy making her promise to keep on living. Her older brother saying he would come and stay if she was worried about being alone.

Joe's heart thumped and shimmered, the room moved around him. The food, a soup he'd never had before, the cornbread a once-familiar staple but his grandfather often put red chile in to spice the flavor; it worked now in his gut, the rough-cob texture threatening to embarrass him.

He focused on that memory, of an old man's hands mixing the meal, letting it wait in the pan to set, creating that crisp outer crust and then the sweet breaking-apart of hot bread, the crunch of the top with a back-spice of red chile. It didn't work, remembering each detail could not shove aside the woman's face, the vulnerable eyes watching him. Even Joe, the dumb Indian who'd never had a woman could read her thoughts. "Thank you for the food, ah...meal, ma'am. I'll sleep in the barn, be gone by morning."

"Mister whoever and whatever you are, you are beautiful." The words came without thought or discretion and Jackie pushed herself away from the table. "Mr. Evans, Joe, I'm so sorry." She cried then, with no reason but that she had hurt a well-intentioned stranger. Joe walked around the table and offered himself; he stood close enough that her tears had a pungent smell over the food, the wet hay, everything but the misery pouring from this woman.

She took a hesitant step and he put a hand to her shoulder. She looked at him, then moved sideways so their contact was proper and he understood the message. Her head was against his shoulder and the crying came from deep inside. He had to use both hands to keep her standing, her knees did not hold, her arms would not grab on to him.

This was grief, this he recognized. It had come to him once as a child. And when he was in his teens and killed Albert Upthegrove, there had been an edge of that barely remembered pain. Now he had little knowledge of what she felt, the past years had dulled him to any depth of feeling. Still he recognized the source of her pain.

Her grief came purely from love.

Joe swiped a paper napkin and gave it to her. They were careful not to look into each other's face as she blew and wiped and he gave her another napkin and she repeated the effort until she could stand on her own.

In silence he picked up the soup bowls and the plate holding yellow crumbs, and put them near a porcelain sink. She turned to the chore, crisp and quick, knowing exactly where things went. She resolutely kept her back to him while she spoke of more impersonal matters. "Joe, I need to take a load of hay to a stable two hundred miles south of here. If you're headed that way, I could use the help." It was an apology and payment, and Joe was suddenly grateful, for his own knees were weak and he too had trouble breathing. This kind of tired was not familiar.

"I'll sleep in the barn. Be ready to go come morning." As he opened the door, he turned around, his face showed that he was digging into a buried past. "Thank you for the meal, ma'am. Fish soup's a new one for me." She let him go this time, but caught him with words as he stepped through the door and had almost escaped; "You are beautiful, Joe, and it's not just how you look." Even with his back to her, Jackie could see him shiver. Her words had wounded a well-meaning stranger.

In the morning, she let him in to shower as promised, and left his washed shirt folded outside the bathroom door. He entered the kitchen shining, holding the ironed shirt as if it would break. She laughed and he frowned, then laughed with her. Eventually he sat and ate eggs and home-made bread, sweet blueberry jam like he'd never tasted, and black-peppered bacon. From her butchered hog she said. Davy built his own smoke house and it was the maple hardwood he tasted along with copious amounts of pepper. Joe smiled at the new word.

It was a simple matter to stack bales onto the flatbed of a much newer GMC. The ropes to tie the load down were quickly familiar and Joe was enjoying the work, the sense of something opening in him. He made the loops and figures, caught each bale under another bale or a lead of rope and then tied off so the rope end would pull free but not slip. She was smiling at him when he finished. "Would you like to drive?"

Here it was; he could tell her no and why not, he could risk the truth but he would scare her from last night's catharsis. Yes he knew that word, he'd never heard it spoken but he had looked it up and understood its meanings. He would not take away from such a sad human being the small offering of peace.

"Ma'am, I've been in another country and haven't renewed my license." A lie, yes, within the shape of truth. He'd never had a license although his grandfather taught him to drive. No one cared in those sand hills if a child drove legal, as long as they could see over the wheel and reach the pedals.

The GMC truck was fancy; individual seats, padded dash, air conditioning and music, yet she apologized that the truck was secondhand and did not have a CD changer but she and Davy had thought this the best for their money. Joe had no idea what she was talking about, more words lost in the wasted years. So he sat in the bucket seat and nodded his head, smiled when it seemed necessary, and felt like a kid again, for that brief moment when all things were new and exciting. She drove well, both hands on the wheel and looked straight ahead even as she talked to him. He could hear his grandfather again, instructing Joe on how to hold the wheel, check the side mirror, especially when hauling anything that covered the back mirror's view.

Impressive, he thought, and was content with their silence. Then; "Where are you headed, Joe? I can know that much about you." This question could be answered with the truth; "I'm going to Gettysburg, ma'am." The truck swerved, she brought it back onto the road without disturbing the load of hay. He grinned; he'd gotten those ropes tied right. At the moment, small victories such as this were all he had.

Her voice cracked; "Why?" He studied the single word, looking for a trap and found nothing; "I read a book and it made me want to go there, to hear the voices of the long-dead and forgotten." He stopped, too fanciful, yet she did not laugh but smiled; "I think I read the same book." "Yes, ma'am. The Killer Angels." It was the only time he had spoken the title and realized that it belonged to him as well. "But why, Joe? Who needs to be heard?"

The name jumped out of him; "Joshua Chamberlain." She nodded, risked a glance at him; "Go on." He obliged; "Chamberlain was every thing good in us, ma'am; he was educated and intelligent and I know those two don't always go together. He spoke of his God with great faith and he volunteered to go to war." What meant so much to Joe about the man was only a few words from being spoken. He had thought these things when he was unable to sleep, going over what he had done, hating himself, until he read about Joshua Chamberlain and began to understand that inside many good men were the seeds of killing.

She had to have seen something of his thought process for her right hand came off the wheel briefly and she touched his forearm. He wiped his mouth; "Chamberlain turned out to be a warrior, the definition of the book title. He knew without being taught and was good at what he learned through harsh experience. And still he went back into peaceful life with no regrets and few difficulties. Hell, ma'am, he was even elected the governor of Maine." It seemed a damned fool conversation, one-sided and talking about a past that had no connection to him. "Anyway, I'm headed to that battlefield."

Joe unloaded the hay where he'd been directed. Jackie had started to protest when Mr. Townes wanted her to come with him to hear about the horses and said that her hired man could finish the job. After all, Townes stated loudly, it wasn't fit work for a lady. Joe let her know he wasn't offended. They understood each other that well.

The farm where she was delivering the hay was actually in Pennsylvania. They raised draft horses, Belgians mostly, and a few of the smaller Suffolk Punches, which Joe remembered from the yard in England. A dying breed even then, Joe had learned, now they were transplanted to this country in an attempt to resurrect them, although a man somewhere in Kansas had bred them in the fifties. Spoken as if something important coming from the state of Kansas was an outrageous concept.

The farm owner was delighted to exhibit his prize stock to Jackie Weeks. He caught up a Belgian mare and foal to discuss the purity of her bloodlines and her correct conformation, while barely mentioning the lesser Suffolks. The owner explained at length that he'd looked into the Brabant, a variety of the Belgian, but had been dissuaded from breeding them by the frequency of a leg edema that could shorten life expectancy. Jackie nodded while her attention remained on Joe.

Done, the ropes coiled and tied and thrown in the back of the half cab, another truck construction he admired, Joe found the side paddock where two Suffolk mares grazed. He leaned on the fence rail and watched them. It was only when he heard the rumble of the GMC motor that he hurried to get his things from the truck.

The man was gone, no lingering to speak kindly with the help. Joe had to laugh, some things in the world never changed. He stood next to the driver's open window. "Ma'am. Thank you for the ride, and the meals." She put the truck in neutral and pulled the brake, opened the door and stepped out. There would be a good-bye and perhaps more and he wanted to run but kept his feet glued to the ground.

He was shaking like a newborn kitten. Whatever had happened to Joe Evans had been brutal yet he triggered and then accepted her grief. Need urged her to grab him if only briefly; common sense said that such a gesture would immediately be filled with sorrow. The wound was not healed, the space not yet secure. She put out her hand; "Joe, thank you." She did felt reassured as he took her hand and gently squeezed, making her aware again of his strength.

"Let me take you to the nearest cross road so you can get on to Gettysburg. It's a long walk from here." He knew better; "No thank you, ma'am. This is a good place to part." He couldn't get his mouth to say the words, that if he got in that cab, he'd go with her and that wasn't right. Not yet. He shook his head; "No, ma'am. This is best. Otherwise we'd make mistakes." She found herself nodding; his wisdom and sense was direct, painful, and the truth.

She got in the truck, and while driving slowly down the lane, she watched him in the mirror. For whatever he'd done, this was a man she admired. And, if she admitted it herself, she most definitely coveted his touch.

Three

The country was cursed with mountains and running water; he had to venture near a large town to find a bridge crossing the Susquehanna River. Then he got stuck following state road Highway 309. Twice he had to step off the road as oversized trucks passed at high speed, leaving a thick trail of odors. The cargo was animals, stacked in two layers, hides and noise and an unmistakable horse stench. When one truck came too close for a brief time, Joe saw a bloodied eye and he had to look away.

Keep walking, don't think on it. Grandfather would take an old or lamed horse out into the sand ridges where small gullies became canyons and the coyotes howled their eagerness. He shot each horse, those he raised, those he saved from others' cruelty; he shot them as the final gift of death without fear.

Three days of walking and Joe was hungry, tired, one foot had a blister, and he could hardly stand his own stench. He was close to Port Clinton when one of the loaded trucks came to a grinding stop next to him. The electric window came down and the man's voice yelled; "Hey bud, want a ride and a few bucks? I got some horses headed to auction and I need help unloading them. Those buckos at the auction, they don't know how to work stock. Now you, you look like a man knows horses."

It was a long speech to yell through a window over the truck growl, and the sad whinnying of the captive load helped Joe decide. The inside of the truck cab smelled as foul as the load, and the man himself was from a different hell. Gaps where there should be teeth, billed cap that partially hid greasy hair hanging to a frayed shirt collar.

When the man drew the unwieldy truck back onto the road, the transition was smooth, even the quick shifting through endless gears caused no great lurch or jump, no sound of panic from the awful load. The driver looked over at Joe. "I ain't that cruel, now some guys they like hard starts and stops, they like hearing them horses suffer. I got a sick missus to home. But I ain't gonna make those horses hurt more'n they have to. Life's short enough. Why I wanted someone who might know how to help. Boy meant to come with me wouldn't do it when he learned where I was bound."

That was the end of any talk. Two hours later, Joe asked one question. "How far is Gettysburg?" The man scratched his head, "Don't know, mister. Ain't never been there. Heard of it though, some kind of theme park, now I took the missus when she could we went to Disneyland, that was enough for me.

Joe'd seen where Gettysburg was, on a map out of the prison library. It was almost straight south and slightly west of the prison. Deliberately he had not counted the miles for numbers could weaken his resolve. It was a place he'd only read about. Grandfather had taken him once to the Lakota battlefield at Wounded Knee. A grievous betrayal so deep that the battle was fought again almost a hundred years later and the government still held on to its prisoners. Gettysburg was the white man's killing ground.

The woman had understood; the driver didn't know why Gettysburg existed.

The land was pretty along the road; farmland with clusters of new houses but still enough in cultivation that a man who loved the land would appreciate the hard work. The driver told him it was the Amish. A word Joe had heard and wasn't sure he understood; what he did know was that they used horses and stayed away from most of the modern world.

The ride lasted an hour more and it wasn't until the truck pulled in to the livestock auction yard that Joe experienced the result of the old-fashioned reliance on horsepower forced to compete with the modern world. Horses everywhere, tied up, jammed in pens, chewing on poor hay, whinnying, some fallen, some fighting with neighbors, kicking and squealing.

They weren't all Amish horses, the driver told him. Lots of folks had horses they couldn't sell, why they come to this auction to send them on to the next place. Like the load he was carrying, from over by the Lakes, the old and worthless, the young, some of the hormone mares and their sad foals, a few horses from the west, good stock, papered thoroughbreds off the track and unsound, too many horses and not enough folks wanting them. The driver tried to explain the economics but Joe didn't hear the droning voice. The sight and smells were enough; he wanted out but he'd accepted a deal, took a ride, and now he had to make good on his word. He got down from the truck cab, shucked off the jacket and tied it to the suitcase. He'd come back for his gear, he wasn't riding in this truck again. As he pulled down the back ramp of the truck, Joe winced. The animals were stuffed in two levels; for the taller horses, their withers rubbed on the ceiling slats.

"Boy, you stop gawking. Soon as we get 'em off, better they'll be. At least they can walk around here, and the auction they's supposed to give 'em hay and water while they wait." Joe shook, his hands barely able to undo the bolt holding the tail gate closed. The driver had backed to a raised earthen ramp so the horse could be funneled into a metal chute where pens awaited. Slick, cement-floor pens, slippery with waste and blood, the lives of too many horses left rotting in the muck. There, the driver said, the horses would be separated according to killer horses or possible riding mounts.

The man asked if Joe could ride; "Anything halfway decent it goes into the ring and sells better ridden. Brings up the dollars." The man quit fiddling with the ramp. Joe nodded; yes he could ride. He was cold, his fingers thick in trying to steady the ramp. Inside the truck body, the horses were motionless, only one head pushed out to see the surroundings. Joe followed orders, numb and furious as he walked along a thin edge of earth and reached up with a whip he'd been given, to poke and prod the horses to begin their trip into hell.

Horses stumbled out of the truck; some on three legs, dragging a broken hind leg, blinded in one eye, bleeding from head wounds where they'd hit the steel trailer sides. Bony horses, sores, swellings, a rotting stench to make a man gag. Loud squeals of stallions fighting other stallions, foals crushed between lamed draft horses. Joe turned his head away as he kept the stock moving.

The bay gelding would have measured sixteen hands at the withers, but a rider would sit on a fleshless backbone, legs pushed against prominent ribs. The hooves were grown out, toes beginning to curl, which forced his weight back on his heels, threatening to pop the tendons. The horse walked in short strides despite the driver poking at him. The driver got aggressive and jammed the prod into the bay's groin. The horse side-kicked and knocked the prod out of the man's fingers; the driver cursed, slammed a hand against the metal slats of the trailer but the prod was gone, and the bay made his cautious way down the ramp to the brief smell of fresh air. Then those behind the bay began to push and nip at him; one stallion laid his head on the bay's rump in challenge. The bay kicked out, even backed up as the stallion reared, tipped over and fell on a mare desperate to protect her foal.

The two-week-old filly was pinned to the trailer slats and the crack of her fragile ribs could have been heard. The bay kicked and squealed until a man slapped him with a long whip and the bay turned to bite at the insult. The horses on his right side shoved past, the mare moved with them and the filly went to her knees, was stepped on by a three-legged draft horse. The filly was hit again and died. The mare whinnied as she was pushed forward.

The obstinate bay slammed into the alley fence, bending the rails but still confined. The bay reared, slipped a foreleg over the metal rail and was shoved by the mass of horseflesh coming sideways past him. The bay spun, hanging by one leg, tearing flesh from bone until the blood slid his leg off the railing and he joined the mass, bleeding and unable to bear weight on the wounded leg.

Near the truck cab, Joe could hear the chaos but not see the misery. The driver, who never told Joe his name, yelled that the horses were out, he'd move the truck, then Joe had to clean the rig. Meantime he could help with the sorting; the livestock vet was there to check each horse as fit to go through the sale. These inspections were a formality; the man on call barely looked up from a list, more intent on making check marks than actually seeing the horses. Each animal had to be able to walk on all four legs in order to go through the sale. 'Able to walk' was obviously a financial decision.

Joe learned that only a few who tended the animals cared. The truck driver's song and dance of sympathy had been meant to keep Joe working for him. Inside the auction ring, a group of people huddled together. They wore clean jackets and sturdy boots and talked among themselves. The driver caught Joe staring at them. "They's the ones, they come here to save a horse or two. Drive up the prices so I don't care but the meat buyers, taking a load up to Canada, they hate them people.

At that moment the vet checked off a bay gelding bleeding profusely from a fresh wound. Holding a gate to allow one animal at a time to go through, Joe considered slamming that gate into the vet, maybe return some of the suffering the horses endured. It would send him back to jail, but the way he felt now it would be worth it. He pulled on the gate with all his anger, until the bay gelding stepped into the lights and noise of the ring itself and whirled back, ears pinned, stumbling on his wounded leg, pushing against Joe and the dented metal gate.

The bay wore an auction rope halter and its lead slipped through Joe's hand. One of the condemned might escape. Joe glanced at the brand, prominent on the bony left hip; Rafter BP; his grandfather's brand. He lunged at the dragging lead and held a horse his grandfather had bred and raised. He drew the bay's head around and studied the horse. Good eyes set well in a wide face, a white star between the eyes. Ears tipped forward then pinned back in fury; Joe dodged the charging bay, got his shirt sleeve and some of his flesh torn by the strong teeth but he laughed. He knew, it was a quarter horse with too much thoroughbred on its mama's side.

His arm ached as he yanked on the line and the bay charged him on three legs. Joe hit the bay on the nose, which stopped the horse hard, chipped hooves skidding on the cement covered in loose shit and dribbled urine. Joe grabbed the nose of the bay gelding to study him. Other than the fresh wound and the half-starved skeleton, the horse looked sound, and certainly had enough energy to pull free and bite at Joe; again he smacked the bay's nose, then tugged lightly on the lead.

His voice was raw but Joe figured the bay wouldn't notice. "You, son, quit it. Mind the manners you were taught years back. I ain't taking guff from no sand hills bronc." Behind him chaos roared; the auctioneer calling out for another horse, the truck driver demanding that Joe ride the bay in never mind the wound, it weren't much, and the supposed veterinarian squalling at the rough treatment from the bay and the slamming gate.

It was a battle moving backwards through the frightened horses. Joe yelled and elbowed and the bay's temper helped, terrifying those struggling horses being pushed from behind to get into the sale ring. He found a pen, empty except for one animal down flat, no rib cage moving in great breaths, well past all suffering. Joe knelt and studied the bay's wounded leg, found the flesh and hide were there so if he wrapped his fingers around the soaked tissue, he could draw most of the wound into a shape that fitted where it had been torn. No need for stitches, not much of a scar left if he could get the wound treated now.

Behind him, on the other side of the pen fencing, the driver yelled at him to get out there and run that horse through the sale goddamn it. Joe straightened up; "You damned son of a bitch." He choked, coughed, spat. "I'm taking this bay as payment for the hell you put them through. You may have bills to pay and a sick wife but I doubt it. No son of a bitch doing this job day after day would have a family at home waiting on him." He took hold of his temper then, let out air in a snort. "Write me a bill of sale, for one twelve-year-old bay gelding branded Rafter BP on the left hip."

He could see the man's eyes widen, then he glanced at the bay's hip. Only a genius could read that brand through the caked shit and prominent bone. Joe kept pushing; "Back of an auction flyer will do, mister. You write it that I own the horse. My name is Joe Evans." He almost added his grandfather's last name but he didn't have the right.

It took an hour before Joe could get himself and the bay off the premises. He led the gelding slowly, letting the horse rest before tackling the narrow road to the back of the auction grounds. The vet's office held a few bandages and some ointment and Joe helped himself as the vet turned his back, muttering he had to tend to his duties.

Joe was stiff in the knees by the time he had a decent pressure bandage in place. There'd been no hot water to rinse out the grit and filth, but he'd been able to fill in the gaping wound with a tar ointment and then tie the flesh back into place with the tightly wrapped bandage. For now this would have to do. He had his gear from the truck, and the driver was nowhere in sight, too busy pushing misery for fifty cents a pound or less. It made Joe sick but he could rescue one horse, not all of them, and he needed to focus on what he'd done and what still needed doing. Walking a lame and starving animal more'n a thousand miles was crazy. Joe grinned and slapped the bay's thin neck. "Son, we got to get that leg looked after."

He walked out of the livestock auction yard onto a tar surface running along a ridge toward town. A buggy pulled by a lean bay horse headed straight toward him. Joe held out a hand, the driver was reluctant to pull up. Joe nodded briefly; the man held the reins and barely dropped his head. Then gestured to the horse; "You did not buy a bargain, mister, if you paid more than five cents a pound."

Amish, that was the word; dressed in black, flat-brimmed hat and half-cut chin whiskers. The man stared at Joe, which he was getting used to but still didn't like. The accent was clear when the man finally spoke; "What is it you want, mister?' Joe patted the bay's neck; "He needs a good vet and I figured you would know."

"It is veterinarian you go a mile into town and turn right onto Flag Street. It is there. He is good." The man doffed his hat this time, then asked his own question. "You are an Indian, what the English call Native?" Joe agreed. "I have never met a man such as you." This time the question was not unkind or rude, a simple query from another outsider. Joe raised his head, thought he'd tell a truth out loud to a man who was curious and decent enough in asking. "I am Lakota." His Amish companion smiled quickly; "You are more than that. What is it, yes?" Joe had to decide. These were words he had not spoken for years. "My father was Welsh, I was born in Britain."

The man smiled. "I wish you well. Dr. Junker will take excellent care of your horse." Another nod, a light slap of the reins and a chirp and the dark bay stepped instantly into that slinging gait that would quickly cover the miles.

They reached a compromise, Joe and the bay. The grass alongside the road was richly green; Joe allowed the bay five minutes of grazing, then tugged on the rope and the bay reluctantly followed. Another stop, another five minutes. It took them an hour to find the vet's clinic, and a man was turning a key in the front door when Joe brought the lamed bay down the narrow lane.

He heard the man sigh, watched the shoulders sag as he unlocked the door and gestured to Joe. "Go 'round to the side. I'll be right there." Joe studied the building as he led the badly limping horse. When the overhead door began to roll up, Joe held tight on the lead, figuring the bay would try to bolt. The horse followed the overhead door's ascent until his head was stretched high, but the animal was never afraid. He had to be sired by that almost black quarter horse Grandfather called Brown Ike; fearless and intelligent and hell to train.

The vet watched; "Nervy son ain't he. What the hell happened?" The man walked around the bay and Joe, stopped, raised his hand to his mouth. "Oh." He'd seen the auction sticker. "Well let's get that leg cleaned up. Bring him inside." The clinic was clean and sparse. Two horses stood in large stalls. One was on intravenous fluids; the other had a thick bandage around his neck and stitches on his face. Neither animal showed interest in the new arrival.

Joe knelt and unwound the awkward bandage. "Sorry for the mess but I didn't want him walking without something to keep out the dirt." The doc shook his head; "You did it right. That auction, usually they just shoot them, or use a pulley to get them on a trailer and headed north before anyone says a word." The voice was neutral, intended to cover real anger. Joe stood and held the bay's head, feeling the horse tense as the doc got to work with a bucket of hot water and a mound of soft clean cloths. The bay pinned his ears and tried to pull the leg away; Joe spoke gently, cupped the bay's muzzle so that the teeth disappeared and the soft lips were held in his hands.

The doc grunted. "Nasty tear but you got it held together. He'll need a few days of antibiotics or the leg'll rot. Goddamn place is filthy." And in the next breath; "My name is Junker, said with a soft 'j'. Karl Junker. You've done a good deed here." Joe's voice was soft; "Joseph Evans." The doc smiled very briefly as his hands worked the wrapped bandage; "Why'd you take a risk on this one? He's three hundred pounds underweight, probably wormy and now that leg. He's going to cost just to get him back out the door."

The only thing Joe could think of was to make a damn-fool comment; "I like them…the bushes you got 'round the building." The doc grinned as if he'd heard the comment before; "My wife's project. Anything to keep her happy." Then the doc stood up and they finally shook hands, feeling the strength of each other. "You seem to know horses, Mr. Evans, and I have these two that came in last night." He laughed. "At least it wasn't four in the morning." The bay pushed at Joe's arm and he winced. "Now, take off your shirt and let me stitch up the bite. That gelding seems taken with you but it looks like he had to brand you first."

"Where do you want him?" The doc pointed to an empty stall filled with shavings and what looked to be good hay. The man laughed; "With those bones, he'll think he's been led into heaven." Joe took the bay inside the stall, and then had to fight to get the rope halter off as the bay tore into the abundant meal.

Seated in a chair, arm tingling with a bath of alcohol, Joe held himself quiet as the doc took neat stitches. He felt each one, tried not to count but there was time between the tugging of the doc's hand and occasionally he could see the glint of the curved needle. "Why'd you buy that bay? It's a lot you've taken on." The vet spoke against the rhythmic pull of the needle, creating a distraction.

It interested Joe that twice now the question had been 'why bother' with a wreck like the bay. He thought about it, studied on it, this was a time and a place where the truth could not hurt. "He's branded with my grandfather's brand." There was so much more, and the doc held up the needle as if waiting for the rest but Joe shook his head. "Oh." The doc took the next stitch, pulled harder than usual and tied off in a knot. "There, take out the stitches in a week and you'll hardly have a scar." Joe looked up to see if the man was making a joke. But Doc Junker had turned away.

His arm ached lightly but it was uncomplicated. The bay was safe; there was no more yelling and fighting, only peace inside the cement walls of the clinic. He grabbed the shirt and shrugged back into it. He saw the blood and torn fabric on the sleeve, which meant mending and washing. The doc sterilized his instruments, placing the scissors and thread in a cabinet. "Mr. Evans, I would make a deal with you." If he listened carefully, Joe heard a ghost of the Amish speech. The doc sighed and Joe realized he was expected to answer. "What?"

"You sleep here, listen for the horses. That dark bay especially. They got hit by a car, damned fool tourist so busy taking pictures he ran two buggies off the road and that bay turned over in the shafts. Don't know about him; the other one, the chestnut, his face looks bad but he'll be fine." Joe studied the man as he talked. It was his turn; "Why?" "Because the horses need tending at night and I need to sleep and my staff doesn't come in until seven in the morning and we open at eight. You know horses, and you need a place and time to let the bay heal. I'll send out supper. And there's a pot where we brew the worst coffee in the county. Help yourself." "In trade for taking care of the bay? And me?" The doc nodded.

Joe discovered the wash stall. There was a hot water hose, cold water and body shampoo and even a coat conditioner. A rubber mat, drains, a thick towel barely used. He spent a few minutes picking off most of the hair, then gave it up as nonsense. He was considering the shower, fingers working on the top button of the torn shirt, when the door burst open and a boy stood there. He held a thermos and a paper bag out at arm's reach, rattling them slightly; a teen-age boy, maybe fifteen, who looked like the doc only with the unformed softness that spoke his age.

"Pop said to bring you supper. Here." The kid put the bag and thermos down, shook his head as he studied Joe carefully; "Hell you're nothing but a 'breed." He went back out the door, slamming it hard enough to startle the horses. Joe sat down to unscrew the thermos top, got the scent of vegetable soup and he smiled. In the paper bag was a sandwich, ham and cheese, thick ham, lots of mustard, dark green lettuce. Joe took a long drink of the soup, chewed on a few vegetables. Then he put the thermos down, wiped his mouth on a napkin from the bag. A woman put together this meal for an unknown human taking up residence in her back yard. He silently thanked her.

He used a metal bucket turned on its rim to hold the thermos, and his hands shook as he held the sandwich; he would have laughed except for the pain in his gut. He was in truth a joke, an outlandish combination. Like mating a Shetland pony to a Tennessee Walker – to produce an animal with no place of its own. He needed to get these thoughts out of his mind and pay attention to finishing the soup, at least eating the meat out of the sandwich, and taking a shower to cleanse his flesh and soul of that terrible auction.

His damaged dignity still allowed Joe to laugh at the absurdity of being buck naked, feet curled around drainage mats, holding on to a stainless steel nozzle with a flexible rubber hose, washing with equine shampoo and tomorrow morning he would whinny when the vet walked into the clinic. He was cautious in not letting the hose spray directly on his sutured arm but he was warm and gloriously soaked, a generous sensation.

The bay gelding had eaten the hay and was watching Joe with ears pricked forward; life already revived in the abused animal. Knowing the sire's temperament, or at least having a good guess, Joe imagined all the scenarios of that bay fighting his riders, handlers, hell anyone who tried to make him behave by force. The two injured horses stood there, heads hanging, barely able to stay on their bruised legs.

Shaving wasn't much of an issue for Joe, he was like his father and once a week was enough. For the first time he was uncomfortable with the church-donated clothes. The cotton underwear felt greasy although he'd washed them, the shirt colors were harsh, the jeans sagged and even the boots were uncomfortable as he pulled them back on. Being soap-and-water clean changed a man's perspective. There was a cot in a back office with blankets but no sheets, a pillow with no cover. Joe dragged the cot into the clinic itself. Grandfather's bay whinnied at the noise; the other two might have twitched an ear but truly didn't care. That worried Joe, so he spent time in the stalls, standing propped against the wall near each drooping head.

The bay on the IV barely opened its eyes. It had decent conformation, one of those pacers he thought, from the slant to the hind leg, the angle through the hip and stifle. He touched the horse lightly, rubbing inside the mouth. The bay sighed occasionally, and when Joe stopped, the bay raised his head and pushed against Joe's arm. He smiled, pressed his forehead against the bay's neck and rubbed inside the mouth until the gums turned pink with blood.

When he entered the stall of the chestnut, the horse was alive enough to gently brush Joe's hand. He rubbed the muzzle, then the flat jowl, up to the ears and the horse sighed, letting its head drop so that Joe could rub the loose ears inside and out, stroking the horse until it dozed. He then checked on the wounded bay; the horse's eyes were clearer, and the gums were still pink. He rubbed the bay's mouth again, then its ears and left the horses alone, certain they would survive the night.

Only then did Joe lie on the bed, without shirt or socks and boots but still in his jeans; he didn't know who would show up, or when, during the night or early morning, and he intended to retain what dignity was left by at least covering himself.

Four

The doc had called to tell both assistants he had surgery scheduled for the morning, and by the way he'd found someone to stay with the injured horses. So they weren't to be surprised when they found a strange man setting with the patients, probably cursing the coffee and looking for breakfast. Of course Dr. Junker, being a man, said little about what he'd found to stay at the clinic. My god he was something to look at. The horses had been fed, hay and fresh water in their stalls, the night's load of manure in the manure basket but the man was what a woman dreamed of while a below-average bar pickup serviced her.

In Amish country, pickings were slim for an English girl who didn't finish high school and had a child at home by a nameless father. Wish it had been this man; she said it again in her mind, my god he was something. He seemed to be sewing on a torn sleeve with one of Doc's curved needles and the finest of poly thread. A man who could sew, and wasn't a doctor. An amazing specimen.

But he couldn't dress himself. That striped yellow and green and purple shirt was a sin, although the colors were great against the dark skin. She smiled and the man, hand in the air, hesitated until she walked past him, then he gave her the slightest of nods and went back to sewing. Sandy wanted to be nearby when Vanessa got in. Now that girl, she might be pure and righteous but Sandy knew how she looked at the doc, that stupid moony-eyed gaze as if a married man like Doc Junker would notice a vet student who couldn't get into college. For Sandy, working here was a job, for Vanessa it was the hope that a good reference from the vet might swing her a place in line. No fun in that, to Sandy's mind. Sandy scrubbed at her arms and hands, wanting to learn more about the man while knowing she'd lose her job if the doc found his morning list unfinished.

Instruments sterilized, the recovery room pads sanitized; she'd done that yesterday after the doc had sewn up the chestnut's face. Driver totaled his car and as much as Sandy didn't care about horses, well they sure didn't deserve this kind of torment for patiently doing their job. At least, as the doc said, at least the owners wanted to try and save their animals. It wouldn't be cheap, but the doc was optimistic. She heard the ring of metal against the metal frame; a fire door the doc called it, part of the regulations of having gas and chemicals inside the building. It meant that Vanessa was coming to work and Sandy floated toward the main clinic, needing of course to see to the chestnut in the far stall.

Sandy positioned herself in the perfect spot to view Vanessa's face.

Vanessa stopped abruptly, and from one of the stalls came a bark. That had to be Sandy, which meant something was up. Goodness but who was this, as the man stood, holding on to an empty cup, smiling as if she had been expected. "Morning." Vanessa jumped again. "I didn't mean to upset you. Doc Junker, he's got me here to keep an eye on the horses." Ah, the doc's call, she'd barely listened to it past the 'don't need to come in tonight.' Oh well.

"Thank you." She managed that much and fled into the warren of back offices. 'Thank you!' She snorted; where did that come from and it was Sandy in the far stall, laughing now, knowing first that there was a man in the office, a man who looked like nothing Vanessa had ever seen. She wasn't a virgin, not like Sandy thought. And she would never correct Sandy's impression, for being teased about sex was bad enough; if Sandy knew how Vanessa had been treated some nights, she would be unmerciful. But as the doc said, Sandy took surprisingly good care of the animals.

There was surgery scheduled this morning and Dr. Junker had promised that Vanessa could assist. So it was up to her to check on Sandy's layout of the instruments, and the cleanliness of the facilities. It was a black Labrador who'd swallowed several large rocks now impeding its digestion. Silly dog, but it loved to chase rocks, and evidently thought that swallowing them was part of the game.

Voices in the main clinic drew her attention. She put her head around the corner of the doorway, listening and watching. Sandy was intending to enter the stall of a strange bay horse who most definitely did not appreciate her attention. The man's voice was clear, with an undercurrent of annoyance. "Ma'am, I asked you not to go in there.

The bay belongs to me, I'll take care of him. It's part of the deal." He hesitated, sighed; "With me and the doc."

Typically, Sandy pushed into the stall and the bay tried to bite her and the man laughed as he shook his fist at the bay. "You contrary son, leave her be." As if the attack was only play, the bay snorted and went back to eating. The man turned and saw Vanessa. He nodded and again she thought she'd never seen anything like him. Then the doc came in, smiling like all this was all quite normal. Vanessa ventured into the clinic room, and the doc nodded. "You ready, that rock hound'll be here soon enough." He didn't wait for any response but turned to the man. "Good morning, Mr. Evans. It appears you have found the few amenities our clinic offers to humans. And the horses look as if they survived quite well. I'm glad to know my faith was not misplaced, although my son tried to convince me otherwise." There was a stop here, a hesitation the girls knew too well whenever Kevin Junker was mentioned in any discussion. "The boy knows only his own kind and they can be merciless." The truth finally, and spoken to a stranger.

The man laughed and accepted a greasy bag. "Breakfast," the doc said, and disappeared into his office to prepare for surgery. Sandy tended to her chores; Vanessa went to make any last minute changes to the operating room.

Joe checked the standing bandage and then ran his hands over the bay's entire body, avoiding the attempts to bite him by tying the bay's head. A threatened kick received a smack on the rump and the horse snorted, then lifted his tail to dump fresh manure. It was ribs and hipbones and each knob on the spine, too close to the hide, too easily found by gentle fingers. Joe winced as he finished the inspection; it was cruel neglect from owners who knew nothing about horses and, more than likely fearing the bay's temper, they tried starving him into submission. The hooves needed trimming and he'd seen the right tools in the clinic. Joe untied the bay and led him a few feet. No limp now, no fussing, so he rolled up the sliding door and took the bay outside.

A woman came from the house and Joe sighed, led the bay close to her, using the horse as a shield to keep a good distance.

"Ma'am, I take it you're the one to thank for that soup last night. And the sandwich. Your effort was most appreciate for I surely was hungry." It seemed enough for she smiled and walked to her car. "You're welcome."

Joe was napping under a tree when the doc came out. The bay was back in the stall, his hooves trimmed and Joe was pleased; there was a good sole and thick wall. Most of what had begun to turn up was dried toe that he slowly carved off. The day was soft and Joe had rare time to himself. He reluctantly opened his eyes and then stood up as the doc approached. He tried to do it right; "How's the dog?" The doc grinned; "Mr. Evans I sincerely doubt that you have been worrying about the insides of a stone-eating Labrador."

Then Joe's host took in a breath, expelled it; "What does a man like you think about, Mr. Evans?" Joe eased back, drawn tight in his gut, fists lightly clenched. No one's business, no one needed to care. He had no answer, nothing that was suitable and would allow him to stay here for the few more days that the bay needed. What truth could he say; he was thinking about sex, about the girls who worked in the clinic, the women he met on his brief journey. He'd be thrown back in prison for his thoughts even as the young females working for the doc dressed in tight clothes and stood so close to Joe that he could smell their power.

He forced a smile; "Not thinking much right now, doc. The bay's leg looks good, I took the liberty of putting on a new bandage, reused the leg wrap. The skin's pink, and there's no more bleeding. I gave him a shot like you told me. And hand-walked him some, did his hooves, hope you don't mind me using the rasp and nippers. I didn't want to bother you in surgery. He's attacking that hay. I figured it's better for him than the rich grass. That could colic him and he'd never live through an attack." Keep talking, Joe thought, keep the words coming to cover what he truly thought.

The doc interrupted; "Where are you going?" Joe shrugged; "Taking the bay to where he was born." Junker turned his head, "And how far away is this home?" Joe grinned; "'Bout fourteen hundred miles dead reckoning." He stood there on the grass lawn making small talk with a man decent enough to take in a drifter with a wounded horse; he stood there and thought about sex.

"What'd you do to the horses?" Joe choked; "Huh?" "Last night as I was locking up, I was figuring to find a dead horse or two this morning. They were sewed and cleaned but road rash causes shock in many cases and I thought one or the other, or both, would be down. It was why I wanted you there. Someone was needed through the night to call me. Hell, man, their gums are pink and they're both eating well. What'd you do?" Joe shrugged; "Something my pa taught me. Rub their ears and their gums, if they'll let you. That's all." The vet studied him closely and Joe was uncomfortable. But it wasn't superficial curiosity. It was deeper, as if looking into all that Joe kept hidden. "You want a job here?" "No." Junker looked away; "Of course."

First it was the brash one, Sandy, barging in to the clinic at dusk. She smelled of cheap flavored brandy. She found him, walked to him where he sat, sipping at another cup of the terrible coffee. She took the cup and put it on the upturned bucket and kissed him. A kiss that made him stand up, her mouth locked on his, no hands, no other contact than her mouth and he was stunned at what went through him. As he was about to erupt, she knew and pulled away. Thrust her breasts forward, played with her hair, grinned at him. "Well?"

The physical distress was terrible; he could not sit down or stand near her. He wanted her gone so at least his humiliation would be private. "No!" She laughed and stepped closer until he put up both hands and she cursed; "You bastard son of a bitch." He'd been called a lot worse and in his case the words were true. He narrowed his eyes and doubled his raised hands into fists and she stomped her way out of the clinic, slamming the metal door hard enough that all three horses whinnied.

When he heard the retreating putt-putt of a cheap car he knew he could relax. There was a toilet inside the office area where he took care of himself, shamed into needing the release. Women were hell ran through his mind as his body shivered with urgency. He took another shower, not because of sweat or manure or hay stuck to his skin but because the girl had made him feel ugly. Joe shook his head as he tried to drown his thoughts in ice water.

She was terrified and knew exactly what she was doing at the same time. Her last boyfriend had hit her to get aroused; this man who was so good with the horses would not do that. She was not bold or brave, she was not pretty or particularly stacked or dressed to provoke men but for once she would ask for what she wanted. Tonight she had stood for a half hour in front of the mirror, naked, washed clear of the day's surgery and clean-up. Studying herself; her hips were wide, and that thicket of curled red hair embarrassed her, so dark and different against her white skin. Men told her it was attractive, even sexy, but to her the hair and its contrast were shaming.

Her breasts were moderate, not hanging yet like her mother's. Perky one man said and that too was an embarrassment. But she understood enough of the male libido that what might bother her was what turned men on, curves and weight and a narrow waist, those pale, blue-veined globes made respectable by loose tops and sturdy bras.

Tonight she wore a light jersey top and no bra. Her belly showed where the top did not meet the low denim shorts. She had bought these shorts when Bobby was with her. Currently he was in jail for assaulting another woman who refused his brutal advances. Vanessa had not realized his behavior was wrong until the other woman pressed charges. And she had not known Bobby cheated on her. She had always accepted his violence.

She knew how to open the surgery door without making much noise. He was in the shower stall and she didn't know whether to call out or retreat. His back was to her and he was beautiful. Strong buttocks, a torso with no pimples, scars or tattoos; wide shoulders, muscle in relief as he raised the nozzle overhead. She could smell the chilled water; there were stitches along his forearm and she recognized Dr. Junker's careful work.

He turned around and his eyes narrowed but he did not hide his sex. Vanessa was fascinated by the slow thickening, for she had been too shy to watch and Bobby only needed a slap, a bit of rolling her around and he was inside as if she wasn't there at all.

Joe had taken care of the urgent need and washed away the shameful results, and now this innocent girl wearing almost nothing let him stare at her while his body responded again. He had no idea how to proceed. She came to stand under the cold spray next to him, until her hair flattened, her nipples were outlined by wet jersey. He let go of the nozzle to touch her and she quickly shut down the water flow.

It was her body laid against him, shoulder to knee, her belly pulsing as she moved oh so gently until he knew he would explode. Here was a woman who wanted him. He kissed her softly and she breathed into him. Then he slid a hand under her jersey, holding the weight of her breast. She slipped out of the jersey, and he unbuttoned the shorts, tugged gently and they slid down. She wore nothing underneath. He let his hand rest on the curled hair and she giggled. "Let's use the sofa in Doc's office, it's probably wider, and safer, than that cot."

Joe took a long breath and kissed her neck. "You are beautiful." His voice rippled her skin. She giggled; "I'll lock the door from the inside." Both of them knew what she meant. He stood naked in a veterinarian clinic, with an erection that hurt it was so full. The woman who had brought him to this degree came next to him, took his hand; "Come with me." Those were the sweetest words Joe'd ever heard.

This was how it felt; slippery and warm, muscles tightened around him, muscles he didn't know existed. He learned to rock into her, pull back out, respond to her hands on his butt as directional commands. A suggestion that he could kiss her breast, that he could suck on the nipple until she cried out and he worried but she said in a hurried whisper that he had not hurt her, would he touch her there. And her hand guided his fingers to that warm place, touching heat and rubbing as she asked until she cried out and her body arched and she pulled him back into her.

She rested her head on his chest, felt his rapidly-beating heart. He had filled her, never hurt her but kissed her gently until she asked for more. He listened to what she wanted. It couldn't be, he was too good-looking, too kind but something impossible occurred to her.

His heart rate eased, his lungs took in air, and she felt him smile when he pressed his mouth to her forehead. As she rolled into that gentleness, she found that he was hard and she wrapped her hand around him, felt his body jerk and heard him stutter. "Again?" She was smiling as she rolled on top; he didn't know.

Joe lay there, a woman sitting on his hips and belly, and when he looked up she was smiling so he leaned forward and kissed each breast. It seemed that she liked the kisses for she moved her hips to capture him and then rode up and down. Everything quickly focused on what was around him and his own back arched, his hips rose and fell and she kept that motion between them.

Vanessa wasn't surprised when he fell asleep. His arm was still around her but he snored lightly and she kissed the side of his face. There was a quilt over the sofa back and she covered Joe; taking one moment to study him, she felt faint spasms through her pelvis. She would never let a man strike her again. And she knew that she would not sleep with this particular man a second time. When they met inside the clinic's sterile walls, it would be difficult to not turn red with embarrassment, but he was leaving soon, that's what the doc said.

After dressing in the dark, she went back to check on him. He still wore the quilt as he slept, snorting when she tucked the material close to his face. Vanessa was smiling when she let herself out of the clinic. She had folded his clothes, leaving them near the sofa. So there would be no further reason for embarrassment if anyone came into the clinic this late.

There were two people in a tan SUV waiting with a litter of puppies when she got to the clinic in the morning, and inside Doc and Joe were working with a cocker spaniel bitch passing blood and crying. Neither man looked at her or spoke and she understood, even if ignoring her felt like an insult.

He surprised her later; she smiled, he said 'hello' in a quiet voice and picked up the wadded sterile cotton the doc asked for. When they met again, alone, working in the operating room to get it ready, he was different. His looks still amazed her, and her memory could not be that poor – last night, well, it had never felt that way before. Vanessa made a silent vow to never again accept less. He smiled shyly and she finally understood. It was her duty so she lightly touched his arm. "You never asked last night but I'm on the pill." His expression showed he didn't understand.

"Birth control," she said. "Babies." His eyes widened; "Oh." She put two fingers against his shoulder. "Buy yourself condoms. At a pharmacy or grocery store." She got silly, trying to help him relax; "Now that you know, you'll need them!" He actually looked offended, so Vanessa stood on her toes and kissed his mouth lightly. "Women will be all over you." She wanted to say more, to tell him that if he treated them like he'd treated her last night, he'd never sleep alone.

Looking into his eyes, though, she was certain this man held things close to his heart and would not choose the intimacy of a constant woman, or the casual effort of one-night-stands. She found herself feeling sorry for him, then shook herself, time to get to work.

Doc Junker lost his private bet. He thought it would be Sandy, and had more respect for Evans that he would turn away the girl's easy sexuality. But it did surprise him that Vanessa found the nerve. He'd heard her walk the driveway, heard the metal door open. He deliberately didn't oil the hinges for he wanted to be aware if anyone tried to break in.

The two of them were another surprise in the morning; no simpering from Vanessa and only straightforward work from Evans. Stalls cleaned, bandages changed, bedding spread out back where his wife had her composting bin. He must have spoken with her; she only liked certain types of waste. Vanessa held herself differently, walking with confidence. Whatever happened last night had been good for these two people. He might be married but Karl Junker was no prude.

The spaniel bitch would recover; her owners wanted to leave the puppies with her, even though they couldn't nurse. It was too much, they said, to be expected to feed the puppies every two hours. There were five of them, they explained, as if that number were high enough to absolve them from tending to the puppies' survival. Doc suggested they could make arrangements with Joe Evans, that for a decent fee the man would care for the puppies until the mother was able to nurse. He saw that glittery edge in the wife's eye as she turned to study Joe, and thought what constant hell Evans must go through. But Evans paid the woman no mind as he listened to the husband's briefing. A handshake and Doc guessed his temporary hired hand would make a few more dollars. From what little talk he'd gotten out of the man, he had a long walk ahead and nothing to fill his belly.

What impressed Karl was that Evans didn't seem to mind the task he'd set for himself.

Five

He'd been half-afraid all morning. Sleep like that scared him; he'd been gone inside so deep he'd felt nothing but the light sweep of that quilt she'd drawn over him, and the even lighter touch of her lips. Sleep like that was dangerous. Doc showed him how to feed the new pups. There was a syringe with a thin soft tube, and he could draw in the right amount of formula, then gently insert the tube into the stomach. His hands were thick holding the small instrument. The trick was, Doc told him, not to get the tube into the lungs. He had to listen to hear belly rumbles and not breathing before pushing the plunger very slowly.

They were what the doc called party cockers, three colors. They fit into the palm of his hand, on their backs making squeaking noises and legs wagging. Eyes shut of course, life barely begun. Their silky coat felt like feathers and he smiled as he named each pup silently, so as to not offend whatever listened. His grandfather had taught him the importance of names.

They thrived, every two hours a small amount of warmed formula in their bellies and he could see them grow. Just as he could see improvement in the bay's leg and realized that in a few days he would leave. She hadn't come back to him and he was glad. If she leaned against him, he would dissolve and lose the need to move on. Abstinence was his penance, the incredible pleasure belonged to other people, not him. Nothing belonged to a man who'd taken another's life even in righteous anger. He could not put the two acts together.

One morning he got up and did his chores, and saw that the bay was half-healed, the puppies able to suckle from their mother. Doc Junker had papers readied for him, and a lecture; "He's been wormed and doesn't need anymore antibiotics. You will however need proof of a negative Coggins test, which I've already pulled, and here's my testimony that he's healthy and not carrying any virulent diseases." The doc studied Joe.

"You did a decent job when you took the rasp and nippers to him. He's got good feet, and if you walk all those miles, you might not need to trim him again." It was close to a joke coming from the doc.

Joe allowed a small grin. "The Warners will pay me for the puppies' care so here's what they owe you, plus a bit more. I'd not mind if you stayed. It's been surprisingly good to have you here." Joe figured the man was serious even while being kind, something he wasn't willing to accept.

He shrugged; "This is more'n fair." The envelope held twenty dollar bills and folded papers; his whole life in a bill of sale, his release papers, and a dog-eared copy of an old certificate from the Rosebud Agency. No proof anywhere of his first ten years. Joe shrugged again, looked away. "Thanks."

"Oh, Joe." Doc had one more word. "I wrote up a diagnosis for the bay. How he came in to the clinic and what you've done with him. How he looks now is an improvement but we both know it's going to be a long time to get full weight on him. Some eager fool might challenge you for starving him." Joe took the paper; another kindness he couldn't repay. Then the doc's wife gave him canvas saddlebags with the weight and smell of foodstuffs inside. She too asked him to stay. Vanessa helped him pack his few things. The horse kept nosing at the bags, then pushing into Joe, making him laugh. Hell and damn, he thought, the bay's actually playing. He'll be a handful leaving the clinic.

Vanessa held the bay, and Joe stepped back to study his companion for the next thousand miles or more. There was the beginning of flesh across the ribs but the backbone protruded, and the rump had deep grooves through wasted flesh. The bay nipped at Vanessa and Joe spoke harshly; "No you don't." The horse glared at Joe but kept his lips over those long teeth. Sandy brushed past, carrying a bucket half-full of loose stool. "Waste of time, that horse is. You'd do better buying a junk car and getting wherever it is you're going." She didn't expect an answer, and they were the only words she had spoken to him since he'd refused her.

Earlier he'd done one last feeding for the puppies. Their fur, the milky smell, still pleased him. He'd keep them as the full memory of his almost two weeks in this safe place. When Doc came out to watch as Joe laced the canvas bags over the bay with two worn-out stirrup leathers that Doc found in his old tack trunk, Joe had a question; "How far is it to Gettysburg?"

Watching the bay gelding lurch then sull, trot sideways, kick out on occasion as the pair proceeded down the narrow lane out into the village and beyond, Doc Junker declared that they had all met a truly unusual man. Most of his clients were normal, some funnier or smarter than others, but very rarely did they get a truly unique character like Joe Evans.

Seventy to ninety miles, Doc had told him. Straight way was the highway or turnpike but Joe shook his head. No main roads, no nearby cars racing each other to get somewhere else too fast. Common sense told him they'd best go around larger towns and cities. Joe had to go west but needed to drop down to avoid those lakes and then he'd face the river crossings.

The doc made a few suggestions as to travel. Joe would want to miss the town of Lancaster, so he'd best go east first to the corners and turn south to Mount Airy and on to White Horse and the Gap, then to Christiana and he'd be going west. That should take him a day or two, then he'd been going alongside 373. What the doc couldn't tell him was how to cross that damn Susquehanna River again.

Walking took more from Joe than he expected. The bay's sire, Brown Ike, sure enough passed on his temper and after a half-hour Joe wondered why the old man kept using the horse at stud. Two hours later, and maybe five miles of Joe walking, the horse jigging, stopping to eat and then a fight over moving on, and Joe figured they'd both die of exhaustion and some poor soul would push their bones into a ditch.

He caught sight of a pond with high cattails growing against the edges and led the bay straight through to water. The horse balked but Joe showed no mercy. He snapped the end of the lead until the horse jumped into the cattail mass, pulling Joe with him. It felt good to be wet again; Joe put his head under, came up snorting and quickly looked for the bay, who was drinking, head immersed up to his eyes, unimpressed with Joe's foolishness.

The bay walked quietly after the pond incident. Along the edge of a narrow black top road, cars sped near them and the horse didn't react. But a few drivers, usually teen-age boys, ran their vehicles too close and yelled out the window, pounded on the car doors and cursed with little imagination. The first few times they were assaulted, the bay skittered and yanked on Joe; the eighth car to perform in such a manner got a load of fresh green manure as the bay's response. The boys yelled louder and the bay farted. After that, the road was quiet.

Joe knew word of their journey and its first destination would have gone through the villages and towns of this close-knit area. He followed a narrow road and at its bend there rose an Amish barn painted red, wearing its distinctive sign. There was a horse grazing in the front pasture, and a convenient stone tie for the bay. Joe approached the house and called out, knowing he was being inspected. A door opened in the side of the barn. The man appeared, wearing the now-familiar black hat, those black clothes with suspenders and a blue shirt. Joe was studying the man while being judged himself. It was the man from the buggy. The accent was awkward, the words clear; "There is a pen out back, with water. And you can give him hay. I see that Doc Junker he has done his work. I have expected you since my cousin said you left the clinic."

There was no further discussion, no small talk or questioning. The pen was large and clean, the manger and water trough filled. Joe removed the bay's halter and turned the horse loose. The bay immediately rolled on one side, then sat up and lay down to roll on the other side. The farm studied the horse very carefully. "He is practical." Joe nodded. "You would like to sell him no?" Joe laughed; "Mister, I know this horse and pulling a plow or being harnessed to something isn't what he'd take kindly to doing."

The Amish farmer studied him closely then; "Horses can be taught." Joe thought of the discarded stock he'd seen at the auction. "Wouldn't be worth the fight, and he could never be trusted." "Then we feed you supper and breakfast and you can begin your journey." The farmer nodded his head once. "Come."

Joe had been shown the pump and towels outside near the back door, where he was to wash off the day's quota of dust. They ate quietly at a long table in a huge kitchen. Names were not offered, and no one looked straight at him, not even the smallest of the children.

Prayers were spoken and Joe struggled with what he needed to do. He could not bow to an alien belief and kept his head high, thinking of his grandfather and the sweat lodge, the chant and reverence of the powwow at Pine Ridge. He could not pray to these Amish words since they did not belong to him.

The food was hot and there was more than enough; two women, seeming to be mother and daughter, kept pushing portions at Joe. He finally sat back and put out both hands. "Ma'am, miss, thank you. That's enough." His benefactor, whose name he still didn't know, laughed. "They are used to farmers who eat the product of their work. They do not know how to treat outsiders. You are the first of the English to break bread with us." The man stopped; "But you are not of the English." Joe barely nodded. "You do not believe in our God." Joe held still, having no answer. "It is of little matter. You are going to the battlefield and there are farms like ours with signs to tell you we are Amish." The man was smiling now, in his eyes as well as his less formal manner.

"You will be fed, as will your horse who cannot be made to do an honest day's work. It is for him that we make this gesture. And for you, who intends to return him to his home." The farmer stood, the children and women stood also and the males left the kitchen. Joe picked up a few dishes but was told by the pretty girl that he must not do such work.

He went to the back door, certain that he would be guided to a loft within the barn. There was a small boy, perhaps ten, dressed in the somber black, with bright blond hair and pale eyes, who would be his guide. He too did not give his name but asked that Joe follow him. The barn was enormous, and inside were small pens and layers of lofts, screened rooms stacked with corncobs, another filled with woven baskets.

The smells were of cattle and horses, and pigs. Not goats or sheep, which surprised him. The boy gestured to a smaller room near a series of stanchions. "Here we sleep to wait for a cow to calf." The room held a narrow cot with a blanket, a lumped pillow. "There is the outhouse to the back, and you have used the pump."

He nodded to the boy absently, as he continued taking in the cavernous barn, empty now in summer, still holding the scents and silenced noises of indignant animals. There was a tug on his sleeve and the boy spoke quickly; "Are you a real Indian?" Joe grinned; "Yes. Lakota." "What?" He let out a breath; "Lakota is the name of my people. Like you are Amish." The boy seemed to think on that for a moment. "Then do you believe...?" That question again. "It's for each of us to find our faith." The boy shook his head. "That is not what my father says."

Joe squatted down so he could see into the child's face. Clear eyes, black hat covering most of the bright hair. "Listen to your pa, boy. It's the best way to become a man." Then he stood quickly and made his way through the barn to the outhouse, knowing the child would not follow him with more questions. He had not had a father long enough, he had not listened to his grandfather, and he had killed a man.

He found the outhouse in time, which was a blessing he'd never considered before. There was a pail inside filled with lye and a shovel to liberally apply the disinfectant. Joe had to grin, he remembered one of these from his grandfather's house. He was grateful to go back outside and sit leaning against a post. Fences everywhere, straight lines ploughed into the ground, grass at even heights; life clearly defined. Joe braved the barn one more time, to find the pillow and blanket and make a pallet near the bay's pen, where he slept restlessly with the night sounds and wind, the bay's snorts and grunts. It was the music he understood.

Light woke him; he stretched, felt a hole in his belly but knew the women would have more food waiting. He would eat sparingly, say thank you even as he asked for extra biscuits, and then he'd move on. As he expected, the women fed him well, few words were spoken, and when he stood, he offered his thanks and the family smiled briefly, then separated to begin their day.

The bay gelding walked alongside Joe for a few miles, no pulling or jigging. Then one of those damned cars went by and the kids yelled and the bay reared, nearly hitting Joe on the way down. The rest of the day it was jig and pull, sidestep and yank. Lunch was in a fallow field, no gate at the opening, one decent tree for shade. Joe made hobbles out of a shirt and tied up the bay's front legs. The horse fought, lifting the tied legs as he thrashed his tail, pinned his ears in fury and Joe ate another one of those ham sandwich that the doc's missus had made him, sipped at cooled water in a canteen and paid no attention to the bay's antics.

When the horse discovered he could set back and raise his tied legs and hop a good distance, Joe tied the lead rope from the crude front hobbles to one hind leg. The horse tried escaping again and fell over. Joe left him there while he finished his sandwich, then untied the side-line and got the horse up, tied to the hind leg again and took a short nap. Under closed eyes, Joe could read the bay's tantrum; it was snorts and a few poundings then eventually Joe heard the horse tear into grass, sighing on occasion. Joe smiled even as he kept his eyes shut. Lesson one for the journey.

Their rhythm became simple; walk until tired, let the bay graze, walk some more. Often he found an Amish farm where they would accept him and the horse and feed them, then it was the barn for Joe, a pen for the horse, on their way by dawn.

The Susquehanna River caught him again; he could smell the water, there were signs for the river, and when he came to a straight north road that offered more small towns, he was quick to get away from the major route. He'd seen a map briefly, and this road did not end in a bridge. He fretted on going closer to a town. The bay jerked and yanked and pulled and Joe didn't want to risk too many people at one time while crossing a bridge alongside cars, knowing with a certain amusement that strangers would slow down to yell stupid comments.

It was dirt roads now, and one of those crossroad stores where an old man spoke up at Joe's unasked question. He said to go through the town of Safe Harbor, not much of a town he said, down Powderhouse Road and once he got to the river, let the horse graze in the park. Sit, enjoy the view, the old man cautioned. Horse might even get used to the rush of water across the dam. Tugging at a wild moustache, the old man grinned and told Joe the punch line; "Me, I'd wait till midnight and I'd lead that horse across the spillway to t'other side. Otherwise you got to go north and face them damned highways and the Staties who ain't gonna let you on that fancy bridge they guard. You know they's fearful that horse shit might ruin the shiny surface." His grin was toothless and genuine, and Joe laughed with him.

The old man gave Joe a stale sandwich, a rusted knife and a quart of milk past its 'sale by' date, and said that's what he'd do, lead the horse across that confound spillway. Damn the rules and regulations and the folks what made them; no man wants to swim a hard-flowing river. Inside the small store, Joe heard a distinct woman's voice that scolded the old man and his absurd advice, but Joe shrugged; there were no other options.

Joe did as the storekeeper suggested; the park was quiet, no one noticed that the bay gelding ate their grass and dumped healthy manure in trade. Before beginning the peculiar journey at midnight, Joe scattered the drying piles. When presented with the wide spillway, water sliding over the top, the bay sensibly hesitated. There were no guard rails, only thick wire strung post to post, a guideline more than any safety measure. More'n likely there were other places that might be easier but Joe didn't have the time or patience to find them.

The bay trembled as he stepped over the low cable. The roar of water, its shimmering blowback, was more of a barrier than anything humans might erect. The bay lowered his head, sniffed at the concrete, then raised his head to draw in the wet air. Both of them were soaked when they crossed to the opposite shore. Once the bay felt grass and dirt underfoot, he put his head down as if to graze, and Joe eased up on the line.

The gelding took off with Joe slammed flat on his belly, holding to the line with both hands. Eventually his weight and the bay's lack of condition slowed the horse to a stop. Joe was of the mind to beat the holy living crap out of the gelding, but standing to brush off grass and spit filth from his mouth gave him time to ease his temper. Crossing a river that way was something he'd never do again. Damn. Then he laughed at the godawful pun and the bay whinnied.

There was a small field a half hour later where Joe hobbled and sidelined the bay before easing himself into a pile of old hay. He slept past sunup and woke only because the bay gelding dribbled bits of grass onto his face. Joe groaned, rolled over and felt the ground shudder as the bay hopped backwards.

They'd crossed their first river, and Joe knew two things; he admired the bay's courage and understood now why his grandfather used that Brown Ike stallion, and that he had to find better ways to cross the other rivers, for another escapade such as last night's ill-advised path could kill both him and the innocent horse.

He bathed when he could find clean water and privacy, he lost weight and gained muscle even as the bay put on weight and on occasion questioned Joe's decisions. Each morning Joe ran his fingers down the bay's backbone, testing for muscle and strength. Then they reached a line where there were no Amish, no working farms or ponds. In their place were historical signs and inconspicuous announcements of the battlefield ahead, fine accommodations for those who'd come to pay homage to the dead or to gawk and take pictures.

The roads were narrow and hilly, yet the neatly-fenced pastures kept him from a safer course. He swung to the right before the town and found himself in a wide field, a high ridge ahead of him across a tarred road. He stopped, the horse immediately grazed on the lush grass. The ridge, left to right, held monuments of differing size and design, their outlines harsh against an early sky. A discrete sign announced this was part of the auto tour. Joe shrugged and pulled the horse away from breakfast.

They climbed a winding road, keeping to the edge. A few cars glided past, engines humming in low gear. Joe reached the top and took the road to the left. He stopped at the first monument and read its inscription, to a certain regiment on a certain date, the number of dead, the battle won or lost. The next monument held different text, sculpted in a different manner yet it was the same list of sadness; those who were lost, their numbers and dates.

The ridge separated healthy fields, narrow streams moved through the rich grass. The horse pulled, jerked, half-reared as Joe held to the line and refused to turn the animal loose in what would be horse heaven. They settled on browsing the road edges while Joe walked slowly, stunned with what he saw and still ignorant of where he would find Little Round Top. There was a wide spot where several cars were parked under thin trees. A glimpse of naked land could be seen through the branches. As he angled across tar to study a sign, the first thing in his way was a park ranger in a neatly pressed uniform, telling Joe what he couldn't do.

"You cannot bring that nag onto these grounds." One more idiot in a uniform; he'd come to honor the dead, and nothing he'd read said 'no horses in the park.' The voice came again; "You. Get that horse out of here. He's a danger." That brought Joe's head up and away from the sign. He turned to look at his accuser. Families watched their confrontation; standing by overloaded SUVs and station wagons, not hurried or frightened, only mildly curious, as if Joe and the bay gelding were part of the spectacle.

Joe was careful as he faced the park ranger. He strained to hear his grandfather's voice, to take courage from the unheard sound, knowing he could not risk a fight, did not want to hurt the man, who was doing his job, he kept repeating to himself, struggling to deal with something out of the ordinary. Joe forced himself to nod politely and ask if there was a place he could leave the horse. He had the money, he assured the ranger, he just needed directions.

He didn't tell the ranger that he would not leave this place without getting to Little Round Top even for a moment. To breathe in that particular air, knowing the reality was foolish but the heart of that one man who fought there had become important, a guide on Joe's chosen journey. He could not explain these thoughts, especially to an angry guard.

Ed Kurzynski wasn't certain what the policy would be from the main office but he wanted this man and his mangy horse off the land. It was ludicrous; a man like this on the smoothed grass, around the carefully maintained statues and monuments, stopping to read the signs speaking of horrors now wrapped in sunlight and mowed lawn.

Ed found the work both peaceful and horrifying. He tried describing to his wife how the lingering souls walked with him, how the wind became fleeting cries. He wasn't crazy, other men and women working within the park would very carefully say such things to each other. It was rare that a wife or husband understood. The ranger shifted until he was upwind of the troublemaker, although truthfully the man did not stink. Still, his kind was not meant to be here; dark-skinned and shaggy black hair, belonging to a distant tribe. He finally answered the question; "I know of no such place, mister. You best leave and take that horse with you." Ed stepped back, shaking his head.

Phil George had brought his family to the park to perhaps understand why men kept dying in wars. His ancestors had not fought here, but they were one reason for the battles. It was not their choice, but life changed for them because of two sides going to war. His grandson wanted to go to Cooperstown, his wife had relatives in Atlanta, and his granddaughter wanted to pat the horse. Right now none of those choices mattered.

Phil had been in Vietnam, a very young soldier at the very end of that conflict, and in the dark-skinned man confronted by the law, he recognized kinship. There had been few color lines in his platoon. And he knew this man, dark as he was, had no African heritage. Still he was being attacked by the white law and unfairly, according to what Phil had witnessed. Marla touched his arm and he looked down at her. "Please, Phil, don't." He smiled as she drew in the grandchildren, using them silently as her weapon. The ploy didn't work this time. His mind was set.

They had come to this place to walk the paths, read the strategic signs, then sit and enjoy a quiet lunch.

A black man inserted himself between Joe and the ranger. His considerable shoulder blocked Joe from being able to reach the official. The man looked back at Joe, eyes dark, mouth offering the barest of grins. Joe nodded. The man turned to confront the puzzled white man. "Mr. Ranger, when I followed your roads to get here, I passed a stable where a sign said they offered tours of the Park on horseback." The ranger shuffled his feet, rubbed his face. Joe's champion proceeded; "Now if horses are an advertised Park activity, I got two questions. Why can't this here gentleman lead his horse around the Park and why didn't you tell him about that stable?

Joe was impressed. He glanced over at the ranger, whose face was flushed. They formed a strange trio; the speaker was dark chocolate, Joe's skin copper, and the ranger was fair and going bald. Joe's impulse was to laugh. His savior turned and faced Joe; "Name's Phil. Wife and me, we'd like to share a meal with you. My wife packed more picnic food than the family can handle. And I know my granddaughter wants to meet your horse."

Behind them the ranger made sputtering noises. Phil took care of that also; "When you're done eating, we'll show you where that stable is. No problem." Ed Kurzynski knew to let go. Problem solved, crisis averted. He nodded as he walked to his next situation. He shook his head as he passed the horse; it was already a busy day.

It showed in Joe's eyes, the set of his mouth; he felt it in his gut, the very ends of his fingers. He watched that righteous back march away, garbed in its ranger identification. Then there was a wife, grandchildren, a shiny newer wagon, baskets and thermoses and a small girl's face open in glee. Wanting to reach up and pat the bay's soft muzzle.

He put his hand into Phil's; they both looked down as their hands pumped together, then almost immediately separated as if aware of their obvious difference. Joe said the words, mouth thick, wanting to avert his eyes. " Thank you." His savior had the same difficulty; "It's all right, man. I've been there." Joe forced himself; "I can't. I ain't proper, neither of us are. We're still finding our way."

The truth came hard; "I thank you for the help. Without you I'd have gone back to jail." The very word burned his mouth. He kept his eyes still, watching the other man's face. Phil George nodded; "You take that road and find the barn. It's about two miles walk from here." He pointed south. "Along Taneytown Road, and there's a campground close by."

The man was pure Indian blessed with unexpected manners; he said his thank-you and tugged on the lead to the skinny horse. Phil watched, flooded by the foolishness of his own judgment, then his granddaughter pulled away from Phil's wife and ran after the horse, small hands flailing. The horse spun around the Indian and reared, the child stopped. It was almost funny if it hadn't been frightening; her mouth opened so you could count her back teeth and she fell down crying. Joe with no last name pulled the horse away as Phil picked up the wailing child and comforted her. She waved once at the disappearing horse and the strange man. His granddaughter's body throbbed against him and Phil would wipe away her fear but he would not change what he had done. His wife reached him, their grandson patted his sister's shoe and the little girl stopped crying.

Joe saw the trail off the tar road and pulled the bay across the grass to walk on decent earth. Hoof prints and manure, fresh overlapping old, a few drying puddles, no rocks. Joe let out a coughing sigh; at least he was on the path meant for horses. The sign read 'Artillery Ridge Campground' and next to it 'National Riding Stables'. He walked down a well-used trail that stayed off the tar road as it wove between campers, tents, and large RVs. The stable help would not be expecting visitors. Sure enough when he got to a back set of stalls, a young woman came out to stand on a broken-edged cement slab, one hand shading her eyes.

"May I help you?" Her voice held the smallest tremor. She was in her late thirties, fit and strong; slender, muscular arms, long legs neatly dressed in tan breeches and high brown boots of a military cut. Joe was so caught up in watching her that he forgot to answer. "Mister?" He noted that she had not used the formal 'sir'; he was an Indian in a garish shirt with a rough horse as company. There was no gentlemen here.

"Ma'am." He'd been rehearsing what to say. "Ma'am, I got me something has to be done, and I need a place to leave the horse." He gave her an opening, a place where she could quickly say no, or by her willingness to wait, tell him he had a chance. She wiped her mouth, then pushed back her dark hair. "Yes?" "I'm asking for a pen, water and two feedings of decent hay. He's putting on weight and I don't want him losing none overnight. He can't afford to miss even one meal." There, he thought, put the horse first. "You got room? I've got papers saying the horse is healthy and free of communicable diseases."

She opened her mouth, shut it, tried again. "Where're you headed?" Neutral tone, simple words. She was going to love the answer. "Taking the bay home." "Where's that?" "South Dakota Nebraska border." A woman who thought like he did, in quick terms, made up her mind that quick too. "Oh." Then, "There's a pen out back, where we quarantine new stock. You say you have papers, I'd like to see them."

A first and about time; Joe'd been walking for over a week and no one had bothered to ask about the horse. It took a moment of fumbling through the canvas bag before he dug out the smudged envelope. Inside were those twenty-dollar bills and the vet's report, plus a piece of paper stamped 'negative' across a description of the bay gelding.

"Here, ma'am." An offering dirtied by hay fragments and matted horsehair but he figured the woman wouldn't mind. "My name is Joseph Evans. He's my horse, ma'am. The bill of sale's in there too." He watched her thumb over the money, pull out the auction bill and turn it over to read the scrawled information. Then she read the doc's report, scanned the Coggins test and studied the bay to match up Dr. Junker's description with the real thing. "You bought him from the killers." Not a question. "Yes ma'am." "Why?" There it was. She smiled; "Well?" Joe shrugged; "That's my grandfather's brand. And no horse my grandfather raised gets served as dinner."

Fury roughened his voice, which did not surprise her; the emphasis was harsh at first, then modulated as if he could feel his anger and knew it was inappropriate considering he'd asked a stranger for a favor. Beth hummed slightly. This would be interesting.

Six

The woman walked away and Joe discovered that a woman in good shape looked spectacular in knitted riding breeches and high boots. Then he reminded himself to be careful and remain a gentleman. She was doing him a favor. Her head turned slightly; the words 'Are you coming?' led him through a crazy assortment, of camping trailers and a clubhouse, then sheds with pens, past a small metal barn filled with sweet-smelling hay.

She stopped, offered a choice of hay and Joe turned down the alfalfa; "Too rich, ma'am." She agreed. "My name is Beth, the timothy hay was good this year. You can have use of the pen for twenty-four hours. It will cost you one of those twenties. Hope that meets with your approval." "Yes ma'am." She said nothing about where he could sleep.

The horse tugged and Joe fed out a handful of the good hay. "How far is it to Little Round Top?" The woman studied him. "Now you aren't the regular tourist we get here. It's pretty obvious you've got no one in your family who might have fought that battle unless I'm reading you wrong. So, one more question; why do you care about Little Round Top?"

There were flip words and sarcasm and wildly varying thoughts going through his head except for one that hadn't occurred to him until now; "I've been to Wounded Knee." His voice cracked. She said nothing. "This has to be your white man's equivalent so I need to be here." He shivered; she rubbed her hands against her arms. He explained; "For me it is a vision. I don't know better how to say it."

Soft voice, lovely eyes; she moved closer to where he could almost feel her. "That is beautiful, Mr. Evans." "Joe." "Yes. Of course. Joe."

Life had changed in the lost years. Women were different; each move they made had meanings he'd never understand. The head tilt, the hands, even the way they walked. Joe wasn't sure if the change was better or worse for him. Now he understood, or at least could imagine what he had missed. But the feeling of their flesh, their power over him, created problems. The taste he'd had made him want more.

Having Beth walk away to show him the pen was difficult. Every roundness of form was there, cloth clinging to her as if real skin. Joe held back, fussed with the bay until the horse reared and pawed at the air and the woman had to stop and wait for him. She carried two flakes of timothy hay in one hand, losing a few wisps with each step. At least when she faced him, he could not stare. Too often he was stared at, beginning in Wales and then England and not often on Grandfather's ranch but when he came east on the bus to his mother's, and from then on.

The courtroom had been a particular hell; he was just turned sixteen, tall, thin, a different color than everyone else in the courtroom except for his grandfather. One bailiff had been a black man who took pity on a kid from nowhere. The newspapers and legal staff treated him as something born of a past no one wanted to acknowledge. He had been different then because of his color; now he was a fool, a man in a mechanized world who would walk a horse across the country.

The pen was large enough, sand footing, a clump of trees for shade, a water trough with a spigot and fresh water. "You can turn him in here, Mr..." She hesitated, he wondered why. Joe shrugged; "Ma'am, my name is Joseph Evans. Joe. Thanks again for letting me put the bay up for the night." It came to him that he'd been walking with the stubborn son for what seemed forever and the horse still didn't have a decent name. "What do you call him, Mr. Evans?" As if she'd been inside his head. "Ike, ma'am. That's his papa's name. Brown Ike. And he sure has his papa's temperament." "Do you, Mr. Evans?" "Do I what, ma'am?" She smiled and he thought again how wonderful the female of the species could be. "Have your father's temperament?"

That was a question no one had ever asked. He remembered Llewellyn Evans, known as Lew Evans or just Evans, a quiet man well-paid for his skill. Joe looked at the bay, who was calm now, eyes no longer showing white. "Yes, ma'am. I hope I do. At least his way with horses." "What did he do? With horses?" This was easy; "He trained them for the races. And no, you wouldn't have heard of him.

He stayed small, but made his way well enough." Odd, Joe thought, he could hear traces of his father's voice inside his head.

"What happened? Your voice changed." Here it was, a woman wanting thoughts and emotions Joe did not choose to share. He could not understand why anyone would care enough to know. "Ma'am. He died. Nothing dramatic, it comes to us all." He swung away from her, dragged the newly-crowned Ike into the small pen where he let the horse go. Ike walked sedately for about three strides, then reared up, came down bucking and kicking and running the small circle until he came back to the closed gate, with Joe and the woman safely outside. The woman threw the hay flakes into the middle of the pen.

Ike stuck his muzzle over the fence to touch Joe's face then retreated to paw at the hay pile before eating. Joe laughed; "Guess that leg don't bother him now. I'll change the bandage 'fore we leave in the morning. If, that is, I can buy supplies from you. Ma'am." He wasn't going to let her know how deep her few questions had gone.

She smiled and it was rough on Joe. "I'm sure we can strike a deal, Mr. Evans. I would never allow a horse to suffer if I could possibly help." Common-sense words from a horseman. Joe shook his head and looked down; "He's settled so I'll go find Little Round Top."

She continued to surprise him. "I don't have clients until two. Can I give you a lift? It would seem to me you've done enough walking." A gesture of thoughtfulness; what people did for each other with no expectations of the favor returned. Joe wanted to say yes but common sense said no. He needed to be clear when he got to that place and she already was a distraction.

He did remember to respond; "Thank you, ma'am, but no."

It felt good to move without Ike. He kept to the trail where the smells, the feel of dirt and manure under his boots, was more healing than a tar road or highway. Then the trail crossed into the edge of a field and Joe kept to the tar. She had given him directions and Little Round Top was an easy distance ahead.

He thought momentarily about the family that came to his rescue earlier. Their kindness, the ex-soldier's instinctive bravery and commitment to helping a stranger, was unusual. Joe had the smallest sense of what it might be like to be of that descent and color; he was judged daily, but without the history that Phil George's skin carried, especially at this battlefield. Few were able to pinpoint Joe's heritage, and none understood the Welsh unless he slipped, as he had just done with the woman, and let rare emotion expose a long-hidden accent.

A gracious, moderate sign confronted Joe, telling him to take a narrowed road that went left into more trees. He walked up the slight rise, and there was the usual parking lot drawn from woods and ground, paving over where young men had died. A roughly-laid trail went into the thin trees, then divided left and right, opening into sunlight and an unexpected barrenness.

He went to the right first, to one of those tall monuments inscribed with long-departed regiments and sentiments. Immediately people surrounded him, in small huddled groups, talking or listening, too few taking in what they had come to see. One man persisted in discussing his long-time infatuation with a baseball team. Joe thought to challenge the man and took one step. The man raised his head, studied Joe and abruptly stopped his lecture.

Joe stood at the base of the monument, ignored the words, tried to hear what he needed from the rise of ground, the land below. Where he expected to find trees, a stone wall, an open field, there was only the recent destruction of sawdust, tree trunks, little new growth, no sense at all of the battle.

He closed his eyes and saw the chipped-away foundation of a ruined church imposed on Wounded Knee. Striped pillars guarded the cemetery entrance; stones etched with mournful names, dates, a simple metal barrier around a rising white monument, nothing like this outlandish figure at Round Top. Within a well-used more contemporary cemetery, Wounded Knee had a singular marble cone with names cut in deeply, worn yet still visible. Listing the names of those buried together by murderous soldiers.

Little Round Top was cleaned and sanitized, with trash barrels and warning signs, and rangers who refused a horse on the honored land. Another path connected to another monument; stones built in gothic splendor as testament to the regiment of men who had fought here, held their line, died too far from home. He read one sign, shook his head, walked around the garish tombstone and there it was, another sign overlooking rocks, boulders, a steep slope into the lushness of valley grass. Two boulders lay close together, conjoined by a slab of rock, placed there deliberately as he learned from further reading. It was a Yankee attempt to hide from enemy artillery. Now shadows walked through the brush, fired into the ghost trees and he could smell the powder, taste the smoke on his tongue.

Joe retreated to the parking-lot path where a stone slab lay, much like the one creating shelter from the guns; he sat, knees drawn up, head protected in his arms. Around him real voices questioned and whined, laughed and spoke of the awful battle and Joe sat, breathing in and out, not allowing the outside to disturb him. When he finally raised his head, he had no idea of time or place. He stood, muscles quivering; it was dusk as he retraced his way to the campground, past the awkward trailers and larger buses where family voices could be heard engaged in evening preparations. It was dark now and only the soft whicker of the bay gelding as he raised his head briefly, hay strands hanging from the stilled mouth, guided Joe to the horse, the fence, something he recognized.

It had been an effort but she did not stop and watch him. The temptation was strong and a shock, as few people in her life struck such a cord; yes he was beautiful but she'd known handsome men. It was his hands on the bay gelding's lead, his voice as he quieted the fractious horse, that immediately appealed to her.

Her mother had pushed almost any career other than horses on her only daughter, even as Beth persisted, bullying her way through schools and universities, taking riding, equine management, anything except her mother's preference of English literature and secretarial skills.

Only rarely now did her mother mention the lack of possible husbands, that the men a woman running a riding stable in a national park would meet were married or old bachelors from the military, immersed in Civil War history and not ever seeing the beauty hiding in Beth's sunburned face.

It would be interesting to explain this man to her mother. Beth smiled, an uncharitable thought coming to mind. Describing her recent visitor would by necessity be in sexual terms and these would mortify her remaining parent. At least she knew he'd come back, unlike some of the men she'd dated. Not for her, she wasn't that self-centered, but for that mangy, hard-tempered, scrawny horse with thoroughbred lines, maybe some quarter horse, well-bred and high-strung and it had to be pure misery for both of them to walk the back roads and through small towns.

For the briefest moment, a wedge between common sense and the next scheduled trail ride, Beth considered that she would like to join them on the journey.

He returned late and Beth acted on impulse; "Joe." He shivered, hands gripped tight to the rail. "Yes, ma'am." He answered only to reassure Beth, to let her know the bay was fine, that Joe would keep an eye on his charge. "I'll be gone early morning, ma'am. Thank you for giving us this chance."

"Was it what you were seeking?" Once again she'd asked a question to which he barely had an answer. He talked out imbedded fragments; "They were there. The sounds are the same, screaming and crying, death." He stopped. "Cries?" "Yeah, in my head. Left there from Wounded Knee." He quit trying to explain what he did not understand; "It's nothing."

She surprised him; she quietly leaned in and kissed the side of his face. Her voice was a whisper; "Come have supper with me. There's a place in town. It's not fancy and we can sit outside." His breath inhaled her scent of fresh hay, soap, no tang of manure or sweat. He could not see her face to know if the offer was made from pity.

"I'm asking you out, Joe Evans. Are you game?" He wasn't sure what she meant. "Ma'am?" She hit him lightly on the shoulder, watching him closely. He smiled, "It's a date." He hesitated and she warned him; "Don't you dare." He'd been right to keep his mouth shut but he was grinning.

He knew to open the door and let her pass, but expected behavior inside the restaurant eluded him. When a man came up to them and said "Two?" with a raised eyebrow, her companion had no response so Beth nodded and replied; "Yes, two. Outside, please." "Follow me" was the command, and here Joe stepped back, allowing Beth to go first.

They were seated in a square surrounded by greenery, confined by iron railings. Small tables, neighbors too close, but Beth was smiling so he gathered this crowding was acceptable. A white tablecloth, folded napkin, a man asking if he wanted water or 'something else to drink, sir.'

She recognized the enormous risk and yet his concern for the starving horse told her volumes about the man. Beth took over gracefully, as her mother had explained that one never made an invited guest uncomfortable in new surroundings. They ordered, or rather she ordered for him. Nothing to drink, at least no alcohol he said. He had no taste for it and didn't like what it did to him. She smiled and said the explanation wasn't necessary, a simple 'no thank you' would do.

She kept her voice calm and soothing, as if working a weanling colt. And he smiled in return. My god she thought, good golly as her much-younger brother would say. She had tried all afternoon on the ride to keep her thoughts clear; now that she saw him so close she could study each feature, her mouth went dry. He seemed to know, for he looked steadily at her, then gave her a shy smile. "Ma'am." She frowned. "All right. Beth. I don't know. I ain't...haven't been out much in public." She tried to make it a joke. "So you've been in prison all these years and never learned the social graces."

Certainly she didn't expect his response. His face went pale, even under that dark color the skin was grayish, the mouth pulled thin. His hands held the table's edge and he had difficulty breathing. "It's best I leave now." He pushed his chair back from the table and Beth made her choice. "No. Why were you...?" She couldn't ask but she could offer him a place to explain.

Joe had known when he became a short-timer that the inevitable question needed an answer, telling the truth without detail. There would be no one he could trust to hear the entire story. He hesitated, wiped his mouth. "I saved two lives, and took a life in doing so. I was a child but they convicted me as an adult." It was all he was prepared to say. For what little it said, the short truths were enough. Plates interrupted the one-sided explanation, dinner slid between them; first her chef's salad and fresh bread and then a steak for Joe, with sautéed vegetables and a massive baked potato.

To look at his meal, steam rising from the potato, the red steak juices still moving from the kitchen journey, then look into the most amazing black eyes of the man she had asked to dine with her and he'd just told her he'd killed someone, and Beth had no sense of what to do. Say something inane or ask a question or begin on the salad or get up and run.

"Beth." His hand touched hers. "You asked me and I couldn't lie. I don't blame you. They can wrap the steak, I can't pass that up. But if it's all right for you, I'll stay by Ike's pen and be gone in the morning." He wasn't annoyed or grim or anything, he simply was there. No guilt, no protest; a man standing up, leaving a woman alone in a restaurant. His expression gave her nothing.

Two women seated in the closest table seemed taken by him and Beth felt the words form in her mouth to explain before she actually listened to herself and shook her head at being so obtuse. "Joe. Please sit. I acted foolishly and you gave me an honest answer. That's impressive. Now I'm hungry. Please." He sat awkwardly and the two women looked away.

He didn't know about small talk, he was direct and unsubtle, but he did know how to eat correctly although in the British manner, and his speech was a combination of slang and intellect. He was hungry and yet he ate slowly, cutting the food into small pieces. He caught her watching and smiled. "A lesson learned on the road. Don't eat a big meal in a hurry. It won't stay around long enough to do any good."

She was appalled at the careless information and her face must have showed it for he frowned. "Don't, Joe. It's not a pretty picture but you're telling me the truth again." She smiled at him, this was truly an unusual encounter and if she were smart, she would give herself over to the moment's enjoyment.

Her face was lined, more than he'd thought at first; he laughed to himself, of course she'd been in the sun and wind, working horses instead of inside a house with a husband and children. He wondered about the choice, then she did it to him again. "I never married. My boyfriend was killed on a motorcycle and I haven't found...that again." The sadness drew him. She was living with more than a job and the evening's entertainment.

He realized something soon as the thought entered his head; he'd read it someplace, had to look up the words, at least the main one. And he'd begun to understand what it meant; now, here, it was real. 'Comparisons are odious.' To compare Vanessa to this woman was unfair for both women. He needed to accept rather than judge.

His stomach hurt; he'd already eaten too much. The meat would give him hell. At least the barn had a proper toilet, not one of those endless outhouses that he'd used on the Amish farms. "Beth, let me pay half." The check had arrived when he was thinking instead of paying attention. She smiled again, "No, I asked you. Remember?"

It was dark away from town and its lights. She drove with skill, hands steady on the wheel. She let him out behind the hay barn. "The door's unlocked, feel free to use the...well there's a sink and toilet inside to the left." He thanked her again, impressed with how quickly she sensed things. He took the opportunity of privacy and access to hot water to clean up and eventually his belly was in agreement with the heavy meal and he no longer embarrassed himself.

Lying quietly on the blanket, hands folded under his head, there were moments of peace until he realized a figure stood by the small pen. Ike was the first to know, of course. The bay raised his head and whinnied slightly as Joe sat up, silenced by what approached. Beth wore a simple gown. She was barefoot, her loosened hair shining across her shoulders. "Shhhhh." He didn't have time to completely stand before she bent down and kissed him.

Night air on hot skin was incredible. His flesh was smooth, the ribs too prominent as she ran her fingers over them, and then above to his chest before moving lower; there the hair was dense and tight as if to make up for so little anywhere else.

He would let her kiss him wherever she wanted. As if he didn't know what to expect, what she might want in return. He was kind, but unable to react except for a response he could not stop. She quickly learned to be careful or he would explode before entering her. A kiss to his chest, her face sliding down the tight belly, one hand pining his shoulders, the other holding his erect cock, moving slightly, then kissing the very tip and he groaned, raising himself as she licked the tip where there was a small bubble, a salty taste, fluid barely able to remain inside.

He slipped from her hands and rose above her, braced on muscled arms, one on each side of her breasts. He leaned down and kissed one breast, then the other, then with surprising ease slid into her. Stopped almost immediately and groaned.

"What's wrong?" She had to ask. Once again his answer was the truth; "Condoms. I was told to buy them..." Then he laughed, "You don't want to know that. But I didn't think...this was possible." So he wasn't completely ignorant.

She pushed him off, letting him find a place beside her. It was difficult now, trying to decide but if she went first on him, he might not be willing...or capable. So she took his hand and placed it on her hips, pushing one finger through her hair to the wetness. "And your mouth, if that doesn't bother you." Directions whispered into his ear as his fingers went in quickly, beginning a rhythm she wanted continued.

He slid down on the blanket, moved over her hips and she let him pry her legs apart. "This," he said as he put his mouth onto her and played with his tongue, then took his head away to ask the absurd question. "This?"

He kept it going, the kisses and then the fingers, then kisses on her belly as the fingers, three of them now, spread out, pushing deep he can't have not done this before and she cried out, squeezed his fingers and cried louder until one hand covered her mouth and she bit the palm. Thankfully he didn't stop until her body let go. He made no demands; instead he put an arm under her head to cradle her as she panted, then breathed normally.

She reached across his belly and took a gentle hold of him. His entire body shuddered and she felt it, from her ankles to her neck, and against her cheek where it rested on his skin. She had to fight him to let her roll over halfway, her breasts against his warm ribs, her head moving down as her mouth covered him. His hands on her back, gentle at first then drawn into fists, feeling the entire length of him, cock in her mouth, skin against skin, muscles tight then he jerked and she heard the groan, felt it coming and let him erupt in her mouth; new life emerging where it could do no harm.

She rolled off, wiped her mouth, kissed him just under his arm and smelled his scent. Her fingers caught in his hair, pulling gently on the shaggy ends, coal black hair, thick, uneven, uncombed. Lightly, so lightly it could not hurt, in return he touched her breasts and then her hair, then two fingers inside her, not moving, no pushing or frantic rubbing but as a wonderful intimacy. A gift from a man who did not know what he was giving. She kissed his jaw, touched his lips. Some men wouldn't accept a kiss after this sex but his mouth touched her tongue as if tasting himself.

"That is...you..." "No. Don't talk or tell me anything or think about more than this is." He pulled away, without moving he went rigid, tight; scared, she thought, and then maybe hurt. He was difficult to gauge for his face remained still, his eyes so dark they were impossible to read.

Then he slapped his own belly and laughed very softly, then another slap and another laugh, a full one this time and she quickly rested her head on his stomach and felt it bounce and she laughed too. "What's funny?" "Mosquitoes. Damn, that's a bad place." She laughed too, getting bitten, slapping them, brushing grass from her hair, from his ear, then kissing him again.

He was gone in the morning as he said he would be. And he left her two of the twenty-dollar bills, and a note written in an archaic hand detailing what supplies he had used to clean and bandage the bay's leg.

He did say 'thank-you' at the end of the note, but the words were not specific. He'd found her presents, a decent cowboy hat to replace the stained black hat, a pile of good quality harness leather, one line broken at the buckle, another frayed within the buckle itself and no one wanted to bother with repairs. Joe must have enjoyed the feel of the leather for she'd known he would need it somewhere along his chosen trail, and he would have been pleased with her for thinking ahead.

She had written him a note in explanation of the gifts; he had found a pencil stub and his thank-you was ostensibly about the hat, those leather reins, the supper, her concern for the bay gelding. In between all those words was the silent thank-you for her acceptance.

Seven

His body was calm, no edge, no rush in dealing with the bay or contemplating the world around him. If this was why men and women came together, he now understood. The sex itself was indescribable, sensations only to be found within a woman's body. The aftermath, that too, Joe thought, that too was special. He could see her lying beside him. A man could come to need being whole, wanted for himself. Not for what he'd done or not done, but for his very being. The thought was tantalizing, the new knowledge painful for he considered it a fatal truth; such momentary peace would not come to him again.

The hat surprised him; it was a deep brown, soft but fairly new and it fit, which made it easy to put the charity hat in one of the battlefield trash can and let the new hat settle. He moved deliberately, one foot placed carefully on the shoulder of the road, another pull of muscle, a light tug on the lead, the bay frisking beside him, jigging again, pulling sideways. Full of energy refueled by time to rest and eat, time to gain strength and make Joe's life a familiar misery.

Each step took him away until she became a series of memories. There was no way to get in touch with her, no way to write. He didn't know her last name; he hardly knew an address other than 'Stable, c/o Gettysburg Battlefield, Pennsylvania.' Joe Evans, murderer, wants to write to a lady. He told her and she had been frightened yet she came to his bed and showed him more of the mechanics, the sensations and possibilities for tenderness. Her generosity soothed him, reshaping edges of his irrevocable act.

The road took them over a small stream where the wooden bridge echoed under Ike's erratic hooves and the horse tried to bolt. Joe kept the bay circling until Ike got tired and began to realize the sound did not go away nor did it rise up to bite him.

Then they walked off the bridge properly; Ike restraining himself, Joe walking at the horse's shoulder, the line loose, coiled across Joe's palm. A lesson learned; Joe grunted. Ike would test this lesson and all others Joe would present to him again and again. It was a long thousand miles ahead of them. And a problem was about to present itself that Joe wasn't sure how to handle.

He'd seen the maps delineating great lines of water flowing out of the clustered lakes. And each river had a bridge to cross. Joe knew those men holding minor power weren't apt to be generous. Walking a horse on the bridge across a wide river, where traffic flowed almost as fast as the water beneath it, would not suit a bureaucrat. He had studied those maps, and thought on the problem. There were places where a ferry made the journey instead of a highway bridge. He might be able to lead Ike onto such a vehicle; conveyance was another word that he'd read in the dictionary. He wasn't certain yet how to say it, but a ferry might convey him and Ike to the other shore. Joe smiled to himself, pleased that one word explained the other.

It became a long day of walking more than the usual ten miles. He figured Ike was gaining muscle and endurance so twenty miles a day was possible, stopping for lunch in an abandoned field or letting the horse graze by the roadside. One good thing about a state with lots of rivers, there was no shortage of water and decent grass.

The first night he found the use for the leather lines. After sharpening his knife, given to him by the old man who so gleefully suggested breaching the Susquehanna River spillway in the night, he made slits in the thick leather and folded the cut ends back on themselves to fashion a cuff, and a second cuff, as hobbles for the cantankerous bay. The shaping of these hobbles took several tries until his fingers remembered what his grandfather taught him. Cantankerous was another word he liked and having Ike for company finally gave him a place to use it. Then he wove a sideline from the off foreleg to the off hind and the bay couldn't hop out of sight.

A week of walking, scavenging for whatever he could eat; berries, wild greens, a rabbit or two caught by snares. Not much, never enough but he kept walking. A few times he passed through crossroads, usually a dirt road bisecting a faster hardtop, and he could tie up the bay, buy a cup of coffee and something to eat at a mom and pop store. Once in a while he got a few hours' work and a place to sleep.

He heard the truck well before it turned the corner behind him. Noisy, missing a muffler, timing off by a skip in the pistons. Old, he figured, some kids in their grandpappy's truck. He stopped and turned the bay's head to the road, letting the horse graze but not wanting the truck to come up behind the bay and give him cause to bolt. The truck, a fifties Ford, roared and rattled and there were two boys in the cab, one with his arm out the window banging to something in a patterned slap. The approaching noise spooked the bay, who lurched forward, then steadied from Joe's voice and went back to the urgent business of eating.

Joe relaxed, watched the bay tear into the good grass. Then the horse froze, kicked hard enough to hit Joe's hand and took off running down the dirt road. He heard it then, the high laughter, curse words and cheers; "Look at the sum bitch run." The truck was gone, engine whining through the last gear. A fist-sized rock skidded against a stout weed ahead of Joe, broke the stem and rolled back, came to rest.

The bay's tracks were easy enough to follow but it would take him hours to cover ground that the bay galloped easily. After a half hour, Joe found the tangled leg bandage and a few strides farther there was the cotton from Beth's supplies. No blood so at least the half-healed skin was holding. He picked up the leg wrap, and as he walked his fingers played with straightening the fabric then winding it, until he could stuff the item in a pocket.

Everything that mattered was buried in those two canvas bags strapped to the runaway. More important than the money were his release papers. Joe patted his empty shirt pocket; that's where they would stay from now on. An hour later and Joe had a headache that kept time with his heartbeat, a blister on one heel, and the flattened bandage in his pocket. He'd discovered his right hand was bruised and not broken. The swelling hand throbbed with each step, but he could move the fingers.

He could still see the bay's straight tracks, with occasional stops for grass, once for a long drink in a small creek. Joe knelt in the bay's tracks and buried his head in the water, then soaked his hand until the chill was too much.

Along the narrow wooded road there were bridges built over a wandering stream, often leading to hunting camps set back from the road, a few had lop-sided barns and an acre or two of fenced grass. In several cases the bridge had washed downstream, but there was some evidence of passage.

The bay's trail veered to the right through a shallow stream, the deep holes showed in the wet soil where the horse had bullied through a thin stand of poplar on the distant side. Joe stopped to pull off his boots and waded across, then followed the tracks until he entered one of those open areas, although this one had a horse happily grazing behind the sagging wire fence; a blond sorrel that looked to be a Belgian from her coloring. The mare took a stride and in her shadow moved the bay gelding. Joe yelled and both horses raised their heads just before a voice growled at Joe from a shack he hadn't noticed.

"You leave them two alone. They's mine." Joe was confronted by an old man under the slanted roof of a porch across the front of what had to be a one-room shack. And while Joe couldn't make out his features, he recognized the silhouette of a pretty fancy 30.06 the man cradled. "What the hell you doing barefoot, boy?"

Boots in hand and hands up, letting out a breath, Joe answered nothing but asked his own question; "How long've you owned that bay gelding?" The old man said nothing as he raised the rifle until the barrel was centered on Joe's chest. "Boy, that ain't none of your business. Any fool can see him and the mare're a team."

"You tell me old man what brand that bay wears and who it belongs to and I'll walk the hell out of here." "Son, I ain't got no need defending that horse. Course it's a UU Bar brand, fella name of Consentine why he sold me that horse papers and all."

A full-face lie said like the truth. Joe risked a step; the rifle wove a tight circle with that staring barrel. "Now son, a horse ain't worth your life. I done told you where he come from. Make good on your word and get the hell off my land."

Joe lowered his hands, held himself quiet, eyes looking away from that rifle threat, then he began to see what lay around him. Junk of all kinds, brass hames and harness saddles, trace chains and an ax embedded in a torn stump. Ropes tangled up, laid on top of each other to make a three-foot pile. He sat down on a bent chair with a frayed seat and pulled on his boots, paying no attention to the old man, who began to mumble and then talk.

"I work in the woods, boy, that bay makes a good teammate to the mare, we get us a lot a work done afore winter and we don't freeze." Joe stood, lifted his hat and swept a hand back over his shaggy hair before he responded; "I'd like to see them harnessed. Bet they make a handsome pair." The rifle barrel wavered, the old man righted it. "You don't know Consentine, you don't know nothing."

The canvas saddlebags with his life packed in between dirty socks and wildly-colored shirts were thrown against a pile of rotting work bridles with cracked blinders and rusted straight-bar bits,. Joe rubbed his forehead, licked his lips. The old man was crazy. The canvas bags looked intact though, buckles tight, no tears. He let out a brief sigh.

"That's a nice mare, old man. You ever get a colt from her? Too bad the bay's a gelding." The old man spat, wiped his wet chin. "I said you didn't know much. That bay ain't never been cut. He and Belle, they've had two colts, sold them back to Consentine by god I did. Got good money for them as a half-broke team."

Here was a useful reality; "You mind I get closer, that mare's a right smart-looking Belgium." Joe waited until the rifle barrel went down. "I'll step along with you, son. Not that I don't trust you but you gotta be careful, that ole gal can bite."

The old man's talk held a core, as if the facts were right, only that he spoke of other horses and distant times. Passing the discarded canvas bags, Joe took a risk. "Them bags look useful, mister. You thinking they might be for sale." The old man stiffened and that damnable rifle started to rise, a weathervane of the old man's temper. "I don't sell nothing belong to me." Joe tried a brief laugh; "Now you just told me Consentine bought that team off you."

A bent and cracked hand reached up and wiped spit from the massive beard under the tight mouth. "Hadn't looked at it that way. Consentine he got money, hard cash mind you, maybe that's the difference. And he's white by god, not like you, son. You'd try to pay me in beads and them damned buckskins."

Joe chewed on the inside of his mouth; "The bay, you said you got him from Consentine?" They had reached the wire fence, and the two horses drifted toward them. The mare showed her age by the white hairs on her muzzle and above her eyes. There were old scars from being harnessed poorly, and she was ribby despite the good grass.

The bay gelding came up and sniffed at Joe, then rubbed his muzzle on Joe's arm. "What the hell he ain't taken a bite out of you. That's mighty strange." Joe patted the bay's neck and got a light nip on the arm. He laughed and the bay snorted. As the bay turned to join up with the old mare, he presented his left side. Without anger, Joe spoke; "That looks like a Rafter BP, mister. It ain't UU Bar that's for sure." "What?" "I know that brand. It belongs to my grandfather." "What's his name?"

"Isaac Brings Plenty." "Lives over to Carverville don't he." Joe held his temper; it had been difficult enough to say his grandfather's name; to have him become a ghost in this man's addled mind diminished the effort. "Old man, I need that bay gelding and my gear. Mr. Consentine he sent me to get them. He wants the bay for a week then he'll bring him back." Lying tasted bad, but he had to reach the old man in the glimmering places where Consentine still existed.

"Fine by me, you watch out you go to catching him up. Here, I got a halter might fit." It was the sale halter with the lead attached. And the bay did nip at Joe when he caught him, the mare backed up while lifting a hind leg. Joe slapped her rump; she sighed and went back to grazing. She didn't even raise her head when the bay left her pasture through the wire gate. Ike thought to resist but Joe spoke to him and the bay settled. The old man, though, he couldn't keep his mouth closed; "That's the way, son, you'll learn soon enough how to deal with them horses, they's cranky and dangerous but a great pair in the woods."

Joe walked the bay to the canvas bags, found them wound with the unbuckled stirrup leathers, and he refitted his gear around the bay's belly. His fingers ran down the backbone and there was flesh beginning to cover that bone. Muscle too, along the thigh, down the gaskin to above the hock and in the neck and chest.

"Boy, afore you going walking to Consentine's let me give you a sandwich, I got a slab of bacon too. Give it to Consentine, he likes my cob-smoked bacon." If it were as moldy as this old man's mind, Joe figured he'd carry the gift into the woods and let the wildlife fight over it. But the bacon was wrapped in a thin cloth and smelled clean. He put it in one of the bags and said he'd make sure Consentine got it.

He started out leading the bay, with the horse pulling and whinnying but it wasn't long before Ike moved up to Joe's shoulder as Joe leaned down and removed his untied boots. They crossed the slow creek, turned and went back onto the empty dirt road, where Joe leaned against Ike to pull on the boots and tie them this time.

An hour's walk and Ike stopped, strained until liquid manure poured out of him; a terrible stench, the horse shaking from the effort. Goddamn that old man and his ancient mare. Joe didn't feel that great himself so he walked on, searching until another one of those empty spaces appeared and this one had a sturdy bridge, a wood-fenced pen and no grass, only the shallow remains of a foundation and no sign anyone lived there.

That same stream he crossed so many times in search of Ike now ran behind the property. Joe tied up the bay, and then shucked out of his clothes and sat in the stream on a water-smoothed stone while he washed away grit and sweat, allowing his bruised hand to linger in the cold. He air-dried as he washed out two shirts and three pairs of shorts and considered frying up a piece of that bacon. Instead, dressed and rolled up in a blanket, Joe slept.

His hand quit aching after two days, and Ike's diarrhea settled down without much loss of weight. Traveling was easy yet Joe knew he needed a better way to cross big rivers other than a balancing act on a cement spillway. Right now the streams when he came across them could be forded, and most bends along the road had a bridge. All this would change at the Ohio.

An easy road brought him to one store selling feed and seed, tractor parts, tires and wheels, even a half-way decent buggy. Gas pumps at the front, the store a long building stocked with jackets, hats and gloves, warm boots and the enticement of steamed hot dogs rolling across a constant grill. There was a hitching rail where he tied up the bay and hit the wooden steps, heard their satisfying crack against his weight, and the scream of the door as he pushed it open.

Three men turned to watch him; black men making quick adjustment to who he was or might be. Joe nodded to the trio, walked to the counter and asked how much were the hot dogs, and did anyone have a chore or two they could pay to have done. He was handy with most anything, especially horses.

From behind him, in an angry voice, a man said; "You any good with mules?" Joe turned around and it was a stout man, about Joe's depth of color only more brown than copper. "Mister, if the mules ain't been started wrong, I can work with them." The fellow shook his head; "You tryin' to get out of a job even 'fore I offer it up?" Joe answered, polite but letting an edge show. "Mister, I ain't heard word one about a job, and I gave you a decent answer on the mules. If they've been rough-handled, they're harder'n a horse to settle. Anyone works with them knows that much."

Two men nodded, the angry one scowled. "Some mouth on you what's looking for work." Joe shrugged and paid for the hot dog. "Thanks anyway." And took his food outside, to ease his back end onto the edge of an empty trough and bite into the food. First meal in two days, since that slab of bacon meant for Consentine had fed him one last time.

"You ain't white." Joe couldn't laugh with a mouthful of hot dog and roll but it was an observation to confound him. He swallowed; "Nope." Took another bite and chewed slowly. The son of a bitch was insistent; "What the hell are you?" Joe swallowed again; damnit this got tiring. He turned his torso and left his backside on the trough.

"Now if I asked you that question I'd get a beating. What I am is my business and right now you know enough 'bout me. I'm hungry, damn near starving, and in need of an odd job. You ain't got the job, well then let me eat in peace and I'll get out of your life. That good enough for you?" He took a third bite from the roll, almost snapping his teeth together. Anger rode hard inside and the food got too big in his mouth. The man wouldn't quit; "Well now you stand up whilst I talk with you." That was enough; Joe shoved the last bite into his mouth and stood very slowly, thoughtfully licking each finger clean. The dark-skinned stocky man studied Joe long and hard, and Joe kept quiet under the rudeness, as if he was inside again and this was a moment could go either way. It was getting hard to breathe.

"All right, now it's me asking and I can't figure you either. Tell me. What the hell are you?" This voice belonged to a lanky man who'd pushed between Joe and the quarrelsome one. His voice was generous, no insult intended. Joe answered; "I'm Lakota." All three men closed in as if the name held exotic power.

The lanky man tried again; "Say what?" Joe grinned, he couldn't help it; their faces were identical in confusion despite being very different in color and features. "Lakota. From near the Rosebud Reservation." Nothing. "South Dakota." "Oh hell man you is a long way from home." The stocky man spoke out of sympathy rather than anger; Joe agreed.

The one who'd been silent so far watched Joe closely. "May I ask your name?" It was an educated voice and manner, neither angry nor playful. Joe decided his grandfather would not mind. "My name is Joseph Brings Plenty. I am going home and taking the horse with me."

The stocky one couldn't keep his mouth shut or his temper under control; "How come you're walking when you got transportation, poor quality but better'n shanks' mare." Joe was brief; "He's not fit yet to ride so we walk." The saving words came from the educated man; "This horse, he has great meaning for you or you would not make such an effort. We send such animals to auction or shoot them ourselves if there is sentimental value."

There it was, deserving the truth. "He belongs to my grandfather and I will not dishonor the name by allowing a stranger to kill this horse. That brand is of our family, and it is up to me to return the horse to where it began. Then, if it is so, he will die. But I will walk this horse to the ranch if it takes a year."

The men all nodded, the stocky man wiped his face with a large square kerchief. "You say you're decent with a mule?" "Yes sir." Nothing more. "Can you plow a straight line?" The truth again; "Haven't tried in some years but behind a good team I can manage. That's why I asked if the team was well broke."

They conferred, moving off so Joe couldn't hear. He went over to the bay, knelt and checked the wounded leg. The tissue was holding, the cut wasn't going to leave much of a scar. He felt the tightened muscle, and there was no soreness in the leg, no heat in the front hooves either, so that rich grass back at the crazy old man's place hadn't brought on founder.

The stocky man spoke; "We got a lady, she wants a field plowed and right now we got enough work to keep us busy. The land ain't much and most of it's hilly, like what you come through. She fusses, and is particular, but if you can handle them, she's got a good pair of work mules and she thinks she needs that land plowed under. Pay's decent, she says."

"I'll take it. You tell me how to get there."

There was more he needed to hear and the educated man filled in the story; "Her family took over that place when it'd been let go. Her folk come here from better land during that war, to find safety. Lot of us had folk did the same." A pause before a heaviness came into the voice; "We're all descended from those who refused to fight. Miz Ella she never goes over that line. So we work for her when we can, and this time, well you need the job and we got one. You understand?"

Joe had a few thoughts; "Coming in it's mostly trees and too many hills but a few parcels of cleared land had crops. Nice place, this little town. A decent farmer could make a living on what he grows." The men nodded, Joe asked how to get where he was going. The men laughed, for it was a tough question.

It took ten minutes more of considering all angles before Joe had an idea of where he was headed. Then he asked one final question; "You gentlemen know how I could get me and this horse across the Ohio? I know I'm getting near and it ain't what Ike and I want to swim. I figured if nothing else I'd try at two in the morning over one of those highway bridges. For damn sure the law won't like it."

The men looked at Joe, then each other and laughed. The educated one, Dawson, said it; "Boy, you've been headed south in West Virginia for several days and you're mighty close to Pricetown. How did you get so far off track you missed finding Ohio from that

Pennsylvania auction?" Joe frowned, then wiped a hand over his mouth and shook his head; "Looks like I may have strayed a mile or two."

Decker, the lanky one, said he knew of a fella who ran a ferry. Took across a car or two wanting adventure. Now it'd mean losing miles going north but more'n likely Buck would take his money and let the horse ride for free. Armed with that important piece of information and the possibility of work for a few days, Joe shook each man's hand. The stocky man wrapped his left hand around Joe's wrist. "You a goddamn Indian like you said?" Joe laughed; "Lakota." Then he spoke a few words, in Welsh because he'd never learned much beyond ceremonial words in Lakota. Bert let go of his arm and laughed. "Now I've heard it all." He grunted; looked at Joe. "You sure you was speaking that Lakoty?"

Eight

The house was a two-story peeling disaster with porch columns and a churned front lawn. It was shadowed by a high red barn that needed either destruction or total renovation. Ike shied and pulled away; then Joe heard it, a pop, another pop, three in a row, one lonesome pop, then two more, as if someone were shooting randomly at tin cans.

While Ike threatened to tear Joe's arm apart, he yelled, hoping the shooter would not mistake him and the horse for a serious target. There was silence where Joe heard the lightest rumble, then an engine whined as if the brake and accelerator were fighting for control. Joe ducked, looked for a fast-approaching car and saw only the tail end of an older sedan running backwards, accompanied by more popping. The car shifted and went forward to produce only one pop.

Using great caution, and some force to get Ike to go with him, Joe went around the house and stopped. The car was an eighty's sedan, angular, chromed and rusted, once a deep burgundy now sunburned and dented. Its driver was an old woman who slammed the car forward and then back, sometime changing the angle of the short path.

One pop, followed quickly by another and Ike reared, pulling Joe with him. As Joe figured what the madwoman was doing, he laughed. There were soda cans under the car, some flattened, some barely dented, a few left intact. With well-practiced aim and two more trips, all the cans were squashed. Ike trembled but stayed on the ground; Joe snorted, wanting still to laugh, but as the old woman struggled out of the car, he felt her dignity could not take the insult. He set his face, nodding to her as she straightened herself up before taking a look at him.

"Can't flatten them cans now, hands too bent, feet too tender so I collects them and when there's enough I run them sons a bitches flat. Saves space and then Suzie's Tenney he takes 'em to the recycle center and gets us a few pennies. What you be wanting from me and get that horse 'way from my garden."

Dalton, Bert, or Decker could have warned him; the old woman was rounded and ancient, white hair pulled back and escaping its braid, a man's shirt and pants, high pink rubber boots. Her hands were covered in black filth and the long fingers flew around her face. The woman kept chewing her words; "Not a bad-looking horse you get some weight on him. Why you taking such poor care of a good animal? No animal deserves to look like that even if he can't work a lick. Now you get some weight on that sorry bastard." Finally she wore down, and before she got restarted, Joe figured he best jump in. "Man name of Dawson, and his friends Decker and Bert, they said you needed a field plowed and harrowed. You asked them to do the work and they got a job lined up so here I am." Hell he was already talking like her.

"What the hell do you know 'bout plowing? You're a goddamn Indian. And that bay sure ain't no plow horse." "No, ma'am, he's no plow horse, and yes I've plowed, it's been a few years but give me a decent team and I can keep the lines straight." Plowing the sandy soil to put in a few rows of corn and some squash wasn't a great deal of experience, and it'd been a painful number of years ago. Still, he had not directly lied.

She studied him head to toe and again he was motionless, willing himself to show nothing. "Nervy son of a bitch standing there like honey wouldn't melt in your mouth and you thinking that this crazy old woman won't know the difference. You bring that bay nag along and we'll find out just how much you do know."

The bay for once was well-mannered as Joe followed the woman. He calculated that her silence was a rare blessing. The quiet gave him a chance to study just what it was he might be doing. The barn itself was long and high, half-collapsed, filled with musty hay and the faintest odor of manure. Sunlight came in through shattered windows, laying a quilt across the littered floor. The bay hesitated, then stepped high over the first rays before deciding they weren't worth the effort. At the end of the barn, a mule brayed and the bay gelding came to a rigid halt; head high, nostrils flared. The mule brayed again, the bay pushed close against Joe's side.

The old woman stepped in; "Guess if that there horse trusts you, I can give you a try. Put that horse outside, there's a paddock fence good enough to hold him. You take water out later, after you meet the mules."

They were a matched pair, full brothers, both a dark red with massive bodies and short legs. Not much above sixteen hands, products of a compact breed crossed with a mammoth jack. He took a wild guess; "Suffolk Punches, ma'am?" She grinned; "Son, you're hired. No one else's ever come close. How'd you know?" He described the farm near the Pennsylvania state line and she nodded. "That's where their mama come from. Good stock, and I admire the man purely for his keeping the breed alive even though he be a snobby son of a bitch."

She brushed back a strand of gray hair. "You bring 'em out and harness them. Want to see you plow a line, no point in getting too excited less I see you work them with a plow." The woman went hot and cold; he'd need to remember that. "Yes, ma'am."

The paddock for the bay had what could be called serviceable fencing, but Joe knew he'd work in the evenings to prop up some of the posts and nail a fresh board on top to hold the fence together. For now, he figured the bay was tired enough to stay in one place.

Then he brought out the first mule. Jack was his name, the woman said. Pointed to which harness was his, saying nothing, letting Joe make the determination. From the setup of the lines, Jack was the off mule. He found a brush, and a rusted metal curry, and set about scraping away old hair and manure. The stalls needed cleaning and there was no reason to keep these animals inside other than the terrible fencing. The mule first tried to bite and then kick when Joe got to the hind end. He grinned, prodded the mule's shoulder with his elbow and spoke the short name hard and quick. "Jack!" The hind leg eased down and the long ears drooped. Joe finished the grooming with a body brush.

Picking up the hooves was a chore, finally he and Jack came to an understanding that no matter how hard Jack leaned on Joe, he still had to give up the hoof. It'd take time, but the animal was smart enough, and willing to learn. Tom was not much different than his brother, more sullen maybe, and less willing to relax, but it wasn't much to groom and then harness the animal. The team was well-broke and suited to the task. The harness was a Dee-ring, like his grandfather used; collars, hames, belly bands, lines all found their places. Joe let his hands do the thinking, slowly becoming sure of the memory. He led the team outside and found the plow she wanted used. As he suspected, it was a rusted walking plow and he'd need to spend time and oil to make it slide through the tangled earth. Backing the team, hitching them, the motions came quickly and felt right. The harnessing took a few missteps, the need to shorten the traces, nothing difficult.

Guiding the team while following behind the plow was the challenge. Joe focused on getting a feel of their mouths. Sure enough Jack was light through the lines, and if he had a choice Joe'd put Tom in a Liverpool driving bit but one glance at the old woman striding next to him and he laughed. "What's funny? You finding out Tom got no mouth ain't you. Well I did the best I could but he's a puller and there ain't a bit made can stop him." "Ma'am, you could try a Liverpool." "Sonny I ain't going to England to get this here mule some manners. Best done closer to home now ain't it."

He grinned and spoke to Jack, who seemed to nod in agreement. Tom twisted his head, yawing his mouth so that the bar snaffle would pull through but Joe slapped the mule's near side and as Tom stepped forward with that hind leg and dropped his head, the bit slipped back into place. "You got a good hand with them mules, mister. My name is Eleanor Talliferro. Most call me 'Auntie' but I 'spect that ain't going to suit so you call me Ella. S'what my husband called me. Good 'nough for you?" She had a talent, Joe decided, of finding the holes in him and speaking right to them. "Yes, ma'am. Ella it is and my name's Joe Evans."

Here it comes, he thought, as she stopped walking, demanding he do the same. He brought the team together in a ragged halt. "What are you, boy? Look dark enough to be Native but that face ain't from no tribe I'd know. You got a mama and a papa weren't from the same line." Joe smiled; "Welsh, ma'am." "Thought so, that jaw and forehead ain't Native no sir. Hope it was legal." "No, ma'am. Not even recorded." She laughed loud enough both mules spooked.

"There's the field, boy. Get at it." Joe sighed; it was nothing more than tangles of burrs and dried stalks mostly on the slant of a hill, with a fence line that drooped, putting hidden wire into the mix. He held to the team, then let up on the lines and both mules relaxed. "Ella, we've got some talking to take care of before I work. Pay, meals, a place to sleep, shelter and decent feed for the bay. You quote me an hour rate and how you'll feed me and then I'll clean up that fencing and wire before I put the team to work."

"You much on bargaining?" He shook his head. "Didn't think so. I got a woman comes in to cook, mighty good at what she does. Could put some weight on you. And there is decent hay to the barn out back." She thought a moment, studying him again and he could guess what argument she was having with herself. "There's a room to the house off the kitchen, built just for the likes of you. Got its own bath. Five bucks an hour plus all you can eat and clean sheets with her doing the changing. Even do the wash for you. Looks like it's past time on your clothes, boy." Their eyes met, he saw pleasure mixed in with eagerness in her face that needed to be a warning.

He stuck out his hand and sure enough her grip was strong as a man's.

Joe turned the mules out with Ike. It was a losing battle from the beginning; Jack and Tom wanted nothing to do with the bay, who kept asking to fight. Neither mule cared; they put their heads down to graze and practically walked over Ike when he got in front of them.

Joe went to fixing that wire fence. It was an ugly job, broken wire poked up through the dried burrs, tangled in his clothes, shredded his hands. He cursed and pulled and wound the short wires together. He worked down one side of the fence and when he turned around and headed back, half way and resting on one of the straight posts was a pair of thick leather gloves.

Joe looked at his hands, bloody nicks mingled with sweat and dirt. He pulled on the gloves and went back to work.

Whatever he was, Welsh and Indian and that was a line she wasn't going to cross by asking again but whatever he was the man knew how to work. He didn't put the team to risk on that field till he checked it, walked it, throwing out rocks and pulling wire and never complaining or cursing or slowing down.

Worked like her man, hard at it beginning to end. Killed her Mr. Talliferro, killed him right in that goddamn field but then he was maybe fifty year older than this young buck. He stopped, found the gloves he did, wiped his hands on his shirt front and she could see the pale streaks on white striping, but the gloves pleased him and he went back to work.

There weren't no sense to why she wanted that field finished. It had belonged to Mr. Talliferro by his work although her family owned title going back some hundred years. Mr. Talliferro would hate seeing the burdocks and weeds, knowing the tight wire he'd strung had come loose and she didn't have the gumption to nail it back up. This one would, he'd finish the repairs and staple the wire to posts already straightened and tamped.

Suzie would cook double tonight, and Ella herself would check on that back room. This boy looked tired already, ain't been eating too good, walking someplace with that ugly rack of bones he called a horse. Have to ask him 'bout that, and other things, once they got comfortable with each other. She recognized her garrulousness and how it scared off day workers. But she didn't much care, a pair of ears, however unwilling, had to hear each word.

He sure was pretty though. Even Suzie, black and middle-aged and well-married, content with her work for the missus and the house she provided for the family, Suzie and her husband Tenney, and their three children. All the kids got through school, done well and two was going to a local college. Nothing slow or stubborn in that family. Nothing at all. Even Suzie had looked out the window to where Ella pointed, and nodded. "Right pretty like you said. And the man surely knows his job."

When he tried peeling off the gloves, they stuck to his skin and the simple act became tedious. He'd come to the kitchen door by the smells, and when he knocked, a deep voice told him to get on inside where he could wash up 'fore supper.

A black woman the size of Bert ruled the kitchen, but Miz Ella sat in a ladder-backed chair and seemed worried. Then the woman told Joe her name was Suzie and he was to call her Suzie and nothing else. He said; "Yes, ma'am." And she laughed; "It's Suzie." He nodded. "Wash up, boy. Those hands'll infect you don't get them clean. Hot water and lots of soap. After supper I'll tend to them. 'Yes, ma'am' came into his mouth but he saw a glint to her dark eyes and only grinned. The old lady pointed, still in her chair, still fretting. "Back there, boy. Your room and where you can wash up."

He stepped down a short hallway and found an open door to a tidy room. A single bed with two pillows was covered in a hand-made quilt. Towels were laid on a chair next to the bed, and a small door opened into the bathroom. He started with soap and hot water, a mild torture as he laid his hands under the steaming water and scrubbed with a lightly scented soap.

He found out quickly that it wasn't going to be simple carving up the steak they were intent on feeding him. His hands throbbed now and the palms were swollen. He managed though, not about to let either woman cut his meal. He thanked Suzie and the old woman too, and went out to the barn to see to the animals and bring in his gear.

"What'd you think on him, Suzie? He's gonna bring this place to life again I know it he's good with the mules and..." That raised hand told her she was hurrying, not seeing what Suzie would understand so easily. The woman's hand rested on her shoulder and both of them knew, could feel Suzie's younger strength against the fragile bones. "He sure is pretty, Miz Ella, but he's not your man and he's not going to stay. Look to him, he's been shut up somewheres and now he's free and no one can hold him. It'll have to be a mighty pretty young woman to lock that door."

The old woman smiled up at her friend and touched her hand; "Nothing says we can't enjoy his company the time he's here, is there?" Suzie laughed; "No, ma'am."

Hard work and good food eventually created straight furrows. The bay was putting on weight as well, bucking around his solitary pasture while the mules worked. Watching that bucking, Joe considered how he intended to ride the horse without a saddle. It had been since his childhood in England that he'd ridden bareback. Grandfather Brings Plenty demanded his grandson use a light saddle, said it gave a better ride to the young stock and didn't force the rider to grab with hard thighs or hold to the reins instead of letting the saddle steady the rider's balance. Yes, Grandfather said, the old ones rode without benefits of saddles, but they would, and did, kill to take a cavalry or stock saddle. That had been Joe's first lecture on the myths of his split heritage.

Miz Ella brought him lunch when he was working the far end of the field. She rarely brought anything for herself but liked sitting in the heavy August sun and listening, she said, listening to the land and watching Joe eat. Once in a while she'd try a question about Joe and he found easy ways around a straight answer. Eventually she gave up and sat with him purely for the company.

He finally had to work on the harrow, which was rusted shut, tines bent, dulled on unforgiving rock. Oil and some pounding with a blunt hammer would bring the machine back into use. Like shoeing, he thought, and breaking rock or working the roadways; hammering at inanimate items until they suited a specific use. It took him two days before the harrow worked to his satisfaction. He suspected the mule team enjoyed their leisure. Both women came out to watch, and even Bert, Decker, and Dawson rolled up in a fancy new truck and parked next to the field. Dawson waved, Bert scowled and Decker finished his coffee.

The mules hitched easy of course; they knew what came next. You rode a harrow so Joe climbed up between the mules' massive hindquarters and found the shaped and rusted seat not as uncomfortable as he'd imagined. He pulled back on the lever that raised the tines and they came up squealing but ready to work. It was simple enough to put the mules straight; they had a plowed line to the distant fence. He dropped the tines, asked the team to move off, and got broken applause from the audience. Joe lifted a hand and waved, then grabbed the lines and directed the team part-way up the hill to keep the harrow level.

Half the first line of the field was harrowed and turned before Tom stepped in a nest of ground bees. Joe saw the first one come out of the opened earth and he cursed, spoke to the mule, eased on the lines to hold him but Tom would have none of it. A kick at the swarming bees, another kick back that scraped Joe's boot sole and Tom took off, bucking and hollering and dragging Jack with him. Only thing that kept it from becoming a full blowout was Jack's weight against Tom as the mule attempted to follow Joe's commands.

The harrow rode at an angle across the plowed field and went over sideways, sending Joe flying as he fought for control. All his weight hung on Tom's mouth as the ground came up and Joe rolled into a fence post. There was a haze of worried eyes, the old woman's white hair, dark faces and strong hands lifting him. He coughed, choked, rolled over and let whatever it was flow from his mouth and damn it was blood red.

At the local clinic, he was diagnosed with a cracked nose, smashed mouth, a few extra bruises on his ribs but nothing broken. Not much damage. He got told to be quiet a day or two, had a concussion but the doc said it looked like he might have had a few of those before. Bert drove him back to the old lady's house, and Joe mentioned how smooth the new truck was. Bert had him a big grin. "Yeah," he said. "Told you we had us a good job. This's the perk. We get to use it for our transportation. She ain't bad."

Joe half-fell from the truck and made a slow trip to the side of the veranda. Miz Ella's head could be seen over the edge of a flat-backed rocker. Chair not moving, head still. Joe pushed himself to get to her as her body slid forward. "No. Damn it." He held the old woman's hand in time to feel the smallest quiver.

It was three days before she was buried. Joe and Bert, Dawson, and Decker dug the hole. There was some grumbling from folks about town that a white man, well a man not an African-American or whatever they was called now, a man the likes of that one hired on to work for Miz Ella was digging the burial hole with them...and here the whispering set in, no one wanting to say the word they'd been brought up on yet when they were troubled it's what came to mind.

Time had to pass and each friend or acquaintance had to have their say but eventually it was pointed out the man wasn't white so it didn't matter.

More than two hundred-fifty people showed up for Eleanor Talliferro's burying. They crawled, hopped, strolled and marched over wet ground to get to the family plot backed up onto the steep banking of a railroad bed. No one spoke of the accident but there were thoughts that the shock of being witness might have put her heart in overtime. She wasn't young you know, and lived alone. And then those heads shook, the eyes looked into the distance as their hearts grieved.

Her lawyer and the local minister were pall bearers along with that man who wasn't white or black, and the three grave diggers, who'd sometimes worked for her and always did errands that needed doing. Suzie cried the loudest, her entire family surrounding her. The lawyer already told her the farm and buildings were hers. But those buildings weren't Miz Ella, and Suzie had known the woman most of her life. No children, no brothers or sisters on either side so the land belonged now to the descendents of those who first worked it.

Joe stood alone. Digging the grave had been a penance. The hole bore scars of deep roots that shovel blades cut through; above the hole stood some kind of swamp pine, offering shade and companionship. Joe knew what he felt and couldn't get rid of it by thinking or talking to himself or to the bay gelding and the bored team of mules.

When the burying was done, and folks were up at the house telling stories about the old woman and her ways, Joe harnessed the mules to the harrow, which hadn't bent a tine or broke a wheel during its brief flight. Eventually folks inside the house heard a peculiar noise and some thought to look out the window. There was that man, neither white nor black, setting high on the harrow's seat, driving the team neat as could be up and down and across the land Miz Ella had wanted plowed and harrowed until it was smoothed and the sun hit fresh dirt clods. Most turned away from the sight, a few smiled as if they understood.

"The boys and me we took up a collection. Miz Ella always paid her debts and you gave her a joy I didn't see since her man went on. She's there with him but this here's her last debt and you take it now, it's what she'd want." Suzie stopped herself, smiling with tears in her eyes; "My goodness I'm talking just like her." She took Joe's hand, turned it palm up and opened his fingers, folded them fingers over a thick envelope.

"Your palm is pale like ours. But you aren't..." For a bunch of people who lived and worked and died breathing the same air, they sure 'nough had trouble with saying who they were. Joe stood up; "I am Lakota." He spoke the word clearly. The black-skinned woman, who was really lighter-skinned than Joe, smiled and he stepped back, fearful she might hug him.

Suzie gave him rights to an old saddle and girth that belonged to Miz Ella's husband's boy by his first wife, the boy dead in Desert Storm, the wife long ago hit by a car. Life was never fair for some people. There was saddle wax in the barn, and an old cloth dried into hard folds. Saddle soap, water, and hard work and he got the leather clean enough, added the wax and worked it in with his fingers.

The plate under the left front of the saddle said 'Barnsby, England', which made Joe grin. He'd ridden a child's version of this saddle a long time ago. Miz Suzie apologized for it being English and he didn't try to explain. Time spent searching through the barn discovered the leathers, the irons, and an old sheepskin saddle pad. Riding, however, was going to be a whole new adventure.

Miz Susie also gave him a warm jacket that the old man had used, stained canvas with a wool lining. A fleece hat and thick gloves, a couple of blankets. His first inclination was to refuse but when he looked straight at Suzie he figured the fight wouldn't be worth it. And despite his guilt, he'd earned the money and needed the warm clothes. A cowboy hat in mid-winter froze a man's ears.

The saddle settled on the bay perfectly, and the horse snapped at Joe when he did up the girth, gently at first but snug enough the saddle wouldn't slip. He stepped back, studied the bay in his new gear, and it looked right.

Still, Joe thought, it wasn't time yet to ride; he wasn't steady enough and the bay wasn't fit. Better manners and more muscle would come along slowly, then he would ride Ike inside a fenced field, the smaller the better that first time.

Nine

He walked away from the farmhouse and met a truck turned sideways in a ditch. Another truck was parked too close and two groups of men circled each other. Since this was the only road to where he was headed, Joe kept walking. Sure enough it was Bert, Dawson, and Decker, surrounded by white men, one of them holding a rifle. How the hell did anyone get anything done if they always fought each other.

Joe led Ike right through the close group of white men, letting the bay's temper and size push the men back. He stopped, nodded to Bert and Decker and asked Dawson how they got the truck stuck that way? Didn't look too bad, and since these men weren't about to give a hand, could they use any help getting it loose?

Behind him a man laughed and Joe felt the lightest nudge of a rifle barrel. Fool. He threw the bay's lead at Dawson as he reached behind and took the rifle like no one was holding it. Spun it stock to his left hand and held it, cocked the trigger. Faced these men and shook his head. "Never get that close to a man with any weapon 'cepting a knife, it's too easy to do what I just did." Then he laughed for the words 'Mexican standoff' came to mind and added a whole new dimension. These folks, none of them including Bert and Decker, looked like they would be amused if he explained his thoughts.

"Get along, boys. I'll leave the rifle to the store, when I get there." He turned to Bert; "First thing we're going to get this truck out of the ditch and we don't need these boys hanging 'round making life a misery. Don't appear to me none of them could be much help anyway." Bert actually nodded and the others seemed to appreciate Joe's perspective.

Those white men got in their fancy truck and roared off without any more trouble. Guess three black men and one Indian holding a white man's rifle were more than they expected. Joe stood guard, rifle laid over his arm, a bullet in the chamber and his finger light on the trigger. Couldn't count on those boys to use common sense, Decker told him. And Joe believed the man.

It was push, shove, yell and gun the engine, and finally the big tires caught in the greased dirt and spun out globs that spattered every man but by all that was holy the truck crept forward onto the road. There they stood, covered in mud, each man wiping his face while staring at the others. "Here." Joe let off on the trigger, gave the rifle to Bert. "Best leave it to the store, I gave my word. Now how far is it to where I'm going, and where the hell am I going?"

Bert knew a man up near Sistersville, still in West Virginia but right up close to that Ohio River Joe was fretting on. It might be a long walk, Bert said, some hundred miles or more and just how many miles did Joe figure he'd walked so far. He told the men he'd started in upstate New York and when Decker said he had a cousin in prison up there, Dawson kicked him, real polite but a kick that told the man to shut his mouth and Decker didn't say 'nother word.

If Joe hadn't known Decker, he might have fought him, wiping out the implication about prison even if it was the truth. But he'd learned Decker wasn't devious; blunt and not careful of his thoughts, but not mean. Damn.

He let out a gust of air; "I figure I've walked over four hundred miles, got a ride in a truck for more'n two hundred. Must be it's been six hundred miles so far. I looked it up once, about sixteen hundred from where I started to where I'm going. Then add on an extra three hundred miles for going 'round big bridges and fancy highways. But I've got the time."

Hearing his own voice line out the numbers scared Joe. They made what he was trying to do seem impossible, but he'd gotten this far. Time had no real meaning excepting he wanted to be almost to the Dakotas before the winter storms. Dawson spoke up real quiet; "I know me some folks in a small town sort of on your way. Decent people, I'll let them know and they'll put you up a night, feed you and that fearsome bay enough to keep you for a few days more."

Dawson added his own thoughts; "I'd not go sending him to that Newport Bridge up by St. Mary's. That horse, well, the bridge's noisy and I figure that Ike wouldn't like it. Taking that ferry north of there, it ain't easy neither, but some safer 'cause it's short and slow." A lot of words for Dawson, and Joe knew to listen. He wrote the directions on an order for lumber, and then didn't know how to leave. They weren't friends, him and these men, but they had more in common that any differences. They talked nervously, fighting the same uneasy sense. He best know the land was timbered mostly, a few hard-fought fields and a small cluster of house pretending to be a village. There was always water, enough grass for that nag, not much for Joe but he'd survive till he got to where he was going. Joe nodded his thanks again, Dawson looked away and Decker almost put out his hand, then withdrew it, head down, eyes closed.

Their voices drifted with him for a hundred yards or so and then faded. He didn't look back, didn't stop at the store or turn around; he was headed north and west to Sistersville, one hundred and forty miles according to Bert's reckoning.

They were easy roads along single fields between thin woods; places for the bay to graze, a pond or stream where the bay could drink while Joe filled his belly, then leaned back against a tree as the bay grazed between weeds and sumac. There was food in the canvas bags, clothing, a warm coat and hat, those damnable work gloves. The air was warm and he wore the cowboy hat to remember the woman's touch. It would be early September now, he thought, and soon enough he'd be glad to have the extra clothes.

It surprised Joe that Dawson thought so much on the matter. "You might take a left off of Campbell onto Indian Creek", Dawson had said. That road led to the village of Lima, where he could get a meal, a place for the horse. Ask if Honey was there, he'd know. Joe had thanked him, Dawson said don't bother, what he'd done back there with the truck was enough, and he'd be sure to return the rifle.

They walked, the horse ate, Joe sat; they walked some more. The few houses were set back off the hard top; the world the way Joe Evans liked it. Then the road made a slow curve and there were two people, leaned forward from the weight of packs they carried, hats stuffed over long hair, jeans and boots and talking fast, no sense at all that Joe and a horse were behind them.

He heard cursing and Joe stopped the bay, who whinnied and the pair spun around, which excited Ike so he kicked out. The woman, a girl now that Joe could see her face, got wide-eyed and stepped closer to the boy. He was a youngster not yet twenty, thin beard, pale skin, stringy hair that spilled around his face as the boy leaned down to protect the girl. They made him nervous but Joe kept walking,

The girl's face turned high-color; the boy wrapped his arm around her as they faced Joe, covering the middle of the road so he would have to pass close to them. He drew the bay's head down, played with the muzzle and the bay relaxed. "Morning," he said, loud and clear. The pair jerked, pulled back; then the boy answered. "Morning."

Over and done with and Joe walked on, leading the anxious bay who went back to jigging sideways and pushing at Joe. Horse was 'bout as bad as Joe around strangers. Thankfully the two had stepped to the side as Joe approached. They were babes, he thought, carrying a full load complete with a tin cup and coffee pot tied to the boy's pack.

They were babies running away. The concept made him smile and the boy got defensive; "What the hell you grinning at, mister?" Now that was purely unnecessary. Joe shook his head and kept walking. He was careful to keep his own body between them and the bay, who reared and Joe struggled to bring him down. A few yards off, beyond the kids and their rattling gear, the bay steadied. Then jumped and scooted forward, kicking out high, yanking Joe almost off his feet while he was cursing. The voice drifted to him; "Sorry there, we must of spooked your horse, mister." He damn well knew they'd thrown a rock. That was twice now and both times done purely out of meanness. They had no reason to punish the animal for the fact of Joe and his one-word greeting. To hell with them; he let the bay hurry, and when he finally looked back there was no sight of the boy and girl.

"Why'd' you do that?" "What?" She hit him on the jaw, intending the blow to hurt. He winced and rubbed his face and she thought again that he wasn't much. All she had, though, to get away from her ma who blamed her and her pa who hit her.

"Why'd you throw a rock at that horse? I was planning on making up to that man, he's got food and other things we could use, maybe even cash. He's alone, him and that damned horse, and a little sugar, he might give us what we need. You sure as hell didn't think clear when we run off. You brought books for god's sake, and your iPod and what good're those going to do us up here?"

Even his voice rubbed her wrong; "I can sell 'em, get us some more cash. You'd like that." Laurel stepped back; Kyle was dumb but useful. Now that man, he was like nothing she'd seen before. Too old but still...those canvas bags looked to be full and between her and Kyle they had clothes and his damned books and not much else.

They walked until it was dark, and that came on too early, she was damned hungry and all Kyle had to offer was cold cereal. Not no milk or nothing but bits and pieces and they was stale. "It was what I could find. Pa ain't been working steady..." Yeah right and who cares, at least he had a pa didn't beat on him. Eventually it occurred to Laurel they weren't following those toe-deep prints alongside the dirt shoulder no more. Man and that horse had stepped off the road, some place nice she bet, water and a bedroll laid on soft cushions and he was cooking good meat over a fire. She grabbed Kyle's arm, made him stop walking and hit him when he asked her why. "You listen good. We got to find him."

He'd been spoiled, sleeping in a real bed, hot food ready for him, coffee come morning, a bathroom of his own, and clean clothes. He was learning it didn't take long to ruin a man's resolve; it took exactly one night of half-raw bacon, cold beans and all the stream water he could strain through his teeth.

The bay was resting, front and side-hobbled, saddle removed, damn but he wished he'd thought to look for a bridle back at the old woman's place. And damn but he missed her, cantankerous and long-winded and kind. Joe shucked out of his boots and shirt, loosened his jeans but stayed dressed. Another thing about sleeping in a bed inside a house; a man could rest buck naked under clean sheets without fear.

Sleep came from exhaustion but he heard them as they whispered, trying to work up the courage. He rolled over, snorted as if still sleeping, hunched his back away from where his belongings were stacked. What he didn't expect was the girl; she had a thick branch, short enough it gave her a good swing. He heard the noise and rolled toward her. The branch hit his cheekbone just as he slammed into her legs and brought her down on top of him. She screamed; the pain spread quickly and Joe kept rolling, expecting the boy to literally kick in.

On his feet, dazed, feeling new blood drip onto his chest, he saw them. She still had that branch in her hand and the boy was behind her. Joe's eyesight overlapped from double vision. Squinting didn't help but at least the blood dripped past his mouth. The girl stood up; "We're hungry." Joe grunted; "Hitting ain't how most folks ask for supper." The boy put a hand on her shoulder; "We didn't know you..." The girl shoved his hand away. "I'm hungry and you have food." "A man's life's less important than your full belly." "Damn right," she said. Joe grunted; "Girl that tells me all I need to know."

He easily took the branch from her and broke it over his knee. Blood still dripped from the wound but he wasn't going to let her know it hurt. She tried to hit him again but her light hand was easy to deflect and he grabbed her wrist. She winced, then quit struggling.

"You, girl, you set there." He pushed her toward the tree "Boy, you go put your arms around that tree. Hold them hands together." They were scared enough now to do what he said and he tied up the girl's arms behind her back, then tied that rope to the tree. The boy, he tied his hands together in front of the tree and left him enough room to slide down to the ground.

"I'll feed you and you'll spend the night there, I'll be gone in the morning, and I do hope one of you thought to bring a knife. I'll make nice and leave it between you and it's up to you to cut yourselves loose." They'd proved themselves dumb enough he could get the hell out of here before they sawed their way free.

Early morning, after a restless sleep and waking with a throbbing headache, Joe didn't listen to the girl's shouts and the boy's whine. He washed up in the thin stream, careful around the open wound, swollen enough he could see the flesh. He kicked the cold fire apart, and then saddled the bay.

It was a strange moment, suspended in the months of strange days and people. A girl of no more than seventeen, a pimpled boy of nineteen and they would have killed him over bacon and two cans of beans, a wrapped packet of cold biscuits. He checked their bindings, discovered the girl had loosened hers. That cleared his conscience. He left the knife between them, and scattered their belongings. He glanced once at the girl and saw her knowing eyes; he grinned and she cursed him.

The girl struggled, yelling words he'd only heard in prison. Then she quit, her eyes got huge and her face paled; "Damn you." He saw, he could smell it, knew what happened. He knew the boy had humiliated himself the same way during the night. He inhaled the raw acrid stench of urine. Joe shrugged; it'd been their choice.

Her screaming started up again and already he was tired. He studied the bay, saddled, canvas bags tied to the saddle front. The lead hanging from the halter was long enough to circle the neck, and tied it could make crude reins. He was out a few lengths of rope and a half-pound of bacon and he saw it as fair trade for his sorry life.

Without thought and certainly with no common sense, Joe tightened the girth, checked the stirrup length and climbed up on the bay who immediately reared. Joe leaned forward as he sought the off stirrup; when he was set, he pulled the bay's head around, kicked with both heels and the horse jumped forward. They hit the roadbed at a run, skidded the corner and Joe figured ah hell and kicked the bay again. Tire the horse, and then they could work on road manners and obedience.

A half hour later, the horse came down to a short walk on his own, still throwing his head against any effort to guide him. Force did nothing but aggravate the bay. Joe grinned as he said that word out loud. Aggravate; another first-time word that certainly fit the situation. Ike jigged and fussed sideways across the hardtop, bare hooves scuffling, and Joe thought to be grateful for no traffic as he couldn't control the horse, couldn't direct or turn him unless the bay agreed. The jig set off fireworks in Joe's head. He didn't touch the scabbed wound, didn't want to know if the bone underneath was broken. He could still ride though. The gallop had been doubtful before he found the rhythm, let himself relax and move with the horse's stride.

Eventually the bay stopped, gave a huge sigh and dropped a load of manure. Joe used the time to step down, found that his own legs were shaking, and when the bay was finished, he untied the lead on the off side of the halter and the journey by foot started again. It surprised him, that initial ride brought everything back; now he could let go of one fear and enjoy what had been his pleasure as a child.

He probably had five miles on the two would-be outlaws tied to their tree, and it might take them an hour to get loose. More'n likely they would seek another direction and leave him alone.

Before the town of Jacksonburg, the road's shoulder was littered with broken rock; a layered wall rose above him yet he didn't move to the road surface for there was a car coming up fast behind him. A square rock fell, striking the ground just in front of Ike, bouncing onto the tar where it skidded and stopped. The horse leaped sideways, reared and the car passed so close Joe could see the frightened passengers. The driver leaned on the horn, sending Ike into a bucking fit as Joe tried to pull the bay off the road. Eventually the horse stood, neck bent, trembling, the one eye Joe could see was rimmed in white, the horse gulped in air.

Without further incident, Joe and the horse reached the village of Jacksonburg on the state road where Dawson had told him that the dirt road by the name of Buffalo Run turned from the town and went into Campbell Run and then the Jacksonburg Road. They were good dirt roads not well-traveled. Turn right on Indian Creek Dawson told him and it was an easy walk to Lima.

Honey was the name to remember.

The land swung unevenly into hollows, the road followed a twisted path. There were fields encircled by rails moving at a zigzag along the tree lines. Thin dark wood, weathered in places, lighter rails stacked between the old ones. Trees grew around old walls and tired fences, scrub trees spread into what had been fertile pasture.

He'd ridden the bay unexpectedly hard much earlier, and now the horse walked quietly, almost as if for both of them the act of riding and being ridden was done and they could quit worrying. He knew he was imposing human emotions on the animal. Still the bay moved obediently, sweat dried along the neck and under the halter. Joe too breathed easier; he hadn't fallen off or disgraced himself and his ancestors. Still it felt good to have both feet on the ground.

There was a word, he'd never heard it spoken but read it in a book and looked it up once. The dictionary told you how to say a word, but you had to already know what the symbols meant and that frustrated Joe. He couldn't remember the word now, but he knew it was there. It meant applying human thought and emotion to animals.

What his grandfather had not needed to teach him, and his father thousands of miles away and from a different culture would agree with, was that animals were thankfully not human. They were to be revered for their qualities, not forced into a human mold demeaning what they were and what they gave.

He was walking comfortably; early afternoon, easy dirt road, little dust but a nice give to the surface, cupping his boots, covering the toes with fine powder. Trees lined the road, hiding behind them were fields valiantly created out of thickening forests. The road dust powdered the greens; weeds, leaves, and needles, softening the contrast of colors. The bay's head often swept against his arm and Joe on occasion rested his hand on the bay neck, feeling the coarse black mane hair and the silky hide and marveling at a rare sense of things being right.

A cluster of trees, a peaked roof, thin sounds of distant work, these intrusions woke Joe to the fact he might have reached Lima. There was a congregation of small houses with low roofs, sheds out back containing a freshened cow, a single bawling calf. The horses at pasture were mostly draft stock. Trees surrounded the tight village, waiting to claim back their own. Obviously the farmers intended to keep their land, using machinery in constant battle with new growth. A truck and a Farmall tractor sat free of weeds close to a three-story barn needing paint.

It was a low-set house also needing paint. An older man waited near a front gate; he bowed as Joe approached. "Good afternoon to you, Mr. Evans. My name is Honeywell Daggart." Joe stopped short, the bay rubbed against his arm. Joe spoke quickly; "Mr. Dawson called you 'Honey'." The man smiled and it was a real smile. "Yes indeed my friends call me that. Dawson said to expect you but by his reckoning it would be closer to evening."

The man was white; tall and bent, lean, drawn face, vivid blue eyes and thick white hair going sideways under a John Deere cap. The man's smile broadened; "So Mr. Evans, you have just shown me your own expectations, believing that Dawson would have only one type of friend. While I do not fit into that particular color schematic, I can see why Dawson spoke of you as your skin is a fine addition to our own irrational colors. It is our private joke."

It popped from Joe's mouth with no thought or barrier; "What is the word when we apply human emotion to animals?" The man pulled off his cap and swept his fingers through the tangled hair. "Now Mr. Evans I do believe you have asked a question, which I can answer for you, that has far exceeded what I was led to expect."

Joe kept his mouth shut as 'Honey' studied him; "Ah there, Mr. Evans. You've taken a bad blow. My wife can help for she is a nurse practitioner with the county and will be home in a few hours. In the meanwhile, the word you ask about is anthropomorphism, which in its own right has a fascinating history but the fact that you wish to know it delights me even more. Please, come in. We'll put the horse out with our cow, and I'll make you a cup of tea."

The old man sounded like a relative of Ella Talliferro's or maybe it was getting to a certain age and living where no one else understood most of your thoughts. The word he'd needed to know, and that this man quickly spoke of it, sounded like what it meant and that gave Joe pleasure. He could accept the talking if it gave him small things of value.

Honey was quick to see the brief smile. "You are enjoying yourself, Mr. Evans? Dawson did say you seemed to have a peculiar way of expressing what few thoughts and feelings you might share." Manners demanded an answer; "I like the sound of that word." Honey shook all over; "I also, Mr. Evans, I also like the word. It says what it is intended to say in vowels and consonants so that we understand completely what it means."

As they talked, they walked to the high barn, where Honey accepted Joe's canvas bags and then the saddle and blankets, to be placed carefully on a rounded peg. Along the wall were bridles tied with a buckled throatlatch, which held the reins close to the headstall. Someone knew horses, for the tack had been properly put up. But that had been in the past; the bridle leather was thick with dust.

Honey followed Joe's gaze, and his good humor visibly dissolved. "Yes. Well. Those belong to our daughter. She was killed in a fall. Our son lives in Richmond and is an accountant. We have chosen to live here because there are no memories." Honey stuttered and for once in his life Joe had the urge to touch another man. The man straightened himself; "We each have our story, Mr. Evans. I do not know yours, and I would not, will not, ask. You are a traveler in need of food and medical treatment, and the occasional definition of an unusual word."

The house was plain and spare, everything carefully packed into small spaces. Honey suggested that Joe sit at the kitchen table. They usually entertained in the kitchen, Honey said; it was the biggest and most comfortable room downstairs. Up against an inner wall was a fireplace, consisting of mismatched stone. Joe looked closely. "Yes, Dawson and Decker and Bert helped us install that surround. Some of those rocks are indeed petrified wood. It was quite a project. More than any of us expected it to be."

Joe listened to more lonesome chatter as Honey Daggart boiled water and measured leaves into a brown stoneware teapot. Eventually as the man spoke, Joe shifted through the jumping words. It turned out that Dawson and Honey had both attended the same college. As Honey explained, it had since gone out of existence; "Due to an excess of drugs and immorality as well as fine professors and eager students. We ate and drank through the fabric of life as it were and destroyed everything around us. However, although Dawson and I were not there during the same years, we knew many of the same professors, and ah yes, the town girls. Dawson quite literally stood out in that particular academic environment."

Only then, with the brown teapot steaming, two mugs, sugar and a small pitcher of cream on the table, did Honey Daggart sit across from Joe and take a long look. Being studied like an insect or a museum exhibit had been part of prison life; Joe knew to sit and wait.

"You are extraordinary, Mr. Evans." Honey rubbed his face and shook his head. "I imagine that is a commonplace you hear frequently. It is true nonetheless. It is the combination of your remarkable skin tone, which leads one to believe you are of Native background, with decidedly English features, except perhaps around the eyes."

Joe did not respond; Honey was gracious. "Let me pour the tea, and while it cools, we shall apply hot water and a cloth to see if some of that dried blood, and whatever else with it, can be removed from your wound." No way in hell Joe thought even as he nodded agreement. He felt it through his body, the cheekbone that fascinated Daggart beat in time with Joe's heart. It was too late for stitches. Treatment would be cleaning and applying some sort of balm to prevent infection.

Daggart sighed; "For now, Mr. Evans, we will wash away the filth. It will be for Mary to make the final determination."

Eyes closed, hands gripped hard enough on the chair arm he thought he'd crack the wood, Joe would not moan but my god heat laid on the opened wound made the swelling throb like crazy. Eventually he smelled a female scent and instantly pulled back. It hurt to even open his eyes, but Joe knew his manners and a lady had entered the room. He stood, turned slightly and she was smiling down at her husband.

Wild graying hair around a good face, no artifice; in all respects this woman was her husband's counterpart. And Joe expected a low voice, thoughtful words, no surprise or condemnation. She kissed her husband's upturned face, and only then looked at Joe. "Dawson told us you would be a surprise, Mr. Evans. However I don't think he meant to include such an ugly wound. Honey, thank you for doing the right thing. I'll get my bag from the office. Please, gentlemen, do finish your tea."

Joe sat, wrapped both hands around the mug and drank the tea as ordered; spices and herbs and it tasted all right. He was letting the heat of the tea sit in his mouth, head tilted to the wound so its warmth softened the pain, when she returned with a black bag and snapped it open, brought out a long, half-rolled tube with a name on it he couldn't read. "It's an antibiotic cream, Mr. Evans. We use it for everything, including the cow's udder when it gets chapped." She laughed, to let him know his surprised grunt was expected.

Her eyes were beautiful, a mix of green and gray and gold, he thought, with dark lashes showing a few gray hairs. She held his chin, turned his face where she wanted it and he let her. No one had touched him like this, even in the recent sexual explorations. This woman cared, her touch was light, her breath smelled of peppermint and he tried not to let his own breath reach her. He had been using twigs to scrub his mouth, but not this morning, in too big a hurry to get away. She smiled gently, bit her lower lip. "You know, I think I can take a stitch inside, not across the surface, there's nothing we can do for that scar. But it will heal quicker and cleaner if I take a stitch, here and here."

The tip of her finger brought back the fire; Joe shut his eyes. "Ma'am, you know best." The pause went on too long and Joe opened his eyes. She had moved from the chair, was standing behind her husband, and in front of them sat a squat bottle of some aged liquor.

Honey told him; "Mary doesn't carry any anesthetic. She's a nurse practitioner, not an MD." Joe looked at the two of them, worry mirrored in the other's face. Mrs. Daggart spoke; "The liquor, it's to steady you when I take stitches. If you twitch or pull away, the results will be disastrous." Joe looked up at the low ceiling; beams running across the room, hard plaster between them. Almost like the cottage where he'd lived with his father. "I don't drink." Honey put out a hand near Joe's darker hand, and Joe pulled back. "Is it alcoholism, Joe? This will be a one-time thing and more than likely so painful you won't want to drink again."

Judgment based on skin color; Joe thought Honey Daggart with his colored friends and liberal education wouldn't have such outdated concepts. Truth would push these well-meaning people away from him but he would leave with his grandfather's legacy intact. He felt an outsized anger and it loosened the wrong words. "I don't drink. I never have. I've been in prison most of my life and being drunk there gets a man into bad trouble."

He waited, conscious of quick glances between husband and wife. Joe looked steadily at the woman, for she would dictate what happened next. She only nodded; "You're afraid of how you might behave, since you don't really know, having had no experience with quantities of hard liquor." The core, naked of surrounding facts, and the truth as he feared it.

"Yes, ma'am." He had an ugly memory of Albert Upthegrove even as Mrs. Daggart patted Joe's hand. "Don't worry, we won't let you get that drunk. This is to dull the pain, it will not work completely, that's a fallacy of stories and the movies. But it does help. And the pain itself will help burn off the effects of the alcohol." Honey poured out a short glass. "Here, drink and don't stop even as you wonder why folks give up their lives for this stuff."

Ten

Joe swallowed and gagged, took another swallow and his head didn't hurt much, another swallow and her voice told him to sit still. Honey stood behind him and put a hand to either side of Joe's head. He was in a vise from the work-strong hands, and the whiskey made resistance too complex.

They were both right; he felt each stitch go in, come out, pull, go in again and his mouth opened to protest. There was one terrible groan that couldn't have come from him yet she frowned and the unseen hands held him tighter. She was done suddenly, smiling as she kissed his forehead and he jerked away.

"That was for Dawson and Bert and Decker. Dawson told me you'd never let me near you so I thought, while you're drunk, only slightly drunk of course, this seemed as good a time as any." She smiled down at him and her face had two mouths, both speaking; "While I'm at it, you want me to give you a haircut? At least let me shorten the front so you can see."

His eyes didn't want to focus and his brain couldn't take in what she was saying. But he understood about cutting the hair and never again. He would wear it as his grandfather wore his. He shook his head as her hands pulled at his, drawing them across the table. She touched his face and it didn't hurt; "Thank you, Joe Evans, for taking care of our friends."

He woke in the dark, wanting to sit up but he'd learned to know exactly where you are and under what circumstances you were sleeping before moving too fast. A triple bunk, a close ceiling or beam, any of those could clobber a man senseless. Joe rubbed his mouth, and thought of a skinny girl with a broken branch.

His face throbbed, his whole body ached and he was naked under clean sheets covered with a light blanket. Slowly he made out certain shapes, a table and its lamp, the soft dark from an uncovered window. He sat up, resting his head in both hands. His naked feet settled on a bumpy surface, curled toes told him it was a braided rug.

A shining-white terrycloth robe lay on a nearby chair. He shrugged into it, tied the belt and ventured out the narrow door. His eyes were open, seeing where the stairs were, the handrail of smoothed wood. He could feel the house's age with his bare feet; no roughness in the floor boards, no splinters, each tread having a dip where his foot rested naturally.

They were downstairs and in the front room, sharing intimacies Joe did not understand. He couldn't interrupt or listen, and he was off balance, still drunk he thought, so he sat midway down the stairs to wait.

It was where she always wanted to be. Nested against Honey's chest, held in the sweep of his arm, on the left side where she could feel and hear the beat of his heart. She remembered too clearly how she'd been held in this special manner after Chloe's death. Honey made her listen to his heart and the inevitability of the next beat helped slow the pain.

Five years ago they had given up his law practice and moved here; Honey worked the land, raised most of their food, bartered when he could, and helped the locals with small legal problems. Mrs. Daggart did well as the county nurse practitioner so they survived. And they did not have to live with the visual loss of their daughter.

She could feel her husband's words. "Dawson wouldn't have known this, otherwise he would not have sent him to us. The man's decent, and he told the truth. According to our beliefs, Mary, he's paid his debt and it is done." They pulled closer, she whispered the unthinkable; "It's not often that our beliefs come into conflict with reality, is it?" Honey reminded her; "When the whiskey hit, his manner never changed. He didn't bluff or brag. He was polite even though cleaning the wound obviously hurt. If he was irrationally violent, he could have easily injured either one of us."

Honey sighed. "The worst is that I couldn't do anything if he had wanted to hurt us, Mary. It's the first time I've realized what we've done. There is no one close by to help." He sighed and she felt a shift. "Chloe, now this; I've not kept my word to protect our family." She touched the back of his hand. Honey continued after a long pause; "There's one thing we can do. I'm signing us up for weapons training. Most of the people here have rifles and pistols and a few know how to use them. Only in an emergency, but I think it's wise."

She felt him nod in agreement with his own words and she settled back against her husband's warmth. "Dawson told us Joe Evans is good man. He is, despite what he said. I'd like to know...no, I wouldn't. He has given us his trust, we must do the same."

His arms were folded over his knees, his forehead resting there. He was dozing, hearing some of the words and hating himself, falling back into a sleep, waking quickly, instantly terrified. And they kept talking, dwelling on if he was dangerous, what could he have done, how they must learn to defend themselves. Their depth of fear found company with Joe's ancient regret and self-hatred. He resolved to get the bay gelding to his grandfather's land and then disappear. He was not fit to take up space.

He was asleep, head on his arms, when Mary went to check on the back door while Honey broke up the fire. She gasped; the white robe had split over his legs, against his dark skin the whiteness glowed. He was indeed a beautiful physical specimen but she was as drawn to his beauty as she was terrified by his being.

Their guest barely lifted his head when Mary rearranged her robe, a pretty floral thing with a matching gown, a gift from Honey. His words stung; "Ma'am, I'll be gone before you wake. I didn't mean..." He fought himself, she watched the struggle. "I don't hurt people. I'm not what you need to fear, it's those who smile and pretend friendship while they take everything." The sad depth of his belief appalled her. "You can't go through life..." He interrupted, noting that Honey had joined his wife and she had backed into him. "You two buy those guns and learn to use them. They aren't who you are, they are proof against what might come looking for you. They ain't me either but I can't prove that to you. If nothing else, the truth might save you."

He stood carefully. Inside this house where only peace and quiet were acceptable, there was no room for a soul-less drifter. He'd been defeated by compassion. "Night, ma'am. Mister." He climbed the stairs, conscious that they remained in the hall, staring up at him. More'n likely they were holding each other in fear.

Joe was up before five and found Honey in the barn, milking the cow, its calf bawling from nearby confinement. The bay gelding was in the adjoining stall eating good hay and what appeared to be a handful of oats.

"Joe, we did you a disservice last night and for that we are both ashamed." Honey kept his head butted into the cow's flank and she on occasion slapped him with her stained tail. "Mary has breakfast ready. Please accept our apologies." Joe looked away as Honey stood up, holding the half-full bucket of frothy milk. "Mr. Daggart." Honey lifted a hand, palm out. "Joe, it's done. You can stay until the stitches come out. Mary and I agree. Please."

It was twenty-five miles to Sistersville and the ferry. Joe left after the stitches were pulled. Under protest, he accepted a decent bridle with his choice of bit, and enough food to feed him for days if it didn't go bad first. He would not take a portable cooler or any such luxury; how in hell would he carry such a thing, but he did take the bridle and his choice of a bit was a thick-mouth loose ring snaffle, which surprised Honey.

"I thought the bay, well he seems to have a temper and is that enough bit to stop him?" An easy question for Joe but a painful memory for husband and wife yet they asked the question as a peace offering. He had been wounded by discussions he had not been meant to hear, and it wasn't that he intended to listen but still the words, the frankness of their concerns, had shaken Joe.

"He's scared." Joe's blunt statement obviously startled the Daggarts. He thought about all the ways he could mess up; "He's scared of being hurt." That wasn't any better. "If I put something harsh in his mouth, he'll feel the severity." He stumbled over pronouncing the word but it meant what he had to say. "He's beginning to trust me. A harsher bit will fret him. He's got the whole country to run and I'd rather ride out a runaway than risk hurting him." There was more; "When he trusts me, he'll listen to my cues and we'll agree on where to go, when to stop. It will be from trust, not pain, that he'll make a fine riding horse."

They understood finally, searching each other's faces for confirmation. Honey ventured into the wrong territory; "Chloe used..."

Joe shook his head; "Children get taught wrong some times. It's feel, a sense of the animal through the hands and seat, and it comes to those who care. Your daughter..." He had no right to speak of her. "What, Joe? You have a sense of her we never understood. Please." Mary, hand light on his forearm, peering up into Joe's face; the lines deepened around her eyes, her mouth tight. "Please tell us."

He had been given the knowledge from his grandfather, and his father, both men who understood the passion. "I saw her trophies and the pictures. In that room." Honey said emphatically; "She never slept there, it's where we put...her things." Joe nodded. "She's a rider anyone would be proud of. And she would understand why I want that easy bit on the bay."

He'd thought on this, perhaps the right words could help shatter what he'd started that night. Spoken out loud, the thoughts soothed his hosts and helped clear Joe's conscience.

The papers and the brand inspection, the negative test and his release were all buttoned into his shirt pocket now. Mary Daggart had given him two shirts that belonged to their son. "He doesn't visit often," was all she said and everything was in those words. Joe had the sense to thank her, and when he finished getting all his gear on the bay, he walked out of the barn and they were standing at the front gate. He led the bay about fifty feet, turned back and there they were, husband and wife, arms around each other.

He found the courage to retrace his few steps, lean over the gate and kiss her cheek and it was the first time he'd offered such affection. She blushed and patted his face well below the still-swollen wound.

Honey hugged Joe briefly, no offense, no closeness.

He walked the bay for a mile and the horse jigged while chewing on the unaccustomed bit. Even though he was walking beside Ike, Joe held the reins and had the lead clipped to the bit and tied to his belt. If he came off or the bay bolted, and it would happen one of these times, he didn't want Ike disappearing again. The horse looked almost presentable enough to be stolen.

Joe was beginning to understand why the bay ended up at the killer sale. No walk, no manners, no mouth or listening to the aids. Broke to sit on but basically unusable. Maybe having to walk for sixteen hundred miles would change his attitude. It sure was mending some of Joe's errant ways.

He lunched under a tree after hobbling the bay to give them each an hour's rest, then bridled up and said 'ah hell' and tightened the girth, fitted the bit carefully, hearing his father's words; "One wrinkle only, at the mouth's corner. We don't want that metal banging on his teeth, lad. Make a rogue out of him it would."

The bay wanted to rear as Joe mounted but he plow-reined Ike's head to the right and kicked with his heel and the horse had to turn rather than go up. Straightened out, four feet on the ground, Joe urged the bay into a walk and the horse began to jig, go sideways, kick out, try to rear and Joe was persistent, go forward, easy, light reins. When Ike burst into a bucking gallop, Joe put his heels to the horse's sides and forced him to run longer and faster than the bay wanted.

They eventually came down to a reasonable trot, finally a walk, for about five minutes and then it was jigging again. Joe decided, since he would need a tired horse tomorrow, that running the bay each time he jigged was useful in two ways. Tire the horse and help him understand that jigging brought on another long run. By the day's end Joe was exhausted, his head throbbed, the wound itched and the bay had discovered that if he lowered his head and walked easily, he and Joe didn't get into any more running discussions. Joe dismounted and found he was stiff and sore.

Then it began to rain.

It was a hard and miserable downpour, no gentle rain but a deluge that soaked him through the canvas jacket and down his legs, filling up his boots until he sounded like a bottle being poured at every step. The bay dropped his head, his ears tipped sideways and he'd stop, shake his head, refuse to step forward until Joe tapped his hindquarters with the end of the lead.

They were deep in woods on a greasy dirt road, the bay sliding, Joe's boots picking up mud; pure misery for man and beast. By time and distance Joe guessed they were close to the town of Sistersville on the Ohio River but he couldn't risk walking into town, a bum leading a horse. He needed a house, a barn, some shelter, anything to get out of the wet and let them dry, clean off the muck.

An opening in the line of old trees showed him a field grown in with bushes and high grass and there it was, a barn's pitched roof. They could wait under cover until the storm ended. He hurried the bay, both of them trotting, the bay shaking his head but feeling Joe's urgency.

Down a short lane tangled with vines and brambles; Joe pushed through, dragging the bay, briars stinging them both. One raked the cleaned wound and he thought he'd go down but the sight of that pitched barn roof kept him upright. They reached the high sliding door and he pushed, amazed that the door moved. More rain pelted him as the door opened; the roof timbers sagged, the walls were gone, only the front quarter of the barn stood. Unsafe and leaking; damn it was no refuge at all.

Joe groaned, the bay tried to hurry inside but Joe grabbed the door shut and swung around. There, to the right under a wedge of trees was a small house. Joe ran, the bay pushed ahead of him. An intact house; windows boarded, front door leaning slightly so that Joe could shove it aside, four walls still standing under a tilted but not yet fallen roof.

Ike snorted, stuck his head through the opening then walked in past Joe. By god the roof didn't leak, at least not in the living room where they stood. A rug padded the sound of Ike's hooves; there were chairs, tables, an empty bookcase. No wires, no sign of electricity, dust and rodent droppings in every corner. The room itself was a marvel of high painted walls above what appeared to be carved leather panels; hell even the ceiling was painted with garlands. In one corner what appeared to be linen hung down under a wet spot in the ceiling. Too bad, Joe thought, the house was a wonder, for the moment appreciated only by a soaking wet drifter and an irritable horse.

Joe left the bay in the front room while he explored. There was a bathroom filled with rusted plumbing, dead insects and mice trapped inside the high-walled tub with clawed feet. He backed out, closed the door, shutting off the musty stench of stale usage.

The kitchen was no better. Rotted food molded in the icebox, dead things in the sink, a chair leg recently gnawed. A desiccated rat carcass exhibited spilled innards. He didn't open cupboards or look in anything; instead he closed the peeling door. Meanwhile the bay had wandered into another room filled with a long table against the wall, two chairs fallen sideways. A cupboard of printed china and silver pitchers rattled as Joe backed Ike from certain disaster. It was odd to sit down on a half-chewed velvet chair and talk to a horse. "Son, we can stay here till it dries…" Ike lifted his tail and deposited a full load of manure at the edge of the frayed rug. "I'll clean that, yeah it's stupid to worry, no one's been here in a long time but it won't be us that ruins the place." Ike brought his head down and Joe rubbed the bony head just above the bit and under the cheek pieces of the bridle.

He stood, stretched. "Time to get you dried off. And me too." He'd seen towels in a hall cupboard; if he was careful to remove them without disturbing the rodent nests, there might be enough material left for a good rub-down. There was a woodstove in the living room; Joe rattled the chimney and nothing screeched or fell into the stove itself so it would be a risk he'd take. Fire couldn't get much of a hold in this rain.

The bay dozed unburdened by convention. Joe pushed the furniture to the walls, leaving room for the bay to lie down. Outside the kitchen door was a lean-to shading rotted cordwood. He carried in two armloads; then, since the rain had slowed, Joe ran to the half barn, hoping for an armful of almost decent hay.

Mounds of brittle grass smelled of mold as Joe drifted through the barn, careful not to push against anything. The roof disappeared and he kept looking until he found a pile of baled hay. When he broke open one bale the inside was sweet-smelling, no longer green but with few weeds, and more than likely palatable enough to satisfy the hungry bay.

He brought in three sections and placed them on the floor, away from the woodstove and not on the faded carpet. The bay jerked awake, put his head down and nosed through the offering to find the bits he would eat. Next it was a fire in the stove. Joe rolled up two pages of newspaper, dated almost twenty years ago, and held the flame near the blackened exhaust inside the stove until thin smoke was drawn into the flue. Then he used discarded hay as kindling, pulled out the damper rod, lit the fire and prayed. Sparks filled the box, then he gloried in the crackle of burning wood.

In the depths of the canvas bags, Joe discovered biscuits of course, and two thick slices of bread, one the heel, with pats of butter wrapped separately. There was a container of stew, a can of hash, a box of cereal that needed water and boiling to be edible. And as a treat, a sealed bottle of maple syrup.

He raided the kitchen for a small pot, stood in the rain and let the downpour wash out years of cobwebs and dried beetles. Then that rain filled the small pot and it occurred to Joe that the bay needed watering even as they'd been impatient to get out of the weather. He made another run to the collapsed barn where he'd seen an upturned bucket. Wiping out cobweb and debris, he set the bucket by the kitchen door. It wouldn't take long before he could give Ike a drink. Then maybe he would gather water for himself, heat it and wash the wound on his face.

Water boiled quickly on the stove as he added more punky wood; it burned well enough but too fast and he'd need to bring in more armfuls before settling down for the night. Adding cereal by guess, he stirred the mess with an ornate silver spoon lifted from a dining room drawer. The cereal thickened, he sat down on the sofa, poured in the syrup and the meal was delicious. He read the box and it was grained wheat, and according to the maker's information he was eating healthy. Joe laughed; he was eating hay, ground up and made palatable by the syrup, and he considered pouring some of the maple flavor onto the bay's hay pile as the horse kept pushing away the dried stalks, hunting for a decent meal.

Sometime in the night, the bay gelding spread his hind legs, arched his back and pissed on the carpet. The splashing noise almost woke Joe but he recognized the sound as harmless and went back to a dreamless sleep. Stench and bright sun woke him. He jumped up, startled, quickly remembering, and pulled the horse out of the dining room again. There was a filled bucket on the porch, he let Ike drink, then hobbled and sidelined the horse and turned him loose on the overgrown lawn.

It was sunrise, steam or fog rising from soaked ground, the trees leaked wet air. Joe stretched, took himself to the woods to take care of his needs. Being buck-naked outside, total freedom denied for so long, was unsettling and perfect at the same time. He watched Ike lie down, even with the hobbles, and roll in a sandy spot and considered doing the same but that would damned foolish of a grown man.

He then came back to start up the fire, heated water and scraped away what little beard he had. He dressed quickly in one of their son's shirts, freshly ironed and then wrinkled from the canvas bag but better than the mud-stained red and white shirt or the wildly striped one. The purple shirt had been left in the woods with the boy and girl. He was too aware of today's difficulties, of the need to convince a commercial operation to go outside the rules and accept a man with a horse as passengers across the river. He needed to at least dress conservatively.

As if he was being watched, Joe cleaned up Ike's mess, scrubbed out the carpet, rinsed the towels and hung them off a line out back, found an overflowing water trough inside what had been a pasture fence and watered Ike again. He shoveled and rinsed and scraped, trying to return everything to the proper drawers and cupboards.

Breakfast was reheated cereal with more maple syrup and he ate it all, licking the spoon, then using his finger to wipe the pot insides. Wash again, pot, spoon, his face and hands. There was a mirror in the bathroom but he didn't want to see his face. He would have to bluff, and use the bay's obvious temper to excuse the swollen wound. Carefully, washing only around the edges, he felt the swelling that immediately radiated pain. Joe grimaced and finished packing.

He had a moment's struggle with returning the silver spoon to the drawer. No one would miss it but it did not belong to him. He closed it in the drawer and left the house, pulled the door almost shut.

The horse stood as Joe mounted, and they eased into a trot, moving down the shaded farm lane and out onto the road taking them to the Sistersville ferry.

Eleven

A sign told him 'Population 1,506' and from the look of the empty storefronts, the loss hadn't been recent. Ike trotted easily down the slow hill. Brick buildings, some showing their English heritage, others from the turn of the last century, imposing banks and churches and dry goods store fronts, they all framed a quiet street.

The ferry landing was downhill through an older neighbored, on a one-way road and a steep ramp leading to open water. The tarred surface gave way to rounded pavers, small rocks and weeds were pushed to each side. As they closed the distance to the inbound ferry, a tractor-trailer pulled up, its driver let loose with the air horn; immediately Joe felt Ike stiffen, his big heart pounding.

He eased Ike onto a grassy area and stroked the bay's neck to soothe them both. In the water, a small house, painted white with red trim, floated easily on the ferry's wake as the big truck glided on board. The bridge house, with its captain visible through the high window, was attached to the ferry by a swinging arm. A boy approached Joe; skinny, his eyes covered by a hat brim, shaking his head without knowing what Joe wanted.

It had begun even before Joe got off Ike and asked politely. Still Joe had to try. He dismounted, took Ike's reins over his head; "How much is the ticket for both of us?" Might as well be positive. The boy didn't look that sure of himself. Joe focused on the face; thin, pale skin, damp hair slanted across a pimply forehead. 'Bout twenty years old, he thought, never had amounted to much and the way he was going, he never would. Chest hollow, arms too short, bandy legs and already afraid. If the boy knew how to read, he'd see that a good blow to the face and Joe would go down.

Joe glared, narrowed his eyes, turned his face so the wound in all its bruised, red-lined glory was staring into those watery eyes and he asked again. "How much's the ticket?"

Hank Lofton knew that kid since he'd started grade school and there wasn't an ounce of sense or compassion in those underfed bones and strangled brain. He best get there before the kid did something damned foolish for that man might have a broke face but he was dangerous and the kid wouldn't know danger until it bit him.

The one day old Skrondahl, who spent his retirement opening and shutting gates on either end of the ferry's narrow body, today the old man coughed so hard even the captain had trouble understanding on the phone that Skrondahl wasn't coming in to work. Ritchie hung around the ferry, watching and waiting and today was his first day. Gonna be a beaut if Ritchie didn't mind his manners.

Hank climbed down from the cab and signaled up to Joseph Rumsey, known as Buck, who manned the pilot boat. Buck nodded back and disengaged the gears. Hank heard the squeal and thought he might mention later that the entire system needed a good oiling.

He meandered up to the silently dueling pair, admiring the lines to the bay horse, curious about the odd pairings of gear, and the raw attitude, shaggy hair, and that neatly pressed, freshly wrinkled fine light blue shirt glowing against the man's dark skin, badly bruised face and generally disreputable air. That was a lot of thinking for Hank, but he stepped right in.

"Cars are four dollars, me I pay per axle 'cause I never know which truck I'm driving. It's worth every mile I save getting to wherever in hell I'm going." It was the best Hank could do, make a fool of himself and give these two fighting cocks a chance to back down. Hank already knew the darker man, mostly Indian he thought, was holding back while Richie, well he'd fight anything threatened his first taste of power.

"I figure a man on horseback's more than a foot passenger and less than a car." Hank turned to the boy and easily, without fuss, slid himself between Richie and this odd man who looked like wounded or not he could take on the whole damned world.

"I'd like to pay the gentleman's toll, Richie. I spoke to Buck and Mr. Rumsey agrees. Since it's only me and my truck, if I want company it's fine." Hank gave the boy five dollars, pushed it into Richie's damp hand and made a spinning turn on his boot heel, to stare into the unwelcoming face of his company for crossing the mighty Ohio River.

Joe heard the lie; there had been no words between this man and the so-called 'captain' of the ferry, but this kid didn't seem to understand subtleties and Joe wasn't going to explain, not when they worked to his advantage. He thanked the man, even offered his hand. "Hank Lofton" was given in return, and Joe responded; "Joe Evans." Shook the hand and each man had that look, knowing they'd met someone of their own strength.

Lofton was tall, a thick man with a loose face. His skin was faded tan, speckled with clusters of dark spots on one cheek and across his forehead. He smiled easily, long used to instant friendships that last an hour or a few days.

Lofton in turn studied the man with the absurd horse, equal parts protruding bone and hard muscle, patchy beginnings of a winter coat and a scruffy tail. Man and animal were disreputable and in need of decent food. Lofton did not recognize Evans' features or coloring, Indian yes but with something else. Hell, Lofton thought, we're all mongrels of one sort or another. "You're a long way from home, Mr. Evans, you plan on riding most of the way?"

"Been walking up till a few days ago." The man, Lofton, instantly understood. Joe waited, curious as to what he might say. "Yeah, he needs groceries but you got his feet trimmed down. Nice job." An odd compliment. Joe liked that someone paid attention to the bay. "Livestock auction?" Joe nodded. "I've been to one, they're hell." Joe touched the bay's neck

"You come on then, Capt'n Rumsey wants to keep to his schedule." Lofton laughed, Joe found himself smiling as he led Ike across the brick pavers to the edge of the ferry ramp. Ike stopped there, put his head down and sniffed, Joe stepped onto the ferry and Ike followed. They came in by the passenger side of the truck, as Joe figured the gyrations of the side tug would scare the horse.

The engine rumbled, farting occasionally, and Ike pushed against Joe. The water lapped close with gentle waves. Ike might be familiar with trucks and their noises but flowing water was different. When the ferry pushed away as the ramp gates were closed, the bay trembled.

Hank Lofton sat on the cab step and studied his traveling companion. His own body was bunched and ready to jump into the cab. He quietly blessed the half-height metal railings lined with advertising, which should keep the horse contained. It seemed to him that the man had to be pushed by a desperate force to risk this manner of navigating a river. The ferry crossed on the Long Reach, the eight-mile straight stretch of the Ohio where the water got up to speed. It was why the wheelhouse and engine were on the down-side of the small ferry, set at the end of a folding steel beam, able to push and draw back from succumbing to the river.

The horse was visibly terrified, eyes showing far too much white, but the man kept stroking the bay's neck and whispering until the animal began to relax, first the ears, which lowered as the eyes were shadowed without any telltale white. The neck muscles softened, the head came to rest on the man's shoulder.

The bay arched his back, grunted and deposited straw-colored manure. Hank cocked his head toward the steaming mess. "You need feeding that horse better, Mr. Evans. That don't hold much nutrition and your boy there, well I ain't one to criticize but he needs good food, sort of like you do. Wait a minute."

Second-guessing that Evans would take offence, Hank climbed into the truck cab and got out his battered red and white cooler. Emma packed it the night before a trip, always with the same food. A store-bought pumpkin pie if she could find it, and two large Cokes. He liked pumpkin pie for breakfast and couldn't stomach the taste of coffee. Maybe had him three cups in his entire life and those three times it'd been heat he needed, not the coffee.

Hank always carried a knife, so he slit open the plastic top and cut out a quarter of the pie. 'Bout all he had in the cab were paper towels and a fresh supply of cotton kerchiefs so he laid the slice on a towel and put that pie right in front of Evan's face and managed to scare the hell out of the bay who snorted and tried to back up, then smelled something good and pushed his nose into the pie crust.

Evans broke off the crust and fed it to the bay, then started at the pointed end and chewed his way through the whole damned quarter without stopping. Done, he looked up at Hank and smiled, and despite that lousy half-sewn split on his face the man was a handsome devil. "My thanks, Mr. Lofton, haven't had pie in a long time. I can see why you want it for breakfast but I'd take coffee over soda any time."

Hank finished his first slice, licked his fingers, wiped them on his shirtfront and slid down to sit on the running board again. "Now Mr. Evans, just where're you and Bones headed this time of year? Hope it ain't far. We're gonna get a lake-effect snow soon and they can be bad enough to freeze a man in his boots. Then some poor soul comes along hunting firewood and mistakes that froze human and tries to chop him down. Gets messy, it does. So, where are you headed?"

It was interesting to watch the dark face; it held still mostly, muscles tight, despairing of emotion or kindness. Man had been in tight places, no pun intended Hank said to himself as he assessed the width of his truck, the size of the bay horse and how close the river water came to the ferry's edge. He waited, considered the second half of the pie and found he didn't want to be too generous. There weren't many places along this run that sold a decent store pie.

"South of Rosebud, actually in Nebraska." Hank's head jerked; "What?" "Where I'm headed." "How the hell far is that place?" Evans touched the inflamed skin below that wound. "By my reckoning, another thousand miles or so. Maybe less." Hank rubbed his jaw; "Where'd you start?" There was one of those moments, Hank knew them, used them himself when he needed to be careful telling Emma 'bout his miles on the road.

"Picked up Ike here at an auction." Well that had to be true, the horse looked like one of those nags went the last-resort trip to slaughter. Hank ran into some of those double trucks on the road if he was sent east instead of over the Ohio River. Just the stench made his gut turn.

"You figure on riding him to Rosebud?" Joe shook his head; "I don't ride him that much, we walk mostly, I let him graze when the grass is decent. So far I've found a few places where I worked and he got proper hay and a rain-proof shelter at night. The weather hasn't been a problem up to now but it's almost fall and we're a long way from getting there."

The boy had no sense of time. "Son, it's October already, seventeenth if I'm right. You got to head south a bit now. That lake-effect snow, I wasn't fooling. Them storms're killers." Evans shrugged; "Not too far south. I need to get him home." The word 'home' was hard on Evans, Hank could see it in those eyes, the sudden restless movements of the hands as if Evans needed to break something. Sad son of a bitch.

The ferry jerked, Hank saw the dark face tighten as the bay raised its head, eyes showing white. Hank tried to ease the worry; "It's the Capt'n again, current here's strong, we're more'n half way to Fly and the river wants to claim us. Capt'n Rumsey's good at fighting back. He ain't lost a car or truck yet." Hank patted the green with gold lettering on his truck door.

Evans was again touching the animal, soothing it with those unheard words. Music-like, nothing that Hank exactly recognized. Rumsey swung the pilot motor up against the ferry's side and began pushing and the ferry glided onto the slope of Fly's Landing. For once Hank wished the trip was longer than five minutes shore to shore.

He watched as Evans led the bay horse to the ramp edge and the horse put its nose down to check the peculiar footing. The animal trembled, pulled back and Hank figured to get down off the truck and maybe help move the horse along. Evans, however, had a different idea.

The man tightened the girth, pulled down the stirrups and only then did it come to Hank that this supposed Indian rode one of those flat English-type saddles. Hank had expected such as him to be riding western, boots, hat, and all. Guess it was the cowboys who trucked up in all that gear. Funny how a man could live with preconceptions he got out of movies and television, and didn't notice when the real thing stood next to him.

Evans patted the bay's neck and slipped into the saddle. The horse thought to rear, Hank knew that much about the contrary animals, but Evans played with the reins and the horse stood a moment. Evans sat relaxed in the saddle, no pull or kick that Hank could see but the horse walked forward and then jumped high and wide over the ferry end and the land's beginning. Evans must have figured on it for he rode the jump leaning forward.

Man lifted one hand as the bay trotted up the landing slope alongside the crowded diner been there a year now. Hank bet most of them folks were bunched to the windows, watching a horse go by. Then Rumsey pulled on that rope and the ferry blasted a warning. Hank laughed, climbed into the truck and started forward through the gears, making his way from Fly to Parkersburg and points west.

Joe had seen a map, so he turned Ike left, hugging the roadside away from the river, and sure enough a dirt road came up, with a sign saying 'Skilfinger Run' and he turned Ike, kicked him into a lope and sighed as the horse bellied down to a gallop. He needed to head away from cities, back roads only; Ohio was too civilized. After letting Ike run a mile or two, Joe eased up and dismounted, hobbled Ike and slipped the bridle so Ike could graze. A ditch carrying muddy water had a nice grassy area where Ike settled in for breakfast; Joe rested himself against a tree, to give his gut time to digest the unusual early meal.

He also needed to find work for a few days, and a place to sleep out of the chill. He had the two hundred dollar from the prison release and didn't want to spend any of it. And he still had a few dollars left from Suzie's generosity and the Daggarts' conscience payment, more uncounted dollars for taking care of those cocker spaniels, a long time ago it seemed. Sitting here, though, on the edge of a dirt road cut in shallow curves, he didn't hold out much hope for a farm house or work, not even an abandoned house for tonight.

A puzzle had come to him this morning, when he briefly answered his pie and ticket benefactor's reasonable questions; he was not born into the Lakota tribe, he was not part of the Rosebud Reservation yet he consistently told people that was where he and Ike were headed. Then he would become uncomfortable and speak of Nebraska. So far no one challenged him on his change of direction, but the indecision bothered him.

He sat and watched Ike and thought perhaps the confusion belonged with the horse. The brand was from a Nebraska registry, yet the owner was a Rosebud native. Seemed to Joe, who knew only the ranch, that he kept trying on the identification of an Indian like a store-bought shirt but it didn't fit. Ah hell, he thought, it also didn't matter where or what he said, he was returning the horse to Isaac Brings Plenty.

Hank Lofton, now he'd driven that rig onto the highway out of Fly and into Ohio's middle to any destination where his dispatcher sent him and it didn't matter where. Joe shook his head, got up and started walking, leading Ike, stirrups run up on their leathers, hobbles strung from the off-side dees. Woods, trees hiding the sun, then fields let go, trees coming in on all sides. It struck him that farming all across his journey was less and less an occupation, leaving the land to grow back, and food to be brought in by folks like Hank Lofton, paying extra dollars for what could be grown in most back yards.

Joe was unexpectedly tired, his face hurt with each step but he kept to the job, one foot down, the other raised and pushed forward. Ike however had a new sense of energy and jigged beside Joe, pulling against the lead, shaking his head when Joe kept plodding. It was a long rough morning, and only when the sky hit its mid-day height, reminding him how far off he'd been on time and the heavens, he stopped, found more good grass to tempt Ike while Joe picked through what was left of the food those kind people in Lima had given him.

They walked on into late afternoon and there were no houses, few fields, a slow stream where Joe and Ike watered. One field held promise; high grass waving in the descending sun, shade trees, a small pond overgrown with rushes. Joe started the routine of freeing Ike from his various burdens. First he unbuckled the throat latch to the bridle until Ike yanked his head away, intent on something Joe could not see.

The horse turned his head, inhaled, listened. Sweat broke out on Ike's neck and at his loins. Then Joe took in the scent, raw and ugly, fresh dung, rank urine, almost sweet. Ike reared, pulled backwards; Joe watched where the horse was staring and saw the enemy; a bear rising on its own hindquarters.

Slowly, fingers numb, Joe redid the bridle, climb on Ike's back and it took several tugs on the reins, a hard kick to the ribs to get the horse walking. Joe steered away from the bear, wanting instinctively to run but keeping to a steady walk. Ike tried to twist his neck and look back, but Joe held the reins and kept the horse moving.

Nothing followed to threaten them, except when from distance Joe heard a low 'woof'. Then he leaned forward and kicked Ike, who was glad to bolt from the small field, taking them quickly away from the retreating bear. An hour later, almost full dark, Joe came across a small pen, a leaning barn, the bare outlines of a charred chimney telling him what happened. There was room in the barn where Joe could sleep and a stall for Ike, who fussed all night, restless and worried despite the bucket of stream water Joe hung in the stall, and an armful of pulled grass.

Joe slept through the bay's ruckus. He woke hungry, before dawn, and when he looked at the stall, he could only see the tips of Ike's ears. The horse was sleeping now that it was time to get moving. They met the sunrise when Joe felt the early promise of warmth on his back and then the chill that came before the sun was fully exposed. Joe let the bay trot easily, they were headed west.

Ike felt good, and the roadside grass was mowed, thick, offering a place to run. Speed was a pleasure for Joe as well as the horse, until an object below them, a dark mound set in a half-plowed field, spooked Ike and Joe came close to a head-first spill. He pulled up the panicky horse, then let Ike stand to regain his senses.

"Sorry, mister. Didn't know no one was galloping through. Such ain't too common here." A hesitation, time to get his breath, and the voice started again; "My grandson he brought me breakfast I been out here plowing for an hour. Nice to see daybreak with coffee and a scramble of eggs and sausage in a biscuit. You want, come down here, join us. We got plenty."

Joe led Ike down a steep bank, then saw what he'd been talking too; a toothless man in his mid-sixties setting on a pick-up tailgate, a boy next to him, legs swinging just above the ground. Between them were containers and a thermos, cups, paper plates and a wonderful aroma of good food.

The farmer poured a cup of coffee, which was strong, well sweetened and laced with cream. The man apologized which to Joe was unnecessary; "The wife likes it this way so that's what I get most mornings. Less of course I fix my own. But she likes doing for me and I surely don't want to hurt her feelings. We been married only six months, she's a good woman but trying too hard to make up for me losing my first wife."

The boy muttered something, then his grandpa spoke up; "This here's Donny, he's my oldest boy's youngest son. Gets confusing sometimes. Joe nodded to the boy, who couldn't quite look Joe in the eyes. "This's Donny's new truck we're using as a breakfast table." "Thank you, Donny." Joe grinned at the boy, whose face turned a deep red.

"How many miles would it be to a place a man on horseback can cross that Ohio River down into Kentucky?" The farmer grinned as he gave Joe the last of the hot coffee. "You might head on down to Stockdale and then to Higginsport's one way. Ferry there might take you across." Joe had one more question; "And how far is Stockdale?" "Son, now that I almost know by heart. Take's me, oh hell you can't use my hours on your way of traveling." He pointed to the bay and laughed. "'Bout a hundred miles more or less, depends on how you cover it, lots a good dirt roads 'round here, you're getting into farming country, son. The breadbasket of our country." Here the man's face changed; "Leastways it used to be."

Joe swallowed the coffee, every last bit for it tasted good and seemed to energize him. Then he ate one of the stuffed biscuits. "Thanks for the coffee and the directions, mister." The farmer nodded; "You and that horse, you'll get where you're going soon enough." The boy looked down at the space between his muddy boots.

Twelve

With three days of decent weather, Ike covered almost seventy miles, then it turned cold and rained one day steadily and half of the second in intermittent showers, until Joe and the horse were soaked, both shivering hard enough Joe had to walk to keep his own body warm, to encourage the bay not to fight, or turn his backside to the slanting rain and stand, with that endless animal patience, to wait out the storm.

There was nothing for Joe to eat but enough graze that the bay was holding his own. Joe's gear was soaked, the saddle covered with the canvas bags in a pitiful attempt to save the leather. Sleep was impossible, so was following any road at night, and the days had shortened until Joe knew November was close. And there was no way to tell where he was, no signs of distance or villages; just rain and more rain until it was fields, pastures, and a few equipment sheds where he could hide for the night, and possibly find old hay for Ike. No place for a drifter and his cantankerous horse to seek sanctuary. He liked that word, it sounded exactly like Ike's attitude most of the time. And 'sanctuary', well he'd been looking all his life for what that word supposedly offered.

As he kept walking, hiding in a shed about half the time at night, Joe realized he was sleeping too long and it was harder to wake up and get going. He was starving to death, looking at sleep to comfort and then take him. Finally a vehicle came up and he almost put out his thumb until Ike yanked on the lead and Joe laughed at the impulse. The driver went by too fast before Joe realized the truck pulled an empty horse trailer. Damn, he thought, he could maybe have persuaded the driver to give them a lift.

He trudged on, the air became thick, no light, just the road beneath his feet and Ike's breathing. Hunger ached through him, right down to muscle and bone, cold and no more energy. He would not think of the past few days, he'd keep walking until he fell into another branch of that damned ubiquitous river. That made Joe laugh; he had no idea how the word sounded out loud but he'd loved the spelling and the look of the word, and especially its meaning, and now he had the opportunity to apply it to a river that had already and was going to again give him fits.

Ike pulled back, and Joe raised his head to see taillights blinking, reaching through the rain as brief vivid points. Slowly he realized it was the trailer that had passed him, now with one tire flat. And a figure stood, hands on hips, studying the sagging vehicle. He stopped a good distance off, wary of startling anyone. "Hello, can I help?" He was getting tired of trouble. This time he'd be more careful.

Of course it was a female voice; "I don't think the jack will hold. The wheels keep sliding in the mud. Can you help me find a few big rocks to put under the tires? I think I can finish the job once the rig is stabilized." She paid no attention to Joe. Then as he moved and Ike came with him, she spoke. "Oh, I passed you earlier, I'm sorry if I got you wet." He coughed, wiped his mouth; "Ma'am, that would be hard for even Noah to do."

She was laughing when he tied Ike to the trailer, away from the road. The woman opened the half side door and Ike poked his head in to where a net hung, filled with good hay. "Thank you." She only smiled, "He looks about as wet as you are." "Yes ma'am, only his hide sheds the rain." There was an edge off the shoulder, held by a retaining wall built of good size stone. Joe skidded down the embankment and grabbed a top stone, sighed as it came up easily into his hands. He lugged the stone back up to the trailer and propped it under a tire where she suggested. She thanked him, he nodded. No names, nothing but trying. Safer this way, he thought.

Three more trips, his boots thick with mud, and he had only the near-side front tire to brace before beginning to jack up the trailer. His muscles shivered, he struggled, fingers bleeding where they scraped against flaking rock. He caught the rock, got it halfway up the slope and heard voices. There was a truck behind the trailer, one he hadn't heard.

The voices suddenly didn't sound right; male voices, anger and fear in the woman's tone. Had to be two men against one woman. Joe dropped the rock, wishing it was could be a weapon. He went to Ike, into the canvas bags and got out his knife, patted Ike to keep him quiet and held the knife blade close to his thigh as he stepped around the end of the trailer. A man had her pinned up to the trailer, fumbling at his jeans. Hell and be damned, Joe thought, right here on the road in the rain and they were assaulting a decent woman. The other man stood too close as if waiting in line. Joe walked forward and laid the knife blade to the back of the one man's neck under the left ear, close to that pulsing vein. "You tell your buddy get off her or I slit you from ear to ass."

Lucy had been too focused on this strange man who'd come out of the rain leading a horse. She worried on his third trip for despite the darkness of his skin, he was pale and breathing hard. She said something and he reassured her it was the mud and nothing else. When the truck cruised up behind her trailer, lights off, engine quiet, she had been relieved for it meant someone could help her savior and they'd all be out of the rain quicker. Then one of them put a greasy hand over her mouth and told her to shut up. She wouldn't call out and endanger the man helping her; let them do what they would and get gone. She closed her eyes and pretended it wasn't anything more than an obligatory gynecological exam.

One filthy hand held her face, the breath was terrible, his fumbling hand produced an almost non-existent penis in partial erection and it was all Lucy could do not to laugh. She bit her lip, let a small cry escape but knew that laughter in such a situation could only get her hurt worse than what these miserable specimens had in mind.

The single word, "Stop!" was barely heard, but the threat was clear and the man vainly trying to rape her lost interest. She wanted to grab him, two against one wasn't right. He threw her to the side and went straight at the man who'd challenged his buddy. There was a cry, some cursing, and she could hear blows, see bodies twist around each other and then two of them ran back to that truck. No one followed. It was silent, the truck engine caught and the diesel rattle and stench was overwhelming. Lucy sank to her knees, leaned against the wheel well and couldn't look up as the truck roared into fog and more rain.

"Ma'am we need to change the tire. Then if you could..." He ran out of breath so Lucy went for the jack and placed it where she hoped it would work. He got the wrench on the lug nuts, she joined her strength to his to spin the wrench. She tried thanking him while they worked but he shook his head as he turned the wrench. The tire came off surprisingly fast, he positioned the good one and they spun that wrench again and he suggested she have a gas station tighten up the lugs when she had the chance.

It was only when the man lifted the flat tire to where it would be screwed back onto the trailer that Lucy understood; he bled from his mouth, a ceaseless trickle made worse by the rain. The rain stopped, the blood kept coming. He coughed, held his left side and blood erupted between his fingers. His words came as a shock; "Ma'am, you got a place we can put the bay. 'Pears I need a hospital." "But you, you had the knife." He grunted; "...had his own. A place for the bay?" He dropped the flat tire into the mud.

She shoved the wounded man into the front seat of the truck, gave him a thick towel to hold over his side, another one to clamp in his mouth. She always kept such supplies in the truck. The bay loaded without trouble, she left him loose in the trailer, in too much of a hurry for the niceties. As she pulled out onto the slick hardtop, she called in to her husband, telling him why she was late and that it wasn't any injury to her, but a man who'd stopped to help her needed a doctor. Meet her at the emergency room entrance, she said. With the car. She had a horse on the trailer. She'd stay with the man till the docs told her about his chances and all.

Joe heard meaningless noise so he let his head rest on the truck seat's high back and tried to keep his hand on the towel at his ribs but it got heavy and his fingers seemed to lose strength so he drifted to where he was dry and warm and his side didn't hurt, his mouth wasn't thick with blood.

Lucy knew too many of the staff and doctors at the hospital so when she phoned and said she had an emergency, the doctor on call immediately thought it was about Deana and it took some explaining; no she didn't need a breathing tube or a wheelchair, or a dilator that would clear Deana's air passages. She had a man she thought had been stuck with a knife, she didn't know exactly where and he wasn't talking now.

He coughed again and more blood poured from his mouth. The towel at his side was bright red, enough blood she could see it spread onto the woven upholstery through the saturated weave. She told the dispatcher she believed the injury might be into a lung.

Taylor had already arrived with the van, Deana asleep in back, strapped into her car seat. Daisy, their Springer Spaniel, was snuggled next to Deana. The dog was Deana's companion, able to comfort her those few times she was alone. Deana didn't wake when Taylor transferred her, seat and all, to the truck. Daisy jumped in beside her charge.

"Just put the horse in a stall and take off his gear. I'll tell you later. Thanks, dear." She stood on tiptoes and kissed him. She'd been scared earlier for herself, and more scared as she shoved the man into the truck and drove him to the hospital. If she told all the miserable details to her husband right now, he would never leave. He hugged her and spoke into her muddy hair; "Long as you're all right."

Attendants were attempting to move the man onto the gurney. He was holding his ribs and fighting them one-handed until they backed away and one attendant, Tim Wedgefield, called to Lucy for help. She hugged Taylor again and ran.

He wasn't going with folks he didn't know. Done that before, hurt too much his side was on fire and he wasn't lying down on that bed. Her face he remembered and he smiled. She put out her hand and said something but he couldn't hear; heart pounding like it would fall out of him. 'Please' he understood and he let her come close, take his right arm and lead him to that damned bed after all.

Joe lay down wanting to ask about Ike and where was the horse, who was taking care of him. But they hooked up a needle in his arm and he drifted off before he could speak the words.

Once inside, it started. "Mrs. McLaren, we have forms...you know." She was tired and wanted to wash her hands but Accounting was relentless and she didn't wish to upset them. They certainly weren't going to like what she had to say.

"His name, please." "I don't know." The response was perfect, the mouth an '0', the eyebrows high enough to hide under rigid bangs. "You what?" "I don't know his name, we never had time to exchange such pleasantries." Thankfully her usual doctor approached and when he lifted one eyebrow at Rhoda, the woman settled back in her chair and rolled away, leaving Lucy with one word, Accounting's version of a threat; "Later."

Dr. Edwards had the same questions, only he also had opinions and information. "He stopped to help you change a tire? How in hell did he get a knife slice through the ribs and into the lung? Another inch and it would have nicked the heart." When Lucy couldn't answer, Edwards smiled at her. "Your would-be savior's one tough man. What's his name, Rhoda at the desk said you wouldn't tell her." Lucy took a deep erratic gulp.

"That's because I don't know his name. It was all about keeping the trailer from sliding, and then those...men." Her hands shook so badly that she clasped them together, but Edwards wrapped his big hands around hers and she looked up. "Well whoever he is, we'll take care of him. We can't have Deana's grandmother worried. How is our girl? We were concerned when you called, thinking something else had happened to her."

He was in hospital for a month. That first week was lights and noise and trying to tell people he couldn't pay but no one listened. It hurt to breathe but other than that he was fine and sat up one day to show them. Got pushed back down and something was injected into a drip that went through him quickly and he slept. No pain then, only strange dreams and odd faces peering at him and always those questions.

First time a face made sense to him it was the woman from the rain. "You all right, ma'am?" For some reason the words made her smile. "You can speak English." Joe thought that over "Course I speak English, ma'am. Why would you say that?" She smiled and her eyes glittered, her mouth was half-open; one hand took his and held it to her chest. "You've been babbling for a while. We still don't know your name." Ah, he thought; "Joe Evans. Ma'am?" She held on and he saw his own skin, saw it was pale, copper but pale as if not enough blood ran through him. "Lucy McLaren, Joe. It's nice to finally meet you."

He fell asleep with the woman holding his hand.

Next time he woke, she was there, and propped up in a wheelchair was a child, he couldn't guess the age. And when...her name was Lucy, now he remembered, when Lucy saw his eyes were open, she rolled the chair closer and Joe found himself looking into eyes like his own. Black as night, thickly lashed, black hair to match. He blinked, the child struggled to lift her head and they stared at each other.

Joe finally grinned, the child's head tilted, the smallest amount of spittle ran down her chin, and she too smiled. He tried to reach for her and his hand wouldn't move. With Lucy's help, the child's brittle arm and hand landed on him, weightless with pliable fingers.

Her mouth contorted and sounds came, nothing from any language but he felt a different weight as if she had pushed down on his hand. He had to look away and saw Lucy's face. "This is why you helped me, Mr. Evans. She is the reason." The small hand with its tentative weight helped him close his eyes and he slept again. The doc told him the few times Joe'd been awake, the nurses lectured him; he needed as much sleep as possible. He'd been fighting pneumonia as well as the lung puncture.

Taylor McLaren sat at the table, elbows braced on the scarred maple top, holding a fresh cup of coffee. Lucy sat curled up in Taylor's reading chair. He took a sip of coffee and shook his head. "The hospital knows we can't pay this bill. It must be enormous by now, and on my salary, and yours, we..." He couldn't say it, had said it too often. They had battled departments and resources, funds and hospitals, to keep Deana as healthy as possible and in a warm and loving home. Now to carry the burden of a stranger, one to whom they owed an enormous debt that money could not touch, would bankrupt them and take away what meager security was present in Deana's life.

"I'll call from school, there must be some way we can work out payment."

There wasn't time to make the call until almost noon, when Taylor despaired of finding anyone in the bursar's office at the hospital, or to reach Dr. Edwards, but he promised Lucy he would try. Dr. Edwards came to the phone immediately; "Taylor, glad you called. Our patient is doing well..." and the voice went on describing the wound and how it was healing, the peculiar old wound on the man's face needing a bit of plastic surgery and Dr. Leveritt had donated his services. Taylor listened, impatient and wanting to know but uneasy breaking into Bob Edwards' soliloquy.

Taylor finally had to interrupt; "Bob you know we can't pay this bill. Lucy's worried...we can't take anything from Deana's trust." Edwards' voice was rough; "Oh hell Taylor. I forgot to leave the message. The town council, the mayor's office, the hospital board and several civic organizations are combined in their decision that as this year's ..." Here Edwards hesitated but Taylor heard the unsaid word and thought that this time he would not let pride provoke him into refusal. "Their chosen charity this year is to pay Mr. Evans' hospital and medical bills. There. I thought you and Lucy already knew."

Taylor very carefully put the phone down. He leaned back in the fake-leather principal's chair. He must call Lucy; however, he had a moral dilemma that he'd been avoiding and now it had to be addressed. Taylor had gone through the man's belongings in an attempt to ascertain a name or any family. He had found papers telling him an awful truth. Released from prison, having served his full sentence of fifteen years for murder two with... He had not told Lucy, not even the man's name.

Taylor lied to his wife, calmly and deliberately and while it felt terrible, he also was protecting her. Taylor knew it too, the weight of an enormous debt; life offered up for a stranger was uncommon. He had seen Joe Evans exactly three times; it was Lucy and now Deana who sat with him while the weakened man fought what were, in Lucy's vivid description, demons of a terrible nature.

The phrase 'paid his debt to society' had become Taylor's mantra. Taylor picked up the phone, this time to give his wife the news that for once their debt was reduced, not expanded.

He was up and holding to a walker when Lucy wheeled Deana down the hallway. He was taller than she expected, and now that he was straight up and down, and the bandage had been taken off his face, she was astounded at his looks.

When he walked toward her, Deana jackknifed in her wheelchair from excitement. He stopped, the nurse bumped into him and he grunted but made no complaint. As Lucy hurried to settle her child, Joe Evans made his way in awkward lurches until he reached the wheelchair.

Bending down, hand steadied by the nurse's grip on that walker, Joe was able to put his face close to Deana and kiss her. The child squealed and her hands and legs thrashed the air. Lucy laughed, until she saw the stunned look on Joe's face and lightly touched his arm. "It's all right, she's telling us how much you please her. That's the sweetest thing..." Her voice broke, tears started and Lucy worried about Joe for he seemed frightened by the commotion. It was time to explain all this to him.

She thought to tell him now, but the look on the nurse's face alerted Lucy to a different crisis. The nurse stood just back of Joe and her face mirrored what must be in the minds of others witnessing this meeting. Joe's buttocks were bared as he touched Deana in a total lack of concern for his dignity, the same lack of concern he had shown when Lucy herself was attacked.

It was obvious from the nurse's face that she had stepped out of her professional demeanor. What was in her eyes, and the looseness of her mouth, had nothing to do with medicine. Lucy spoke sharply; "Help him." The woman's face changed and she closed the opened edges of Joe's gown, unable to meet Lucy's stare.

By the time Joe was settled in bed, he was exhausted. Lucy gripped the handles of the wheelchair and turned it on one wheel, headed for the door. Joe's voice stopped her; "You were going to tell me." He spoke each word with a gasp. "Please."

It happened four years ago, when Taylor was celebrating his sixtieth birthday and talking of retirement and his plans for their thirty-three acres, the crops he would grow in the old manner. He even had a deal with a man about a good team of half-Clydesdales, harness and all.

Four years ago a truck slammed into the older sedan holding Deana McLaren, her mother Cathy Star McLaren, her father, Hyatt McLaren, and their son Tim, killing mother and father and brother, and making a quadriplegic out of their beautiful six-year-old daughter. Taylor had taken the job as principal of the local high school and Lucy devoted herself to Deana's welfare while picking up editing jobs on the computer. It was battle after battle, insurance and health care piling up astronomical bills they could never pay, and then dealing with agencies and groups and any and all organizations that promised help and assistance to the families of children in need. Lucy became adept at stating their case and pleading for help without demeaning herself or making Deana a mark of false sympathy.

Eventually a small trust was established out of the meager insurance from the truck company. It wasn't enough but it helped.

"Yes", Lucy said, as Joe studied her, "She is part Osage." Joe smiled, his hands seem to ease on the white sheets and Lucy touched the back of one hand. "I knew when they brought you in here. Even covered in blood and filth, I knew you and Deana would see each other."

It was mid-December when they brought Joe home. He could walk unaided and he was gaining weight but not fast enough for Bob Edwards' satisfaction. "Good cooking, and lots of it. Much as you can get into him. He's restless but seems enchanted by Deana and that's good for her, like her having...." The doctor swallowed hard.

They had talked the night before Joe's release. Taylor couldn't look at her as he spoke; "Too much was going on and we owed him, still owe him so much. But he will be in our house, making us vulnerable so I need to tell you." This was not a good beginning to any conversation. Taylor asked her to sit in the wing chair while he continued.

"There were papers in his belongings, I lied about finding them." She wanted to shake him; "For the Lord's sake, Taylor, tell me what's bothering you." He sighed, and rubbed his hands together as she'd seen him do at school; "He was released from prison this past spring." She gulped and her hands rose involuntarily to cover her mouth.

Taylor delivered his words with a relentlessly pedagogical tone normally reserved for academic chastisement. "He served fifteen years and the papers were quite specific. He was charged with and found guilty of murder in the second degree. He received only fifteen years because of extenuating circumstances." The term, 'Extenuating circumstances', its designation fascinated him and he had no answer when Lucy asked him what else he knew.

He did mention that from his looks Evans must have spent most of his adult life in jail. For a confessed killing, the courts would treat fifteen year olds as adults. He had given his age as thirty-one. This simple notion of half a life in prison intensified their apprehension.

She said the single word; "Murder." Taylor echoed her. Both shook their heads.

They knew; he saw it in her face. They'd gone through those damned canvas bags and they knew. He was quick to ask, pretending to pack as if he was in a hurry to go with her. "How's Ike doing? He can be a handful." He could not look at Lucy as he said the words.

So, she thought, he's guessed. She listened to him, heard within the words that he was aware of their fear and was planning to leave and it was up to her to stop him, gently, without judgment. "Deana has a pony. So Taylor is used to horses and had little trouble when he took your horse to our barn." That caught him off guard. She kept going; "It's why I had the trailer with me. We take her and Gus to a riding program three times a week. I'd been going to get the brakes done when..." He nodded; 'Oh."

Joe had no warm goodbyes for any of the nurses, no doctors that came in to check on him. An orderly settled Joe in the wheelchair and pushed him in silence. On the way out, Joe made a stop at the bursar's office, where he promised to make payments when he got home. Lucy heard the hesitation over that last word, and for an instant she felt an enormous pity. Rhoda listened without speaking. Then

Lucy glared through the glass cover and Rhoda seemed to find the exact words extremely difficult, as if needing to swallow after each syllable. "Mr. Evans, your bill is fully paid."

He stepped through the sliding door, glad to be out of the mandatory wheelchair. About the dumbest and kindest thing he could do now was to ride out. Holidays were coming, time meant for families and loving friends, and these people were terrified of him. He'd seen her face, and now the husband would greet him at the farmhouse and Joe had no answers that would satisfy them.

They were seated on the sofa close together, the lit fire burned down to warming coals. Daisy lay stretched out on the braided rug and Lucy took a mental step back from the bucolic picture of how they would appear to an outsider. Here it was, a reminder that what looked perfect often was troubled underneath.

Joe Evans came in from the bedroom, stood briefly at the corner of the fireplace. Daisy sat up, snuffled over to him and insisted, by reaching up to put her nose under his closed fist, that she was to be patted. He squatted and a spasm went across his features. He looked at the dome of the spaniel's head, where the silky ears spilled around her neck, and he gently played with them, lifting and rubbing, until if Daisy had been a cat she would have purred.

He kept his eyes down stubbornly, studying the floor, however his voice was clear; "You can ask me what you want, what you need to know. That don't...doesn't mean I'll tell you more than what's in the public records. But you can ask." She watched him stand, and once again was surprised; Joe Evans, dark as Deana's skin, black hair almost to his shoulder; and how he'd fought them in the hospital when for sanitary reasons they wanted to cut his hair. Those eyes were kin to her beloved grandchild and yet they were not related. She wanted to ask him what tribe he was but the question seemed inappropriate.

Taylor spoke abruptly; "Who did you kill?" Lucy gasped, grabbed Taylor's hand, not yet ready for such a demanding question with no possibility of a polite answer. Joe answered; "My stepfather." Taylor waited; Joe's eyes did not drift from Taylor's face. Taylor was relentless. "Why?" "He was going to kill my mother." A deep indrawn breath; "And my half-brothers." That let out some of the tension, but Taylor wasn't done. "Why didn't you go to the authorities before...?" The question could not have a one or two-word answer. Joe hesitated, one fist tightened across the knuckles until there was no color.

"Who would hurry to a drunk's house before he killed his family?" Not an answer, but a question to provoke more careful thought. Taylor pushed; "How old were you?" "Fifteen when I killed him, sixteen when I was judged and started serving time." He fascinated her; voice steady, no fuss or restless movements, only the glitter in his eyes to betray that each word took its piece.

"Would you do it again?" Lucy gasped, this was cruel. Joe's body tightened, his mouth pulled down. "Yes." He hesitated, "Under the same circumstances. Yes." Taylor was relentless; "Doesn't killing a human being hurt you at all?" There, some feeling in Taylor's voice, an allowance that perhaps Joe had been correct in what he'd done, but the moral issue asked for a different reaction. "No." Taylor waited, but there was nothing more than the one word. Finally he gave in; "No to what?" "I won't answer, Mr. McLaren. My feelings have nothing to do with what happened or your safety with me in the house. I won't be here long. I can't live with your moral judgment."

There, he'd said it. After all the years, he'd told one man, and a more sympathetic woman, exactly how he felt about a world that ignored what had been building in the family until a child had to take action and they punished him for the family's survival. The words felt good even as they would drive him from this house where he needed to be until he gained strength.

As she listened, Lucy heard the steady rhythm of Joe's answer, the rehearsed words that kept him separate from his act until that final statement. She rested her hand on Taylor's thigh and squeezed. She spoke this time, hurrying past Taylor's half-opened mouth; "You don't frighten me, Joe. You have told us what we needed and nothing more, as you said in the beginning of this...inquisition." Taylor shifted under her lightened caress and she patted him. In truth she had been terrified, first of Taylor's revelation and now Joe's answers.

Joe looked directly at her and she became aware of the peculiarity of their situation; she and Taylor sat in warmth and comfort on their sofa, once again the dog was snoring on the braided rug. The room was lit only by intermittent embers. Joe seemed to know what she was thinking for he took three logs out of the cradle and placed them on her grandmother's andirons.

He spoke while feeding the fire; "Ma'am, you can protest all you want but I see the fear. You and your husband owe me nothing, what I did was for a stranger. Not you, not Lucy McLaren." His body sagged and she jumped as if to catch him. He straightened, grunting softly. Lucy stared at him.

This was the moment, her choice, when what she feared in this man's past would determine how they dealt with him. Lucy was a believer but not a church-goer, and she was thankful that the town had seen fit to extend their Christmas charity to the hospital bills. It was not because this man meant anything to them, it was for Deana, and Taylor and Lucy herself. Right now, she had a rare opportunity, where she could rise above her selfish fear and offer a gesture of trust.

She glanced at her husband, and Taylor's face seemed to reflect Lucy's confusion. She knew Taylor, knew his generosity, sometimes lost in the strict educator he'd become by necessity. Taylor's face was in the shadows, his eyes hidden from her. She stepped closer to him, touched his knee. His fingers swept over the back of her hand and she could just see his smile. It was all right, she could go ahead.

"Joe, I'm going to heat up a bowl of stew. We haven't had, none of us have had supper. Excepting Deana." She could see Joe's dark hand, steady and slow, putting that spoon to Deana's lips and the child smiling, opening her mouth, Joe placing the food gently inside with what had to be an act of love. Nothing else elicited such tenderness.

She became aware that both men were waiting, she'd best finish her statement; "No supper is inexcusable. Bob Edwards was adamant on making certain you gained weight. It's the least I can do." She was talking too much, letting out her nerves. She marched past Joe, lightly brushing his turned shoulder and she smelled the stench of fever. Before she disappeared into the kitchen, Lucy stopped to study the two men. Taylor sat alone, hands on his knees, Daisy's head resting next to him. Joe had not moved, still using the hearth for support.

Taylor watched his wife walk away, then looked quickly at the man who caused so much trouble. The situation had become a test of humanity. And it bothered him that he did not believe under such circumstances he would have risked his life for another the way this stranger had. Taylor's mind and heart were split between fear and forgiveness and the overwhelming debt he owed another being, a man who in more normal times would be no part of their lives.

He admired his wife for her determination, and when she tapped his hand, he knew that she was asking and he had to give approval. It was a difficult decision, and he make it more difficult by smiling at her, then nodding to the strange, dangerous man who had rescued the best part of Taylor's life.

Thirteen

Joe fell asleep on top of the neatly tucked covers, still in jeans and a shirt that smelled now of body heat and sweat. He found the barn that next morning, slipping twice on the icy path. Once inside the well-kept stable, he whistled and spoke the bay's name and got a resounding whinny in return.

There was a chestnut pony who looked out over the half door, saw Joe and snorted before returning to his fresh hay. Ike kicked the wooden wall hard enough Joe thought he might have cracked a two-by-six. "Hey there, Ike" he said as he opened the stall door and he was scolded; first his hair got pulled, then the collar of his borrowed jacket was chewed until Ike shifted to the front of the jacket and pulled the line of snaps open. Then Ike butted Joe, knocked him against the wall. That hurt and Joe put out a hand, which promptly got bitten. Not hard enough to draw blood but held, teeth firm, head shaking. "Enough." Ike snorted and let go; Joe squatted; needing to catch his breath and Ike rested his muzzle on Joe's head, pulling occasionally at his hair.

When he eventually stood up, he was dizzy and grabbed onto Ike. Guess he wasn't going anywhere for a few days at least. He would not think on last night's grilling, an apt word for how he felt, burned beyond recognition, seared by questions he could not tolerate.

He entered the house by the kitchen door and immediately Lucy McLaren reminded him to remove his boots and they'd have to get him a decent pair of slippers. She chattered on. 'Yes, ma'am' was all he had to say. Then he saw Deana, tied in a motorized chair by vivid nylon straps. The black eyes glowed and he felt himself smiling, so he knelt down to fuss with his boots.

When he stood, Lucy handed him a spoon. "When you're done, I'll have lunch ready for you." He started, almost dropped the spoon. Lunch! And he'd been thinking about breakfast. "Thank you, ma'am." She smiled and it seemed genuine; "Feed her, Joe. She eats more when you feed her. For Taylor and me, that's a relief and a blessing."

As Lucy returned to her chores, she decided that there was no right time; "What tribe are you, Joe?" There was a note in his voice when he answered. "Lakota, ma'am. And Welsh." Let her chew on that for a while.

He fed Deana, he brought in firewood, he learned where the barn implements were kept and very slowly was able to take care of the two horses. There was no winter riding for Deana; as soon as the snow stayed, the program closed down. No indoor arena, no facilities to protect the adults and children. Lucy spoke of her attempts to get a shelter built but the area was poor and the funds had yet to be raised. It was a pity, she said, for everyone in the program benefited greatly.

For over a week, Joe ate, did chores, slept, and fed Deana. This was a great help, according to both Lucy and Taylor. They never knew each breath hurt, and at night his heart pounded irregularly. The child made him laugh, the two horses whinnied whenever they saw him. And Mrs. McLaren fed him well, while her husband asked no more questions.

Each time he used paper to start the fire, he noted it was a day closer to Christmas. Thanksgiving had been lost; then again, the holiday meant little to him from either side of his heritage.

"Ma'am, you and Mr. McLaren, you haven't said...I won't be joining you..." She looked up from the cookie dough she was rolling out; it was Deana's favorite, gingerbread. The child bounced in her upright chair, colorful straps held her against the misdirected energy of her frantic muscles.

"Joe." She kept rolling out the gingerbread; she'd learned that not looking directly at Joe while they spoke allowed more room for discussion. "Taylor and I usually take Deana to friends. They have a daughter who loves Deana. They're very gracious." She glanced up in time to see relief in those startling eyes.

"Thank you, ma'am." She'd given up asking him to use her name, and he didn't call Taylor anything at all. The two men had a truce, unspoken of course, where their talk was kept to a minimum and Lucy asked about the easy things like what size boots to get from the Thrift Store and did he like Brussels sprouts.

It was his for one day; an empty house with a dog and two horses in the barn. Joe slipped on the thrift-store boots, put on the more durable canvas flannel-lined chore coat and went to the barn. Daisy came with him, leaping into snowdrifts and barking at him to play.

When he turned Gus out, the pony stood fetlock-deep in snow near the barn. When he brought Ike out, the bay leaped forward up to his knees in fresh snow, digging his head underneath and throwing up snow, kicking out, squealing and then falling, rolling over, legs waving until Joe had to grab his side from laughing and even old Gus got in a buck or two. Joe went inside and brought out two big flakes of hay, which he shook out and separated and laid them well away from each other. "Merry Christmas, boys. You've earned it."

Lucy left a roasted chicken, a slice of apple pie, a potato to be reheated, and fresh green beans waiting in a Tupperware container. She had taught him the refinements of the microwave and he put it to good use. After eating what he could, which still wasn't much, he knew enough to wrap things and put them in the refrigerator. Then it was his intention to start fire in the fireplace and take a nap.

He picked up the paper to tear into starter strips until he read the headline. 'WEST VIRGINIA FAMILY TERRORIZED.' Joe knew immediately what had happened. The names jumped at him; Honeywell and Mary. His vision blurred, then he blinked furiously and read the most important bit...'the Daggarts are resting comfortably.' He expelled a hard breath; according to the reporter, the husband and wife were in the local hospital while the young woman, who seemed to have been the ringleader, was at a hospital in Wheeling with serious wounds, and the boy had surrendered to the first person in the small community who responded to the unexpected shotgun blast from the Daggart residence.

He stood again, Daisy sat up but he told her to stay. Right now he didn't need company, he needed to be moving. The girl's face, that branch coming down on him, the terrified boy. And the Daggarts who had discussed in expected privacy whether or not they could trust Joe in their house, giving him his first real taste of how he would be perceived.

The Daggarts were 'resting comfortably' only because they had feared Joe enough to buy themselves a decent weapon. One mark for him, Joe decided. He pulled on the new thrift boots and the canvas coat and skidded down the driveway to the main road, well-plowed from yesterday's fresh snow.

No one was out, all the locals were at home or with friends, eating and laughing, knowing they were loved. No one was here to celebrate that Joe Evans had done something of immense value which saved lives instead of taking one.

The car seemed to glide up behind him and only when the driver honked, a brief tap so that he didn't jump too high, did he turn and see a face that was almost familiar, a woman's face, dark hair loose around her high sweater, smiling at him through a frosted windshield. Then the car stopped and she leaned over, partially opened the passenger-side door and made a silent offer. It took some maneuvering around the snow bank to slide through the narrow opening and get all of himself inside the car. Now he knew who she was, one of the hospital nurses. She smiled and he was certain; "Where're you going, Mr. Evans? There's not much out here close enough to walk to." He shrugged and she shifted gears, started along the road.

She remembered him, they all remembered him. Even the one male nurse spoke about what an extraordinary man their patient was. Beautiful, a married nurse said, the first to put it into words as she had a husband she loved but told the girls a woman could always admire when male beauty came along. After all, such beauty was so rare it was worthy of being noted.

After a disastrous meal with her mother, Lois had escaped and found herself a Christmas present. She smiled and he quickly looked at her, head tilted. She hesitated, worried at being rebuffed, but then she could always ask him to get out of the car. Her hand on his thigh was the answer. He remembered her from the ward; he even remembered her powdered scent as she rolled him onto the unwounded side, washing him while preserving his modesty, talking past the intimate actions of her hands.

He looked down at those hands now, pale, long fingers, short painted nails; her fingers closed lightly on his leg and she was smiling as he leaned in to kiss the side of her mouth. He could feel her lips move in pleasure as her hand slid up his thigh. She spun the wheel and directed her SUV down a narrow, barely plowed road while Joe kissed her full on the mouth and Lois giggled. It felt funny, so he kissed her again and got another giggle.

They were out of sight from the road, with a light snow brushing the vehicle. She left the engine running, the heat on low. Without looking directly at him, she said; "The seats fold down." He kissed the side of her mouth again and nodded his head at the same time. Her reaction was to slide her hand under his shirt against his belly. He shivered and they both laughed.

The seats had buttons and levers and then they were flat and she had a blanket folded in a corner. "We can use a jacket as a pillow, Joe." He took her face in his hands; "Merry Christmas, Lois." He finally had remembered her name. They crawled through the opening of the seat backs and then he leaned into kissing her as she became busy with zippers and buttons and removal of anything that might get in the way.

As he rose above her, erect and aching, she spoke words he immediately regretted. "Do you have any protection?" Joe pulled back; "No ma'am." He tried to grin; "I don't even have a driver's license." There was a hesitation, then she laughed; "There are other ways, we'll just have to...lie down beside me, Joe. We've got to keep each other warm."

When they were settled, skin against skin, she placed her order; "Well you, come here." And she took hold of his head, pushed him down the length of her body as his mouth tickled her flesh and she laughed even as her body responded. He was quick enough to use his tongue, pushing inside and against her flesh until it was almost too much to bear and she used both hands as leverage to move him but he persisted while she went into spasms that lasted over and over until her entire body was shaking and he simply laid his head on her belly.

When she could breathe again, he kissed her belly button, saying nothing while his own need poked her leg. She drew him up to her and tried to double herself to reach him with her mouth and she bumped up against the wheel well and fell on him.

"You taste good," she said and nipped him gently under his arm. His body jumped, the head of his erection finding a corner of her hip. They both laughed. In order to take full advantage, she had to brace her buttocks against the front seat, lean over his entire torso so he could nibble her breasts while she took in his cock, right to the base where her mouth was distended and he shuddered, his hands shook as they cupped her breasts. His shudder became an eruption, he tried to pull away from her, a sensibility she did not expect.

Then she asked with gestures and the slightest moan if he would do her again, his release had triggered more wanting. This time it came slower, deeper, and when they were both exhausted and rolled up into each other, it was an extreme effort to untangle clothes and get dressed. But it was cold now, fresh snow piling on the edge of the windows, in layered patterns that were both beautiful and a stern warning.

Before they climbed into the front seat, she turned Joe to face her. "There is nothing beyond this, you know." His answer, amidst kisses on her hand, her eyelids, even at her neck and then down to her covered breasts, was a nod, a deep sigh. Two words spoken just for her; "You're wonderful." And then a nod; "Yes."

She left Joe at the McLarens' house, right up to the barn as he needed to bring in the horses, he said. He leaned over the console and kissed her one more time, making her regret her earlier statement.

"I know," he said. "Me too."

Joe refused to look back as the SUV engine whined into reverse; he rushed through the barn, found both horses standing at the back door, head together, an inch of snow rising from their rumps. Ike rumbled while Gus ignored him. He brought them into their stalls, took the necessary time to dry off their backs, made sure they had enough fresh water and more hay and finally admitted to himself he was exhausted. If there wasn't the possibility of a fire in the fireplace and a soft sofa where he could stretch out, the hay pile right here, next to the horses and smelling of a familiar sweetness, would be tempting.

He was asleep, the fire burning, Daisy curled on the sofa with him, when the McLarens came home, pushing the wheelchair into the house, appreciative of the freshly shoveled pathway. Even as Deana screeched and fussed as they washed her and put her to bed, Joe didn't move. Daisy raised her head, wagged her tail a few times before resting her muzzle on Joe's thigh.

Lucy put two logs on the embers; kneeling there she watched Joe, his face almost relaxed, body at ease. She smiled up at her husband, who now stood behind the sofa. "Taylor, he doesn't frighten me any more." Taylor smiled; "I know. Let's go to bed." He had that look, and despite wine and too much to eat, Lucy smiled at her husband.

Then it was after the New Year and Bob Edwards called; time for Joe's follow-up visit. Taylor drove him; it was still Christmas vacation and school was closed. The two men weren't comfortable with each other; the brutality of those first questions remained an invisible boundary. They tried sometimes and it almost worked.

"Joe, I had to..." "Protect your family. I know." Silence, a few more miles. "Do you have any other family?" That inevitable pause, then a brutal statement. "I don't know." No place to ask, no reason to push; if he didn't know, then he had no answers.

"Where will you end up?" An open question, without purpose or answer, McLaren's slow attempt at civility. Joe tried, mostly because of Deana. "I grew up on a ranch outside of the reservation. My grandfather." Here he stopped, fearful of even speaking the words. "He is old, was old when I was sentenced." Truth thickened with terrible thoughts.

McLaren coughed; "How many years?" As if he had forgotten. "Fifteen." "Nothing for good behavior?" "The first years were juvenile hall, school and all that." It wasn't an answer but Taylor didn't pursue the fact. Now education, that interested him. "How'd you do? In school?" Evans' answer truly shocked Taylor; "I'd never had formal schooling so it was rough in the beginning."

McLaren's return question surprised Joe; "What did you enjoy most about learning?" "Books, reading. Anything I could get my hands on. Fiction, philosophy as I got older, geography, biographies.

Anything. Even the dictionary." McLaren steadied the big truck on the slippery on the road. "That surprises me." Now it was time for Joe's questions. "Why, do you think I'm ignorant or dull because I was never inside a school formally?" The man smiled; "No need to attack me, Joe. It's just that, well..." He knew the pause, the difficulty over what to say next, how to call a man who killed another human something other than killer or murderer.

Joe decided it would be a kindness to give this man an out; "I killed a man, Mr. McLaren. But I am not a killer. I did not commit murder, and it isn't semantics. I defended my family, and words like 'self defense' don't cover that; 'self defense' sounds like a face to face fight and does nothing but assign a label to me." The next words were barely a sigh; "I was a child."

Taylor had nothing more to say. The man had condemned himself as the world condemned him with incarceration. There was nothing, not even a twitch from his passenger. The truck pulled up in front of the doctor's office away from the hospital. Taylor let him go; "I've got papers to read."

"Don't you think of leaving. I can see it in your eyes, Joseph Evans, and despite how much better you think you feel, there's still inflammation in that lung. You go out there and lead that damned horse to wherever it is that's so important and they'll find you froze to a tree or in a snow bank somewhere."

Laid out, said, peeling away what Joe had wanted and hoped to hear. Tied now to this place, for Edwards would tell Lucy and McLaren exactly what he'd just told Joe and they would use Deana to hold him.

He slid back into the truck seat and McLaren's head jerked up, eyes wide behind those glasses. "Well?" Joe looked out at the cold late sun; "When winter breaks."

Spring had to come soon; Joe was restless, anxious, no longer satisfied with the simplicity of the McLaren house. Walking helped, miles on the roads to build his strength and stamina. And walking let him have the small hope that a rusted SUV might glide up beside him and the door opened one more time. The air began to have a different taste, lighter, more delicate. In a few places snow had melted, up against a wall holding some warmth, and the surprising yellow of early flowers encouraged him.

Then she filled his dream and drove that grinding SUV next to him, opening the door, smiling as he climbed in. "No more back seats, Joe. My place?" He nodded, this was more than he expected.

It was warm inside her place; she unbuttoned his shirt and licked his chest. "Never mind what I said...I want this to happen." He sat on the bed to remove his boots, struggled with his jeans and she bit his neck gently. "Take off the socks too. It'll be warm with the two of us. She offered a packet of condoms as he pulled his own supply out of his jeans back pocket. He blushed, she rubbed two fingers against his belly. "Now look at that!"

The struggle under the comforter got confusing, each time Joe found her hips, brushed his fingers across that mound of hair and readied himself to enter her, a corner of the comforter intervened, an edge of folded fabric, a cold foot against his thigh. He swore and she laughed as she used both hands to capture and draw him in, slow at first, making him stop, wait as she squeezed, raised her hips, then let him slide closer until he simply pushed through her hands, impaling himself, finding her smiling as he thought to kiss her mouth, then her neck, then her breasts as his own body moved in and out and in deeper until neither of them could bear it; she gasped and raised them both, he used his arms, hands grabbing her shoulders, pulling her impossibly close until they came apart shuddering, Lois crying as he pulsed and was captured and she had no guilt or fear but to find more of him and hold him until she let go from exhaustion.

They eventually crawled out from the comforter, him at the left side of the bed toward the foot; she popped up on the right where the pillows were skewed sideways. They looked at each other across the blue-patterned cover and he lunged for her, ass high, pouncing like a cat but my god his butt got cold quickly, so she rubbed his cheeks with her hands, back under the down comforter, finding that impossibly enough he showed signs of being ready again.

She waited in the SUV, heater running on high, watching until he was inside the McLaren house, where only one light downstairs showed that anyone might think to wait up for him. He turned his head and nodded once, then let the door shut. My god, she thought again as she shifted the gears and her fingers had clear memory of his body, my god he was beautiful.

Inside the McLaren farm house, Joe stretched out on the sofa, eyes turned to the flame, head cradled on his arm. He could smell her, them, mingled on his hands, even in his breath. He wouldn't wash off that smell. She had kissed him gently when they were finished the second time; no fireworks, no antics and contortions but him lying on her, supporting himself, moving in and out slowly, watching her face to see what pleased her most.

He woke when his hands were cold and Daisy pushed her wet nose into his face and he realized it was late night, maybe predawn and the air had changed. He got up and closed the damper over the gray fire, let Daisy out and stood in the freshening wind without a jacket. He gloried in the new air that did not bite or scratch his lungs. The late winter freeze was done.

He told the McLarens that morning he was getting ready to continue his journey. It was March and despite the possibilities of more snow, the air would warm, ice melt, snowdrifts disappear and he needed to make the miles. He used Deana's computer, with her help; directed by where her eyes landed, they discovered how far it was from Stockdale in Ohio close enough to where he was going. There was no name, no town or village, but neither Valentine, Nebraska nor Rosebud, South Dakota were far away from the ranch and he used those points for directions.

Deana was quiet around him now, her eyes watching but she no longer reached out with those battered fists to push at him. Lucy McLaren smiled frequently, cooked hearty meals but did not engage him in any discussions.

Taylor, however, came up unexpectedly with an idea. "Do you have a driver's license, Joe?" That was easy, and he remembered using it as a line with Lois and how in hell was he going to leave her? He shook his head violently and Taylor raised a hand; "It's all right, it's just a question." Taylor continued; "You've lived here three months now and I'm sure the local authorities would allow you to take a driver's test."

The comment, so simple, a part of every American male's life, dug right to that place where he'd been stabbed. As if it were now the spot accepting all new wounds and especially words. He tried, choking on the poor explanation; "I've driven an old Jeep and a tractor, and my grandfather's truck." He and McLaren studied each other; how often it was that a simple question came around to what Joe had done before his life stopped.

"Well then, let's give you a refresher course."

A week later, with hours spent driving through the McLarens' fields before venturing out onto back roads where the local law didn't patrol, nights spent reading the driver's manual, Joe passed the test and was given a proper driver's license. Taylor McLaren had more to say; "The rest of this, Joe, is that a friend of Lucy's is bringing a pony half way to keep Gus company. She's from Indiana and called asking if we knew anyone needed a ride for their horse going west. I told Lottie 'bout you and she said she'd risk giving you a try. Or throw you out on your own; it depends on your driving."

Joe folded his hands together; "Mr. McLaren I've never driven a rig." "Joe." The man gave a huge sigh meant to chastise Joe for sticking to formality. "Lucy's got the rig hitched up, it's actually simple. You keep the trailer in line with the truck body, you don't speed up on a corner until the trailer's in line, you don't slam on the brakes and you don't let fools hurry you."

He called Lois wanting to see her. He was polite and asked her to dinner. Said he'd come pick her up and that yes he had permission from the McLarens and he'd been doing odd jobs locally, earned a few dollars so he could ask her out. His treat.

Joe didn't tell her; he couldn't face another absurd truth about his life, that this was his first real date. She surprised him; she opened the door but would not let him inside. Her voice was harsh; "Everyone in town knows you're leaving." He wasn't sure what was expected.

Her eyes told him she had crossed the line she herself had drawn. 'Never again' she said that first time. In the SUV with the windows steamed from their activities. 'Never again' as they played under the quilt in her apartment.

That he was leaving seemed to change her; "A dinner, Lois, it's only dinner." He made a plea, unsure if it was proper but he wanted more time with her. Not just in bed, but talking and looking at each other. She was about to slam the door in his face. He tried again; "I made no promise, you told me not to. I don't know your rules."

She did close the door, slowly, not hitting his face but removing him, making him step back. Her voice was low and filled; "You told me, I told you. But telling isn't enough, Joe. As a friend used to say, 'Write when you find work.' Good bye." He didn't understand as the solid door closed and he heard the lock twist into place.

It was Lucy McLaren waiting for him this time; he had carefully parked the truck, backed up to the trailer as the McLarens preferred. He felt more confident about a new skill of handling the big truck. She asked him to come sit in the kitchen, they needed to talk. Then she sat and studied him.

Sudden tears flooded her eyes. "We don't want you to leave, Joe. Especially Deana. Others in town, they've gotten to know you." She didn't ask, knew better, and it was an odd sensation, of being accepted. "It's the middle of March, the pony will come in two weeks time, Joe." Two weeks, an extension, no chance with Lois but he needed to get Ike moving. "Thank you, ma'am. That saves me a lot of miles." Lucy smiled, even as she wiped her eyes, no shame or looking away, a gesture of simple sadness.

"Do you want him shod, we know a good farrier." "No thank you, ma'am. I rasp his hooves the way I want 'em, and traveling keeps them that way. I found an old rasp in your gear to the barn, and a pair of blunt nippers I put an edge on, same with the hoof knife I carry. Simple tools, I learned how from my..." He was doing it now, talking over any feeling that dared rise to the surface. She countered with; "Have Taylor ride with you while you practice driving the trailer. I told Lottie you could help with the return trip since she's going so far out of her way to deliver this pony. You don't want to make a liar of me." They sat across the table from each other; neither willing to leave yet each acknowledging no more words were possible. Too much had happened, growing too strong a bond between them. "You will let us know when you get to your grandfather's." It wasn't a question, so he nodded, remembering that he'd made the same promise to another family.

"Joe." She paused and he knew but wasn't quick enough. "Thank you." He raised his hand, his voice brittle; "Don't you thank me, I did what I did on instinct, you and your mister, you've helped me out of moral necessity. If I'd thought on it, studied the situation some, I might have stayed behind the trailer." Joe left the table then, heard her sob as he cleared the living room and down the hall to his small room that had begun to feel like home.

He had two weeks; he walked Ike for an hour each day that first week, learned the horse had gone back to jigging sideways and Joe let him. The second week he saddled Ike, turned the son loose in a small paddock, and got what he expected. He'd already suggested that Lucy bring Deana out to watch the show. Ike was no disappointment; the son of a bitch bucked and pitched, reared and snorted and ran kicking, shaking his head, sometimes squealing in anger.

Eventually he tired, sweating along his neck and chest, at his loins, lungs moving as bellows, nostrils wide to draw in air. Beautiful in his high-bred way, fine hide beginning to shed the winter, mane and tail grown out, black hooves trimmed. Joe approached with the bridle and Ike considered rebellion but Joe shook his head, laid the reins on Ike's damp neck and the horse sighed as he lowered his head to accept the bit.

The riding went easy, except that Joe felt a twinge deep inside, and guessed he would be wounded by that hole for a long time. Walking was best for him but he needed to know Ike was amendable to accepting both the bridle and Joe's direction.

Deana was cheering, arms waving, legs thrashing, her mouth wide in that smile, her eyes the brightest black stars. Joe brought Ike up close and the bay stuck out his nose, lightly touched her face despite the flailing hands. Then Joe backed the horse, put him into a circle where they trotted and cantered and he even asked for a flying change across the circle and Ike surprised him by making the change feel easy.

After a break, for Joe and his breathing, they tried flying changes every three strides while Lucy held on to Deana and told her the horse was dancing just for her. It was enough; Joe gulped air and dismounted, had to hold on to the saddle, had to let his feet find steady ground, as the child behind him flailed her fists and laughed and Lucy laughed and cried.

At the evening meal, Lucy described what had happened that afternoon, giving Taylor all the minute details, then Joe said he was leaving in two days. Their friend had called and Joe took the message. Two days.. Taylor's face changed; "Aren't you going to see Lois one more time?" The bluntness deserved its own brief answer. "No. She shut that door." It was not their business, but concern came with family ties. Joe wasn't going to allow that closeness near him again.

It was a different wound, a betrayal of the kind Joe did not understand. He knew rage, and fear, and knew death far too well. But this sense of loss, of possibility denied, was a raw complexity. He didn't like it, didn't want other people to confuse what was a simple idea, to walk a horse back to where it had been born.

Fourteen

Ike loaded easy and Joe's gear didn't take up much room. He shook Taylor's hand and leaned down, briefly laid his face against Deana's cheek. No eye contact, barely touching and even that little was too much. Lucy waited in the truck, hands on the wheel, no impatience, no sign of any emotion. Good, Joe thought, her withdrawal will make the trip easier.

He climbed in the truck, sat close to the door, heard her push down the automatic lock and put the truck in gear; it was a moment of backing, turning the wheel hard first right and left to get the truck and trailer in line and then she eased up on the brake and gave the truck enough power to move forward evenly, with no scrambling hooves or whinnies from an alarmed horse.

They traveled through the outskirts of Stockdale and onto a highway headed to Cincinnati, and then, finally, Lucy spoke to him without taking her eyes off the road. "Lois's broken-hearted, you know." He kept his eyes outside the truck cab, sensing the land, not listening or hearing her. The woman had shut the door, not him. He didn't know how to say it without being mean.

After that one comment, they drove the more than one hundred miles in silence. Land and roads, small villages and highways he did not have to walk leading Ike, or attempting to ride. He needed to thank the woman for so much and the right words weren't his, neither written nor spoken, unexpected words of gratitude. He risked a glance at her face in profile, mouth tight, eyes refusing to leave the long road's yellow line. She drove well, easy and constant, thinking only of her passenger in the trailer, no concern for Joe.

The sign worried then confused him as Lucy seemed to know exactly where she was going. "Kentucky?" The question slipped out. "There's no city, I thought we had to go through Cincinnati but there's nothing except trees." "We cross the Ohio twice here, Joe. Look, there's Cincinnati? Joe was stunned; "It's like those ads Deana likes for Disney…" Lucy smiled; it was the only mention of Deana from Joe since they'd gotten into the truck.

Lucy paused, trying to find the right words. "I couldn't think of a way to say thank you again, Joe, except to get you across the Ohio these two more times." She risked a glance at him; he was studying water and trees out the window and his lack of response saddened her. He had so much still to learn.

"We're going to be early at the meeting place; I planned it so we could eat before you and Ike change onto Lottie's rig. It's a much longer trip to Pana. All the way across Indiana you know and most of Illinois." She was polite and friendly as if no bitter words hung between them. He took in a breath, let it out; "Yes, ma'am. That's kind of you."

Fast food they called it; a parking lot big enough to park the rig, and Joe followed Mrs. McLaren inside. Stood in line with her, ordered what she did and she glanced at him. "Are you sure?" It was a salad, damn, but there were chicken slices on top so it wasn't too bad. She sat across from him as they ate, where they could see the rig and keep an eye on Ike.

"Ma'am, I'll send Deana a post card. And pictures of the ranch." 'If it's still there' was a silent echo but he wasn't going to let those words escape. "Lois." Lucy had only that one word. Joe felt his face heat up. "Lois shut that door hard. Ma'am." Lucy reached into the large bag she tended to carry and handed him a paper without looking up from her salad. "I hoped, no I knew you were sad to leave. Leaving's natural, Joe. It's only that you, well what happened to you was wrong and it has changed your life. Taylor and I, we want you to know that you will always be part of our family."

Words could dig holes, enlarge them, stop breath and heart. Joe had to spit out the piece of chicken, knowing it was rude but impossible for him to chew and swallow. The single sheet of paper held names, an address and phone number.

"Thank you, ma'am."

Eventually a bright red truck towing a white trailer pulled up next to the McLaren rig and the conversation ended. Lucy left Joe to dump the food, which he did after watching other folks take care of their messes.

He drank her coffee and took two pieces of chicken from the piled lettuce.

He let the women chat while he walked to the new rig. Around back he could see a spotted rump, a rat tail hung over the tailgate. Appaloosa. He smiled, what his grandfather had to say about the breed was unprintable. "Joe, this is Lottie." Short, wide, chopped hair, broad face tanned and lined, hands that knew hard work. He nodded at her. "Well by god Lucy you and Taylor weren't lying but I'll behave and he'll make it clean to Pana and where he goes from there, it's up to him." "Lottie!" The women studied each other. The sturdy woman laughed; "You knew well enough I can't hold a thought to myself. I know what this man done for you and yes he's special so I'll behave but by lordy above he's a terrible temptation."

He was too tired to be embarrassed and realized he was getting used to such comments. He'd never suspected that women looked at men this way, never had time or reason to think about it until recently.

The horse transfer started smoothly, and then a very official man stormed out of the restaurant when the appy gelding, a varnish roan of some age, stopped to produce an amazing pile of manure. They got the appy promptly onto the trailer where the pony chewed into the hay Ike had left. Almost immediately there was an attack; "You'll clean that up, I can't have such a thing...why this is a restaurant, a place of business." Joe placed himself in front of the two women, Lottie with a manure folk in hand, Lucy holding the rope-handle plastic bucket.

"Mister, this's a goddamn parking lot and they're about to clean up the pile, which by the way smells better'n the food you served us." The man bristled, stood on his toes, hands on his hips and that's where he lost Joe, who snorted and went to the back of the red truck to sit on the chromed running board and laugh.

Lucy McLaren found him and he stood up while she put her arms around him, laid her head on his chest and he could hardly bear the contact. She whispered into his shirt front; "Thank, you, Joe." Then pushed away and did not give him a chance but waved to her friend Lottie and got in her own truck to go home.

"It's six hours give or take a half hour from here to my farm, Evans. I'll drive out of the city and over that damned river again, Lucy told me you and rivers have a bad history. She says too you don't have much experience driving in town but that you grew up with horses and know how to pilot a rig once you're on the road. Did you know we're going through a bit of Kentucky right now?" Please, Joe thought, give me miles of silence. He wanted no thoughts, for there was a deep ache in his gut and no way to absolve himself of the pain. It was new, not physical, almost worse than the killing, sentencing, those years in prison. He could move there, keep moving, fight if he had to; this stayed deep and felt permanent. He coughed, looked out the window.

"You ain't much of a talker." He grunted, didn't look at her. "S'fine by me, Lucy and Taylor they warned me. Breed warmbloods, I do, a Holsteiner stallion and some damned good mares I got off the track real cheap. These well-bred mares get raced into no legs, no more winning and I pay two maybe three hundred..." She went on, about horses and bloodlines and some of the names were familiar but he didn't bother. Wasn't worth it, getting close to people took something from a man. What he needed was to be on his own, to walk the last six hundred miles leading Ike, to expect nothing at the trail's finish. No one to care, but one bay horse turned loose on the land where he was born. Odd, Joe thought; the horse had more claim to the Brings Plenty land and heritage than he did.

It was all main roads, the luxury of speed, crossing rivers with ease on spanned bridges. He smiled to himself, remembering the man with the pumpkin pie and the tipsy ferry sliding onto land. Her farm was south of an empty town and when asked Lottie said that it was filled with older folks, mostly women, with families leaving to find work. Too bad, she said, it's a sweet place to live. The land was fertile, and her farm supported almost thirty horses with low taxes and good home-grown hay.

He didn't ask, didn't want to get her talking but she told him anyway. "I admire Lucy and Taylor and what they're doing with that child, she and I met with a group trying to keep trails open across the three states and hit it off. That appy has the soul of a saint and will be good company for Gus who's getting on in years as you already know." His head felt the cool of the window glass and he nodded slowly whenever she stopped for air.

He never got to drive; she kept talking, driving easily, muttering and explaining and Joe slept, woke, shifted in the comfortable seat and dozed again. She didn't seem to mind.

Wet ground, patches of drifted snow, muddy horses in dirt paddocks all whinnying when they saw the rig. A few broke into a run, slipping on greasy footing, kicking out, heads high, filled with spring fever.

Unloaded, quivering, nostrils widened to take in the scent, Ike looked like a pony near these massive animals. Holsteiners, she said again and started to explain. Joe was too abrupt; "I know, ma'am. Been 'round them before." The biggest owner at his father's small yard kept a Holsteiner to hunt. He was the biggest in many sense; owning ten of the fifteen horses his father trained, and weighing, ah damn he couldn't remember the conversion into stone, but the man had to weigh near three hundred pounds.

She was standing too close, looking at him oddly; "Boy you going fold on me or can you get your own horse into a stall and private paddock. Let him unkink and eat well 'fore you two head off to wherever it is you're going." It was a passive question, and he answered; "I'm riding up near Rosebud Reservation, on the South Dakota Nebraska line." He took a leap, more hope than fact; "There's family on a ranch there."

Lottie was intrigued by this young man; she knew parts of the story, that he had saved Lucy from a terrible ordeal and had almost died in the doing. To ask more than that was impolite so she held her tongue for once. "Guess these past five hundred miles or so were a help." "Yes, ma'am. They're most appreciated." They studied each other; "Ma'am, a place to put Ike?"

And of course he wasn't there in the morning, no matter that she got up at five and brewed coffee, took a cup out to him. He'd found the stale coffee from when she had a farm manager living in the small apartment. Smart son of a bitch, she thought, and drank the coffee black, not like she enjoyed it but it was to hand and she was cold. Might be almost spring but this part of Illinois was chilled at night, and slow to melt the winter snow.

It was mud and damp air, Ike jigging, traveling sideways, then ducking his head and slamming Joe who cursed and struggled with his own balance. Forward, out of this goddamned town and state where all the mud in the world sucked at his boots. He blessed Lucy McLaren for their purchase from a thrift store, good enough for the likes of him. A man bent on returning a horse no one knew was missing. His packer boots, resoled and cleaned, were stuffed in one side of the canvas bags, along with new socks and shorts.

He was pushed by a private clock, knowing that to cross most of Nebraska and up into South Dakota he needed water and in springtime there were surface ponds, wet springs and sometimes decent graze. Not like the east and Midwest where rains and rivers produced lush grass all summer long. Crossing the Mississippi came first, the biggest of his troubles now that the Ohio was to his back.

Last night, in digging through his canvas bags, he'd found what the McLarens had done. An envelope of bills, so many that he didn't count them. He couldn't see but felt them with clumsy fingers. It was more than enough to get him to South Dakota and still have those damnable two hundred dollars that held him prisoner.

Daytime was all dirt roads and clinging mud. He'd looked at a map at the McLarens' home and still hadn't figured out his travel route. The bridges were highways, the ferries all south of him and he needed to head north now, into Nebraska and the sand hills around Valentine.

Railroad bridges were useless, too great a chance for Ike to catch a hoof between a tie. Highways were an exceptional danger for they were patrolled by super-vigilant state troopers, and he remembered the signs, and his grandfather talking about them, that the law had no understanding of horses. 'No pedestrians, motorbikes, led or ridden animals.' Not posted in every state but the silent law was there. Grandfather would snort and make a disparaging comment about such restrictions. Joe smiled, knew that the word 'disparaging' would please the old man.

Joe rode south out of Pana to avoid Springfield, and got off course skirting a college town. He ended up in Chesterfield and still had no idea how to cross the Mississippi, or the Illinois River for that matter. After he forded a creek, Joe found an old man at a store outside of Rockbridge, who had some kind words about the now-tired Ike. Joe took the chance and asked the only person he'd seen all day.

Just how would Mr. Grunwald, as the old man introduced himself, how would he get such a horse across the Illinois and then the Mississippi on the way north into Nebraska. Grunwald spat to the side, rubbed his jaw; "For the Mississip' and the Des Moines since you headed north and west, why I go up to Keokuk, 'bout hunert fifty mile from here, go north and west mind you, till there's signs. They's got a bridge cross that river, it's a state highway mind you and the police don't take kindly to a led horse, but hell boy, you've got a saddle on him. By the look to you, riding's what you know to do."

The two men looked at each other. Grunwald spat again; "Now you's close to the Illinois River and even closer to a ferry takes cars and such across." The man grinned; "For free, mind you, which I 'spect ain't a problem. Only trouble will be that there bronc stepping on to a river ferry."

It was enough to make Joe laugh; "Mr. Grunwald, Ike's already a veteran, we crossed the Ohio out of Sistersville on their ferry." Grunwald nodded; "Thought that might be a smart horse." Joe patted Ike's neck, the old man nodded again as if pleased. "Yup, he looks to have speed, and them cops, well they ain't too quick to pick up on what's happening in their faces." He laughed, coughed, spat again. "I ain't putting notions in your head you mind me, just thinking out loud."

Then he went to that motion again, rubbing his jaw and looking thoughtful; "The Des Moines, it comes right in near to Keokuk. Two rivers with a town between 'em. Probably the place for you to cross. If you set on going north." Grunwald then offered directions to a fenced pasture, a small grove of trees with a rock ring; no invite to supper or a house, just a safe place for Joe and the bay. Grunwald had given him a final word; "After you take your ride on the Kampsville Ferry, go north and keep that Route 136 in sight, boy. You'll miss most of them cities and hit the Montebella State Park. Bridge's in there someplace, I ain't never crossed it, don't care much to travel, got what I wants right here. Wife's in the backyard, been there thirteen year now. She's good company and I don't plan on leaving here afore I join her."

Time stretched then; Joe wanting to get going. Grunwald sighed, said; "There's one thing. When you get through Keokuk and hit that Des Moines River bridge, they put in a walled sidewalk, wide enough you and your bronc'll fit. Safer than riding down the road's middle." The old man nodded.

He thanked the man, and got Ike walking again, following Grunwald's directions. Ike thought to jig but it'd been a long day; one reprimand with the lead line and the horse settled to a decent stride. About time, Joe thought. Tomorrow and for a few more days, till they crossed the river, he planned to ride some sense into the horse. Police cars and angry cops were no laughing matter.

Old man Grunwald showed up the next morning as Joe boiled coffee on the fire ring. Grunwald tipped up a tree stump, sat and looked expectedly at Joe, who shrugged and raised the only cup he had. Grunwald dug out a tin cup from a pocket in his loose coat. "Pour, sonny. Ain't had coffee boiled over a fire long time now."

A raven had visited Joe late last evening and now the curious bird returned, settled in a branch above Joe's head, to squawk three short bursts before cocking its head. Grunwald shrugged. Joe squawked back three times. The raven cawed again, four this time, and Joe mimicked him.

After several exchanges, the raven didn't stop but cawed up to twenty-five, then his squawk broke, he attempted two mores caws, coughed out a pathetic sound and quit. In the silence, Grunwald opinioned that the raven was cawed out. Both men laughed; the large bird unfolded its wings and left. "Insulted by God," Grunwald suggested. Joe poured the last of the coffee between the two cups.

They sipped in a comfortable silence, both hands wrapped around the mugs. Until Grunwald took the last sip and spoke; "Got me something needs doing, mister. You look sturdy 'nough thought I'd ask you." Joe sighed, smiled at the old man. "You're used to being caught like this, ain't you boy. It's how you been paying your way 'cross this country."

It wasn't much as it got explained to him; Grunwald had an engine wedged under the seat of a long van, been keeping it there for storage. He'd finally gotten to the point where he needed that engine to put in a truck he was helping rebuild for a useless grandson. Or at least he was supervising that rebuild. Trouble was, he couldn't get at the engine. Damn thing was jammed under the front seat of the old delivery van pretty good and it needed to be pulled out. Winch and pulley would do the trick, but his bones and what muscles was left in him weren't up to the chore. Stored the engine there maybe ten years past, seemed to have taken on a life of its own and didn't want to leave. Boy himself, the grandson, he wasn't bright enough to work a winch or find a good place to hook the chain. The engine might be going to keep his truck running but the boy wasn't perking up to be much help.

Joe said he'd be along in a half hour. The old man got back in his truck, one of those Studebakers sold right after the war. Engine sounded good, truck body was rusted all to hell. Joe cleaned up best he could, pulled burrs and dried grasses off Ike's hide and tail, then saddled up and packed his gear. To hell with it, he thought and climbed on Ike who thought to buck. Joe laughed and put the horse into a strong trot.

He got to Grunwald's place, which was easy enough to see for a mile in any direction. The man had cars and trucks everywhere. Pulled to the front, alone among the chaos, was an International van, faded green, long body, tires flat, the doors open to the back. And there were newer vehicles with license plates parked at angles to the house. Neighbors, Grunwald explained, friends who'd been helping him on the project.

Of course they were old men in varying states of ability, some on canes, some with all their teeth, others' mouths drawn in, hands trembling, but they were sharp in their quiet looks as Joe rode up. There was a place to tie the bay, and he could leave his gear on the front porch, so he was told.

Grunwald came at him, leaning hard on that cane, shaking his head. Stood feet spread apart, used the cane to pick up an edge of Joe's hair. Longer now, untouched, uncut, thick and black. Lois had liked it, Lucy McLaren had tried to give him a haircut, and most men shook their head. Hippie was a word he'd heard, sissy-boy, tough; none of them knew his reasons and he wasn't going to share.

Grunwald, he used that cane tip to hold out a length of Joe's hair. Joe thought to push away the demeaning gesture, but it wasn't Grunwald's way to hurt a man; "You pretty much Indian, boy. Something else and I ain't asking, ain't none of my business but by god you work inside that van and that goddamn engine you be wanting to tie up all that hair, cobwebs and grease, hell. Too early in the spring for bathing yet, I don't recommend it." The circle of more old men rubbed at their raw mouths and let the words pass.

Grunwald watched Joe as he took care of Ike. "Boy I wasn't sure on you last night or this morning nevermind that raven's comments on your character. You ain't from here, easy enough to see that. But you handle that horse quiet so I thought to myself all night, you might be one I could trust. Get this damned job done. Cody now, he's right anxious 'bout the truck, said he'd be here soon." He stopped and even Joe could hear it, the rough skip of a truck needing work on the timing and valves.

"Cody's here. I keep telling him 'bout that truck but he don't listen." The truck pulled up in a skid, showering two of the old men with dirt and they were cursing when the boy got out of the cab. Behind him a thick stream of white smoke settled to the ground, adding its stench to the piles of garbage.

The boy, tall, lean, blond hair and light blue eyes, grinned at his grandfather, stopped suddenly and took in Joe's appearance. "Who in hell're you?" Posturing and that tough-guy stare; ah hell. Joe shrugged, raked his hair back and jammed down the worn cowboy hat.

There wasn't a real step to the back of the van, only a steel office chair with a mouse-chewed seat to lean on as he climbed inside and took the winch chain with him, unfolding it down the long body. He figured Grunwald would take the kid in line and as he crawled along the sloping van floor, he could hear the thunder of that old voice alongside and over the kid's few words, the boy's tone going high and thin.

Grunwald stuck his head in the van; "Son, you pay no 'tention to Cody, his ma done spoilt him and I been trying to get him growed up." Joe drew the last of the chain to hook the engine block. Big son of a bitch and it had been there a long time. As he crawled out backwards, he asked over his shoulder; "Ole man you sure this engine's worth the trouble? It gonna run you think?" Grunwald snorted, as Joe knew he would.

"You're learning our lingo boy, might do to stay around a while. Yeah, I know, you got a place to be with that damned horse but..." Joe felt it, the foolishness of how he looked, butt hanging out of the van, legs and back inside, trying to keep the chain from kinking while some unseen old coot in a big Dodge was driving the winch, slowly tearing up the van floor and moving that big engine through the shreds of an upholstered bench seat.

Grunwald spoke a quick truth; "You best get out boy, 'fore that 440 run over you." Joe backed out, one leg seeking a step, a bumper that wasn't there and he remembered, thought ah hell as he grabbed sideways for the chair. Some kind soul had moved the chair; Joe hit it mid-fall under his outstretched arm above the elbow and he heard the pop, felt it as the burn of a branding iron. His feet found the ground and he was able to stand, the half circle of wide-eyed old men moving in cautiously to surround him, and one gut-stupid kid grinning.

The boy had no idea what had just happened. The old men all knew and Grunwald came to Joe; "I'll call me 911 though it takes a while to get them out this far." Joe barely shook his head. His left arm was useless, elbow bent back, arm hanging wrong from the shoulder joint. He'd seen his grandfather deal with it, knew what to do, tried to make that first terrible move.

"It's out ain't it boy?" Grunwald or one of the other old men asked the question; Joe couldn't speak. The boy was laughing, then quiet. Joe blinked, dropped his head. Took that breath, then used his right arm to lift the left arm at the elbow. One old man, face tight, stepped up, took the arm, twisted it as Joe pulled back and the snap was loud, tearing through the innards of any man gone through the same thing. Grunwald's grandson heard the noise, his face went white and someone yelled 'man down' as the boy pitched onto his face, lying in the dirt unmoving. No one was inclined to check on him.

It went in, bone to the joint, right back to where it belonged but tendon, muscle, and nerve were screaming and Joe needed to set down. Grunwald shoved that goddamned mouse-chewed office chair up to the back of Joe's legs and he sat. The old-timer who'd helped Joe, whiskey veins across his face, held out a flask, Joe drank half of it, swallowed and finished the rest. Sat there, head down feeling the pain recede as the whiskey spun his brain.

Then a mad clunk, the ground shaking and a hard whine, a banging and the old coot behind the wheel of the Dodge finally turned off the winch 'cause that damned 440 was pulled against the front of his vehicle, trying hard to go through the grill and hood.

Joe spent the afternoon drunk, the evening in bed, woke in the morning groaning but his arm worked. Weak with a hangover and offered another day of resting but he was determined to get the hell away from these ancient madmen and their schemes. Ike had been curried and fed and even the old Barnsby saddle had a nice rubbing of wax but none of it was enough for the wreck in his shoulder and the loss of a full day's travel.

Joe wasn't going to give in even after Grunwald stuffed some bills, greasy and wadded, into Joe's coat pocket and said by god he could stay a day or a week or two till that arm quit torturing him and by god he was sorry for the trouble. Joe thanked Grunwald, said he needed to ride on and Grunwald answered that's what he kinda expected.

They parted quickly, Joe struggling to climb on Ike's back and Grunwald leaning on his cane, eyes to the ground, knowing what he'd done and sorry for it with no way to fix the mess. One of those times when an apology and money meant nothing.

Fifteen

Ike got fit quickly; he'd come to life on decent feed for the winter. Now that there was an edge to the bay, it made the walk almost impossible, so it was mostly the trot with a few attempts at bolting. The ferry at Kampsville had been nothing; Ike snorted, then walked right on. No arguments from the captain or the deck steward about a horse as passenger, just a curt nod before going about their business.

North then was back roads and villages. Each step was a torture for Joe; the arm nerves continued to scream, putting him off balance. It was unfair to the bay but leading him was worse. Joe finally stopped to buy relief. A small man in a small store was terrified by Joe's appearance on that high-strung, prancing horse and sent out a teen-age boy to ask what Joe wanted, fearful that if the horse got tied in front of the store there would be consequences.

Joe pulled out a few bills, greasy and mangled but legal tender, and said he needed the biggest bottle of whatever worked best on pain, and a cup of water could the boy spare it. The kid grinned; "Hangover?" Joe glared at him and the boy ran back, came out with two bottles of something said take two every four hours so Joe took six and drank them down with water from a plastic bottle. Cost him eighty-nine cents, the kid said. They didn't give out water for free no more. Grunwald had told him of a dirt shortcut where he could pick up speed. The turnoff became a straight line with almost no tire tracks disturbing its surface. The bay pulled at the reins and the pills began to work; Joe was finally distant from the nerves in his left shoulder down to the numbed fingers and weak hand. What the hell he was stoned now, all injured nerves deadened, so he leaned forward and kept a feel of the bay's mouth but it was time the old boy showed his stuff.

At first Ike traveled sideways despite Joe trying to pull him straight and urge him forward. Eventually the bay took a twisting leap and then it was a race against nothing but the length of stride, the power of the hindquarters, the need to move the way a horse was designed to move; full out, ears flat, tail flying.

When it felt like a mile had passed, Joe sat up and steadied Ike, brought the horse to a rough trot that made him gasp, but he'd gotten this far, might as well use the miles ahead of them. So it was trot for a quarter mile maybe more, then another gallop, this one controlled, until Ike's breathing was harsh and Joe brought him to that trot again. They repeated the pattern until Joe felt the rapid heaving of Ike's barrel and figured the horse'd had enough.

When he pulled up, Ike was willing to stand quiet while Joe dug out the bottle of pills and took five more, knowing he was hurting his insides but he couldn't stand the jangle in his arm and hand. They walked on then, Ike on a loose rein, his easy stride almost comfortable for Joe's battered shoulder.

Eventually he found an empty field, no crop this year or last year, no signs of haying, no sign anyone cared enough to say 'keep out' and most of all, no old men with ideas on how they could use a younger man's ignorance. He unsaddled Ike, hobbled him, hung a tree branch at the opening to the field, and went to find himself a stream or puddle for drinking water and maybe soak his shoulder, his whole self for that matter.

Spring run-off brought the clear water high enough it came up the bank and carved out an island mid-stream. Joe shucked his clothes and lay down full length in the rushing water until he no longer felt his body. Those pills gave him an edge; he could tolerate most anything since he couldn't really feel the parts that hurt.

They covered ground for four days in this manner and suddenly there was a sign for Hamilton, ten miles away, and Rte 136 to Keokuk, thirteen miles. He stopped at a gas station outside of Hamilton, where he would get the usual jokes about 'gassing' up the bay, or refueling and Joe wouldn't bother to smile. He was stoned, nothing hurt, but he knew his mind wasn't working well neither.

Joe dismounted and pulled the reins over the gelding's head but Ike followed willingly into the open bay of the garage. The mechanic jumped up too quickly, hit his head on the underside of the car on the lift. He expected to hear 'hey mister, get that nag outa here.' Joe only needed to buy a road map. He'd learned the sad lesson that nothing came for free.

This man surprised him. He put down his tools, walked to the bay and put out his hand, let Ike sniff him. "Nice looking sort, you ever run him?" Those Nasrullah lines of Ike's mama showed up to anyone who knew race horses.

They talked some, after Joe backed Ike out of the garage. For once when asked where he was headed, Joe told the man. The mechanic grinned; "I got relatives in Chadron, went to school there. Pretty land, too bad your folks got given the worst of it." Both of them went silent then, Joe wishing he could get the hell away from the man's unwanted compassion.

"Here." A can of Dr. Pepper and a fingerprinted road map of the two states. Man had even circled Hamilton and Keokuk and the high bridges over the two rivers. The mechanic grinned, wiped more grease onto his face; "You look pretty rough to me, mister, so I done pointed out best way you can cross them rivers. Good luck to you."

It was two in the afternoon according to the repair shop clock when Joe headed west again, only a mile or so to a quiet space, another lapsed pasture where the fences were enough to hold the bay, and the gate this time actually was there to be pulled shut. He read the map, drank the Dr. Pepper and took more of those pills and then a nap. He figured to ride through the outskirts of Hamilton and across the Rte 136 Bridge into Keokuk about ten hours from now.

He slept fitfully, hungry, bound by his clothes; using the saddle as a pillow had to be one of the most uncomfortable things he'd tried. He woke to stars that said it was maybe midnight, and Ike was dozing peacefully not ten feet from where Joe sat. He called to the horse, waited until the head came up and he could see that Ike's eyes were open. Joe stood, made noises until Ike advanced a few steps, then waited as Joe bridled him.

Ten minutes later the bay was packed, canvas bags tied down, gear stuffed so nothing rattled or threatened to spill out. It wasn't much past midnight when they picked up the state road above Hamilton and spiraled along the banks to the bridge over the Mississippi and Des Moines Rivers. Joe intended to drop off into Missouri where there were fewer cities in the way, and then come back up into rural Iowa.

A quarter moon gave horse and rider enough light, along with street lamps set closer together as they rode through the top edge of

Hamilton. Ike's bare hooves made little sound on the hardtop or cement sidewalk, which kept folks from peering out through a pulled-back covered window to see a horse and rider out of place.

As he turned down alongside State 96 to where it picked up 136 again, a car passed and then slowed down. Joe tensed up and Ike instantly fussed. Four boys out to raise hell and sensing an easy target, they shifted their muscle car and pounded on the doors, tattooed arms and loud voices meant to spook the horse. Joe angled Ike toward the car, right up close enough he could reach down with the doubled lead rope and slap one of those arms, even caught the edge of a leering face smart enough the child cried out. The car swerved and Joe let Ike move into an easy lope up someone's drive and behind their house, scurrying to the ridge top, leaving behind those boys moaning and cursing and telling each other what they would do when they caught up with that fucking cowboy.

He could hear the car engine strain with the climb and he was enjoying the adventure for the first time in days; his arm didn't hurt much, he'd gone through almost the whole bottle of those little pills. And he was headed in a different direction than any road those boys might choose to follow. They sure as hell weren't going to call the cops on him.

He came down the edge of a pleasant tree-lined street, which ended at a park and roads going right and left. The river took up his field of vision; even at night the power plants were bright, ghostly; Ike stopped abruptly and snorted. Joe sat quietly, letting the horse draw in the different scents and turn his head, ears swiveling.

There was no way to get across the Mississippi River except direct, trotting alongside the river, turning with the road, then tackling the great expanse with water rushing under it, and those lights, the power grid that so fascinated Ike. It took a brief kick and some cursing before Joe got Ike's attention and the horse crossed the tar road, swung left away from the power plant, trotting easily on the grass side. The road bent to the right, trees hid the river. Then a brick building came up to street level, a sign proclaiming it the home of the American Bee

Keeper Association. The absurdity of that title made Joe laugh, and Ike pinned his ears.

The bridge itself was a shock; taking that step into air over rushing water. Joe wanted to turn around, Ike swung his head as if agreeing, but they kept straight down the yellow line; no traffic, no problems. Until a slow police car passed Joe going in the other direction and that was trouble. He pushed Ike into a long trot, heard the vague sound of the police siren behind him and blessed the fact that they'd passed the halfway mark and the police car had to get to land before turning around.

They got across the Mississippi before the cop had his vehicle in hand; Joe would have yelled in celebration but he needed to keep Ike pointed straight, then a turn in Keokuk to duck under the bridge and go along the banks far as he could, up a block and across the main street, to hide for several hours in city neighborhoods. Let the cops search for him; no tracks, no sign of horse and rider.

He found a quiet street, let Ike walk, felt the bay's sides heave, but the horse moved freely. Then he stopped Ike, sat quiet, the horse not fussing or pulling. A car went by, siren muted but the lights spinning. Joe patted the horse's neck and thought maybe they'd wait a bit longer, till Ike had fully recovered and the cops were completely confused. He knew this wasn't over; one more bridge and there'd be cruisers already on their way, Joe was sure of that.

Joe's edge was that he didn't need roads to follow; he just needed the bridge for a moment before he disappeared. An hour later by reckoning on the stars, Joe picked up the reins, asked Ike for an easy trot down a sidewalk that seemed to parallel that South 17th Street he needed to get to the bridge. The enclosed sidewalk was there, just as Grunwald told him, but at the far end of the bridge two cruisers sat nose to nose. Two cops who thought they were clever; they stood by their cars, guns drawn, waiting for the moment.

One of them used a bullhorn to yell at Joe as he leaned over Ike's neck, asked the bay son to run like his mama's grand sire and they flew straight at the cops, who would be country boys, too good-hearted for shooting a horse and the stupid bastard riding him. Joe counted on that generosity and lined Ike at the touching grills. At the last moment he whooped and kicked Ike and let the reins slip and the horse jumped right across the middle between the two bumpers and slanted hoods and Joe looked at upturned faces wide-eyed, lips moving, pistols pointed to the ground.

Ike stumbled on the landing and Joe leaned back, let the horse find his balance and as Ike lumbered into a run, one shot whistled past and the other cop yelled what sounded like 'you goddamn...' Joe guided Ike off the tar road, down the embankment into soft ground partly covered in trees.

No roads, no way the cops could follow him. Once he could no longer hear the sirens, Joe angled Ike back up onto a tar road, with a nice shoulder and groomed lawns that met up with the sidewalk. He sighted down the line, looked like about a half mile of these pretty houses before the countryside came back in. He was grinning despite the hour, his shoulder, and knowing that the cops wanted him; he trotted and then loped Ike across the front lawns, on two occasions they jumped a low wall bordered with flowers. Twice Ike lifted his tail and left behind fertilizer for those dedicated gardeners.

There'd be head-shaking in the morning when each house spat out one individual to walk right to the mail box where the daily paper rested. Horse manure, soft hoof prints; some kind of peculiar goings-on while the neighborhood slept.

Now that they had passed the last of the houses and a few farms, the land was barren; wired fences that sagged, deeper footing, brush alongside the road, a few animal corpses, some badly decomposed, that had Ike snorting as he stepped around the mangled flesh, ears cocked but quiet. Finally the bay gelding had run out of rebellion.

Joe agreed with the bay; his head throbbed, he could breathe but his side and that lung ached and the pain in his shoulder was pure misery. He kept Ike traveling at an angle away from the highway, Rte 61 he thought. For once he searched for a hard road and let the bay walk, leaving as little mark as possible of their direction. Different state, different side of the second river but he wasn't looking to fend off the law.

He found a closed gate, rusted but unlocked; behind it was grass, trees, a small creek; heaven for an exhausted horse and rider.

The sun woke him coming straight into his eyes. Ike was sleeping, legs curled under him, tail fanned out, eyes shut, ears loose. Joe grunted and the horse grunted in return. He thought about getting up, rolled over onto his bad shoulder and cried out. Ike opened his eyes, shook his head against a few flies and grunted, lay flat out and went back to sleep. In a moment the horse was snoring. Joe went back to sleep almost as quickly.

A woman's voice startled Joe. Ike was up and at the fence, sniffing a woman's outstretched hand. "Mister, he's a pretty soul isn't he. I hope you don't mind my patting him." Mind, Joe thought, Ike sure had mellowed for he was more into biting than patting when Joe dragged him out of that killer auction. He stood up, conscious of being filthy, crusted in dried sweat, and that his arm hurt like blazes and the pills were at the bottom of the canvas bags. It would be impolite at this point to go rooting for them, washing them down with stream water before he could be human again.

"Mister, I can see you are in distress. Is there anything we can do to help?" It was the 'we' that finally got his attention. He wandered over to Ike and saw that besides the young woman, barefoot, bare legs, a long skirt, loose blouse and free hair, there were two other women and they all carrying woven straw containers filled with flowers and weeds.

The boldest of the three, who'd been playing with Ike, spoke for them all. "We are part of a group and live a mile down the road on our farm. You are invited for a meal, mister, and a good grooming for your horse. And it looks to me he needs a trimming; your riding has thinned him and chipped his hooves. He is in need of better care."

She was smiling as she made the comments, and then pacified Joe's growing temper by an offer; "You too are suffering from an injury, and perhaps too much riding. Come with us, we can care for you." This was almost a dream, one of the fairy tales his father read to him in lyrical Welsh, about young women rescuing travelers out of kindness.

"Yes, ma'am."

They weren't a commune, Nibbana explained to their guest. They were people with common ideals who bought an abandoned farm for the taxes and were making a successful life. Yes the locals did not choose to accept them, but they did not demand acceptance, they believed in the life they'd created, with its potions and herbs and compassion for all living things.

No, she continued, they were not vegetarians for most of them had tried that life and found their own inner spirit shrinking from the diet. They honored the animals raised to be eaten, they were treated kindly, fed well, warm in winter and out to pasture in the summer. And when one of these animals was slaughtered, it was done with compassion and a ceremony to bless the giving of life through death.

They raised sheep mostly, and vegetables, special herbs for tonics and tinctures. They had cows and goats also, but no pigs. It had never been discussed but they all had an aversion to pork. Joe listened, nodded and allowed them to lead him down the road. Their group footprints of bare feet and sandals would mangle his prints and Ike's. And he was tired, the pain in his shoulder taking over his entire being.

The farmhouse was a handsome brick two-story home set on a rise, with a stout barn and sturdy outbuildings, pens for goats, a pasture with three cows in it. A team of horses plowed a field in erratic lines and Joe was too damned tired to comment. The team was halted, brought in to the barn and stripped. The man came from the barn, two more men appeared from various buildings and Joe was uncomfortable.

One man, short and slight, with wisps of a beard, longish hair pulled back under a straw hat, stepped forward; "Nibbana says you are in need of a meal, sir. And that your horse needs tending also. Please, rest here. There is plenty of food, we have an abundance of winter root vegetables left, and one of the cows has freshened. If you don't mind roast lamb and turnips, then welcome, let us feed you."

Joe knew his mouth was open. The McLarens, they'd taken him in for what he'd done for them. These people offered compassion out of selflessness and he didn't trust it. However a large man walked with Joe to one of the smaller barns, where he was told he could leave his gear, and put the bay out on pasture with the team until there was time to tend to the chipped hooves.

As Joe bent down to disentangle the canvas bags, the man placed his big hand on Joe's shoulder and he came around out of blind pain and struck the hand, threatened the man who immediately stepped back with no intention to fight. A voice came from behind him, a different man; "Sir, we will have to ask you to leave. Violence is never the solution."

Joe hunched over, gasping at the command to leave, knowing he could do nothing right then. A woman's hand appeared, resting lightly on his right forearm. It was the one named Nibbana and her voice held no reprimand.

"Your shoulder, it is injured. How? And what have you done for it, when did it happen?" She turned to the big man and spoke quite firmly; "Michael, this man is hurt, not violent. You still do not understand the enormity of your strength and most likely have touched an injury that could not bear your weight." She then turned her temper on to the slight man; "Fern, he has been offered our hospitality. Now we must heal what hurts him so terribly."

The men were silent as they escorted him to the house, staying too close, unwilling to allow the women any contact. Once in the warmth and privacy of the neat, bare kitchen, they stood with arms crossed, scowling while quick female hands unbuttoned Joe's shirt and slid it from him. The undershirt was more difficult as he needed to raise his arms and the left arm would not move.

He ended the struggle by taking a knife from the table and saw the men stiffen, hands moved down to become clenched fists. He used the knife tip to poke a hole in the thin fabric and slit it, tearing up to his left armpit and then through the seams at the neck. The knifepoint pricked him and he felt the blood but it barely mattered against the pain going into his useless left hand.

It was unseemly and they had all taken vows but she had never seen such beauty. The clear black eyes muddied only when the pain became too much, the thick black hair down between his shoulder blades fanned across the dark skin. Naked from the waist up, barely enough flesh on him to cover his ribs yet he was well-muscled. There was evidence of a crude cut above a professional incision on his left side, much too close to his heart.

Obviously his shoulder pained him, no opened wound, no break, but the muscle had already atrophied, and Nibbana would guess that he had dislocated the joint recently and had not sought treatment.

She touched his face gently and he looked straight at her with those eyes. "You have damaged your shoulder, yes?" He nodded, almost shrugged and then a blast of pain reminded him. "I...that is we can help. Do you know about acupuncture?" Whatever was done would be the group's decision. Nibbana let the very tips of her fingers touch what seemed to be swollen tissue around the shoulder joint and his body quivered.

"No, ma'am." No what, she thought, and then removed her fingers from the smoothness of his skin and remembered her question. "It is an ancient method of using very slender needles to bring blood to the site of an injury. It moves energy through the body. A few treatments, a week of rest and you will be able to resume your journey." She was speaking too much, taking charge when she needed to be silent but the men only glared at this unwanted interloper and the other women seemed without a thought in their head.

Nibbana smiled; it was as she suspected. They might have given a vow of celibacy but this simple purity, the beauty of his dark skin and the hands, even the left one coiled and stiff and held gently in his lap, his very soul reached into all of them. His scent was sweat and tired and enticing enough she licked her lips and hoped that Rose and Edwina didn't understand her behavior.

Finally Michael seemed to have recovered his sense for he spoke over Nibbana's words, re-explaining the concept of acupuncture and offering the group's hospitality for a few days while the man recovered. He stood, shining copper against their white-painted kitchen and their own pale shirts, tan pants, work boots, long faded skirts for the women. He looked at each one of them in turn; nothing showing in the black eyes except a fading curiosity.

"Thank you. I'd admire to learn what this acupuncture can do. Never hurts a man to know something more." She wasn't sure if he was making a joke out of pain, but the corners of his mouth turned up, and he looked straight at her. "Ma'am."

It took two of the men several minutes to replace the shirt on their visitor's back. The undershirt was useless and Fern finished cutting it away, to be washed and used as a rag. Here nothing went to waste.

They shared an awkward supper with their guest, whose evident discomfort forced them to talk more than normal. Once their guest praised the tenderness of the roast lamb, Willard took it upon himself to describe the sheep-raising aspect of their farming endeavor. The exact words were lost, but Nibbana remembered their visitor's surprise that the lamb was so sweet as he spoke about eating mutton with the Navajos.

It had been Willard's idea to try raising the Katahdin sheep, a breed developed in the fifties from a band of wool-less sheep imported from Africa. Willard found his voice and he over-explained to their visitor. The sheep had a hair coat, not one of wool, Willard said, which gave a much different taste to the meat as there was no lanolin in the sheep's genetic make-up, creating a more delicate flavor in the meat. They did raise sheep for wool, and sold those lambs early in the spring as was traditional. But the Katahdin lambs could be allowed to mature through the summer, and when butchered in the fall they kept the sweet, nut-like flavor to the flesh, instead of the tough and gamy taste Joe remembered in connection with mutton stew.

It was a long and boring lecture but it got them through the evening meal. And it tired the man so he was eager to leave the table before dessert. Dear Michael took him out to the barn and showed him where he could leave his belongings and rest for the evening.

Michael reported back to his friends still seated at the table, that the man thanked him for his efforts to make him comfortable, and to please thank everyone in the house for their hospitality. The six of them exchanged glances, silent as to their thoughts but explicit as to their concerns. They were not used to strangers, and this one in particular unnerved them.

Sixteen

They decided everything by consensus brought on by discussion, selecting this chaotic manner over voting, which seemed destined to become a popularity contest rather than the true wishes of the community.

In the end Nibbana was appointed to do the treatment. She had studied acupuncture long before either of the other women, or any of the men, knew about its possibilities. She had the most experience; the man's injury was already set in his flesh, and it would take skill and patience to effect healing.

It was this aspect of the discussion that prompted the men to give their approval. Nibbana and Edwina both could see it in those male eyes, blue, brown, and a dark hazel, eyes that narrowed as they watched their 'guest', eyes that studied his very being and took offense at his obvious appeal. They were practical in their choice; the sooner the man was healed, the sooner he would be gone.

The following morning, after sharing coffee and breakfast with them, Joe was taken into a small room, white walls, a few chairs, and shelves of jars containing dried herbs, roots, leaves, stems. Each container was labeled but he did not care to read them. He hurt; his arm rested in his lap and he sat quiet, hardly breathing as each effort seemed to intensify the pain. He'd run out of those store-bought pain pills and asking these folks for such relief was pointless.

She helped him unbutton and shrug out of the offending shirt. She held it like an unsavory specimen, careful not to remark on the fact it desperately needed washing. Something cool was rubbed on his shoulder, the top, along each side, then she picked up the arm and laid it on a table padded with numerous towels. "Mr. Evans, you need only to breathe easily, think of what pleases you and try to refrain from tightening your body. I know that sounds as if I am warning you in advance and you will of course tighten, but you will feel only the slightest prick and if there is pain, let me know and I will remove the offending needle."

He sat quiet, head hanging, listening to her. Then; "Let me see these needles you're intending to stick in me." She resisted; "Mr.

Evans it's usually best if the patient does not see them, it can make you uncomfortable." Joe pulled back; "Hell lady, you're about to make a porcupine out of me and the arm hurts like crazy, I'm miles from nowhere and at your mercy and you don't want to upset me?"

This was most definitely not going according to her training. Most of her patients came willingly because they knew the treatment worked. This one, however, disturbed her on so many levels she almost wanted to push him away and put the needles back in their sterilizer. Yes she knew that because of AIDS, most practitioners used disposable needles but they were not as effective and in her world, AIDS was not a consideration, for those who took partners, took them for life and did not stray or experiment.

Once again she placed her hand very gently on his injured shoulder and felt the flesh draw away. Her hand was pale against his dark color and she felt the softness of muscle and skin even as he moved in some discomfort. "Mr. Evans, if you don't accept this treatment you will continue to be in pain and that is a waste of your time and the energy your body needs to heal. You are already too thin, and I gather there are miles still remaining in your journey. You are being foolish."

"Ma'am, all I asked is to see one of the needles." Nibbana laughed, truly that is what he'd asked and here she was lecturing him. She took the needle she intended to first insert, brought it around in front of him, with the warning that he was not to touch it as it was sterilized, and as he could see, she wore gloves to protect that sterilization.

He said nothing, his head moved a few times. Then he nodded. "Thanks." Nibbana began her treatment, finding those places where the energy was blocked, tapping in the needles, only the slightest amount in some places, deeper in other and while on occasion a muscle rippled, he made no noise, no deep sighs or quickened breath. She was impressed by the discipline.

The six friends had come together slowly, finding each other in a larger group of little faith. They made a loose organization based on the readings of Mother Ann Lee, with one specific difference in their understanding; that if love, not lust, grew from their cohabitation, then they would move on to the level of a nuclear family with sexual union and children.

Under her hands was a man who could divert her from these beliefs by his presence, even the pain he endured through raw humor. She worked on him, face close to his skin as she impaled the needle then turned it. When she'd finished, he sat quietly with eighteen needles rising from the fineness of his shoulder and back and down the smooth muscle of his arm.

Even when she picked up an herb bundle, lit the end and held it to some of the needles, he was still. His head lifted to catch the scent but for now he asked no questions. However, Nibbana felt a need to explain; "If the heat is too much, Mr. Evans, let me know and I will do otherwise."

Her hand was shaking the very slightest amount, a remnant of her body's response that her mind denied. As soon as possible she retrieved each needle, cautious because she felt her agitation and did not want it transferred to his healing. "There, Mr. Evans, be quiet for a while. Sit here if you wish. Do nothing with that arm for at least a few hours. We will do another treatment tomorrow."

She fled, terrified of her betraying flesh.

He wandered around the farm after sleeping hard for three hours, a sleep that held no pain or fear. First he checked on Ike, then he went out to the field where the man, Michael he thought it was, the big man with excess strength, was plowing or rather trying to plow, working the team against each other, lines literally crossed in the harnessing of the stolid Shire mares.

His approach was cautious, since basically with the reins turned around, the man had little control. "Mornin'. That seemed a good beginning to Joe, but it didn't work as the surly answer slammed him. "It's afternoon. Been that way for an hour or so. You missed lunch. Nibbana said to let you sleep."

Joe shook his head gently; "Guess I slept longer than three hours." He got no response. "Those're good horses. Where'd you come up with such a fine team?" Michael hauled up on the lines and the off horse went sideways to muffled cursing. "None of your business." Joe hesitated, then approached the team and their very angry handler. There wasn't much to lose; "Mister, I'll be gone quick's I can. But I ain't leaving until I show you a thing or two about those horses. You I don't give a damn about, like you feel around me. But you got a few things to learn and I don't care if you hate me enough to skin me alive, you're gonna listen 'cause I know what I'm doing with horses and you sure as hell don't."

He presented himself wide open to the big man, close enough one blow from that fist and he'd go down, for he wasn't going to fight those who were offering help. But kindness and tact weren't this man's way of thinking so Joe put out the challenge and waited.

"All right. For the mares." Joe approached the off horse, a good eighteen hand black roan mare. He reached up and stroked the big jowl. The dark eye rolled back at him. "No blinders, good for you. But the bridle's buckled too tight." He pressed on the black's poll and the big head came down so he could loosen the cheek pieces two holes on each side. The mare flapped her lips and sighed. Joe spoke without looking away from the horse.

"Bet it was tough getting that bridle on. Now, watch." He unsnapped the rein, crossed it through a different dee on the harness saddle and then the hames and snapped it to the near horse's bit, then did the same with that rein, ending up with the lines crossed. "Easier this way to turn them, no hauling or yawing and they'll listen quicker when you want them to halt."

The men stared at each other. "Okay, you showed me and I understand now so let me get back to work." Joe held on, looked down at the torn ground, glancing back at the uneven furrows. "Mister, you plan on farming this land, you'd do well to plant a straight line, it's easier to weed and harvest. Fixing the lines'll help, but you got to feel the ladies' mouths, their response and temper, and keep them headed forward and straight, not wandering all over hell and gone."

He'd stepped in it this time by swearing again but the man only came up close to Joe, head tilted, eyes wide but not threatening. "Show me."

She couldn't help but worry, for Joe Evans was standing up to Michael and they were talking, Michael waving his arms and the shorter of those two enormous horses seemed upset. Joe actually put his hand on Michael and she thought she would witness mayhem.

Instead the two men went to the back of the horses, between those massive hindquarters and the plow, and Joe picked up the reins, the lines she'd heard them called, and she wanted to tell him not to pull back as Michael did when the team got it in their mind to head in a different direction, for he would undo all the good the morning's treatment had begun. Unexpectedly he knotted the lines together and draped them over his right shoulder, then stepped behind the plow, resting both hands on the extended wood handles. It made more sense this way, than Michael standing to the side, putting uneven pressure on the plow while he fought the mares.

Another surprise, as the team stepped forward, straight and true, the plow went in deep, pushing aside a smooth fold of dark earth. It was beautiful, that line of moist loam. She watched, fascinated, as the two men walked in close to the plow, Joe holding the plow and pushing down while the mares moved straight ahead for him. There was no tug at the speckled black's mouth, no sign of a lolling tongue or any other resistance.

Then he draped the lines around Michael's shoulder, and those big hands didn't want to close around the handles so Joe held Michael's hand and seemed to be explaining something for Michael's head was tilted. They made the exchange and the outsider stepped aside, letting Michael take hold of the plow and push down, lean back to steady the team as they dragged that heavy plow in a line almost as straight as the one they'd just opened.

Nibbana watched all this while smiling. She admired the big Shire mares; it was difficult to know how they did it, but these two behemoths, despite their impressive size, were distinctly female in attitude and expression. It pleased her that their identity was obvious as she stood beside them and the black mare lowered her head to sniff at Nibbana's outstretched hand. She could see, and feel, the gender response even as the long Shire whiskers tickled her palm.

It was a rare human who could stand up to Michael and make any point. The man was an ox and Willard had once joked they could yoke Michael to the plow and save on feeding a team. There had been two days of sullen quiet until Willard finally got his friend to understand the suggestion had been meant to be a joke. They had learned then how Michael was sensitive about his size; like all of them he had been an outsider. Each of them had their private torture, and they were learning to be gentle with those raw places in others.

She met Joe as he went to the pasture where his horse came up to the fence; exactly how they had first met and that was only yesterday. She was shy and thought to return to the herb garden and dig through the winter's growth, pick out the dried weeds, plan where she would put each new herb she'd chosen out of the precious seed catalog. Her only winter's reading.

But it was a treat to stand here, in the sun, next to this unusual man, who had tamed Michael and the team of Shires, who sat still for needles, who had ridden many miles and yet was only halfway home. It took careful questions at the meal last night to have him give up any of those answers. Without looking at her, or waiting to be asked, he told her; "Ma'am, the shoulder feels fine. I can ride on now, save you more trouble. You folks've been good enough to me, I don't want to be in the way." She smiled, looked down at her hands clasped together. Without looking up, she spoke to him from her heart; "Mr. Evans you need a second treatment and we are delighted to have your company for however brief a time. Please share the evening meal with us."

Joe watched her leave, bare feet digging in the barn dirt, long skirt moving easily with her body. She was small, barely up to him mid-chest and she smiled easily as she talked, with a voice he could listen to for a long time. She was lovely, and it seemed she had flirted with him, looking away, smiling, telling him, not asking but telling him that she wanted him to stay.

This was new to Joe, this lowering of the eyes, the sideways glance. So far it had been the woman who let him know, either by clear words or through hands taking what they wanted.

That evening he studied them; passing bowls, offering meat, pouring out fresh milk or clear water, tending to another's need as if each gesture was a gift. He did not understand them, their choice, their manner and determination. The meal was pleasant, the food plain, even the winter squash tasted good with the simple addition of fresh-churned butter. He offered, as he had once been taught, to wash the dishes or help clean up but Nibbana gently pushed him away. "You are a guest in our home, Mr. Evans. We would never ask a guest to do such chores."

The opportunity for washing was expanded to Joe's person, with Joe not involved in the discussion. He listened, agreeing that he needed to get clean, but there were thoughts and considerations that had never occurred to him. Eventually, it was Michael who stood outside the downstairs bathroom, where the women did their laundry, and where a large tub of heated water awaited. Michael was grinning as he opened the door and gave Joe one towel.

"You hurry, mister. We don't hold to uncleanliness here, even if it's from plowing a straight furrow." There was a hint of laughter in the man's eyes as Joe took that towel from the oversized hand.

He managed to wake for breakfast, and this time they let him move empty plates from the crowded table to the tin sink. Then she put her hand on his arm, below the elbow; "Mr. Evans, we will work on your shoulder again. Come with me."

There were no explanations, no soft cajoling voice, no small gasp as he easily slipped out of his shirt. He wore nothing underneath for that had been his last tee shirt. Her fingers were light on his skin as he took in shallow breaths and felt a pressure in his groin. She began the needles; he felt each tiny prick, then the twist. And finally the burning herbs that she held to the needle and made small noises of contentment. "It helps, doesn't it, and if you're careful the shoulder will heal. What did you do? I never asked."

He described the situation, making a joke out of it, even through putting the bone back in its joint with an old man's help and how the tough kid fainted. When he looked up to catch her reaction, she was crying and he could not believe it. He stood, needles quivering as they tingled in his flesh, and he gently touched her face with his right hand.

"Ma'am, there's nothing sad about that story. Worse has happened." She stopped her crying; "I can see that, Mr. Evans, and it is heart-rending to know that a human being can take such punishment and find humor in it. I suppose you find this all a grand amusement."

Her fingers touched that knife wound and Joe leaned down to kissed Nibbana's mouth, very gently, knowing that it wasn't sex but tenderness the woman needed. She pulled away and rubbed at her mouth. "That cannot be, Mr. Evans. Sit, I will finish up and you can leave." He was confused, knowing once again he had misunderstood what a woman asked or didn't ask from him.

She said nothing but continued on as if they had not spoken or that he had kissed her. She was firm, her touch with the needles stronger, more demanding and he was relieved when they were slipped from his hide and she handed him his shirt. "Get dressed, Mr. Evans. We are done." She suggested then that he spend the day doing as little as possible, and that she intended to work on her garden, which would be too strenuous for him. She stopped a moment over the word and took time to explain its meaning; "It would be asking too much of your arm as of yet, Mr. Evans. I will see you this evening."

That night he didn't sleep but ran over and over what had been said, what each touch might have meant, what he'd missed or misunderstood. In the morning, he woke to breakfast being over and to find that Michael was paring and rasping Ike's chipped hooves, not too short, for the horse needed to travel with some support. Doing what Nibbana had suggested, the big man said. Since Joe would ride out today. He packed his meager belongings, found that the red and white shirt and the vividly-striped one were missing, replaced by two muslin shirts, well worn and patched but they fit. Only one shirt belonging to the Daggarts' son was still decent enough to wear.

Edwina opened the door when he knocked. She smiled, a plain woman whose eyes were clear blue and they gave her a beauty he had not noticed before. "Mr. Evans, thank you for teaching Michael about plowing and the team. He is a good man, stubborn only because of what has been expected of him." Her smile was generous and Joe thought that maybe this time, since it meant nothing to him, that he might be reading the signs correctly. He smiled at her and nodded.

"Yes, Mr. Evans. Michael means a great deal to me but I cannot tell him. We have taken a vow and it can only be changed by all of us, not through one person's desire." She hesitated; "Or any outsider." She touched his hand lightly. He bowed his head. "You were beginning to mean too much to Nibbana. She told me yesterday and I watched her during the evening meal. It is best you leave without seeing her. We are bound together, the six of us, and there is no place here for you."

Clear, he thought, level and well thought out and detailing for him why he was not wanted. "Yes, ma'am. Good day to you all." It was done, he thought. Edwina's kind explanation would make leaving Nibbana and this place easier. He held to that thought until a man came out to where Joe stood, the one man who'd barely spoken during his stay. No questions at mealtime, no demands or orders. This man, whose deep brown eyes studied and seemed to know everything, led the small group through his quiet depth of purpose.

"I am Fern Miville. Here." Joe was handed another sack of food, as if all the people he met recognized his need for sustenance and the improbability of him finding steady meals. "You are more than halfway there, Mr. Evans." The man hesitated; "I know she is bound by her emotions, but when the time is right, I will take care of her." No name, no need for one. Joe thanked the man for his thoughtfulness.

Ike was eager to move on and when Joe mounted, his arm and shoulder gave him little trouble. He didn't look back, held no thoughts of these people; he was gone, riding out into a different life. Maybe one time, some time in the future, he would learn what women and men sought in each other and how they knew it was right or wrong.

He rode an hour north and west past a town named Wayland and then a sign on a patched tar road told him he was on County Road NN. He followed the track; it was grassy footing for Ike, an easy lope, some trotting, a few stretches of walking. Joe's shoulder no longer hurt but he was cautious about using his arm and hand. Then a shallow river cut under the road and it was going more north so he stepped Ike off the formal road and went with the river itself, along the banks, using animal trails, footpaths, moving away from the river when it was heavy with trees but always keeping its silver glint close to him. It would take him into Iowa, it had to, and Iowa was one state next to Nebraska. He was only two states from home.

The thought of home had become bitter.

Joe kept to the river for two days, figuring he and Ike were making thirty miles a day. Then there were growing signs of towns, people and smaller, newer houses, driveways instead of farm lanes; maybe he'd crossed the border into Iowa. So he let Ike have a day to graze, roll, sleep, stand and do nothing. True to his nature, Joe washed himself and his clothing in the river and near to froze his feet to the sandy bottom. Painful, hurting cold but he hated the sweat and dirt of constant riding. And wondered where along this long trail he'd gotten to be so particular. In prison a shower was more danger than a pleasure.

He slept, ate the remains of the food that the Miville fellow gave him, boiled up sour coffee, sipped at the terrible brew and watched spring pop up around him. A day of sunshine and he could almost see flowers open, grasses grow at least an inch every two hours. It was far different from where he was going, more like where he'd been born. Green grass, more hills, steeper grades, fog and cold and wet from the ever-present seas. He barely remembered specifics now, except for the sound of his father's voice, a big hand against his back to steady him, and the constant scent of horses.

The signs were there; a town of decent but not excessive size, where he could find the exact whereabouts of those damned rivers. He knew, he remembered; the Missouri River lay between him and the barren land of the western plains. That meant finding a way to cross another expanse of water and this time he wasn't willing to try the run. Cops weren't stupid and they had a web of information going town-to-town and state-to-state and he suspected there was a lookout for him. Not much of a description because of the dark but how many riders traveled through the countryside now. Head down, quiet and respectful and he might get to where he was going.

Gas stations hung at the edges of most towns and cities. He let Ike drift along the road shoulder with easy footing and not many cars. He had time to admire the land, the rich fields, some of them plowed and waiting. Decent farms from the distances between houses, still human in scale.

Then it was houses closer together and finally what he wanted; a garage that worked on tractors and rakes, the big combines, and these mechanics wouldn't be surprised by a man on horseback asking directions. He stepped Ike onto the grass verge to avoid colliding with a motorcycle. He watched in amazement as the biker roared past, one hand steering his mechanical monster, the other holding something that he scrubbed across his teeth and Joe realized the gentleman on the Harley was brushing his teeth as his bike gained speed.

His jaw dropped; the man bit down on the toothbrush, waved at Joe then returned to his endeavor as he pumped through the bike's gears and roared into traffic. Joe watched him until the bike disappeared, but the sound of that engine still rattled back thick with exhaust.

Three men sat at a picnic table, elbows resting as they chewed through thick sandwiches and Joe heard his belly grumble. He rode in not too close and dismounted. A man on the ground wasn't as intimidating as a man mounted and looking down. That word, intimidated, made him think on a pretty woman who didn't want feelings for any man. Joe shook his head, while Ike grazed on the rich grass near the garage.

Seventeen

"Afternoon to you, mister. Can we help? You caught the noon show, I see. That Red, he's gone to see his girl, don't want his wife to know, don't have the time to 'freshen up' as he calls it so he's figured out how to take care of his morning coffee breath." The laughter wasn't mean and even Joe smiled.

The men went back to their lunch. Joe spoke quickly, aware he was treading on rough ground; "Thanks. Yes. I need a map. Need to get me and Ike here over the Missouri without being on the wrong side of the law. It's hard to know where the best crossings are for a horse." Joe knew he had to get their attention or he'd receive a brief nod, a map handed out for a dollar and then these buddies would finish lunch, talking to each other and easily ignoring the oddity staring them in the face.

"Oh." One man stopped chewing, smiled showing a missing front tooth. "Hell mister, it were me I'd go down into Missouri and over on the Brownville Bridge. Guess it's called that, depends on which side of the river you're on when you cross it. Joe nodded; the man chewed a moment, a different man spoke up; "They's ain't many police 'tween here and Brownville, mostly farming country. Peaceable folk, unless we don't get their tractors or combines fixed right." The men laughed and went on eating.

"Mister?" It was the first man, head tilted to one side. "Now my missus she puts in an extry sandwich or two so's I don't starve. Think she's done well, don't you?" He patted an ample belly. "Here's a half sandwich I was holding for later. If I gets hungry then I'll call Eloise and she'll bring me piece of pie or a cobbler. 'Pears to me you could use the feeding."

Before Joe answered, the second man pushed forward a glass jar of milk. "Set, mister. We ain't gonna bite. You looked too lean and tough for us to barbecue." The third man, who hadn't said a word, pushed over a bag of chips. He accepted their invitation as the second man slid on the bench to give Joe room. He held to Ike's rein and sat down. Reached for the half sandwich that was handed to him. Saw the man's skin, close to his but different. That brown almost black tone, dark but not copper like Joe.

"Where you from, mister? Ain't seen many the likes of you 'round here." Joe chewed quickly, swallowed, hesitated and wiped his mouth. My god that was good; thick roast beef with a horseradish sauce. He nodded. "Headed up into the Dakota Nebraska line. Where the horse's from, thought I'd bring him home."

Silence, thoughtful seconds as each man chewed and puzzled over Joe's words. Then the first man smiled, real and wide and he slapped Joe's arm. "Mister, that's as good a reason for traveling I ever heard. Let me get you that map." Joe ate, trying not to be greedy or the men would give him more and that was begging in his way of thinking. The milk was cold and delicious. The man got up, true to his word on producing the map, and he was a big son, all belly and broad shoulders.

"Now I don't know how you chooses a place for the night, but not far west of town, a few miles out of your way, we got a mighty pretty state park and they got campsites and water and even open land your horse there could use for supper and breakfast." It was the quiet man who'd offered up the milk. "Kids and I we fish to Buck Creek come summer. Cold now, but I don't think you'll complain. And it ain't near as cold as winter. They got covered fire pits and I'm betting you'd do fine."

He put out his hand; "Name's London. How do." Joe replied in kind, accepting the handshake. "Joe."

He rode out after an hour's visit and a few more bites from shared meals offered by other mechanics as they drifted over to see what was happening. Some were white, more were black; none were American Indian but no one in the group seemed to take notice.

His belly was achingly full, he had two extra half-sandwiches and a plastic bottle of fancy water, compliments of a boss who had no idea of his employees' generosity. The directions were simple, the roads clearly and frequently marked to guide all possible tourists to the park, which of course was empty; it was almost dark and early April he'd guess. Not exactly the height of the tourist season.

There was a convenient back camp spot, so Joe filled out a ticket and paid the fee on the honor system, stuffing the envelope in a locked box. Names; Joe and Ike Evans, home the Brings Plenty Ranch near Pine Ridge in either South Dakota or Nebraska. Let the park ranger figure that one. He'd paid the fee, all that was necessary.

As he front and side-hobbled Ike, he heard the odd noise of a struggling vehicle. Joe paid no attention, not his business, nothing he could do to help for he knew little about engines. He found enough dropped pine needles to make a soft bed, laid out his blankets, wadded up his winter coat for a pillow, no more of that saddle nonsense, when a female voice called out.

"Anyone there?" Women again. Joe held his breath, hoping it had been imagination instead of reality calling. "Anyone there?" He sighed, went over to Ike and tested the hobbles, patted the bay who barely looked up from grazing, and went in the direction of the voice.

Well look what calling out in the dark brought to a girl. My my. Sheila elbowed her friend hard in the ribs. "Are we both having the same dream?" Penny laughed; "Wow!" The man stopped sensibly enough not too close, half in the dark and he still was gorgeous. What luck. And they had fan belt trouble to boot. Penny was the brave one as always. And she was sober since they'd been driving across state and both were wise enough to know the risk wasn't worth the penalty. There was plenty of time and vodka waiting in the old bus. It was their spring break and they'd decided on an all girls' road trip, not the beaches to the south or coast but across the belly of the middle.

Now Providence had brought them a reward for being sober and marginally virtuous; Penny moved as if stalking something wild and Sheila admired the tactic. Eventually the man turned full-face, stepped forward in fact and she studied him closely. Tall but not too tall, lean as if eating wasn't a regular occasion. That black hair, the eyes, the color of the skin told her Indian and she didn't mind at all. Neither of them had ever drawn that line, and now it was theirs to willingly cross. 'Course they might ask the gentleman if he had similar intentions.

And they best be cautious, they'd known when they came to the campground that it would be basically abandoned, with the idea of getting stoned in private. Now the fan belt and this particular man's appearance pushed everything into a new direction. Sheila needed a bit of time to discuss her ideas with Penny, but then she and Penny usually thought alike which was why they traveled together.

Penny's voice was clear, no seduction or teasing. Must be something she didn't quite trust about the man. Sheila walked up to stand next to her friend and from the expression on Penny's face it was more confusion than fear. This close the man's face was angles, planes of light and dark, a full mouth and that black hair pulled back. A delight, tantalizing; Penny wondered out loud if he knew how to fix a fan belt.

"Yes, ma'am. One of the few things I know 'bout vehicles." An interesting accent she could not place. Perhaps it was a tribal element but there was the British Isles in certain sounds. He smiled as if knowing what worked through her mind. "Let me take a look." Sheila glanced at Penny, who shrugged as they started toward the old bus. They heard a horse whinny, and as the man walked to the bus, there was the distinct smell of horse following him. Which made sense to both women.

It was a Volkswagen, a joke on campus where its box structure was highly visible among pickups and muscle cars. Neither of them used it often as there were enough boys to guarantee local rides. But for trips like this, where no one knew them or cared what they did, the bus was perfect.

The man was perfect; he even came with a horse so he had to be kind. As he leaned over the bus's exposed mechanics, Sheila and Penny signaled to each other and moved in, one to each side. There were other mechanics more important to them at the moment, like how they would divide him. Did he have the stamina, was he shy? Or perhaps a bully. They both licked their lips and laughed, and while his back twitched, he did not respond to their teasing.

He was in over his head and knew it. The fan belt had loosened and was frayed. He'd suggest the girls buy a new belt soon as possible.

Certainly it took no more brains than the use of a wrench and the ability to tighten or loosen a screw to fix this now and replace it later.

He recognized the urgency of their leaning in so close to him that he could feel their breathing; it had to be sexual. For once he had to be right in reading sign. Joe stood back, closed the silly VW hood and wiped his hands on his jeans. "That's done. Now what do you two want?" He didn't know any other way but to be direct. These girls were tough; one of them, with the red hair spiked in some unimaginable manner, stood on her toes to kiss him.

Full on, no delicacy, no gentle pressure but mouth, lips, something hard through her tongue but he didn't mind. He grabbed her, still careful about his arm but he was ready. Hard, pushing against Red's belly and she laughed and stepped away from him. "Here, try Sheila. She's game too." Same kiss, full and deep but she was taller, nothing hard in her tongue, and her breasts pushed into him, free, loose and full, so he pulled open her shirt, kissed the top of each breast, holding one hand on her back. She pressed into him, laughing, calling to her friend; "Penny he's more than willing."

The woman gasped, her friend came up behind Joe and rubbed on his butt, hands grabbing hips, then moving one hand forward to find his erection and he groaned. "You do that and it's over." Each one stepped back, touching him with a hand, one on his belly, the other over his mouth, but they smiled past him to each other.

Getting into the bus was easy, the side pulled open, a mattress covered the entire back. Joe was pushed in, the girls followed, hands all over him. Between his legs, up under his shirt. Kisses in the small of his back until he lay face down and the women surrounded him with shed clothing, panties and a flimsy item that had to belong to Sheila. It quickly became impossible to keep them straight, what body parts belonged to which girl and it didn't matter for all they wanted was his cock, his fingers, or his mouth, in any number of wet places.

Exhausted, drained, mouth tasting of salt, Joe lay on the mattress. He recognized that he was naked, that two women lay curled next to him without their clothes and all three of them were satiated, filled with the pleasure of complete sexual release. One of them picked up his sticky useless cock, held it like a child would hold a butterfly.

Her voice was as gentle as that child; "Wow." Her fingers closed on him and he couldn't believe it but the skin tightened, the tip rose and she rubbed two fingers across the very top. "Man you are something. Penny...ah hell I'm too tired." Penny's voice was thin, "Me too."

He laughed, it was all wrong. "Ladies, me too, I'm tired but that...guess the body doesn't always know." He took her hand away, patted her belly and the sticky wet cunt hair, let his fingers rest on the inner flesh. It's what the girls told him to call it; an unpleasant word remembered from prison, the only time those years entered his mind during all this but the girls insisted. Tough girls, yet they were generous.

He knew though, that after this he'd never use the word again. Too ugly, the opposite of what it was meant to describe. They sighed in unison and then laughed. Sheila found a quilt and pulled it up and, twisted together, trusting each other, they slept.

There was no immediacy in the morning, only good coffee in a French press, toast on a grill and eggs browned in bacon fat. Ike whinnied when he heard Joe's voice and Joe grinned, thinking that for once he'd had a better night than the horse. The girls were in the process of trying for a repeat when a park truck drove in, stopping long enough at the honor box for the ranger to take out the preceding day's fees, giving Joe a chance to subside, and the girls to straighten their hair, and for Sheila to redo her bra before the law came asking questions.

It was 'good morning' to the girls and a lecture for Joe who dared to bring an animal into Buck Creek State Park. The park law finally clued in to what might have gone on last night and demanded to see the girls' licenses in order to prove their age. Joe had a moment of panic until it was shown that Sheila and Penny were twenty-one and twenty-three respectively. When the same law asked to see Joe's identification, he shrugged, said he was riding his horse and was about to say he didn't have a license when he remembered that the McLarens had forced him to take the test.

It took some digging and his heart quit when the prison release papers came into view, legal stamps and the formal name of the prison right there on top, but the girls were flirting with the ranger and Joe slid the papers under dirty shorts. The license proved he was real; it even had an address, so he immediately became less of a threat. Joe forced a smile and began to groom Ike.

The ranger couldn't quite get his eyes or mind off the girls who were posing for him, instinctively knowing that they were saving Joe's butt and what a nice butt it was. It meant no good-bye kiss or anything more adventurous but it had been a night and no one back at school would have a story like this one.

Joe let Ike run, the quickest way to escape temptation. Nothing in his entire life, growing up, helping his father hold a stallion to service a mare, listening to the bragging in prison, nothing prepared him for these sensations, tastes, moments of agonizing pleasure. He actually kicked Ike, who shook his head and pinned his ears but extended his stride and got them the hell out of town. The map showed him where to go, south angling west toward another goddamn river when all he wanted to do was stop and rest.

Driving east, Sheila told Penny she was too sore to keep lifting her legs on the clutch, brake and accelerator. Penny said she wasn't much better and they could trade in an hour or so. But Sheila crawled into the back, where the quilt and mattress reeked of sex, and burrowed herself in so deep Penny could see only wisps of red hair under the pale yellow pattern.

She licked her mouth constantly, felt her hands tighten around the steering wheel and dreamed fully awake and driving about a man whose skin was smooth, whose mouth seemed to know, and who gasped as he plunged in deeper. Finally she pulled the bus over at a rest stop and crawled back there to push Sheila aside and hide under the quilt.

They had played around with each other before, never with much interest, more curiosity than anything passionate. This time they hugged, and smiled, and told each other what he'd done and how it felt.

There had been undercurrents he still did not understand. Nothing was overtly wrong, the girls had made no complaints even when the man was over by his horse and they could speak freely about what might have happened to them.

Fred Washburn had been a ranger for eleven years now, and had the feeling that whatever it was he'd just encountered, he would neither understand it nor meet up with it again. The man, however, there had been a bulletin issued about a man on horseback, the description vague; black hair, presumably dark skin, a bay horse, that much the one state cop was certain of. Said he knew horses and it was a bay gelding.

Can't be too many of those riding around the country, even with an Illinois driver's license, so Fred called in to his boss and gave his report. That they'd taken in nine dollars for last night at Buck Creek and he thought he'd run into the man riding that horse. Couldn't be sure, but he had a name, Joseph Evans, with an address in Illinois, which seemed peculiar since he was decidedly moving west.

Joe rode for three miles by his reckoning and discovered he was sore. Too sore to be galloping through the rich cropland and small clusters of forest or scrub moving in to what had been farm property. He slowed Ike from the now customary morning run, and had the gelding walk. Slow, long even strides, head down, and it was after some adjustments and a change in how he sat on the saddle, that Joe realized the horse no longer offered to jig or go sideways.

All the miles, all the roadways and fields, streambeds and highways, even that foolish jump over the troopers' cars and the bay gelding had learned to listen. Whatever faults born of poor treatment and misguided training that had ended with Ike at the killer auction, seemed to be gone now, worn out through more than a thousand miles of travel.

He dismounted and walked Ike, following a hardtop road for over an hour and not one car passed them. Not wanting to push his luck, for he carried a sense that the park ranger would put out Joe's description and the fact of him riding a bay gelding and perhaps was wanted, Joe kept to the hard surface of the road, leaving behind no print, no sign of passage except to the most watchful eye. And he doubted that his crime would call up the hounds and trackers and the state cops with their technological power.

It was a relief to find a narrow track grassed over so Ike's prints wouldn't be more than flat areas that a day of sun and light wind would bring upright, disguising their illegal passage. As the track turned a corner, it opened into a small meadow with a half-collapsed house, which reminded Joe of that rainy night inside with only Ike for company. He laughed, feeling that maybe the world would be all right with him for a day or two.

He went through the tasks quickly, having done them so often; hobble and side-hobble Ike, strip the gear, get it up and off the wet grass. The house had a decent front porch, good doorway, solid front walls; it was only the back ell that had collapsed, even the kitchen where it had been attached had withstood the fall, boards splintered and pulled off but beams and corner posts intact.

This rotted, half-collapsed house was a monument to one man's skill from maybe a hundred years ago. Joe spent time picking through the rubble, finding hand-forged nails, wooden pegs and floorboards showing the edge of a hand adze. Joe was impressed, and saddened, for soon enough wind and water would finish off the small structure.

There was a pump out back; with some priming from a nearby stream he got a bucket full of water. Easy enough to clear a fire ring and set up a tripod, boil water for a decent bathe; he stood naked in the small field, enjoying the mid-day sun, warm water, even shaving which he usually didn't bother with, that too felt good, taking away the past night's outrageous activities, the women's smells inside his mouth, on his belly and fingertips.

Once a helicopter flew overhead, not too low, not searching for anything in particular. Joe resisted the urge to wave. He slept easily, after a supper of grouse, new ferns boiled with a few wild onions. Spring growth would feed him, but he dreamed of a fine meal, a white tablecloth. A bed, all the incidentals of a decent room, even a shiny clean toilet that flushed, where a man could sit and read and relieve himself with some dignity.

In the morning he boiled up the stale coffee, picked at the grouse carcass then dumped everything out of the two canvas bags, which sent Ike flying even side-hobbled. When the horse and the dust from the bags settled, Joe eased himself down, tender in certain places, and pawed through the collection of dirt, clothing, bits and pieces and wads of money that he'd managed to accumulate.

Now, suddenly, time held new incentives for Joe; he saddled quickly, noting that Ike's coat was shedding to reveal a rich dark bay hide. He even heard himself singing, from his father's memory, songs in a different language and as he realized he was completely alone, he began to bellow. Ike shied and birds flew up out of trees and brush and Joe laughed, breaking from the song, then finding it again.

The license and the wad of bills were buttoned securely in his front pocket, where they wouldn't bother him while riding. Some of the bills were greasy, some new, counted finally and creating quite a surprise. Gifts going all the way back to the Junkers even, and then the McLarens, Lottie, even old Grunwald had contributed to the impressive numbers.

Two days in the small meadow had given him a sense of ease. No one was on the hunt for him. Ike was sassy and Joe's body responded to food, rest, and the remembrance of folks who'd cared for him. The counted bills came to over three hundred dollars and that didn't include the ugly twenties, ten of them now folded in with the prison papers. Packed in their dusty white envelope at the bottom of one canvas bag, they were no longer his identity, not what he had to show if anyone asked.

He trotted the bay around the field twice in each direction before going down the dark track to the road. There he allowed the bay to run that first mile.

It was two hundred miles to Brownville, eight plus days of traveling at a trot and canter, with breaks, walking, long drinks in farm ponds or streams, crossing land that included ridges and gullies, run-off and freshly plowed fields. Then the land eased, flattened out until he saw a green line in the distance. Bottomland enriched by spring flooding, cottonwoods lining the river's course.

The biggest surprise was the large towers capped with a small head and three revolving blades; these terrified Ike. Joe knew what they were, machines intended to capture wind. But how did you tell a horse that the wind farms were a good thing. The towers were scattered in a vague pattern alongside the Missouri banks. Joe had read about them, but it never occurred to him he'd be riding a high-strung horse through an actual farm. Eventually there were only a few of the towers to contend with. Ike spun, bucked, shied; Joe never pulled or kicked but kept the horse going forward. Then a road sign told him 'West 136', with more of those towers behind small hills on the road's other side. Ike moved easily at a lope, finally bored with the turbine wars.

According to the map, Joe was back in Missouri and riding up to the Brownville Bridge. Built in 1938 it said, a wispy layer of steel girders bank to bank. Ike stopped at the bridge, snorted and put his nose down to touch the edge. Then, when Joe asked with a gentle nudge of his boot heels, the horse trotted onto the Brownville bridge and Joe didn't like the two-beat gait so he asked Ike to walk and they covered the span, stepped off gently onto a hard-top road with a wide edge that brought travelers into town. Only one car crossed in the other directions; the travelers waved and cheered. Too bad the other river crossings hadn't been so easy.

It turned out to be a very small town set to one side of the main road, surprisingly hilly and tree-lined, filled with amazing buildings as if the past century barely existed; brick stores, straight houses set back on green lawns, cars, people walking. A few nodded to Joe, a man on a bicycle raised one hand as he passed too close in front of Ike, who shied and it took Joe a minute to get the horse settled.

He let the horse walk, resting one hand on his thigh, the other having a loose hold of the reins. He and Ike walked down Main Street, saw a pale building announcing books and a café. No one yet had complained, yelled or bothered him so he angled Ike toward the building. He dismounted, trying to decide if he dared tie Ike to the glossy black hitch post. A horse in a space outlined for a car seemed a fool thing but he was hungry and had the money to actually buy a meal.

"Sir, if you wish to come inside, then perhaps that tree behind the fence would better suit tying your horse." Joe lifted his head; it was a common sense suggestion spoken in an even voice, with no fuss about Ike who'd just deposited a steaming pile of green manure.

"Thank you, ma'am. Yes I'd like a meal but I don't quite trust Ike in the center of town." He looked up at the voice's source. It was a pretty woman, dark blond hair, slender and wearing an apron, and she smiled very sweetly, pointing; "Take him around the fence. That tree is nicely shaded and he looks like he could use a rest."

Joe left the horse tied firmly by the halter and lead. He was curious, the building appeared old yet the signs were new. Inside the café was simple; hardwood floors, clean windows, tables in two rooms, a counter with a wall behind it offering a variety of liquors.

Several tables held groups of men, farmers in overalls, and they were eating salads, sandwiches, talking easily with the pretty woman and she teased them back. She looked up at Joe; "Take a table and I'll be right there." He sat close to the wide front window, wishing he could see Ike but he'd listen for any trouble. The woman approached, handed him a menu; "What may I get you to drink? The specials are on the board and the quiche is particularly good today." She smiled at him, as if not certain he would understand.

He smiled, nodded to her; "The quiche, ma'am, and a big glass of water." It occurred to him that clean, fresh water was as much a treat as the food. She brought him the food, placed it in front of him but a few words on a sign had caught his attention and he didn't even grunt or remember his manners. She waited, then finally had to ask; "Anything else I can bring you?" He forced himself to look at her, tried a smile. "What's a book town?" This surprised Helen, who saw her newest customer as a wild and uneducated individual riding into town as if such an event were commonplace.

She gave the usual talk, about a generous man's wanting to sprinkle 'booktowns' throughout the world, stocked with secondhand books and meant to revitalize fading small towns and generate discussions, lectures, anything to promote reading and the adventure it brought to the individual. As she spoke, she realized this most unlikely person was following her lecture, nodding in the right places and appearing more interested than most people. "Thank you, ma'am. That's quite an undertaking." He put his head down and began on the quiche, looking as if its appearance were something out of his usual fare.

The café filled up, more farmers come in for lunch, tea drinkers, a few in to read the paper. Finally Helen went back to her customer seated in the far corner, staring out the window. "Sir, is there anything I can bring you for dessert?" His answer startled her. "Who came up with this idea, miss? About the book towns?" That was different than the usual flirtatious comments so she answered with the facts; "A man in Wales, from a small town called Hay-On-Wye. Mr. Booth calls it the International Booktown Movement..." She'd lost his attention. His black eyes had gone blank, his face, his entire body, was too still.

"Mister, are you all right?" The question seemed to shake him. "Yes, ma'am." He hesitated; "Is there a place I can board Ike for the night, maybe a place where I could stay too?" She thought about it, hesitant but curious. "I live with my father just out of town, and it's a small town so that's not far away. Dad used to have horses for my sisters and me. There's a decent shed, turnout, and a few bales of hay in the loft. Dad enjoys having horses around the place at times."

He smiled vaguely. "Thank you. Is there a place in town good enough for me to stay?" She looked at him in surprise. He smiled widely and she had some momentarily interesting thoughts. He was gently teasing her and she enjoyed the give and take. He stood up, "Ma'am, I can appreciate a nice bed, good linens, and a decent meal. You've tempted me. I've never had a better quiche." That statement almost made her laugh. "I've been looking for a treat. This place has a feel to it. And I want to know more about the 'book town' project."

She realized how tall he was, and too thin despite the wide shoulders. Another good meal or two, a decent sleep; she smiled, betting that women from sixteen to seventy, no, she thought, eighty, reacted in the same manner. "Mr...?" "Evans, ma'am. Joe Evans." Welsh, hmmm, he didn't look it of course, he had to be part Native but Evans. "Yes?" He was quiet, standing, waiting for her answer without distress or impatience. Helen smiled at what she was about to turn loose; "There is a bed and breakfast a block down Main Street, and if you ignore its appearance, RG's on the bridge corner serves a fine meal. You'll be well taken care of here."

She would have let him go then, but her conscience pricked her; "Mr. Evans?" He stopped, turned, smiled and Helen shook her head. "My father is a bigot, but it's the only place in town where you can leave a horse safely. I will speak to him, but I want you to know." That took courage, Joe thought, as he nodded to the woman and decided that a prejudiced father was not enough to force him to leave town without spending more time with the daughter.

Several of her regular customers looked at her, the obvious question in their eyes but she didn't give them a chance to ask. She had no idea who the man was, or why he chose to ride a horse into town, but he was intriguing, and these farmers, the few tourists, they already wanted to know everything.

Helen stood on the front verandah and watched as her customer checked his horse, tightened the girth on an English saddle of all things, mounted and rode toward the bed and breakfast. Helen thought to call Caroline and warn her of what was about to arrive, but the man was well-mannered and the surprise would do Caroline some good. She took her antiques and her lace and linens far too seriously; this lovely man with the Welsh name and the beautiful face would jar Caroline out of her proper demeanor.

She did call her father back. She felt it was important that she give a simple description of the man that wouldn't set her father off on one of his rants. It had come to her slowly, over the years and even now she often forgot, that her father was a bigot. Oh well, Helen thought, as she heard Dad's voice and tried without success to remind him to be on his best behavior, Mr. Evans appeared well able to take care of himself.

As Joe untied Ike and fiddled with the gear, reluctant to leave the café and the woman, he surprised himself with his thoughts. He'd been riding for almost a year, been wounded, half killed, chased and ambushed. Yet each physical wound had healed or was healing, each raw place of fear and anger at himself had softened, maybe healed too was the right word. He no longer felt that edge of being on guard, and now this woman had slipped past all his defenses, and he was smiling as he rode Ike in front of the café and down the main street, certain the woman was watching him, and it was a pleasure without fear to know she was interested.

Hay-On-Wye. He'd been born there, live there with his father for a time. The Hay, a town his father adored, stores filled with books, and the Norman castle remains that Joe had loved as a child.

The girl's directions were clear, the B&B was easily found. A good sturdy post held up a front roof so he tied Ike securely. The door rang over his head as he entered, startling him and bringing a woman quickly from the back of the house.

Eighteen

This would not do, Caroline Markham thought. He was dirty, smelled strongly of horse and was, well, dark. Native with the hair and eyes and oh my but she hadn't had a guest in three days and the electric bill was overdue and here was money. At least she expected he had come in for a room; he most certainly did not look like an antiques buyer. Why he would have no way of carrying anything. Oh dear. She put the back of one hand to cover her nose and mouth, and breathed in her lavender cologne.

He smiled and she felt faint; "Ma'am, may I have a room? I promise I'll behave and I sure don't expect the horse to stay in the room with me." Caroline forced a smile; "Certainly sir, we have an exceptional room at the back, with a private bath and entrance." Quick Caroline, she thought, how much is the bill, think. "It's $65 with tax, and that includes a full breakfast at whatever time you choose."

He had seen the calculations and must know she was desperate, trying to balance what such a man could afford and how badly she needed a guest. It wasn't the season yet, even a roughneck like he was could understand that much. Bless the man he paid in cash, even the exact amount and did not ask for a receipt. Although the bills were greasy, they were real. She showed him the room, which had once been the laundry and servants' quarters and then a sleeping porch. It was her biggest room with lots of windows curtained with blue and white check material. It was as masculine as her small establishment could offer.

Mostly the men who stayed with her were accompanied by wives who sighed and fussed and bought a few antiques and said how lovely the house was and wanted to know its history. This man, who signed the book as Joseph Evans from Valentine, Nebraska, asked no questions, and said breakfast at eight would do him fine. He brought in the most disreputable set of canvas bags, and was polite enough to ask if she had a sheet he could put down on the floor where the bags wouldn't ruin the freshly polished wood. She obliged him and sighed with thoughts close to pleasure that the man had enough sensibilities to understand her concerns.

Done with the flighty woman, Joe led Ike up a hill straight up out of town then a right turn and an older house on the left. There was a small fenced pasture, and a decent shed where Ike would be safe. Joe grinned; walking up and down the hill could be a challenge.

Hiram Ilfield wasn't as accommodating as the woman at the bed and breakfast, although he accepted Joe's horse as promised. Helen was the only child home after a bad marriage. The other girls barely spoke to him but Helen kept trying, as if her sweetness might back him into a corner.

She'd said this son of a bitch was dark but not a black and by god she was right. Goddamn Indian and he wouldn't have such in the barn never mind the house but he'd promised Helen and she was hell on wheels if he got foul-mouthed and opinionated when she'd made a promise for him. He stared at the man, studied the horse. Good looking thing, that bay. Brand seemed familiar too. Nice lines, racehorse breeding crossed on a Quarter Horse. The man, though, he too was a breed, two different lines and in humans it produced nothing but trouble.

"Mr. Ilfield, you daughter told me 'bout you. Ike's done nothing but be a horse so you can't blame him and I trust your daughter's word that you will take good care of the animal." It was quick this time; the two of them on their opposite ends, their individual anger thick for no reason other than habit. "Ilfield, I know men like you. You run scared and what's different frightens you."

No son of a bitch talked to him like that. Then Hiram shook his head; the words were stronger, crude enough but what his daughter told him all too often. "All right, Mr..." He couldn't remember. "Evans, Joe Evans." "Oh yeah, Indian like you with that name." He shook his head and the son of a bitch stood his ground.

"I was born in Wales, old man. It's my father's name and you're damned right it's not your business. Hell I'd bet you've never been in that bookstore and as soon as I'm sure Ike's going to be all right, that's where I'm headed. You want to come along?" Hard words and all over a bookstore Hiram refused to enter and Hiram had some smart answer when he really took a look at the man. "You go on, I'll care for the horse. I know the brand." He'd remembered suddenly, could see the wiry, white-haired Indian who'd sold fine working cow horses up near Valentine. The boy's face got tight but he nodded and left. Could be the horse was stolen; he might get in touch with Roy up to the State Police, see if anything was out on a red-skinned white man.

Joe quickly found a chair in the second room of the bookstore, away from the few customers in the main room. There he could draw in smells and sounds, even to the hard wood floor and the height of the stacks. Memories from twenty years ago wound around the past fifteen years, all of it impossible; a lifetime's journey from a British stable yard to the upstate New York prison and then a return to Nebraska.

Even the titles were familiar; Joe went to one particular book, its spine well-remembered and his fingers ran over the leather boards before he gently opened the book, which seemed to have barely been read. He inhaled, turned each page carefully, knowing when he came to the next illustration exactly what he would see. A treasure given by his father, long ago lost. A silly book of a talking paint horse and a witch horse who cast spells, Yorkshire Tamworths with double names and a man named Horace who couldn't say 'aitch' in any of the right places.

Hildebrand, by John Thorburn and illustrated by The Wag. Published first in 1930, so that the copy Joe had known was worn and old and fragile, unlike this one which was pristine. Joe grinned, another word had found its rightful place; pristine. "You like this book? No one's ever even looked at it except me. I read it, it's quite funny and yet it speaks to class and judgments...how interesting this is the book you would find." It was her, Helen, taking time from serving meals and talking with the clients. Joe turned and forced himself to smile but he couldn't stop the betraying words; "Yes, ma'am. I read this when I was a child."

Helen studied him as she thought over his answer; a man who looked like he came out of Hollywood casting, riding a horse across the country, staying at a bed and breakfast and now he's holding a book published in England eighty years ago, talking as if he'd read it yesterday. "Mr. Evans, may I join you for dinner tonight? I've already recommended RG's."

She stopped, face immediately flushed; asking out a complete stranger who was only riding through. Then she smiled; 'riding through' was what interested her. All these peculiarities in one man, on his way from here to there while she stayed in the middle, in this rigidly quaint small town.

He bowed slightly, and when he brought his head up and looked at her, she thought what a pity it was that he would leave so soon. "Yes, ma'am. I would be honored if you'd join me for dinner. On me, of course." She thought to object but the look in those eyes told her he meant his words. She smiled, bobbed slightly and said "thank you kind sir." He actually laughed.

"Ma'am, I need to sit here a while, then I'll check on Ike and yes I'll not start nothing...anything with your father. He's like too many people I've run across on this." He thought about the next word; "...on this odyssey to bother me. I'll see you at six?" Helen agreed as she retreated to the cleared-out café to think about what she'd just done, the why of it, and more importantly what she would wear tonight.

It was a while before it registered; his beginning to use a word and then correcting himself. The singular word, 'odyssey'. That had her smiling to the point that a late customer asked her what was so funny and she made up a story to appease him. It was, after all, a very small town. Joe sat in the cafe for an hour. Occasionally he would get up and go through a stack of books where he found more old friends, more memories, until he had to be outdoors in clean air to get away from the past. Ike's welfare gave him a destination.

Ike was grazing placidly, contained in a sagging fence. Joe slid through the boards, sat with his back against a post. Slowly, taking one bite for each step, the bay managed to end up standing over Joe, allowing bits of grass and saliva to dribble out of his mouth and splatter Joe's shirt and hands.

"Goddamn you get off my land." Ah, seen but not remembered, yelled at for his skin color. Joe wiped off his hands and shirt, stood up and turned; "No sir, Mr. Ilfield, I've been asked to dinner by your daughter, but if you want me to explain..." That dug into the old bastard, cut through his bigotry to the love of a child. She might be grown up but she was his daughter, and Hiram Ilfield loved her. Probably the only thing in the world he loved and she loved him in return. Joe hadn't known this; that unqualified love was what defined a family.

The old man hobbled back to his house, letting the door slam in a vain attempt at arrogance. Joe laughed, put his face into Ike's mane and held in the scent, to remind himself of what he was doing and why.

He was indoors, in the floral chair his wife had recovered maybe twenty-five years ago. The fabric on the arms was worn, exposing the rough brown tweed she had hated but the price on the chair was good enough that Hiram had purchased it over her objections. It fitted his body, accepted the weight of his considerable haunch and had a depth to allow for his massive legs.

He'd had too much time to contemplate the rightness of his buying a goddamn chair his wife hated. It weren't possible to express his opinions to his one daughter that could abide him otherwise she too would leave. Going out with that...here's where he needed to stop but no one in all the years could show him why his beliefs were wrong.

The one step to the private back door of his room creaked. Thankfully the proprietor did not pounce as he moved about the room. He pushed on one of the pillows and it gave satisfactorily and he laughed; here was a man who slept on the ground, in a dead house, in barns and lofts, on hay and matted pine needles and he was considering the suitability of a mattress and pillows in a fine establishment.

Downright foolish; he laughed until he coughed and covered his mouth to stop the impulse. Part of the laughter came from remembering his last time lying on a mattress, sandwiched in the back of that Volkswagen bus between those two accepting bodies. "Mr. Evans, are you all right?" The voice he feared, the question without an answer. He lied; "Yes, ma'am. I'm fine. Thank you." If he opened the door, she'd be there, standing too close, eyes bright with forced sweetness covering fear.

Joe shucked off his boots and lay down; the bed was perfect, its comforting welcome made even the inquisitive innkeeper bearable. While he thought on the use of that new word, he quickly went to sleep. Flat out, hands loose at his sides, head cushioned by the doubled pillows, hair stark against the crisp white of the embroidered pillowcase.

Caroline Markham would be horrified if she saw how her guest was treating the elderly coverlet.

He was five minutes late skidding into the bar. She heard his boots on the wood flooring and then the quiet as he crossed the faded carpet and when he appeared in the room, Charlie who preferred to be called Charles while working, had a startled expression as he guided her dinner companion to the table. Joe Evans stood smiling down at her and his looks were a fresh shock. He wore a pale muslin shirt, hand-made and fitting him perfectly, snug at the belly, wide enough for his shoulders. Almost-new jeans, their softened denim outlining his body. The boots were old but they'd been well cleaned. The hair was slicked back, tied with leather; he looked charming and old-world. His appearance was stunning; no wonder Charlie had that look.

"Ma'am." He was grinning as he sat down. "I overslept." Caroline would be having a fit, this man roaming inside her house, her delicate sensibilities all aflutter. Charles handed her a menu, then very carefully made certain that Joe had a good grip on his own menu. Smiling a bit too greedily, their host and server listed off the specials, before asking if they would like anything to drink.

Joe nodded to her; "Ma'am, whatever you would like." Then he shook his head and studied Charles. "Mister, what've you got for champagne?" She heard the smallest of struggles, as if he'd never said 'champagne' out loud. Charlie was delighted and listed the choices. "We have a nice sparkling wine, similar to champagne, from California, one of a better quality from New Mexico. They are both around twenty dollars." Rarely did anyone in RG's order more than beer or a shot. Only tourists ordered wine.

Surprisingly, the man did not seem interested in the lesser wines. "Mr. Charles, I've never had champagne and it would suit me to have the real thing first time. What've you got that's from France?" Helen was amused, shocked, and delighted. The man knew what he wanted and wasn't embarrassed to expose his ignorance in front of her or the fawning Charlie, and he also was prepared to pay.

"There is a nice Moet, sir. Extra Dry." Charlie made a face as he spoke the two words; it was obvious that Mr. Evans understood the man's distaste. "And in the brut category, we have a Veuve Cliquot." She watched her dinner companion, not even trying to guess what he would choose. And he did it again: "Mister, from the way you're talking I'll take the brut and the Veuve Cliquot on your word and I suspect it's pricey but when a man tries something out of his league for the first time, it best be first-class." Then he turned to Helen and his smile was a wonder. "Ma'am, I do hope you like champagne, for I can't drink a whole bottle of anything."

Charlie went away in a swoon and Helen took hold of Joe's hand. "Mr. Evans, whatever pleases you tonight is my wish." As soon as she said the words, she heard what they could mean, and blushed. He picked his hand from hers, brought her hand to his mouth and kissed its back. "I seen this done in the movies." He was teasing her again.

He liked the champagne although he sneezed after the first sip. It tickled, then the taste spread in his mouth and he could almost chew the bubbles. Not sweet, not heavy, fruit yes but light enough he took a big swallow and got the hiccups and decided the only answer was another swallow of more moderate proportions. He was smiling when she reached out with a starched white napkin and dried a bubble at the corner of his mouth. Her face was close, her eyes focused, intent on her mission and Joe realized they were flirting. This was how it started, not by fingers grabbing at parts. He leaned into her hand, and her mouth was close enough to kiss but he finally knew better.

He learned too that champagne gave the world a different look. And the wad of bills paid for that perspective; he was almost one hundred dollars lighter, not counting the room. And looking across the table into Helen's face, the tilted smile, her slight wobble in the chair and the bottle in its dark glass and fancy label, was the knowledge that spending the money was worth every penny.

He had paid the bill with a grin, tipped the man more than was decent but the champagne advice had been invaluable. Now he knew, and it was brut for him also. He had even stood up and pulled out her chair like he'd seen in the movies, and he was rewarded with the sweetest of smiles.

An unexpected truth startled him; he had to ride out early tomorrow, leaving behind the promise of any possibilities with this woman. She smiled and he felt accepted; he wanted her closer, up against him. Now that he knew how it felt, he wanted her in bed. They had few choices; her father filled their shared house with anger, Caroline Markham prowled the small house she loaned to strangers for dollars, and a woman like Helen did not literally roll in hay. It was all wrong. Joe stopped, caught Helen at the bottom of the hill and turned her to him. Her smile, damn the woman she was smiling up at him knowing his thoughts exactly.

Without any discussion or shyness, they had chosen at dinner not to ask each other personal questions, not to pry or show any curiosity but to talk of what they already knew they shared. Books, stories, history, horses; the West, the land. Beauty in all its forms. Joe did not know he could talk and think this way; she found the words that drew from him ideas and beliefs he'd never realized out loud.

Now they were climbing slowly toward the house where Hiram Ilfield ruled, and the open-sided shed where Ike would be resting, quiet and alone and deep in his horse dreams. She reached up and kissed him. "There's an old garage behind the shed, Joe. I know where Dad keeps his camping gear and there are two bedrolls that zip together." She stuttered on some of the words. He leaned down and brought the kiss back to her; "Ma'am. I'm already there." She laughed through her mouth on his chin. "Me too. We best hurry."

Her breast filled his hand, her head rested under his chin in that hollow made for her. Her fingers played against his ribs as she sighed and told him he needed to eat better. He nipped at her shoulder and she laughed.

They fitted right from the beginning; no shame or hurry or discomfort when he slid into her and she held him as if he was rare and valuable. He moved on her, mouth to her neck and then the line of her hair, down to her shoulder, the top of her breast again all the time her body rolled around him, holding and releasing and holding, letting him in deeper and deeper until they climaxed together, hard to breathe, not caring, wanting more, her hands on him, all over his buttocks, her mouth against his skin whispering his name.

Hiram knew as soon as Helen entered the house. That smell, one he remembered and envied and missed each night and how could she sleep with a goddamn Indian. She went past him, knowing he sat in that ugly chair and when he struggled to speak, she stopped him. "No. You say a word and I leave." Hiram sagged into the chair and bit down on his lip, hated himself for what he thought and could see in his imagination, hated the man for what he'd been able to do. The girl loved an Indian and now Hiram had no one.

The antique bed could never be as soft as that old hay and the two bedrolls but Joe managed to fall asleep under the cover. Clean sheets against his skin, wishing she were with him. He got up after four hours of drugged sleep and was quiet as he packed the canvas bags with all the gear. He considered a shower, but wanted her smell to be with him.

When he got to the barn, Ike whinnied and Joe hurried in to quiet the horse. He fed out good hay, filled the water bucket, and while the horse ate, he stood just inside the shed and stared at the house as if his wanting could reach inside and bring her to him. As he saddled up the horse, fitted everything where it belonged, Joe was glad, he said to himself and then to Ike, glad she hadn't come out. He'd never leave if she had and he needed to get Ike returned home.

She watched out the window, knowing her father was suffering. He'd been up walking most of the night, his bulk made the floors shift and groan and she hadn't slept until dawn. Now he was downstairs with his bitter coffee and his hard mind and she didn't want his company. The bay horse tried to buck on the slippery hill but Joe pulled on one rein and spun the horse and Helen could see the wide smile on his beautiful face. He should have a hangover, they'd finished the bottle of champagne and then had brandy with dessert and he told her he didn't drink much. But he was in good form on the horse; she wanted to go with him.

Hiram too was watching; that son of a bitch could ride and he was headed north over to Seventh Street and then into Nebraska proper. Probably going to those damned sand hills and onto reservation land. That's where the brand came from, that old Injun named Isaac Brings...hell brings something, one of them names no white man would tolerate.

No wonder this one used Evans, probably had nothing to do with his birth but Brings whatever was too much a mouthful. He'd call Roy and report the overnight visitor. Horse and rider were out of sight now. Maybe Helen would come down the stairs and sit with him. Then it was past seven and Helen hadn't appeared to join him or maybe she had slipped out to be at the café and he needed to call Roy and see if the law had any interest in that damned Indian.

It rode with Joe, taunting him, what he was leaving behind. A woman who laughed with him, who knew about books and horses and her fingers were gentle on his skin, never taking or demanding; offering sensations he'd never known existed, and so far past just sex that it was a different world. Twice in the first ten minutes Joe turned the horse in tight circles. He used the excuse that Ike was being contrary. If he went back, he would not fulfill his promise to the bay gelding. If he turned back, he wouldn't know about his grandfather and his two half-brothers. If he went back, he would fall in love. It had taken only a few hours, and then the night, which made no sense to him but she wasn't like anyone else.

He had nothing to offer her, no skills, no life beyond prison and almost a year of traveling. Book learning, yes, lots of pages turned, words pondered, looked up in dictionaries but that didn't make for an education and he had no way to earn a living. Shoveling manure seemed to be the best he could do.

He found a dry trail headed north and west, so he let Ike run and this time he made no attempt to rate the horse. He realized then that he'd left his hat, the cowboy hat from the woman in Pennsylvania, left it in the old man's garage and to hell with it. It was from another time, a different innocence. It was four hundred miles to where he was headed, three weeks of hard travel. He'd been on the road close to a year, the traveling seemed to take forever but then again, as he felt wind sweep his face and let the rhythm of the gallop slide through his body, what else would he have done with the time.

The wandering Rte 136 took him west and north, and Joe rode its curves until it crossed a river heading more in Joe's direction. There were some fences, most he could ride around, a few that sagged and he jumped Ike over the wire, which was a fool thing to do, but he was a fool. He'd been learning that lesson over and over on this fool's errand he'd chosen.

Twenty miles to a town, thirty more miles north and west to another town; a gas station, a feed store, a diner. He found the rhythm again of traveling, three days of moving hard, a day of rest for Ike, maybe some work for Joe. A meal here and there, shoveling shit, helping a farmer spade up winter dirt. It was time for the seeds to be placed carefully in the turned ground, the irrigation softening and flushing hard winter earth.

The land he crossed was green edged in brown where the irrigation stopped or a hidden spring nourished ragged trees. He pushed Ike, pushed himself, didn't bathe, ate little, worked for those few dollars that fed him and the horse. There were few regrets on the women who'd taught him. They had been kind, wanting his body, not seeing him in particular but as a stranger; they thought him unusual, those comments on his face, his eyes and hair had so little to do with him, but he had learned from their physical generosity.

The river ran fast and muddy, filled with sediment and unappealing to Joe. It was the North Fork of the Big Nemaha; he knew that from a sign outside the town of Tecumseh where he'd sighed in relief and moved Ike off roads and highways and found their own way along the river. Still he'd found no place where he would want to shuck his clothes and bathe.

Eventually she had to join her father, who grunted but had the sense to not express any opinions. She smiled all that day at the café and the next few days, and those who really knew her tilted their heads in silent question but she had nothing to say.

Her father broke down one evening and asked questions, like where was the man headed, what were his plans, would she see him again? Never a name, never personalizing Joe's existence but she knew. And she didn't answer other than he needed to get the horse to where it belonged.

Memory became a torment; her head rested on his belly, the thump and rise as blood moved through him, her face tickled by that thin line of dark hair leading her to his now-softened cock. If she rolled her head slightly, she could taste them together, her intimate scent on his flesh, the texture of his balls, lightly haired, softer than she would expect. The cock hardened and fitted in her mouth, the hair pressed to her cheek as she held him.

Nineteen

He kept a mental list of the towns; small places, cross streets and road signs, mile markers, few humans, fewer animals except road kill. There was no particular order to the names, just small dots on twisted roads; Adams and the North Fork of the Big Nemaha, Wilbur and Olive Creek Rest Area. He managed to get around the town of Crete on one of the endless dirt roads lined with thin trees

There was a stock tank overflowing from an endlessly spinning windmill; no signs of cattle, the wire gate pulled back to lie on the ground, a deliberate move by a rancher who did not come out of the pasture the way he had entered. Water running uselessly was poor management. Joe snorted; look at him, making judgments about strangers.

He figured it wasn't trespassing since he did not open the gate and there were no signs, new or faded, tacked to any fencepost that said 'don't you dare come inside'. He'd come on to the pasture and the inviting tank from a faded dirt track in open range, so it seemed reasonable that he take advantage of the water. Its scent held on the dry air, damp and teasing. He rode through the gate, angling Ike so the bay would not step into the fearsome tangle.

He hobbled and side-lined Ike in a stand of prairie grass, then shucked out of his clothes and held them at arm's length. There was a wind, unlike New York where the air was soft. Here nothing stopped the wind and his body clenched in the chill, his balls drew up as he danced around the stock tank. First he put a hand into the stream of water coming from the pump; damn it was freezing and he needed to climb in, get to work. The shining surface entranced him. Across from the rushing water, there was a raised cement step, as if other folks came to bathe here on occasion. He stood on the block, feeling the rough texture against his feet. He shivered, shook his head and saw his reflection move within the water. Joe raised his head.

His face stared back, distorted by the slightest ripples, pulling at his jaw line, bunching his eyes, but he was in there, his features, dark hair past his shoulders, freed from the confinement of a bit of string. The hair lay twisted in thick strands, uncombed and greasy. There was a darkening beard, visible even in the water's loose surface.

Joe studied himself, seeing only the shape of his head, the black stain of hair, holes that would be his eyes; his features unfamiliar, the brutal scar on his cheek still vivid despite delicate surgery. He knelt, feeling grit under his knees, then he leaned over the tank's edge, conscious of the cold metal touching his belly. The clothes needed washing so he threw them in, relieved to see his features disappear in the slow waves of sinking material. Now he had to climb over and rescue the shirt, jeans, socks, drawers. There was no choice. Until the waves eased, the shirt floated while the jeans had settled to the bottom, disturbing a thin layer of sand.

There was his face again, reflecting what the rest of the world saw. Even the dark color of his skin, made darker by a year of weather, showed in the pale water. No wonder he got in trouble, now that he could study the features, watch the eyes move, the lids blink, as he cocked his head to see different angles. He did not look like any of the people he'd met.

A voice stopped him just as he swung one leg over the lip of the stock tank and gasped at the cold. He couldn't understand the words, only garbled sounds barely able to penetrate his body's defenses as his skin shivered, his heart beat faster and his entire being screamed 'no' while he sank down on his knees, water up to his chin. Goddamn.

"You. Stop. What the hell're you doing anyway?" Joe let the waves soak him as he scraped his hands across the tank's bottom, drawing up a fist of sand. His bar of soap lay on the cement rim and he really didn't want to use soap in the cattle's drinking water despite the fact he'd seen no livestock. The man approached but was careful to stay literally at arm's length of the tank. Any movement Joe made pushed water over the edge in brief waterfalls.

"Mister this ain't no public bath and how'd you get here anyway? Ain't seen a truck or car, and no fool walks here, we ain't near to nothing." At the prolonged sound, Ike whinnied, lonesome and having eaten all the decent grasses within easy reach. The man laughed, then got serious again; "Where're you hiding that bronc? He stolen?"

Judgment still caught him unaware simply for being so much alone. By choice he reminded himself, and that acknowledgement forced his manners. Joe grabbed for the wet clothes and stood, water pouring off him. "Mister, I apologize for the disturbance. I don't think I've hurt anything and I surely needed a bath." He thought a moment, decided since it was the man's property he owed some explanation; "And, no sir, the horse is not stolen. He belongs to my grandfather and I am returning him."

The body looked like a portrait out of a Curtis photograph Tucker'd seen in a museum his wife dragged him to. She was keen on these things, being from the East and all, forgetting that her husband grew up with the images walking around him. Here was one in full glory, naked and unconcerned, splashing Tucker with his own damned water. The face, though, that was different, as if something foreign had been added. Tucker was definitely curious.

His fault, he'd neglected to disengage the windmill when he'd moved the yearlings to another pasture. He'd gone to a talk up to Bozeman about a way of ranching based on rotation and smaller pastures and he was figuring how to get the fencing up and just lost track of the windmill and it was a poor use of water and he was ashamed of the waste.

This son of a bitch looked almost familiar and like one of those pictures and damned but he was standing there now, upright and naked without shame, the beads of water making his skin look bronzed and he even had a tan line, dark against darker at the neck, around the wrists but the boy was Indian, had to be. Then the boy turned himself sideways and bent over the tank wall to scrub them clothes against each other and Tucker got more of a view than he wanted so he wandered over to study the man's transportation.

It seemed to Tucker that a naked man would find himself at a disadvantage dealing with the owner of land where he was trespassing. This son had no such inclination, and that singular point was downright interesting. Studying the bay gelding, he got a notion in his head and went back to that tank and the tall, black-haired man who was wringing out wet jean and already wearing a quickly-drying shirt and drawers.

"You're a cool one, ain't you." Joe looked up, hands gripped hard to the tough denim, pulling out more water before he could slide into them. The man was leaning up to a sagging fence post and kept talking. "Now I guess you got time to give me an explanation. Why you're in my field using my water. It ain't free out here, you know. Water's 'bout as precious as gold."

Joe spoke hard; "That water's unused and left running a long time." He stuck a bare foot in thick mud, lifted up his toes and the mud slid free. "Waste of water, there ain't been stock in here a good week or so. You begrudging me water just 'cause you've been wasting it?"

The words struck close; Joe watched the weathered face tighten, the eyes narrow but this time he didn't care. Then the man's shoulders let go, and he smiled. Big damn smile showing teeth and pulling up more wrinkles across the stubbled cheeks. The man straightened slowly, rubbed up under his cap; "Well boy that was a mouthful and I guess I won't be charging you for the use of the water but a meal and a night's sleep. That there's Isaac's brand so you have to be that boy he don't talk about. Heard the cops're out looking for you, something about riding your horse over the cruisers and one of them boys he got mad 'cause you disregarded his order to stop. His brother's in our bevy of State beauties and he's got a hard-on for you now." The old man could get talking, but in all those words were two important points; that Joe was close enough to the ranch that the brand and his own existence were known, and that the law did have the word out on him.

A complete stranger knew more than Joe did, but then the man lived around here and knew Isaac Brings Plenty and there was no reason someone this close to the Brings Plenty ranch, an observant man like this one, wouldn't recognize the brand. "Come on, boy. I'm the law you get to face this time 'round, sheriff of this here town that don't exist no more and you're welcome in my house for a meal, Maura, that's my wife, Maura. Now she likes cooking for a man in need. Makes her feel important to see her food going to a good cause."

Joe untied Ike and walked with Tucker Vrooman, for that was the name of the sheriff of the non-existent town, while the man told him a State Police bulletin had gone out detailing Joe's charge down the middle of the bridge and the bay horse jumping the cruisers set nose to nose. Vrooman shook his head; "Now I know one of them troopers here, he's brother to that trooper transferred from Illinois and I can't see him thinking he was going to stop you so easily."

Joe agreed with his slow-moving savior; this time he thought he could speak his mind. "I gambled that they'd never shoot at a horse could jump like Ike did that night. Guess we all took a gamble." Vrooman laughed; "Boy, you done your grandpa proud."

He was clean, well fed, and sleeping in a familiar barn, half-listening to the night animals and the horses, missing Helen and anxious that he was getting close to a place he'd never thought to see again. Vrooman had assured Joe, without specifically being asked, that the old man was alive. Since Joe didn't respond, Vrooman dropped the subject and his wife dished out another helping of stew.

Through the surface elation ran fear, terror if he looked it straight in the face. He didn't know; was the old man half-dead or with a clear mind, the two boys, they would be adults now, maybe with their own families and he would have no place. The land he remembered but the boys' faces were blurred, lost in rage and blood. He wondered too if they knew what he'd done and why. They had been babies barely able to carry a complete thought. What they had seen, what had been done to them had to have left a mark. Would he know them, understand how they felt? They would see him as the murderer of their father; they had been witnesses, they had even spoken in court against him.

Lots of questions, words, silences, had driven from him the notion that he could see the face of his mother in the killing. He had no sense of loss when he was notified of her death. As if by giving birth to two more sons, she had escaped him except as the wet darkness where he was conceived.

Lying in the sweet smell of last year's hay, secure in a familiar place no matter where it was, how or when it was built, a barn filled with hay held safety for him, and yet he could not sleep. Fretful, tossing until finally he got up, fingering the washed clothes to know they were dry enough to pack. Outside surprised him; it was early dawn, not midnight after all. He must have slept but he felt like he'd fought with the devil and had a buffalo running through him all at once. Ike was willing enough to go on, no biting or squealing when Joe saddled him. It was time to get back on the road.

It was another long list of disappearing towns. First he had to ride under Interstate 80, where Ike panicked inside the dark tunnel as cars roared overhead. Joe ducked down to not hit himself. There was a moment when the bay half-reared and Joe felt cement scrape his back and he figured they were both done. Route L80F went north to Utica and the dirt road to Shelby turned into rich farmland, scattered with simple towns alone the tracks of the railroad. Joe and Ike crossed the North Platte River at Silver Creek, a town of about six hundred, which was more people than Joe had expected.

They crossed Silver Creek itself, a fairly clear and shallow bed, where Ike drank his fill and Joe considered another bath, except for the folks in their modest houses, going about their daily routine, keeping an eye on the stranger appearing and hopefully disappearing quickly. There was always one more river, and like so many in the dry Nebraska land, they were thin streams weaving together, making shallow channels so he and Ike had no trouble crossing other than to watch for quicksand. Joe let the bay test each step and they rarely made any change of direction.

It was more miles to the land above Valentine once they rode past the town of O'Neill, the biggest of the endless supply of small towns in these farmlands. Valentine would be closer to the sand hills and almost home for Ike. The small village of Kilgore west of Valentine would be his point of arrival. Up past the town, spanning the Nebraska/South Dakota state line, was the land his grandfather earned, not from his heritage but from hard work and breeding good horses. Where lesser men took out mortgages and defaulted on them, Isaac Brings Plenty played the white man's game of signing a deed and paying full on the note, and he'd won.

Joe found he was riding slower, no more of the long, easing gallops but a sedate walk, a lope now and then when Ike grew restless but the traveled miles were dreamy as Joe became more fearful; stopping to let Ike graze, reasoning to ease his conscience that he wanted the horse to come home in good condition. No one would notice, unless he pointed it out, that there had been a terrible wound on the foreleg or that there were thin, almost unnoticeable scars on Ike's face and his ribs carried more thin scars where spurs had been liberally used. There was a layer of fat and muscle on the bay horse now, his coat gleamed in the new spring light and he was eager to travel.

Joe came to the town of O'Neill, south of a hard top road called 'Cowboy Trail', which he found ironic in several ways; twice police cruisers passed him, turned around and came back for a second look. Of course he still rode the Barnsby and with the color of his skin, he was most definitely not their version of a cowboy. The air was clean, a good sky, thin high clouds and a deep sun. A beautiful day; Joe eased Ike into a lope alongside this supposed Cowboy Trail and enjoyed the freedom. He had to cross a main road with its warning signs but it went north and south and was of no interest. Then he guided Ike into a trot, rising to the two-beat gait, covering ground again, both of them wanting away from the small city and back into the grassland, the dirt roads, the smell of broken sweet grass and horses, cattle, free-flowing rivers.

The powers above had sent his brother out of the town where they'd been born to a high-wind empty place. He now chased escaping cattle and responded to calls about elk or deer in the back yard, even a bear on occasion. Dwayne was still a State Trooper but he was being punished for letting a man on a damned horse ride across their bridge, and being unable, or unwilling as their captain had considered, to actually shoot after shouting the command to stop and being disobeyed. Those were the captain's exact words yelled at Dwayne when the report was sent to headquarters.

Here he was, that son of a bitch give Dwayne all the trouble, more than a month later, trotting pretty alongside the road, headed west, persistent son of a bitch and now he was riding through

Dwayne's brother's town as if taunting the troopers for their multi-state non-performance. The captain even had a call 'bout this son from an angry man over to Brownville. The captain, he dismissed the call after explaining to his command the caller was a well-known troublemaker, seeing conspiracies and terrorists in anyone come through his town. But the description matched what Dwayne told his brother. Right down to the stupid saddle.

Stocky put out a call. Anyone within hearing, they had them a scofflaw riding through town and it was up to the law to stop him. Stocky would bet this man met the profile they'd pulled out of the reluctant law enforcement data bank, of a man let loose from a prison back east maybe a year ago. There weren't too many that fit the description and yeah he'd served his time but he'd managed to break laws all the way through the country, crossing rivers and bridges and sleeping in folks' barns or pasture, no other way he could have made the journey, without no one's permission he bet.

A few bulletins had come in, all the way back to Pennsylvania, answering the description of the man, saying that he'd moved on, leaving no crime spree in his wake. Not on the radar, not one particular matter of law-breaking. But acting irrationally, which meant that whatever went on in this released killer's mind could be murderous to another man disrupting his intentions.

Stocky gunned the cruiser engine, turned on the lights and siren and went sailing after the son of a bitch who dared jump over Dwayne's car, facing two guns and the voice of the law. That outrageous act had ruined a good man's career and the perp needed to pay.

The siren jarred him; Ike scooted sideways and almost lost Joe. The cruiser was too close, the driver an idiot for pushing a horse from a car. The inevitable wreck would have few survivors, with the horse being the first fatality. They certainly hadn't exceeded the speed limit posted anywhere he could see on the dirt track paralleling the tar road. The siren went up a notch, screamed then shut down, screamed again and Ike pinned his ears, tried to grab the bit and run but Joe stroked the bay neck, eased his weight deep into the saddle and brought the bay to a walk, more a nervous jig but slowly, carefully, the horse began to settle. That damned siren blurted just as Joe swung out of the saddle so he could confront the officer and Ike reared straight up; pulled off balance by Joe's weight, horse and rider went down, Joe got kicked and rolled underneath Ike's belly.

The horse went completely over, Joe heard the saddle tree break, felt like his own ribs broke too. Ike stood, mouth torn where the reins were caught in a front leg. Hobbled at least, Joe's mind settled on that one important fact; that the horse was hobbled gave Joe time to stand very slowly, conscious of his left side hurting, tasting too-familiar blood in his mouth. Ike let out a stream of loose manure, tried to raise his head but the hooked rein strangled him and he began to fight, panicked, terrified, rearing backwards, yanking on his already bleeding mouth. Joe reached for the horse's head, caught the bit, spoke gently and Ike swung his head, got Joe in the mouth and this time he heard a tooth crack.

Still he held on, trying to unbuckle the closed reins. With the buckle bent, his fingers shaking, it took too long and Ike began to fight again. A voice behind Joe said 'step aside and I'll take care of him' and Joe knew exactly what the man intended. He kept his back solidly between Ike and the irate police, even heard the cold noise of a pistol being cocked and still he fumbled until Ike relented. The buckle opened, the reins loosened and Joe straightened up. He had to bite his lip as a cracked rib pressed into him.

He was slow to turn around, drawing in short breaths, keeping his focus on Ike, not his own temper, not his fury at the cop's stupidity. Pay attention to the horse, to Ike's white-rimmed eyes, the tight ears, tail lashing, blood dripping from the mangled lips; those were his orders to himself. Joe wiped his own mouth, then used two gentle fingers to touch the torn flesh at the bit. Ike sighed, lowered his head as if accepting Joe's ministrations.

"You! Why in hell didn't you stop?" A second cruiser, then a third arrived; the troops coming to their brother cop's rescue. Three grown men with guns afraid of an unarmed man on horseback. Joe shook his head, felt the droplets of blood stain his last clean shirt. Here it was, the place that terrified him. He tried to look into the cop's eyes and saw only reflected fear.

The face was bland, the man perhaps Joe's age, maybe less but those years had been rough on Joe while this boy ate his mama's cooking and screwed around with his little darling in a hay field. Nothing but a farm boy playing at the law. Joe caught hold of the words before they spilled out. Ike shook his head again, splattering the cop and Joe. Red drops that settled in the boy's skin, one big drop on the thin upper lip. Two more cops, on each side of their comrade, weapons drawn, gun barrels pointed down in gloved hands. A threat not spoken but loud enough to be heard in the next county; Joe wiped his face clear of his own blood. "What do you want from me?"

Stocky raised his weapon two inches. Ned, to his left, shook his head and Ralph, who was always slow to react, said it was what kept him alive, actually put his weapon back in the holster and the loud snap as he strapped the pistol in was a surprising reminder. Ralph paid attention as the man spoke, noting more blood dripped from the torn mouth and the man wiped at it, smearing his face. "What do you want from me? Here I am, you stopped me." Ralph looked at Stocky; "You called us as back-up, what's he done and what do we do with the horse?" These two, Ralph and Ned, didn't know Dwayne; they had come to Stocky's call so it was Stocky's show. He needed to make this man pay for his brother's humiliation.

"Uh, one of you take that horse to the fairgrounds. There's free stalls there, call the manager, he'll meet you to unlock the place." Joe stiffened, shook his head; "This horse needs to see a veterinarian because of your idiocy and I'm going nowhere till a doc goes over him. You got one on call, let him know where we are."

Damned son of a bitch's surrounded by three cops and he dares tell Stocky what to do. Risking his dignity, Stocky looked to Ned and got that slight nod again. "Okay, I'll call the vet. You, Ralph, keep an eye on this son, he's liable to do 'most anything." Ralph doubted Stocky's assessment of the man, but he turned, studied the broken-faced cowboy, nope he was pure Indian. Or maybe half. Still, Stocky had asked for assistance and Ralph had provided backup. He wasn't sure why, but it wouldn't hurt to stand and wait.

Joe stood at Ike's head, gentle with the tired horse. Ike shivered in the warm day; sweat patches showed on his neck, between his front legs, at his loins. Joe wouldn't let anyone he didn't trust take over Ike's care. He'd seen it, felt it, held it inside him now; rage provoked beyond sense or discipline. But it was not a man, not two boys, this time it was cruelty to a horse who'd carried or walked with Joe for over a thousand miles. To weigh one against the other, lives and loyalties human and animal; he wanted to tear the cop into pieces, wrestle the pistol from him and use it as an instrument of ruination on the man's wide face.

The law was grouped close, talking as they watched Joe. Eyes bright, hats pushed back, voices low enough he couldn't hear, didn't want to hear. Then an ancient four-wheel van drove up and the man who got out was the horse doc. He marched straight to Joe, barely bothering to look at the troopers. He stopped, not so close that Ike worried but the bay raised his head, blood crusted now on his muzzle and nostrils. He took in the doc's scent and became restless until Joe had to tug on the reins wrapped around Ike's neck.

"Sorry, Doc. He'll settle. I need to get his halter and lead out of the bags, if you'd hold him a moment." The doc had easy hands, touching Ike's shoulder first, then letting one hand rest under the bay's muzzle for a good sniff before he took the end of the reins and Joe searched through the canvas bags. He couldn't quite remember where things belonged or were stuffed and he went to his knees, head shaking, guts turned. The doc yelled; "Goddamn it Stocky what'd you do?" But Joe was back on his feet before he was in danger of receiving the law's 'help' and found the halter, the lead, offered them to the doc who made the transfer.

Joe took the lead, stood with Ike while the doc's big hands went over the horse head to tail. "Saddle's broke, son, you know that don't you." Joe nodded; "Ike spooked from the siren and we went down. When he rolled, well I heard it crack." "Damn shame," the doc said. "I've ridden one of those Barnsbys a couple of times. Mighty comfortable on a man's parts, you set it right."

The troopers shuffled, the round-faced one opened his mouth and the doc turned, stared at him until the mouth shut and there wasn't a sound from the trio. He continued talking to Joe as if it were only the two of them and the horse. No law at all, nothing they needed to know or would understand. "Your friend here might have some bruises come morning. His legs are good though, clean and hard. That scar's recent, you did a good job on the healing." Then he stood back and studied Joe. "Other than that cracked tooth and a split lip, I'd say you have some sore ribs. Let me..." Joe pulled back. "Why, son, ribs is ribs, horse or human."

He knew before he said a word that he'd come to a place where he could defend himself with words; "Doc, I got stabbed a few months back. And before the law here celebrates some victory over my misdeeds, I suggest they call the police in Stockdale. That's in Ohio." There had to be some reward out of this mess so Joe turned to stare at his silent accusers; "The sheriff in that town will tell you why I got stabbed. And it's not from a gang war or anything illegal. I still don't know why you stopped me."

Then he saw into the law's faces and the sudden knowledge was his release. Two of the troopers were reserved, faces showing nothing. The middle one, who had chased him and Ike, his face seemed to melt. "You and your horse jumped over my brother's cruiser and wouldn't stop on his command. That got him transferred and he's pissed and his wife wouldn't move with him."

The words ended in a whine; the law was human, no better than anyone. Joe studied the man, who appeared to shrink as his flankers moved way. "Oh." Joe turned and gestured to the shivering horse. Turned back and wiped his bloody mouth. "Man I couldn't hear over that siren and my own heart, and Ike here breathing hard. I didn't believe anyone cared that much, there wasn't traffic on the bridge, hell it was the middle of the night." It was as close to an apology to a man he'd hopefully never meet that he could muster.

The doc stepped in front of Joe, his back to the troopers. "My clinic's a mile up the road, you can walk your horse there. I'll be there ahead of you, we'll give him something to ease the pain and who knows, by the time you're ready to ride on, he'll be fine." Joe didn't like the sound of that last sentence. He'd walk if he had to, hauling Ike along slowly like they'd started out. It wasn't that far, and no cracked ribs and a broke saddletree were enough to stop him.

Doc almost hand-led Joe and the horse, driving that big beige van maybe two miles an hour. The clinic was in another steel building and the doc pushed a button, a door raised and Joe led the horse inside. It was much too familiar; the stall bedded, fresh water in a bucket, hay on the ground. A cot rested in the corner, piled with pillows and blankets, and doc's hand guided him. "I spoke with a friend at the hospital, he said to give you some pain medicine and let you sleep. He's coming 'round in a couple of hours so you got nothing to do but rest. And." Here the doc was grinning. "And if you give me trouble, I can always call on that state trooper to subdue you." It was almost funny and as Joe sat down, gently because his side hurt, he grinned up at the doc's scruffy face.

"You sure know how to get a man to hurt himself with those bad jokes." The doc offered him a tablet and a glass of water and Joe swallowed the tablet with the water, then he lay back slow and careful. The doc had the last word; "Something tells me, mister, you don't often do what you're told, even if it's in your best interest." Joe had thoughts on that statement but instead of answering, he slept.

Joe woke and he hurt but nothing like...whatever time it had been when he'd gone to sleep. A second man, slender, graying beard and tired eyes behind wire glasses, tightened his mouth. "Mister, oh that's right, Doc here can't remember your name. He says you called the horse Ike but your name..." They both laughed, long-time good friends, and Joe interrupted; "Name's Joe..." He had a choice now.

"My name is Joe Brings Plenty." Both docs looked at him, the vet smiled gently. "Thought you might be. You've come some distance to claim that name, haven't you." Joe accepted that this man, and others he would come across, knew the story better than he did. The doc was kind; "Joe, you didn't think, did you. You figured to ride in and leave the bay, god knows where you found him. And then move on like you never existed. You've got a name here. You're a story with most people believing in you and not that prison law up to New York."

Joe stood, tight on that left side, panting lightly but not going to listen to a man talk about him. Then, without thinking, he took a deeper breath and the pain was negligible; he smiled and the two men stared. He was rested; he'd slept among strangers and trusted them. Life had shifted for he was almost home, already recognized by those who didn't know him but knew his family.

The doc put a hand on Joe; "Coffee first, it's about five in the morning, boy. Angus here came soon as he could after his shift. Yeah you slept 'most of twelve hours. Got up once and I was here, kind of guided you to the bathroom, got you back into bed. It's been a night for all of us." Ike whinnied and the doc laughed; "Except for your bronc, who's eating everything I could throw at him. Don't think a few bruises will bother him. He's sure one of Isaac's."

Coffee and milk, a hard hunk of cheese and stale bread eaten in small bites and Joe felt almost human. Then, against his useless protests, the two docs pulled off his shirt and Angus, no other name but Angus, gave Joe's left arm to his friend the vet who held it horizontal while Angus examined Joe's side. The process left a man with little dignity. He was determined to give away nothing to these men who were equally determined to save him. Angus kept shaking his head and muttering. Joe got mad. "It's a knife wound and yeah it was bad. All I need to know's if a rib got cracked or broke and it don't feel broke so for god's sake you two let me have my arm back."

They were laughing at him. Laughing, damnit. Angus said very gently; "I read the report on you last night from the law in Stockdale. You're fine, just don't race cops over bridges or you and that horse jump anything for a while. Give yourself time to heal, Joe Brings Plenty. You've got a long life ahead of you."

"Now Joe I want that rig back next time you're in the neighborhood. No hurry mind you, I had to quit riding two years ago but I'm fond of that saddle and I've gone many a mile setting it. It'll do to get you home. Too bad about the Barnsby though, they's good saddles." Kindness, asking for nothing, all new to Joe, fresh knowledge gleaned from this trip.

Joe grinned at the word 'gleaned', another word that pleased him even though no one heard it. The doc looking at him strangely and Joe nodded. The saddle on Ike was an old Monte Forman, worn soft at the seat and fenders, new latigos, good sheepskin underlining, and a thick felt pad with a woven blanket over it. The doc shook his head; "You still can't put a bit to that mouth and I don't own a mechanical hackamore, think he'd ride in a bosal?"

Joe cocked his head, mimicking the doc's concern; "I've ridden him miles in that halter and lead, he'll do fine. But thanks for the trouble you've gone to, I didn't mean to drag you into my mistakes." The doc's face sobered; "Son, a lot of folks here think what happened to you was wrong. You stood up and protected your family. No more thanks, boy, no more apologies. You ride on, there's a lot you've still got to face."

Joe was pointed back to the supposed 'cowboy trail', a track barely visible in places that would take him alongside most of Route 20 and into or around Valentine. Kilgore was another few miles, and then north into the hills and ridges where Grandfather Brings Plenty let his horses roam. The doc assured him yes the old man was still living, and the two boys worked the ranch now.

Ten days he gave himself; one hundred and thirty–some miles to Kilgore and then north along a thin dirt track, between and around the sand hills and a turn only those who knew Isaac Brings Plenty or called to make an appointment to see his horses would know to take. It was the turn with the least traffic marks, mostly horses, mostly barefoot. A few rows of truck tire marks. No fancy iron sign overhead telling the world where one old man lived.

It hurt to ride at any speed but he thanked the veterinarian silently for the loan of the saddle. It had a padded seat, the stirrups swung easy, the flat rigging let him move with Ike if he kept the eager horse to a walk. He had time to think as he rode, no need to pay much attention to Ike, who moved out smoothly, letting Joe rest a hand on the saddle horn and ride in silence, except for the land birds, a few pelicans near surface water and the ground owls. He remembered them as strange sights for a boy from Wales. Oddities to be found in the dry hills, and he never had a chance to ask his grandfather why they were there.

He was that little boy again, fearful of the unknown, at the end of a long journey he never expected to make. The bookstore in that town was a reminder, as if fifteen years had not been lost. Ike shook his head and Joe looked down to see his hand gripped on the lead to the halter, the length drastically shortened, drawing Ike's head too much to the left. He eased up and apologized to the horse. He was going to miss Ike's company. And he was scared; in a land once familiar where it was tall grasses and loose sand, windmills and surface water and no one but yourself for company, he was terrified.

He stopped in the early morning as he came to the fork where a sparse track led to the unmarked Brings Plenty ranch. He climbed down from Ike, tied the horse to a pole once holding up a mailbox. It took a moment to find what he needed out of the canvas bags. Prison papers and ten twenty-dollar bills. Joe knelt not on his grandfather's land but at the county road's edge. He pulled up dried weeds and began a small fire, fed in the papers until the flames touched his fingers and he let the ash fall.

He took each bill, lit a match and held that paper too until his fingers were singed. These captured ashes were raised to the wind and drifted quickly from his hands. There, he thought, I did not use your money. You do not own me.

Twenty

He was an old man and he couldn't see any more, except from the very edges of his eyes; to speak with a friend was to sit side by side and Isaac could see just the outline of that friend's face. He could walk alone, for he could see the ground directly below him. A good solid cane and slow steps, and he could navigate the edges of the ranch yard, to the corrals, the tack room and hay mounds.

Moving into his late eighties and blind, he was still useful; he could pick up the fresh hay and feel it, bring it to his nose and smell it, knowing its winter richness or that it was musty and no good, to be fed out to the half-wild cattle he had always raised. The boys depended on him even as they continued to breed a few horses with the Brings Plenty brand. They were good boys; Quent, the oldest, was married to a Lakota girl and they had built a house on the ranch, a much grander house than the compact and efficient adobe dwelling with its two rooms, and an outhouse, where Isaac had raised his small family. His wife died when the girl was eleven; Isaac knew he had done a terrible job instilling respect for the old ways into his only offspring.

His child had died alone, her boys scattered, one in prison, two sent to live with their grandfather. He at least had been willing to love these boys when they came to him; Quent at seven, Eddie, almost five then, an unhappy young man now, in his last year of high school. Isaac could do little, but he continued to speak out when the boy mishandled one of the colts. A good scolding, reminding Eddie that the animal had not caused Eddie's pain and he could not, must not make that animal pay for his own suffering.

The boy would not talk. It saddened Isaac. As for Joseph, who had been with him those few years, since Isaac could no longer see to write, he had not sent a letter. It was a flaw, a terrible thing to do, but he could not ask Quent or Eddie to write to Joseph, a man cut in half, a man both their brother and the killer of their father.

He sat forward in the chair, leaned on his cane, listened to the beat and rhythm of the approaching horse. It wasn't one of the boys, they rode close and tight, holding the reins snug and no matter how often he spoke to them they did not have enough confidence to ease up. Eddie was in school today, Quent and Dolores at their jobs; he did not know who approached his home. This rider and horse were well paired; the horse moved easily so the rider must have a light hand. When they stopped directly in front of him, Isaac stood, leaning on the cane as he rose and advanced to the top step. Here he waited, listening; the horse was breathing lightly, it was the man who had trouble. "Can I help you?" They were harmless words yet the unseen rider grunted as if in pain.

That the man did not answer worried Isaac, and he considered the difficulties of navigating the steps. He had so far refused a ramp, would not be that much of a cripple, but he could admit that these steps unnerved him. "Here, let me." A voice with an odd manner of talk, a catch, differences Isaac could not define. But he knew the other sounds, of boots tapping the ground together, something tied around the hitch rail, the movements of the horse, restless without his rider.

The hand that cupped Isaac's elbow was dark and heavily callused; he was one of them. But the voice, careful and brief, did not ring true. "Let's turn around and sit. I came to speak with you." Isaac heard a thickness, as of grief, in the voice and he thought first of Eddie, then Quent, then it came to him that the knowledge of his oldest grandson had arrived this way, by Agency messenger, not through the phone but in person. Here was another messenger; Isaac trembled and the man's hand suddenly was hard, turning Isaac so he could sit in his chair.

His grandfather was old, and blind. Those wandering eyes, the impossibility of him seeing well enough to maneuver the steps, the signs were abrupt and hurtful. Still the old man was alive, and by the tilt of his head as Joe rode into the yard, his hearing was a viable sense. It was a physical wound to hold the old man by the elbow, to remember those arms when they first reached for him. Joe bit down on his lip as the old man asked what was wrong. "Tell me," he said, his voice strong as it had been almost twenty years ago. "Tell me what has happened to one of my boys."

Joe cleared his throat, wiped two fingers across his eyes and studied the old man. Then he drew a bench so close that if they breathed together, their knees, their hands, would touch. Ike whinnied then, and Joe spoke to quiet the horse. "You are Joe." The unfocused eyes watered as his grandfather tried to see him straight on, then the old head turned, tilted, and Joe heard the sigh. "You are Joe. You are thin, and tired. But you are my blood."

The old man put his hand forward and Joe accepted its touch, felt the prominent tendons and bone, allowed the long fingers to smooth his own hand, to define each finger while the weathered face smiled even as tears caught in the wrinkled skin. "I wanted to know if you have all your fingers and both thumbs." Joe had to grin as Isaac's hand rose to touch Joe's mouth. "You are smiling, you have not been lost."

Joe's face settled into a mask; he needed to meet up with the two boys. As if knowing what Joe must feel, Isaac began to tell him; "They remember you, they remember what they saw. I do not know if they understand yet and you will talk to them, listen to their anger and perhaps they will begin to accept why their father was killed." Harsh and unforgiving; Joe felt his entire body tighten; sixteen hundred miles to hear what he already knew. The old man removed his hand from Joe's face. "It is a truth, son. But not all of the truth. Here, come walk with me and I will show you what has changed and you will see what is the same. First though, we need to take care of your horse."

Shallow breaths, he thought, hold on, don't let words unhinge you. Listen to him, he knows. Not all of the truth but more than the boys knew. Joe wanted the rest of that truth told. He would wait here, and tell his brothers so they could be released from the prison Joe still inhabited. "Stand up so I may lean on you." Joe stood, winced at the cracked rib's objection, and the old man stood next to him. Bent as if to see the ground before him, yet he took Joe's elbow and they progressed down the treacherous steps. "No," Isaac said, "No I will not have a ramp down the side of the house to show the world I am old and helpless. I can see enough to make my way, I can see for instance that the horse you ride is a bay, with good legs and feet although I would suggest you take a rasp to that chip."

It became harder to breathe; Ike pushed against Joe's arm. The old man laughed; "The horse is fond of you. That tells me what I need to know. You are a horseman, as you told me your father was. And I consider myself a man who is, or was, good with horses. It is a gift, boy, one you have not lost and that makes me proud." Now it was time yet Joe couldn't find the words. It was his grandfather who prompted him. The old man moved his hand from Joe's arm to touch his chest, to where his heart lay under bone and flesh. "It is from here you must speak. You have not come this distance to listen to me. You have completed a warrior's journey."

Stillness, until Ike shoved Joe in the ribs and he grunted. Isaac returned his hand to Joe's chest. "You have been injured. Tell me." Joe shook his head slowly, the old man's hand rested at the point of his jaw. The intimacy of the simple touch loosened him; "This is your horse, Grandfather. He has your brand. I found him in the East when he was to be killed and I brought him here to be turned loose. He has earned that freedom." He had come close to the word but could not speak it. He had brought Ike home.

"Tell me what hurts inside you." "Did you not understand what I said?" The old man's face broke open, few teeth, shrunken cheeks and mouth but he was smiling. "I know about the horse but I ask about you." Joe would not be forced into anything personal. "The bay is twelve, no, thirteen now. He has no white on his legs, only a small star on his forehead. He looks like the dark bay stallion you had, the one you called Brown Ike. And I think his dam is that thoroughbred mare."

He could see her, she had been the only thing he touched his first day here, when he was shoved out of the Agency car by a hand at his back, to face an old man whose words were different and yet the same as his father's. How badly he had wanted to go home, knowing home no longer existed. The man with the white hair, skin darker than Joe's, that man had taken his new grandson to the pens where a mare and her foal waited for them. It was the mare who produced beautiful offspring with hot tempers, and she had to be Ike's dam.

"Her name was White Feather and she was registered. She always had babies that were hot-tempered and I was asked why I bred her. But when a horseman gentled that spirit, they had a horse who would give its heart to the rider. It was a gift only a few ever understood.

"I remember several bay colts from her, how old do you think this one is?" The old man was not as calm as he pretended. Joe laughed then; "Well in the beginning I felt those teeth a few times on my hand and arm, and then I actually looked at them. That was a year ago. He had the beginnings of the groove you showed me. So I think he is now thirteen."

The old man began to tremble and Joe pressed his arm near the fragile hand and Isaac caught him at the elbow. "I wish to walk around this horse. To know if he is the one I remember." They started at the head, where Ike obligingly put his nose up against Isaac's face and the old man breathed back into the opened nostril. Ike snorted, the old man laughed. "Why did you find him, you said he was about to be killed? Tell me."

Joe placed Isaac's hand on Ike's shoulder and as they walked, the fingers felt each muscle, rib, backbone, to the loin and hip and the buttocks, the tail bone and to the other side, where those fingers found the impressed white brand and traced it while Joe told the old man how and what kind of place it was where he found the bay gelding. Ike's hindquarters shivered and his tail swept against the old man's face and Isaac smiled. "I do remember him, he always had his mother's temper. You say he was starving, I imagine he fought and they tried to starve him until he would submit."

Joe held the old man steady while he finished his tour of Ike. "That's what I thought too. He jigged and fussed for a long time before I could get enough weight on him to try riding." He felt his grandfather's body lift then fall in a deep breath. "He jigged and fussed under saddle too and it near to drove me crazy. I figured the long miles might ride it out of him and it worked. I let him run when he was getting fit and when he wanted to quit I kept him going, never too hard, but hard enough until he was willing to listen." He caught himself; it was too easy to talk only about the horse. This time he could see his grandfather as an old man and that his body was tiring despite his protests of being sound and strong.

"I intend to turn him loose. It is why I came back. When I have talked to my half-brothers, I'll move on. My being here is...wrong." He felt the head shaking no, he knew what the old man wanted to say but he refused, by lifting Isaac Brings Plenty up the stairs and presenting his backside to the waiting chair.

"It's time for me to keep my promise."

His boy walked away without further talk. Boot heels always told their story and Isaac heard Joe's last steps before he hit the packed earth. The horse nickered; his grandson and this horse were connected from their journey. There were certain noises, of leather drawn through rigging, a grunt from the horse, the saddle placed on the tie rail. Isaac Brings Plenty might be blind but he could read.

Then another grunt, and the hoof beats softened toward the dirt track. The boy would remember, he would guide the bay up into the hills, dismount and remove the halter and the horse would be home. It was a brave and important thing his grandson had accomplished; Isaac was impressed and pleased with the boy. What happened next would tell him even more. Joe must help his half-brothers as this horse in his great need had helped Joe.

The chair became unbearable, a long time had passed, the sun's warmth told him two hours, and Joe was not in the yard. Eddie would come in soon, walking the two miles from where the county dirt road crossed the ranch track. Now Isaac would fret until at least one boy returned.

Joe lay against the ground, arms and legs wide, eyes closed. The wind blew high grass into his ears, across his face and he didn't attempt to brush the stalks away. Every so often Ike would sigh or fart, and Joe could hear the bay's teeth click as he tore into the sweet grass shoots. It was the world where his grandfather lived. Noise, scent, feeling heat or cold, now these were Grandfather's eyes. Ike lived in the same world of blowing wind and endless grazing, where a horse listened constantly, ears moving even as he ate or slept.

Joe would like to call it home but it was not his choice. What happened next was in the hands of his brothers. He left the rest deliberately unremembered. The sun scalded his face. It was noon and Grandfather was alone. There would be a meal waiting for him in the house, but with Joe's help getting to that meal would be simpler for the old man.

Without opening his eyes, Joe spoke Ike's name and the horse kept grazing. Then Joe sat up, opened his eyes and the bay was a good twenty feet away, rump to Joe, indifferent to what Joe would do next. Good, he thought, Ike's already forgotten me. He stood, let himself settle, his rib hurting if he moved wrong.

There was the temptation to lie down at the crest of the hill and roll; he'd done it on this hill as a boy. Then he considered his condition and his descent was slow and deliberate. Ike never raised his head from eating. The walk back to the isolated ranch house took all of ten minutes. As a child, this walk had seemed like crossing half the world.

The old man was still there, in the chair, under the ramada's cool shade, leaning on the cane with both hands. "Boy, which are you?" Joe laughed, that was one hell of a question. There was no fresh sign, nothing to say either of the two boys had come home. "It's the killer, old man." He stopped, jarred by the rage spoken straight from his thoughts.

"You have not learned to live with yourself. Who have you been all those years? Have they turned you mean, for I remember the gentleness in your hands and voice as you worked with the foals?" Hard questions; Joe toed at the dirt, standing below the narrow steps and he knew his grandfather could see the boots, the bottom end of his jeans. The old man did not fuss or talk; he waited with the endless patience Joe remembered.

"I read." That wasn't enough. The old man grunted and waved a hand. "I read everything they had and asked for more. And I came across a town here a few hundred miles back where a man in Wales sent a woman six tons of books. I'd never heard nothing like it." He wanted to tell Isaac Brings Plenty the rest, about the girl and falling in love and about the man's shop in Wales where Joe'd been with his father.

"There's more you aren't telling me, boy." Joe shook his head. The old man would not let go; "No, that won't do. Something to that town is stuck in you." Damn the old man was good. Joe searched for a neutral answer; "A girl." His grandfather laughed; "Well good for you, son. You have grown into your promise, Joe, to be part of your father, and part of your mother. You will have left a broken heart everywhere you stopped on your quest." His grandfather already knew what it had taken Joe a year to learn.

"Now I 'spect you have some tales to tell. Don't go bragging to the boys, they're young still. And they do not have your father in them. Quent may be married but he and his wife, they're innocents. More'n likely not as innocent as you were just a year ago." Joe didn't know if it was innocence, stupidity or sheer luck but he'd managed to remain intact through the prison system, which he knew was a peculiar thing for a thirty-something man to brag on.

"Yes, sir, I'll keep quiet on those matters." Joe was smiling as he brought out the sandwich he knew would be waiting in the fridge, a glossy new fridge that didn't rattle and complain each time the compressor started. On his grandfather's directions, Joe made himself a sandwich, and brought out two glasses of water. It was quiet on the verandah under the ramada's shade, cool and pleasant just as he remembered. His grandfather ate straight on through, no talk or niceties but keeping to the business of sustaining life.

Halfway through his own sandwich, Joe found he wasn't hungry. He sat quietly but his grandfather knew. "Not eating, boy. Must have been well-fed on your trip, or you got used to not eating." Joe stood up and took the old man's empty plate, added his own and took them inside to set in the sink. When he turned around, the old man was right behind him; "Time for me to rest, you see to yourself."

Joe went back to the hill where he'd set Ike free and the horse was gone. He'd left behind big gouges where he'd lunged from standing still to a full gallop, straight out into more of the sloping hills and high grass. Joe nodded; it was done. He lay down in the grass, where his earlier shadow still bent the tender stalks, and stared up at the changing sun.

Twenty-One

The engine sound woke him. The dense sand hills distorted and misdirected noise but he would bet on a school bus letting off an unsuspecting passenger. If he got up now, moved on quickly, he could walk in with the boy, the younger one whose face he could not recall. He saw the boy, tall now, lean and walking with lurching strides, anger in his long face, the dark skin no surprise for he was a full-blood if only half Lakota. Their shared mother was in his face. Joe skidded down the hill, the sand giving way and he yelled out for the boy to wait.

"What the hell!" The kid kept walking, Joe hurried to catch up and then the bay gelding came down the track at a full run, tail over his back, head up. The boy stopped and turned and said, "What the hell?" again and Joe wanted to laugh but instead he stepped back, to let the bay have his race. Ike skidded to a stop and snorted, trotted straight to Joe and rested his head on Joe's chest.

Joe grabbed Ike's ears and pulled on them, the horse butted him in the belly and Joe grunted. Got what he deserved but he was pleased at Ike's sudden appearance. He swung around, the boy stood there, mouth working. "Who the hell are you? Oh." As if he'd finally taken a good look and knew. "You're that fucking son of a bitch killer."

Eddie's hands ached; he knew who this was, he could see her face in the thinned shape, the length of arm and leg. It was the other man, not their father, who'd given this son of a bitch his straight nose and large eyes but not their color, not the skin neither. That same color he was; anywhere he lived, Eddie Upthegrove with his odd name and vivid temper was an outsider. Never mind his grandpa let them take his name, he was Eddie Upthegrove and the whole goddamn school never let him forget it.

Even back East among them reservation Indians they were outsiders, all because their ma wasn't the right kind of Indian and their pa wasn't neither. Why the damned son of a bitch chose to live away from his kin was something Eddie never got to know. Wampaunoag,

Lakota, who the hell were these outsiders to come in and hold their heritage above the local reservation. He couldn't even remember the tribe's name, didn't want to because when his father died, when this son of a bitch killed him, the elders turned their backs to him and Quent. Said they belonged with their mother's tribe as they hadn't been registered with Albert Upthegrove's clan.

Politics wherever it was and however you called it. But they at least had Grandfather and were accepted here unless Eddie lost his temper and the Agency teacher came to Grandfather's door and they spoke in soft tones, but Eddie always knew what they were saying. Quent had good grades and didn't get into fights, Quent was the good child, Eddie was like his...they never said it out loud, never to his face but he could hear the words. Like his brother the one in prison. Like his pa who got killed hitting a woman. Bad blood, them Upthegroves, bad blood all around.

He studied this feared killer. As they faced each other, the bay horse nudged the man. Where in hell'd this horse come from? It had saddle marks and chipped hooves, fresh scars at its mouth but for some reason the horse wanted the intruder's attention. Without taking his eyes off Eddie's face, the man held the bay's muzzle, pulled the whiskers, then took an ear and stroked it and the bay seemed to enjoy the mauling. "I'm Joe Evans, Eddie. Grandfather knows I'm here, he's waiting for you. And for Quent. He wants us to talk."

Eddie plunged forward, fists raised and repeatedly struck the man's face, his nose, jaw, neck, and the man took the blows with no resistance. The bay horse backed up, then whirled and ran and Eddie wanted to call out for the damned horse to take the cowardly son of a bitch out of here but the horse was gone and the man stood in front of him, accepting the assault without protest.

Then Eddie watched as his fist hit the man in the chest and the killer grunted hard, his face twisted so Eddie hit him there again and the man went to his knees. Blood dripped from the opened mouth, soaked quickly into the sand. Eddie stepped back, raised a foot to really hurt this thing that killed his father. He held his balance, found he could not finish the kick, and put the foot down, knelt and touched the man's shoulder.

The eyes were pure fire when Joe Evans looked up at him and Eddie leaned back, certain the man's rage would set him to kill again. Instead, Evans spat out more blood and spoke; "Feels pretty awful deep in your own gut, don't it, brother. Hurting a man this bad." He spat again, wiped his mouth and almost tipped over. "Finish it, boy. I won't fight back. I'm readied for you, it won't take but one good kick for you to become my killer."

He wanted to, had been given the invitation, earned the right through what this son of a bitch done fifteen no seventeen, maybe eighteen years ago. Paid for it like hell he did. That was only time, not the grief he'd caused.

Joe Evans looked up, staring into the sun now, barely able to see the boy's face. Life or death, he didn't care. It wasn't his decision. He hoped the boy understood his choice. He tried again because the boy was his flesh, all he had left; "What I did saved you, do you know that? What you do now will own the rest of your life like it has for me."

He coughed, spat blood, took a ragged breath in order to continue; "Me, after those years, I don't give a fucking damn but you boy, you're her, our mother. I can see it. He showed me pictures. The old man..." He coughed again and more blood came up, and it looked like the boy had already done his work with a little help from a state trooper.

Eddie choked from uncontrolled tears. He knelt down and faced the man, could smell the hot blood, see sweat on the lean face, heard the slightest groan and he raised his own fist, looked at it closely. The knuckles were raw from hitting his brother. Crying harder, feeling the wet on his mouth, dripping down his chin, almost drowning him; angry and sad and furious at himself, Eddie got one foot underneath his own weight and offered both hands. "Let me help you."

Quent stormed into the house, face blanched of its strong coloring, eyes wild. "There's a pool of blood down the road and horse tracks all over did you get thrown who owns that bay out there? He's got our brand. Grandfather!"

Where Grandfather usually sat, a stranger was seated, head leaned back on the padded cushion. As Quent calmed down, the man brought his head forward and Quent figured Eddie had been in another fight. This one too close to home, though. Must have something to do with the mix of horse tracks. Then he really saw the face, a bruise on one cheek, mouth twisted but he knew that face. He knew what he intended to say, having rehearsed the words never believing they would have a chance to be spoken.

"I saw you kill him. I still dream about it." Quent waited, his big half-brother nodded. There was nothing hateful or angry in the face, only exhaustion as he spoke; "I know." "You sorry?" Now there was a change, a breath that ended with the face contorted as if in great pain.

"No." Quent's gut lurched. The voice was relentless; "No, he was going to kill your ma and then you both. He forgot about me. So, no I'm not sorry, because there's still a family. Grandfather has not been left alone." Silence, a hesitation in Quent's eyes, his voice thinning out. Isaac Brings Plenty sat in a hard-backed chair, hands folded on his cane, looking sideways at each boy. Eddie stood up, walked to his older brother. He touched Quent's arm and his brother flinched.

"Who did that to him?" The last word was spoken as if it encompassed the entire world. "I did, Quent, and then I stopped and helped him come here." Eddie'd always had a temper but he usually got the bad end of a fight simply because he was skinny and picked on bigger boys as if seeking punishment.

Joe Evans, son of a bitch had his father's name, he was leaned down, face drawn but he looked to be all muscle and there wasn't a mark on Eddie. "Oh." Easy enough to read; Eddie's temper blew, and for some reason Evans didn't return the fight. Quent didn't understand. "Quent." That voice, the only comfort he'd known for most of his life. "Quent, boy, your brother has paid..." Quent shook his head; if he was going to get that damned speech about the debt to society, he was leaving the discussion and the damned house. Grandfather's words did not give him that choice.

"Your brother has paid dearly for his act even as it gave you life. Now he takes Eddie's blows and your anger and he waits, willing to accept you simply because he lives his own grief at what needed to be done. You have no right to judge him until you too have a choice, a chance to save lives. Understand what you owe him, not what you think he took from you."

Then a blow that Quent had not considered; "Remember, grandson, he was a boy younger than you are now, his own father had died, his mother abandoned him while she kept you. This is a heavy burden. He could have run yet he stayed to fight for you." There it was, for all of them to think on, each struggling with private furies. Joe leaned back against the chair, feeling as if he was going to faint or throw up; it was not from the few blows but from needing this, needing to be accepted by his brothers despite what had been done. Eddie went to his grandfather and put a hand on the old man's shoulder. Quent stood alone, then made his way to the edge of the sofa near Joe's chair. He put out a hand, asking but not touching. "Joe." Without opening his eyes, his older brother reached for Quent.

At Grandfather's insistence, Quent drove Joe to the Agency hospital, with Eddie holding Joe onto the bench seat of Quent's truck. It was only an overnight this time. And the boys sat with him so Joe was never alone. Quent went back and brought Grandfather to Joe's room, where the old man touched his grandson's hand, his forehead, not seeing the dark eyes that followed his gestures but knowing that the boy again belonged to him.

In his brief dreams Joe walked on ground that had no feel but it held him, he breathed clear air having no scent or taste. He raised a hand to his face and felt nothing; he could watch himself as he walked yet the dust as it rose from each step held no grains of sand.

He woke with bare remnants of memory.

They brought him home to a chair set outside under the ramada. As Quent's truck bounced along the track to the Brings Plenty ranch, the bay gelding turned up to trot alongside, snorting with each stride, flagging his tail and as they came to the small house, the horse broke into a gallop, speeding past the truck and circling into the yard, head high, ears pricked forward..

Quent told Joe; "You know, none of us can catch him. 'Cepting you." Joe grinned at his brother; "Long as he don't cause trouble, leave him be. I brought him here to be turned loose, if none of you mind him using a bit of grass and some water. Humans did a number on him, I figure he's earned his freedom."

Quent looked over Joe's head to where Eddie sat and they nodded in unison.

Two weeks later Joe asked if he could borrow a truck. He'd change the oil, check the fan belts and put on new tires, he said. He had errands and doing them on horseback might take him another year. He even had a driver's license.

Joe waited and finally it was Eddie who asked. "Why you going 'way now that you got yourself here?" It was the question Joe wanted to hear. He was grinning as he gave the two boys and their grandfather a brief summary of what needed to be finished. And he felt his own heart beat faster as he talked about the woman in the Nebraska booktown.

There was a saddle to return to a veterinarian in O'Neill, two letters to be mailed, one to New Holland in Pennsylvania, and one to a family in Stockdale, Ohio. And a woman to see in Brownville, Nebraska. Maybe too when he got there, he'd throw away a fairly new brown cowboy hat, if it still hung in her grandfather's garage. It belonged to a different life.

ADDENDUM

To learn more about William Luckey and for summaries and reviews of previously-published books, please go to http://waluckey-west.com.

Made in the USA
Charleston, SC
12 October 2011